CW00555961

TOURNAMENT

by

HERBERT BAILEY LIVESEY

and

RON HAMLIN

2008 Reprint

HERBERT BAILEY LIVESEY is the author or co-author of twenty books on a variety of subjects, as well as a frequent contributor to such diverse magazines as Travel and Leisure, Playboy and Food and Wine.

RON HAMLIN is acknowledged to be one of the world's top captains in deep-sea fishing. Since 1971 he has won numerous tournaments, accomplished many world records, and holds the Bahamian record for the first swordfish on rod and reel. As an angler, he has four black marlin - each weighing over 1,000 pounds - as part of his own personal record. In 2006 he released his 20,000th billfish fishing out of Ixtapa, Guatemala.

The idea of this novel was his, and his experiences fill these pages.

TOURNAMENT was originally published in 1980 by Doubleday & Company, Inc. This edition, published in 2008, was reproduced by Patrick J. Mansell in collaboration with Ron Hamlin.

Original Jacket Illustrator: Robert Sticker
Jacket Design: Paul Hammond, Studio 41, Boca Raton, FL

ISBN 978 - 0 - 9728564 - 8 - X

Printed in U.S.A.

To all the sick and suffering addicts in this world, if there is hope for me -- there is hope for all of us.

Ron Hamlin

Thank you to the counselors at Mount Sinai Addiction Center for showing me how to be a functional person again and to Tim Choate who made it possible.

ISBN:
Library of Congress Catalog Card Number 79 7870

Printed in the United States of America
Second Edition

This book is for
JAMES McLENDON
and
NICK ALDACOSTA
and
Billy, Brenda, Bobby, Barkie,
Barbara, Fanny, Gene, Harley,
John, Mike, Allen, and Carol

CONTENTS

TOURNAMENT

PALM BEACH

SWORDFISH
(Xiphias gladius)

Greek mythology alleged that broadbill swordfish were descended from bereaved warriors who leapt into the seas upon the death of their leader Achilles. Anglers who have managed to stalk, bait, and hook one attest to the ferocity of the beast. The broadbill makes a habit of attacking boats, and sometimes sinking them. Coveted by sportfishermen for its elusiveness and savage power, the swordfish roams all the oceans of the world and might be the only istiophorid to venture into fresh water. Breeding takes place in tropical waters, it is believed, but spawning occurs further north. Recently anglers have experienced modest success intercepting this south north migration at night off the east Florida coast. Much latitude remains for experimentation in technique. Physical characteristics distinguishing this species from its siblings of the gladiator family are: The wider, latter spear, nearly one third of its total length, its exceptionally large eyes, necessary to life at depths of 4000 feet and lower, the high, rigid, sickle shaped dorsal, set well forward, and the single keel on each side of the caudal peduncle. Colors are variable, but upper longitudinal body hues of bronze or dark blue predominate. The recognized world record captured on rod and reel was nearly fifteen feet long and weighed 1182 pounds.

— THE IAA HANDBOOK

1

The guard behind the high iron gate was skeptical. He ran his pencil down the list on his clipboard, shaking his head.

"You ain't on here," he said again, reaching for the call box on the side column as he watched the visitor through the bars. Guests of the Floridian Yacht Club were rarely diffident, and they didn't drive brown Chevrolets.

Ernest Lichine shifted uneasily under the scrutiny, looking away when the guard spoke into the receiver. He was, he reminded himself, three hours early.

Then the gate was swinging open and the guard was jabbering that the office never told him anything, that they didn't usually close up like this, but with this thing starting today, there were reporters and even TV people all over the place and he hoped Mr. Lichine understood that you couldn't be too careful.

Lichine was embarrassed by the sudden effusiveness. He slid behind the wheel and drove up the crushed shell road bordered by yellow elder and sculptured hedges, half expecting to be halted as an interloper. An attendant was at his door before Lichine braked to a stop in front of the clubhouse. To avoid having to thread his way through the people clustered on the marble steps, he chose to skirt the building. The broad leafed ground cover struck him as unnaturally spongy.

Only a few members were on the patio out back, braving what was by South Florida standards a chilly February afternoon. It was at least sixty-five degrees, but with a fitful breeze snapping the triangular pennants on the flagpole. Four days before, Lichine had caught the last plane out of La Guardia, flying into the teeth of the second blizzard of the year. Just four days from that other life, his real one. It seemed much longer. He shook off the tickle of foreboding. The lawn sloped to the edge of saltwater Lake Worth, which was part of the Intracoastal Waterway. Over near the mainland, catamarans and sunfish danced on the silvered water. Six of the club piers were unoccupied, their boats out on regular Sunday cruises. At the seventh, center dock, five sportfishing cruisers were moored, sterns to, rocking in the wake of a passing Scarab.

Catherine was nowhere to be seen. In characteristic ambiguity, Lichine was both disappointed and I relieved. At least her absence gave him time to savor the fruits of the only overt decision he had made since leaving Brooklyn Heights. The boat at the far end was his, acquired the day before yesterday on agreement to the asking price of $196,750. Plus tax.

Viewed from the end of the dock, the Bimini towers and outriggers were a forest of skeletal aluminum uprights, braces, and ladders. The canopied platforms at the tops of the towers stood forty feet and more above the water. Every boat had long, high foredecks, sweeping prows, and enclosed flybridges above the cabins. And in each of the open cockpits, a single chair with adjustable footrest and detachable back was bolted at the base of its metal column to the teak deck, facing aft.

The fighting chair, it was called.

Paint gleamed, brightwork sparkled. These components were equally shared. But as Lichine walked slowly along the line, variations began to reveal themselves. The first four boats ranged from forty-two to fifty-four feet in length. His was only thirty-seven. The others had simple bench seats and utilitarian radio units and depth finding equipment. His cabin was packed with transmitters, telephones, panels of complex electronic hardware, a wet bar, color television set, Ultrasuede upholstery, and shag carpeting.

But there. were less obvious differences, things he hadn't noticed in the flush of acquisition. The other boats were clearly the more finely fashioned. Wood joinery was impeccable. There was not an unintentionally raised welt, not a parted seam, not a bubble of adhesive, not a patch of grainy finish. Every comer and edge was safely round, every burr honed, every knob and handle recessed. The lapping water produced a series of gratifyingly substantial thumps against their hulls.

Lichine conceded his admiration. These boats were the aristocratic fulfillment of their builders' sole intention - the ultimate sportfishing machine. They compromised not a centimeter of purpose to leisurely weekend outings nor to cocktails in exclusive Bahamian ports. They were meant to transport anglers and crews in adequate comfort to the places where large fish were known to live and to serve with unflinching reliability as the one essential tool in catching same.

On Friday, the yacht broker, a Something Rumfeld, had elbowed him in the side and poked a cigar in the direction of a sleek Rybovich. A honey, isn't she? Custom built down to the last davit. If you ordered a new one today, they couldn't even lay the keel for five years. This one's bigger than what you got in mind, but over there. . . . Lichine had cut him off, claiming he couldn't afford it.

Standing behind the boat he had finally chosen, Lichine remembered his grandmother's word: catchpenny. It was skillfully assembled, true enough. But he saw now that it bore a film of unnecessary flash glossing an inattentiveness to detail. He sighed in resignation, sat on the splintery beam at the end of the dock, and checked his watch again. His new captain and mate were late. Lichine permitted himself an indignant huff. The tournament was to begin in little over an hour. He hoped that their tardiness was not an indication of their reliability.

Catherine Nettles had recommended the two men, and he had hired them unseen, over the telephone in her bedroom. Now he felt a flicker of suspicion. Just how badly did she want to win? Although dismissing the thought as meanspirited, he was nevertheless irritated. Then he heard heavy footfalls behind him.

"Lookit him," he heard someone say. "White as lard and green as grass."

Someone shushed the first speaker. Lichine looked over his shoulder. And stood. Two men approached. The one on the left had a loose limbed, shoulder roiling gait, moccasins slapping. He wore white ducks, a shiny black shirt, and a sueded leather cowboy hat crammed low over streaked yellow hair that curled around his neck. About his own age, Lichine guessed.

The second figure was arresting. He was immense, the slabs and pads of muscle cording and undulating with each step, even beneath the tee shirt and jeans. That strength was built, Lichine suspected, over years of hauling tuna and marlin, not by health club workouts. His copper hair and beard were unshorn, a blazing corona around a bulbous nose and marble eyes. He wore a canvas hat with the brim turned down so that even those few facial features were in shadow. The eyes, however, glittered.

"Mr. Lichine?" asked the younger man, flashing a row of even teeth. Lichine nodded and took the proffered hand.

"Wink Andros," said the man, smile in place. "And this winsome lad is Jeeter Doakes."

Lichine winced as the huge hand ground his knuckles. He met the penetrating stare for a second, but then his eyes skidded away. Jeeter Doakes grunted acknowledgment, then moved past to examine the boat. More grunts. Pacing. Bending. Fists on hips.

"This it?" he rumbled, squinting at the waterline. The hat concealed his reaction.

"It is," Lichine said with a note of defiance. "Of course, it's not exactly mine yet. Buying a boat is a drawn out process, I've discovered. Papers, clearances, negotiation with the owner ... But yes. Mine, for all practical. . ."

"Piece of shit," said Doakes.

"Oh?" Lichine swallowed. "How is that?"

Doakes gave a contemptuous snort. "When did they stop makin' fishin' boats?" he said to Wink. Lichine might not have been there.

"It ain't so bad, Jeet," said Andros. "I drove it over here from Rumfeld's."

"Fuck it ain't," Doakes exploded. "That aluminum hull'll bang like a bass drum at anchor, never mind out on the water. Crew's quarters forward might as well be in the bilge of a tanker."

"I didn't really expect that you . . ." Lichine tried to say.

"Never mind that," Doakes continued, his indignation deepening, ignoring Lichine. "What's it gonna do backin' on a fish? Shake like a bitch is what. Like to rattle every rivet out. And it won't track worth a damn. I rode this model once. The rudders are too shallow. It wallows like a scow in any sea worth remarkin' on. Takes an hour to get up on plane even when it's slick calm. And will you look at that crap in the cabin? Tricked out like a Mexican cathouse. Man who put this together was thinkin' on Vaseline pattycake in Biscayne Bay, not about catchin' fish."

"Since you feel that way, Captain," Lichine heard himself saying, "I don't imagine you'll want to join us."

Doakes swiveled around at the sound and regarded Lichine as if he had only now arrived. He took a step and planted himself inches away from Ernest, who was surprised to discover that he didn't have to look up.

"Wink says you're payin' four hundred a day," Doakes said.

"That was my offer." *I will not step back.*

"Two-fifty for me, one-fifty for Wink, and another hundred for when we got to take on a second mate."

"But I thought. . . from what you were saying. . . ."

"What? Oh. Listen, Mr. Lichine. I won the Master's in a boat that makes this one look like the Queen Elizabeth. Is the split okay or not?"

"If it's customary."

"Good," Doakes said. "Now we got to understand each other. Right here, on the dock, you're the boss. You're payin'. But soon's we're on board, everyone moves to my notion, includin' you. We go where I say and we fish where I say. I'm gonna take you out, hang your bait over Big Mo, you're gonna reel him in, and Wink's gonna boat'm. Far as I hear, you don't know diddly shit about this business, but even if you did, that's the way it'd be. Also. I'm gonna run this boat hard. It's the only way to do it. Can't catch fish if you baby the equipment. Seams are gonna split, bilge is gonna flood, hoses're gonna snap.

"You're gonna have to pay the bills, and I don't want to have to explain every piddle-assed nickle dime repair. Now close as I can figure, we're expected to come out fifth out of five in this horseshit contest, maybe tie for fourth, if we get lucky. Me, I'm goin' for the whole nut, and if you don't think we're gonna do it, you tell me now and I'll walk."

Doakes waited. Wink Andros shifted his weight. Mooring lines creaked, a gull yapped.

"Your stipulations are acceptable," Lichine said eventually, after discarding several other replies. He held the gaze of the glittering eyes, though. This time, Doakes pivoted away.

"We got things to talk: about," his new captain said to his new mate. "Let's check it out."

Lichine was dismissed. He watched the retreating backs.

"Captain Doakes," he made himself say. Too loud.

Doakes stopped and looked back only after Wink nudged him.

"Somethin'?"

"Yes," said Lichine, willing his head not to tremble.

"Well?"

"You were late," Lichine said, feeling foolish even as he formed the words. "I trust we will be ready in time."

Doakes glanced quizzically at his mate, then back.

"Don't you worry none, Mr. Lichine." Just rev your own-self up. Me 'n' Wink'll do the rest."

The tournament was conceived in the aftermath of the annual awards banquet of the International Angling Association, held the preceding Thursday. Fifteen minutes before the dinner, Ernest Lichine found his assigned place on the dais and undertook a protracted examination of the table setting. Anything to avoid watching the scores of people coming through the doors.

Most of the men wore crested blazers with monogrammed gold buttons; the women, bare shouldered floor length gowns in white, peach, and lime. They all knew each other. At twenty-eight, Lichine was younger than they, a newcomer, and unaccustomed to public celebration of his achievements.

"Put you as far below the salt as they could, didn't they?" asked a throaty voice from behind him.

Lichine started and turned. The woman was dazzling. Keen featured, lean, honey haired.

"You're the broadbills, aren't you? Lichine?"

He managed to nod.

"I'll keep you company," she decided, and sat down with the assurance of one who had long ago dismissed the possibility that her presence might not be welcomed. After switching place cards, she appraised her chosen tablemate with a directness that set Lichine to fumbling with his napkin and flatware.

"This is your first time here, isn't it?" she asked. It was just as well she didn't pause for a response, for Lichine could not have managed more than a strangled croak. Instead, he fixed his eyes on the bridge of her nose, for the draped neckline of her dress swooped so low that when she leaned forward he glimpsed the shadowed tip of her right breast.

"Isn't it a horror? It really wasn't too bad a few years ago, in an Ivy League sort of way. Then the whole place underwent what the board of directors chose to describe as its 'plant rejuvenation.' There's oak paneling beneath that dreadful avocado paint, and Spanish tile floors under that bottle green broadloom, and those grotesque drapes with the peonies replaced really fine brocade."

A waiter poured champagne. They sipped. Lichine had yet to speak.

"Ugh," said Catherine Nettles. "Finger Lakes Finest again. Anyway, the Commodore must be whirling in his sarcophagus. That's him over there."

She indicated a painting on the opposite wall. It portrayed a man in blazer and visored cap at the helm of what Lichine supposed was a racing sloop. The Commodore glowered at the gaudy assemblage over a luxuriant mustache.

"Commodore Whitney Triga Somerset himself," Catherine Nettles continued. "The portrait was commissioned on the occasion of his third triumph over upstart challengers for the America's Cup. It's all that's left of his notion of what a proper sailing club should look like."

She picked at the crab cocktail, grimaced, and reached for the champagne.

"The man the Commodore is glaring at is his nephew. Right down there, center front. That shriveled little man with the beady eyes. B. K. Triga. Ever heard of him?"

Lichine shook his head.

"Most people haven't. B.K. keeps a low profile, as well he might. He's the last living billionaire in the United States and never turned an honest million. Hates to be photographed. The only one I've ever seen of him was with Barry Goldwater, whose cause was the most liberal Triga ever supported. B.K. thinks Genghis Khan was a pinko. Sorry. Didn't step on your ideological toes there, did I?"

"No," said Lichine softly, astounded he was able to form words. "I don't know much about politics."

"Well, for your future guidance, you'd be hard put to find anyone in this room who doesn't hew to B.K.'s line. Anyway, the Commodore loathed B.K., and B.K. returned the favor. B.K. also hates boats, fishing, this club, and just about all of the people here. That's why, the day he was elected chairman of the board, he put his wife, Bubbles, in charge of the tasteful renovation in which we are now imprisoned. Pure spite."

The tournedos arrived. Lichine concentrated on the meal, nodding at appropriate junctures in his companion's monologue but daring only an occasional glance at her. Beautiful women rattled him even more than groups of two or more people. A lifetime of days and nights at his workbench had insured both sanctuary and a lack of opportunity to develop social grace.

With the arrival of the strawberries jubilee, the toastmaster moved to the podium to begin the ceremony. Lichine's stomach knotted. Catherine Nettles went right on, lowering her voice only slightly as she rostered the elder Triga's holdings.

"Steamships, copper mines, hotels, cattle ranches, North Sea refineries, among other things. As far as I know, B.K. hates all of them, too. Actually, the only thing he appears to be ambivalent about is baby Horst. Damned if I know why, except B.K. has a grudging admiration for excellence, even if it's in something as irrelevant as big game fishing. Horst isn't much otherwise, but he's one of the three best anglers in the world. And in case you're wondering, dear, the other two are Monty Childs, that gorgeous creature in the blue velvet tux. . . and me."

A change in the toastmaster's pitch from frivolity to portentousness disrupted Lichine's consideration of that scrap of self assessment. He looked down the table at Horst Triga, who bowed his head as he was described as a man who had rewritten the record books of the IAA and who required no further aggrandizement at the hands of the master of ceremonies.

Horst Triga rose to applause. He was inipeccably tailored in a fashion not unlike his great uncle across the hall, minus the cap. He radiated robust health and possessed a full head of snowy hair, the only physical characteristic he shared with his father. B.K. Triga was attempting a thin smile.

Horst accepted the silver bowl that was emblematic of the Association black marlin championship. He hefted the trophy and leaned toward the microphone.

"Unfamiliar as I am . . ." he began, anticipating the interruption of knowing laughter. "No, really," he continued, "after a few times up here," he paused for another ripple of chuckling, "you find that the only satisfactory words are 'thank you, my friends, very much.'"

Catherine Nettles groaned. "Horst," she said, "is as humble and unassuming as a water buffalo in heat."

The next award was presented to Montgomery Childs, for blue marlin. Lichine's hands began trembling. He didn't dare lift a glass to his lips, for then his head would wobble, too. Bowls were given to Theodore Marker for giant tuna and to Catherine Nettles, for sailfish.

Another agonized moment, and Lichine heard the toastmaster say, ". . . and finally, a new warrior on the aquatic field of honor, our swordfisherman of the year, Ernest Lichine!"

Lichine willed himself to stand. His chair fell over. He righted it. His toe caught in a microphone wire. He took the trophy before the presenter was prepared to relinquish it, mumbled his thanks and scurried back to his place. His head would not stop quaking.

"Poor darling!" Catherine Nettles said, placing a cool hand over his. "Was it as dreadful as all that?"

"W-worse." The polite patter of applause lapsed into a sniggering burble as the dinner began breaking up. All three hundred people were laughing at him, he was certain.

"Don't let them get to you, dear," she soothed. "They all hold their peckers when they pee. Come along. This ersatz bubbly hasn't enough zip to gentle a gnat. We'll get some brandy into you. Don't argue, just come on. It's over."

She led him to the lounge off the dining room. At least a third of the banquet guests were there. They hooted over shared experiences and revived gossip. Heads turned as Catherine Nettles and Lichine passed.

Speculations were exchanged. Were the woman not leading him firmly forward, Lichine would have fled.

He ventured aloud that he had never in his life felt so alien.

"There, there," said Catherine. "You are now one of the superstars in our tight little orbit and most learn to grow into the role." She raised her hand, and a waiter materialized with two snifters of brandy.

"Cheers, Ernie," she said, draining half of hers. "Go ahead, drink up. It'll give you an erection."

He did as instructed, but she tipped his glass and he swallowed more than he intended.

"Good," she said. "Now we can go beard our fellow champs."

As they picked their way between elbows and backs, Catherine resumed her commentary. The membership rosters of the Floridian Yacht Club and the International Angling Association were virtually identical, she said. The latter organization was misnamed, for it was devoted exclusively to deep sea, big game fishing. Barefoot boys and trout fishermen need not apply. At the instigation of B.K. Triga, the club had evolved from the Commodore's vision of a southern branch of the gentlemanly art of sailing into a bastion of the despised adversary avocation, motorboating. The current membership called sail boaters "ragpickers," and all lingering wind yachtsmen had now departed for more congenial surroundings.

The other winners had taken up traditional positions at the long window overlooking the boat basin. Tides of friends and relatives eddied around them.

When Lichine and Catherine Nettles arrived, Childs, Triga, and Marker widened their circle. Nettles made introductions. Lichine surreptitiously wiped his palm on his trouser before he took their hands.

"Monty, darling," Catherine said to Childs, "you are a vision tonight."

"What can I say, Cat?" Childs responded with a practiced grin. "When you're right, you're right."

"And you are your usual delectable self, Catherine," Horst Triga interposed. "Congratulations, by the way."

"You can't win them all, Ho," she said.

"All I can do is try," Triga said with an amiable shrug.

"I should explain, dear," Catherine said to Lichine. "Until you came along, the four of us monopolized these things. This year, Horst came in second to me in sailfish. Theo and I tied behind Monty for blue marlin, and Horst missed Theo by one fish in tuna. That makes you odd man out. None of us even came close in broadbills."

"I didn't even try swordfish," said Childs.

"Too frustrating," Triga agreed.

"Needs more patience than I got," said Marker.

"I was just lucky," said Lichine, flattered.

"Indeed," said Triga, with a resonance shading from neutrality to agreement.

"What they ain't sayin', Ernie," said Theo Marker, "is how you 'n' me're the only ones here who had to overcome the disadvantage of workin' for a livin'."

"Spare us just this once, Theo," said Childs. "That rough hewn working class hero number is gritting a bit frayed."

"I gotta sweat, pal," Marker said. "I pay my ex-wives, they don't pay me."

"The price for thirty years of starlet pronging, Theo," Catherine Nettles said. She turned to Lichine, who was staring at Marker.

The man was below average height, with a bristling ruff of gray hair across the top and back of his head. His beard was cropped into a pugnacious thrust, and he was wearing a safari jacket with a kerchief knotted around his throat. No one had ever seen Theodore Marker dressed otherwise.

"If you're trying to place the face, dear," Catherine continued, "Theo makes movies. Two hours each of dismembered bodies and great goops of gore flying across the screen in slow motion. Then he goes on the talk shows and explains how he's making a statement against violence."

"Theo makes films for people who move their lips when they watch," Childs added.

"Beats hell out of sucking up to broads older'n God's wife, gigolo," Marker snapped, the leathery flesh of his neck turning darker.

"I protest the implication that God is a dyke," said Catherine.

Lichine took refuge in his drink. The bantering resumed. Two more snifters arrived, as if divined. Lichine emptied most of his and signaled for another.

2

The warning klaxon sounded at 4:45. Most of the club boats had returned to their berths. Members and guests stood along the seawall, glasses in hand, bantering with the contestant crews and anglers. Lichine alternately watched his new captain and mate in their preparations and scanned the crowd for Catherine. Finally, she was there, picking her way through the onlookers and walking quickly toward him. His face was suddenly hot and before he could formulate his greeting, her arms were around his waist and she was pressing herself to him.

"A kiss," she demanded. He complied.

"Another," she said, slipping a thigh between his. After a very long moment, she pulled away. "Good luck, darling."

She was gone, trotting toward her boat. There was a patter of applause from the waiting crowd.

Activity in and around the boats intensified. Crews made final preparations, anglers settled themselves, the umpires boarded their assigned craft. Lichine observed it all in a daze. Jeeter Doakes was on the bridge, calling down to Wink Andros.

Flying gaffs in the seat? Affirmative. Straight-butt rods aboard? Yeah. Got ice? Beer? Yeah. Enough paper in the fathometer? Wink asked. The captain nodded distractedly, running through a mental checklist. The downstairs steering doesn't work, the mate reminded. Ain't used that station on a boat in ten years, Doakes replied. Again, the klaxon. Two minutes. Wink hopped to the dock, unwound the stem lines from their cleats, then clambered up the ladder to the flybridge, where Lichine and the umpire were sitting. Doakes slid a panel aside and pulled out a microphone, flicking on the radio with the same hand. He adjusted the squelch.

"What's this shitbucket called?" he asked.

Lichine flinched. Wink gave the name.

"Christ," said Doakes, "who'd call a boat that?"

"I would," Lichine answered.

Doakes shrugged, and held the mike to his lips. "We is ready, Oscar," he said. "When you fixin' to get it on?"

"Momentarily, Captain Doakes," came the reply over the speaker. It was Oscar Farrington, the head umpire. A pause. "All boats. We have thirty seconds ... now! Twenty-nine, twenty-eight ..."

Doakes turned to the control console, twisted the key, mashed the starter buttons. Engines coughed to life all along the pier, a platoon of Panzers responding to battle orders. Lichine felt a sharp tightening in his chest.

Five prows inched forward. Decks shuddered.

"Feel like goin' out?" Jeeter Doakes calmly asked of no one in particular.

"Why ain't we left yet?" Wink Andros replied.

"... six, five, four ..."

Doakes eased both clutches forward. At the instant the word "Zero!" came over the speaker, he rammed the left clutch to the end of the slot, jerked the right into reverse, and spun the wheel. The boat lunged, pitched to starboard, straightened. Lichine grabbed at the handrail. The umpire gaped. A curving wedge of white water slammed into the other boats in the rank, throwing bows skyward.

Brain Soup was first away.

Eventually, Lichine decided that the byplay between Theo Marker, Monty Childs, and Catherine that previous Thursday night was merely a variety of locker room conviviality in which people accustomed to winning continued the competition. It made him profoundly uncomfortable, at first. The taunts cut too close to the bone, although only Theo Marker betrayed any irritation. Horst Triga remained tolerant and detached, rarely sipping from his glass and handily deflecting the occasional barbs aimed at him.

An hour passed, perhaps more. With a grave tenacity or tenacious gravity Lichine reckoned the number of cognacs he had drunk. The accounting was inconclusive, so he concentrated on picking up the direction of the conversation.

"Even the greenest tourist can pull in a dozen sailfish a day," Monty Childs was saying. "You just have to drag enough baits."

"And how is that different from blues?" Catherine Nettles answered. "I've boated marlin in five minutes. And I never use anything but twenty pound test line! With the stuff you use, I could haul in an elephant."

"If you had the strength," said Childs.

"I do. And I'll match you, Monty," Catherine said. "Anytime. Anywhere. With no handicap."

"Head for head, you might say," Childs smirked. "How about tonight?"

"Don't be ludicrous, darling. You'd muss your coiffure and it'd take two hours to get it back the way it was. I was speaking, in this case, about fishing."

"I never knew you to turn down a tumble, Cat."

"I don't, too often. A hard man is good to find."

"Did you mean that, Catherine?" Horst Triga interjected. "About no handicap?"

"You bet your thing I did."

"It might be stimulating to put that claim to the test," Triga said, idly twirling his drink.

"Name the place," she said.

Marker and Childs were suddenly alert. Lichine motioned for a refill.

"Is that an open challenge?" said Childs.

"Why not?" said Catherine.

"Could be a kick," said Marker.

"Just us four, you mean?" Childs persisted.

"Five," said Catherine, taking Lichine's arm. "Don't forget the new kid."

Lichine surmised that they were looking at him. He endeavored to focus.

"What?" he said.

"I don't know, Cat," said Childs. "We've all been at this a long time. Lichine isn't. . ." He let his voice trail off.

"Bullshit," she said. "We aren't talking about heart surgery. Experience is useful, but not critical. Balls and stamina count for more. And Ernie has a broadbill record. None of us has ever come close."

"I concur," said Triga. "There is a certain symmetry in that prospect. The five international champions of the year in an elimination tourney."

"A fish off," said Marker, playing with the idea.

"For top angler of the world," added Childs.

"When do we start?"

"No better time than now."

"What will the setup be? Do we get the IAA to sponsor?"

"I say no. They'll just wrap it up in red tape."

"I agree," said Horst Triga. "Let's keep it simple. If I might suggest. . ." He surveyed their faces for dissent, found none. "We have the outline already. Each of us has a favored prey, as demonstrated by the awards we now possess. Depending upon location, the seasons for each species happen to fall in a logical sequence. Swordfish now, sails in April, tuna in May, blue marlin in July, and black marlin in October. True?"

They nodded.

"Very well," Triga continued. "All five of us will fish for all five species in a place designated by tonight's winner in each category. That is, Catherine says where and when we go for sailfish. Theo picks the spot for giant tuna, and so on. We allow two weeks for each segment, with breaks in between to permit repairs and refitting and to attend to personal business. We follow standard IAA rules and agree beforehand on types of equipment to be used, number of crew, and the like."

"Sounds good."

"Okay with me."

"Me, too, as far as it goes," said Catherine.

"How do you mean, Catherine?" said Triga.

"Will it be tag and release or on the dock?"

"On the dock, I should think," said Triga. "To insure verification of catches."

"I figured you'd say that, Horst," said Catherine, her tone edged with scorn.

"But, Catherine, I'm sure we'd all want some way to confirm results. We can't do that if we don't bring the fish in."

"Besides," said Childs, "with a release tournament, a one hundred pound fish counts as much as a thousand pounder."

"And I figured you'd side with Horst," Catherine said. "The two of you are more interested in the killing than the fishing."

Horst was unruffled. "That's unwarranted, of course. But what do you propose, Catherine?"

"Simple. Five umpires appointed by the IAA, to rotate boats for each phase of the contest."

"Oh, now, Catherine, I don't really think that's necessary. We are honorable people..."

"I like it," Theo Marker said, running his hand over his bristly hair. "It'd keep everything straight."

"Lichine?"

"I'm wif 'er," said Lichine, patting Catherine on the shoulder. He was following very little of this.

"Very well," Triga said with evident reluctance. "May I suggest we all get together to iron out details? Say tomorrow afternoon? The *Highlander*? One o'clock? I'll have a light lunch prepared."

"Fine," said Catherine.

"One thing I'd like to settle now," said Theo Marker. "What's the action?"

"I've got ten thousand dollars that says I'll take it," said Monty Childs, flicking a flake of ash from his lapel.

"Make it twenty," said Catherine.

Triga drew a leather memo pad from his pocket and began to write. "I had in mind," he said, "a figure more nearly of these dimensions."

He tore off the piece of paper and handed it to Childs.

"Each of us?" said Childs, cocking an eyebrow when he read what Triga had written.

"Yes," said Triga. "I believe the necessary resources are amply represented in our little group." He busied himself with the preparations of lighting a cigar.

"You're on," said Catherine when Childs passed the paper to her. Marker pursed his lips in a low whistle when he saw it.

"Okay," he said finally. "I guess."

"I'm in," said Childs.

Lichine accepted the scrap of paper. The numbers Triga had scribbled with an insouciant flourish, Lichine was able to discern, were a "one" followed by six zeros.

"Me too," he said, trying to recall the subject under discussion.

Marker finished his drink. "Gentlemen, Cat," he said,. "I think I'd better get to clearin' my decks."

He nodded farewell and left. Montgomery Childs and Horst Triga began the motions of departure. Lichine couldn't be positive it wasn't accidental, but he knew that the hand that brushed across the back of his leg belonged to Catherine Nettles.

By the time they were heading into open sea, the sun had dropped behind the jagged wall of high rise condominiums on the mainland. The sea was placid riffles and the wind was almost undetectable. Wink Andros was below, readying the rods and rigging baits in the cockpit. A hump of milk green water dragged behind, bracketed by writhing twin cords of foam. The nearest outgoing I boats were a mile back. Lichine went down the ladder and perched awkwardly on the covering board, out of the mate's way.

Wink inserted the butt of a rod into the tubular holder on the left side of the chair and allowed it to swing forward to the maximum forty five degree angle. Then he stripped off a few feet of line, the big brass sided reel ratcheting. He picked up a loop of double line from the bait table by the door and carefully tied the ends together.

"Is that a special knot?" Lichine asked, in attempt at conversation.

"Bimini twist," Wink briskly replied. He didn't look up.

"How long is the double line?"

"Thirty feet." The mate tied the end of this to still another strand, this one of visibly thicker plastic monofilament. "And this is an Albright knot. Leader is thirty feet of four hundred pound test." Double hooks about twice the size of a crooked finger clattered on the deck at the end of the leader. "And the hooks are ten oh. All strictly by the IAA rule book."

"I didn't mean to suggest . . ." Lichine trailed off, flustered by the mate's apparent annoyance.

Wink glanced up and grinned. "Me neither, Mr. Lichine. Guess I'm edgy, too. Ask away."

"Why mono leader? Why not wire?"

" 'Cause we drift for swordies and the baits move more realistically on mono. Only need wire for the big fish, so they can't chew through."

"Are we using squid or Boston mackerel?"

"Got both. We'll see what works."

"How far out are we going?"

Wink squinted at the rolling swell of the Gulf Stream. "About another half hour. Twelve, fifteen miles out. Jeet's running south so we can drift with the Stream and not get too far away from Palm Beach."

"How deep?"

"Water'll be about a thousand feet. We'll put one bait about two hundred and fifty feet down, another at two hundred, a third at one fifty."

"Why not deeper?"

The mate paused again, looked sharply at Lichine. "I thought you'd done broadbills before."

"Yes," said Lichine, embarrassed again. "But up North they go for swordfish during the day. And we don't drift. We don't even put out a bait until we spot one on the surface. This is all new to me."

"Pretty new to us, too. Only been the last three or four years we been catching swordies on purpose." Wink pulled a squid as big as a clenched fist from the chest and inserted a hook. "And damn few boated, at that. Not likely we'll see anything near as big as your record, either."

"What's the average?"

"Maybe a hundred pounds. Three hundred, and they send Walter Cronkite."

"But my sword was 546 pounds. . ."

"On eighty pound test," Wink completed. "I know, Mr. Lichine. But we just haven't been seeing them that big here."

When he finished rigging the third bait, the mate asked Lichine to get into the fighting chair. He lifted a rod from its holder and placed the butt in the seat gimbal between Lichine's legs.

"Get into position," he said.

Lichine shifted in the chair, his left hand lying on the back of the reel, which was mounted atop the fiberglass rod, two feet from the butt.

"Okay?" Wink asked. He looked his employer over, decided to adjust the footrest. "You are a long drink of water, Mr. Lichine. We got this almost to the last notch. You have any preference on the belt? Hip or kidney? There's both on board."

"Whatever you think."

The mate chose the one shaped like a fielder's mitt, placing it so it cradled Lichine's hips and buttocks. Two adjustable straps with clasps on the ends ran forward from the comers on the harness. These were snapped, in turn, to the metal eyes on each side of the reel. Buckles were loosened until there was balanced tension between hips and rod. Lichine straightened his legs and leaned back, raising the rod to the vertical, then slid forward, lowering it.

"We're ready as we're gonna get," Wink pronounced, clapping his employer on the shoulder. He unhooked the clasps and returned the rod to the holder on the side of the chair. "Might as well settle back. Gonna be a long night."

Attempts to still the fluttering in his chest failed, so Lichine focused his thoughts on Catherine.

It was the day after the awards dinner, of that Lichine was certain. Nearly. Sooner or later, he instructed himself, he was going to have to open his eyes. He deferred that inevitability by fanning his arm. Cool, slithery. Satin sheets, he decided. A bed, he deduced. Large, because he couldn't reach the edges. Not his, because he wasn't wearing his pajamas. No other person in it, but a presence. Something round and warm between his legs. The air was metallically chill.

He eased one eyelid up and immediately regretted it. Sunlight pierced into his brain. After a while, he managed both eyes. That hurt. His bowels churned. The Siamese cat curled at his groin glared at him. Lichine cautiously reached to stroke its head. It hissed and bounded off.

There were no other sounds in the room. Lichine made himself sit up and swing his legs to the ledge. His head throbbed and he fought down nausea. There was a piece of paper propped against the brass lamp of the marble topped side table. He picked it up and tried to focus on the writing.

"Good morning, darling," it read, in a sweeping hand. "Thank you for the loan of your body, if not your undivided attention. To answer your questions: (a) You are in my house; (b) It is in West Palm Beach; (c) I'm at the club; (d) You are due there at one o'clock; (e) You were better than indifferent but less than spectacular; (f) Yes, I did. Maybe three times.

"There is a fridge in the dressing room. It has orange juice and bloody Marys. Push the button on the telephone and Rosa will bring coffee."

The note was unsigned. There was a gilded clock under a glass dome on the bombe chest on the other side of the room. It tinkled. Lichine padded across to it, conscious of his nakedness, and squinted at the ornate numbers. Ten past noon. The fourth door he tried was the dressing room. It was as large as his kitchen back home, brimming with the scent of her. He took the carafe of orange juice from the small refrigerator and sat on the chair in front of the vanity while he drained every drop. His stomach protested, so he drank half of the bottle of bloody Mary, too.

As his queasiness subsided, Lichine considered the ramifications of his actions of the last twenty four hours. Never had he permitted himself to get so far over his head, and in so many ways at once. He rarely drank, for one thing, apart from a beer or two before dinner. The results of that deviation from pattern were abundantly clear. Until less than a year ago, for another, his only experience with saltwater fishing was day excursions with his brother Jason, on party boats from Sheepshead Bay and from piers and beaches on Long Island. Until last August, a fifty-two pound striped bass was his largest trophy. On a whim it was the day their accountant estimated their joint net worth at slightly over $25 million, he and Jason chartered the cruiser out of Montauk, just for themselves. That was the day of the two swordfish.

However engaging, fishing remained a weekend diversion. He and Jason had work to do. But Horst Triga and Catherine Nettles and the others were, in effect, professional anglers. Catherine said that .the hundred days a year she spent on her boat were far fewer than the totals of either Triga or Monty Childs. Even Theo Marker, for all his protests about the demands of his career, managed ninety. And they had been at it for years.

Further, by the standards of his new rivals, he was merely well to do. When their accountant made his stunning announcement, he cautioned the Lichine brothers that they would be hard pressed to put their hands on even three million dollars in cash. Ernest didn't understand why Jason handled marketing and investment but it didn't matter. He couldn't imagine how he might spend all that, even with concentrated effort. Until today.

And Catherine. Although approaching thirty, Lichine could count on one hand the women -- girls -- he had bedded, and accuracy demanded acknowledgment that he was more often the seduced than not. Never had he encountered a woman of Catherine's erotic expertise. She had shed her waspish, mocking manner as soon as they entered this room and she reached for the first button on her blouse. She had soothed, stroked, guided. When he fumbled, she reassured and restored the pace. When he became over urgent, she quieted him with a touch. When he was premature, she eased him back, then quickened toward unbearably protracted release.

Lichine smiled, half triumph, half wonder. What more might she give him, or he, her? There was the sense of knowledge held back, sensations yet to be revealed. How could she know so much of him, the points and junctures of arousal and relief hidden even from him? Where, from whom, had she. . . ?

He sprang upright, heart pounding. A husband? Away? Dead? Here? He couldn't remember. Lichine bounded to the door, knocking over the bottle. He found the bathroom, showered quickly. The presence in the cabinet of a razor and shaving cream was not reassuring. He swabbed up the spilled bloody Mary as best he could and found his clothes. By then, he was calmer, and he had decided.

Possibly he was mad, certainly irresponsible. But first things first. He needed a crew and a boat. Then he would talk to his brother. And Catherine.

3

Sparky Thomas was the umpire assigned to *Brain Soup* for the swordfish phase of the tournament. He shoved the glass door of the cabin aside and stepped out on the cockpit deck. Thomas bore a head the shape of an egg, with a torso to match. His cardigan, polo shirt, and slacks were various shades of beige, coordinated with a thinning thatch of sandy hair. A black pipe with a curved stem was clamped between his teeth. His preferred attire, Lichine imagined, was tweed.

Thomas walked to the transom, bracing himself against the roll of the boat. He puffed reflectively, first regarding the darkening sky, then the welling wake.

"Splendid spot, isn't it?" he observed, turning slightly toward Lichine. "I never tire of it. Did you know that the Gulf Stream carries more than five times the total volume of all the freshwater rivers in all the world? Isn't that a remarkable thing to contemplate?"

"Really?" Lichine said, his mind elsewhere.

"Yes, indeed. Fifty miles wide, as much as two miles deep, moving northward at an inexorable four miles an hour. You're from up North, aren't you?"

"New York. Brooklyn, actually."

"So I heard. Yes. I am, too, you know. Quite different here, isn't it? Hmm?"

Wink Andros came down from the bridge and poked around in

the cabinet beneath the bait table. He stuffed three green candle shaped tubes in his hip pocket. Each was about nine inches long. Lichine caught his attention, raised his eyebrows in inquiry.

"Cyalume lights," Wink said. "Plastic, with two glass cylinders inside. I bend them, the glass breaks, the fluids mix, and they make a glow that lasts about three hours. Shows Big Mo where the food is. We think. Like I said, we're still experimenting."

He stuffed a tube inside one squid and tied the other two to the leaders on the remaining rods.

"We don't know which way works better. Next couple weeks, we'll try everything."

The radio on the bridge squawked. Jeeter Doakes listened, then bellowed down to Wink.

"*Adroit* and *Redemption* got their baits out. We lost our lead. Put that right stick on the outrigger! Leave the other two flat. We got no moon, so keep one of the baits on the surface. Get your ass in gear!"

Wink dropped the squids of the two chair rods over the stern and free spooled as the water grabbed them and tore off line. When they were far enough out, he thumbed the drags on the reels one third forward and tightened the screws. He did the same with the last rod, which was placed in the port covering board. Then he caught the line just above the rod tip, affixed the outrigger clip, and ran the line hand-over-hand through the pulleys until it hit the end of the gull-wing pole, fifteen feet up and out from the side of the boat. The squid skipped briefly on the surface, a hundred feet astern, then plunged. Doakes throttled back. The engines cut to a low rumble.

It was quiet, almost completely dark. They waited.

At 7: 12 P.M., the outrigger clip snicked open, the line sailed out in a long looping arc, then straightened. Something had decided to eat the squid.

The planning meeting was held that Friday afternoon.

Lichine was no more prepared for the opulence of *Highlander* than he had been for any other experience of the last twenty four hours. Each of the other contestants owned at least one sportfishing boat. But only Horst Triga and Catherine Nettles maintained yachts intended solely for living and cruising.

Highlander was 120 feet long, Catherine informed Lichine as they stepped up the gangplank. There was a helicopter pad above the salon, because Horst liked his Miami Herald and Wall Street Journal with his breakfast coffee, she said, wherever he might be moored. There were gold plated shower heads and faucets, bulkhead to bulkhead carpet, an exercise room, movie projection booth, Corats and Pissaros, pre-Columbian artifacts in glowing niches, live blooms in vases, thriving plants in brass pots, and buttery leather and suede and chrome and alabaster. *Highlander,* pampered and indulged by a crew of seven, preceded Horst Triga to each fishing ground, in seasonal sequence. Catherine doubted that Triga spent a total of seventy days a year in his houses in Coconut Grove and Morgan Cay and Algeciras and God knew where else. *Highlander* was his home. *Adroit* was his office.

"Vulgar and ostentatious, isn't it?" Catherine said as they entered the salon. She swept two glasses from the tray held by a passing steward. "On *Aphrodite*, I have to get by with a week old Newsweek."

"Poor Catherine," said Lichine. He had seen *Aphrodite.* It was a demure thirty feet shorter than *Highlander*, but hardly Spartan.

"I make do," she said with a valiant sigh, a bump of haunch, and a squeeze of his arm against the curve of her breast.

"We will make do."

The preliminaries were predictable. Catherine, Theo Marker, and Monty Childs needled each other mercilessly, the stings deepening in proportion to the frequency of appearance of the steward and his tray. Lichine and the other guests situated themselves just beyond the periphery of the fray. Horst Triga selected an interlude of regroupment to suggest they address the business at hand. Seats were found. Triga introduced the five IAA umpires. Rules were discussed, some in passing, others with heat. Locations of the five segments of the tourney were announced, one by each participant. Catherine chose Cozumel, off Yucatan. Morgan Cay for tuna, said Marker. St. Thomas for blue marlin, said Childs. Cairns for black marlin, said Triga. Lichine picked Palm Beach, as was predetermined. He would have preferred Nantucket.

Triga then proposed that, as he put it, "The pot be made good."

Certified checks were produced from four wallets and one handbag. They were handed to Oscar Farrington, the head umpire. He tapped them even on his knee, placed them in an envelope, and dropped the envelope into a small black attache case. He pressed the clasps shut and spun the dials of the combination lock. Two men with creases across the backs of their necks took the case and left. A stretch limousine awaited them at the end of the dock.

Rules were then discussed in detail. Each of the five phases was to be two weeks in length, commencing Sunday afternoon at five. There were to be two lay days each week, determined by all participants at the sites. The scoring system was simple: ten points for every fish brought to the boat and designated by the umpire as officially caught. All were to be released, with one important exception.

"To illustrate," said Oscar Farrington in lectern tones that set his audience to squirming, "let us consider swordfish."

Average weight was under one hundred pounds. In the interests of environmental conservation, all broadbills under that limit were to be released, unharmed. Over that minimum, however, the angler could choose to gaff and boat the fish. If his estimate of weight proved accurate on the dock scales, he or she would be awarded a bonus of one point per pounds over the limit. If he or she proved to be inaccurate, a penalty of one point per pounds under the limit was to be imposed. Was that fully understood?

There were impatient shufflings of feet. "Christ Almighty," Theo Marker muttered.

"Yes, Oscar dear," said Catherine, "we really do comprehend. Can we please get on with this, love?" Farrington's papery cheeks pinked, but he continued at the pace already established.

Finally, he was done. "If there are no further questions. . . ."

"Oscar," said Horst Triga, "if I might have the floor for just a moment?"

Marker and Catherine groaned.

"I assure you," he said, "only a moment." He cleared his throat. "It occurs to me that we have made no provision to ensure the faithful participation of all contestants."

"Meaning what?" Catherine asked impatiently.

"Merely that it will be in all our interests, and that of the sport itself, if we agree on some means by which we can assure diligence."

"S'pose you sort that out," Theo Marker suggested.

"Simply this: we all desire a true test of our skills. The extraordinary scope of this competition and the time we are devoting to it attests to that. But it also bears the seeds of potential trivialization."

"For Christ's sake, get to it."

"Lacking predetermined sanctions, anyone of us can withdraw and return at any point, willy-nilly. Yet I think it safe to say that we five are in this for the challenge, for the prospect of prevailing over the most able competitors. 'Head-to-head,' as Monty put it. What will victory mean if all of us are not present at all times, putting forth our best efforts?"

"The point," Catherine prompted.

"I propose that anyone of us who absents himself--or herself--for more than three consecutive fishing days be permanently dropped from the tournament. . ."

The others began to protest, but Triga continued ". . . and the entire amount of his or her wager forfeited."

Everyone complained at once, and at length. But in the end and for reasons of their own, they voted to accept Horst Triga's proposal.

After twenty minutes, the broadbill sounded. For a long moment, it had lolled on the surface, its high curved dorsal and the sloping upper lobe of its tail lazily slicing the crests. It was close enough to be visible within the nimbus of light produced by the powerful quartz lamps attached to the flybridge handrail. Lichine thought the fight was over. But then Jeeter Doakes opened the throttles, backing on the fish to permit Lichine to retrieve line. The noise and looming stern startled the broadbill, and now it was gone, swimming down and away.

With great effort, Lichine straightened his legs against the footrest, pushing back against the hip harness. He watched helplessly as two hundred feet of line zizzed from the big, brass-sided reel. He heard the captain curse and felt the boat shudder to a halt.

"That's the way, Mr. Lichine," said Wink Andros, who was standing behind and slightly left of the fighting chair. "Keep the rod high. Make her work for every inch. You're doin' fine."

"Her?" Lichine gasped, clamping his hands on the armrests and straining to raise the bowed rod. "It's a female?"

"Most likely," the mate replied. "We don't see two together very often. And this one you got on is bigger than the first. The female always is."

The whirring of the spool slowed. The line was taut, but now the pressure lightened. Lichine grabbed the handle and started cranking but was able to rewind only a few inches of line before the rod throbbed and bent in a dangerously sharp arc.

"Move it up a little, Jeet," the mate shouted to the bridge. "Fish is right under us," he said to Lichine. "Harder that way. We'll get the line angled out a bit. And remember what I said, Mr. Lichine. Flow with it.

Reel when you swing forward, not when you pump back. Smooth, smooth. One continuous motion. You're doin' fine."

"Easy for you to say," Lichine said, half irritated.

"Sure is," said the mate mildly. "All I gotta do is hold your coat."

"Sorry."

"You want a drink?"

Lichine's tongue was swollen and it stuck to the roof of his mouth. There were dried salty streams of sweat and seawater trailing over his cheeks and neck. He nodded his head, trying not to think about the way his legs were trembling. Every part of him protested the unfamiliar torment of muscle and tendon and joint. After two hours of pumping and cranking against the first swordfish, his right arm was no more than a fibrous extension of his body, without sensation. At first, eye-filling exhilaration kept it working. Now, it was pure will.

Wink went into the cabin, leaving Lichine alone with the umpire, Sparky Thomas. The fish was not moving, but Lichine could not gain an inch. Stalemate. If he were to lean back just a little, or increase the drag, the line would snap. No one would notice. It would be over. There was no dishonor in that. Only one swordfish in eight is ever landed. For that matter, only one out of fifty even took the bait.

"Tiring, isn't it?" Thomas stepped to his side, puffing placidly on the black pipe. Lichine could only grunt. He wound in line. At least five feet, that time.

"Remarkable creatures, these," the umpire continued. "Astonishingly strong, of course, but most billfish are. They are the most mysterious, though. Very little evidence---only supposition, really--as to where they spawn or how far they range. This fellow here may have been off Sicily a few months ago. A provocative prospect, hmm?"

The line was coming in faster. Lichine was bending forward, reeling furiously, then rocking back, bringing the rod up.

"Flow into it," Wink said. He wiped Lichine's face with a damp towel and held the can of beer to his lips. "That's it. Now you got it."

The fish suddenly halted, lifting Lichine from the seat and dropping him back with a jolt The line slanted to starboard, tearing off the spool even faster than before. Fifty yards out, the fish paused, and with a yank at the restraining hook, plunged once more to the bottom. It lay there in its secret place, resisting the tether like a dog on its leash. Lichine held on, breathing deeply.

The bridge radio was silent. They were wrapped in a velvet shroud. No moon, no stars. Not a wisp of land glow nor a pinpoint of ship light. Apart from the band of green water bracketing the stern, with its flashes of small bright fish, they might have been a scrap of cosmic debris floating through emptied space.

The first swordfish was propped against the base of the port transom, out of the way. Lichine had almost forgotten it. He craned to look. It was ten feet long and at least one hundred pounds. A gleaming bronze when they pulled it from the water hours ago, it was black with death now, its hide cracking, the huge eye filmed over. Tendrils of milky fluids and blood curled out from beneath it. The mate caught Lichine's glance. He dipped a bucket of water and sluiced the effluvium toward the scupper.

The rod tip quivered. Barely perceptibly. Then it bounced. Once. Twice.

"Time to get to work, Mr. Lichine," Wink said. "You can't let her rest like this."

Lichine was exhausted beyond imagining, but the rod was throbbing steadily now and the point where the line entered the water was starting to shift. The reel clicked off an inch of line. Lichine rearranged himself in the chair, ready. His heart pounded. It was about to happen.

Another click. Another. Lichine unscrewed the drag lever, eased it forward an inch, tightened it down again. Wink nodded his approval. Lichine was able to make one half-turn of the handle, no more.

Suddenly the rod snapped straight, bobbed, and was still. The line went slack. It was the last thing Lichine expected.

"She broke off!" he cried in dismay.

"REEL!" Wink yelled in his ear. "Reel! Reel! Reel."

Lichine bent over and cranked as hard as he could. There was no need to draw the rod back, for the line merely looped out and disappeared beneath the dark swells. There was no weight on the other end.

"It's gone, it's gone," he gasped.

"*Keep cranking, I told you!*"

The spool was filling. Maybe a hundred feet left. Lichine searched the surface for the skipping bait. Nothing.

Then the line sprang taut, cracking off a sleeve of spray. The rod was ripped from his hands, bucking forward and down. He scrambled to regain his balance, struggling to bring the rod upright.

Doakes cut the engines. Wink was poised at the stern transom, the flying gaff raised high in his hands. A circle of turbulence disturbed the slick edge of the wake at the starboard quarter. There was a rushing sound Lichine did not identify.

Three feet off the stern the boiling, widening circle exploded. The monster fish rocketed straight up, maw gaping, blue-violet sides glistening and undulating. It cleared the water, towering twelve feet above them. The great blue eye rolled back and the broad flat sword slashed about, seeking a target.

Lichine sat transfixed. Wink Andros didn't. The mate swung back the gaff even before the broadbill broke the surface. As the fish reached the top of its leap, Wink sent the cruel hook home. It thudded into the belly-flesh below the pectoral fins. A crimson fountain gushed, splattering the mate. With a keening exhalation, the fish flung its massive head toward its tormentor and fell over the transom into the boat.

As the quarter-ton swordfish came down diagonally across the cockpit, the stern was lifting on a swell. The thunderous impact pounded the hull into the sea. The boat heeled. Water poured over the gunnels. Pots and bottle sand crockery crashed against bulkheads in the cabin and galley.

Lichine propelled himself forward, over the rod. He sprawled face-down at the bottom of the transom, one ankle tangled in the harness. The fighting chair swung crazily on its steel base, its back sheared from the seat as the creature fell.

For a split second the fish lay stunned. The boat righted itself, shuddering throughout its length.

Sparky Thomas had taken refuge behind the ladder to the bridge, but on its descent the sword of the fish cleaved the wooden handrail and crumpled five of the steps. When Lichine looked up, Thomas was pressing himself into the corner where gunnel and cabin met, his face drained, his head jerking frantically about for escape. The fish reared up, its spear passing inches away from the umpire's groin and nearly meeting its forked tail. Wink Andros was gathering his feet under him when the tail flashed down again. He was caught between deck and tail and Lichine heard only a gasp followed by a long sigh.

The fish humped in the middle, standing on its tail and the point of its spear before it toppled over away from Wink and Thomas. Toward Lichine.

With the ladder gone and the fish immediately below, Jeeter Doakes was frozen on the bridge. Now there was room. He dropped to the deck and snatched up a billy. Thomas was trying to escape to the cabin. They collided. The deck was slick with blood and they lost their footing, collapsing in a tangle of arms and legs and skidding toward the fish when the boat canted.

One of the hooks was imbedded in the jaw of the fish. The other was loose, whipping about, three inches of steel from point to shaft. At the instant Thomas slid against the fish, the hook lashed out and buried itself in the calf of his leg. It tore through the muscle and lodged against the shinbone, dragging the umpire toward the stern.

Lichine could not see the cause for the first howl of pain. He was still on his back, protected momentarily by the remains of the fighting chair and its bolted down metal base. But the shriek became an unending scream, lancing his brain, blotting out terror. He levered himself up, balancing on his free foot as he wrenched his other ankle from the tangled straps of the harness.

The rod tip was snapped off and dangling by the line, but the butt was still in the seat gimbal. The fish continued its frenzied attempts to return to the water, its bill ripping deep creases in the deck on each down thrust and flashing at Lichine when it came up. Thomas flopped about the deck, the hook holding fast, sawing through flesh. Blindly, Lichine yanked the broken rod from the holder, raised it above his head and brought it down with all his force. The heavy brass reel bounced off the shoulder of the fish; but the second blow found the point where the sword broadened into the head, and the third hit the cheek, and the fourth, the great blue eye itself. Lichine did not stop. The line curled and tightened around him as he brought the reel down on the head again and again. He panted with effort and skidded in slime and nearly fell overboard but went on clubbing and clubbing until the sound was that of thin ice crunching over a mud bog and he sensed Jeeter Doakes standing there, watching.

4

As it was past the agreed closing hour of 5 A.M., the four other boats were already returning to port. None of them had boated fish. Doakes and Lichine packed Thomas's leg in ice and applied a tourniquet above his knee. Then the captain called to arrange for an ambulance. When they arived, Catherine was waiting at the club dock. The other anglers had left.

Theo Marker had an appointment. Alone in his car, he took the turn at the designated mile marker and searched for the entrance to the side road. There it was, marked by a lone mailbox with the faded name "Dublin"on its side. He turned the Mercedes onto the shell road, trying to avoid the branches of the scrub pines on either side. After the small orange grove, there was the farmhouse with the screened porch on three sides. And after that, the road curved right, now little more than two ruts with walls of tangled brush on either side. He cursed as the car scraped bottom but noted the odometer reading. After exactly five tenths of a mile, he stopped. And he waited, trying to suppress his mounting anxiety.

In ten minutes, a gray Ford rounded the bend and continued toward him until it filled his rear-view mirror. It halted only when the bumpers were touching. Marker kept his eyes on the mirror, but remained in his seat. As instructed. After two minutes, the driver of the other car got out, hitched up his pants, and walked to Marker's door.

"Good morning, amigo," he said, leaning over and smiling.

Marker caught a whiff of mouthwash. He nodded.

"Please move over," said the man.

Marker did as he was told. When he was in the passenger seat, the man opened the door and got in. He looked at the dashboard and console and stroked the leather upholstery admiringly.

"Very nice," he said. "Very nice." He shifted around, pulling up his right leg and cocking his arm over the seat back. "And how are you, *amigo*?"

"Fine, fine," Marker replied. "You?"

"The same, my friend, the same." The man shrugged. "Except for a woman who cries a great deal for no reason!"

"Too bad," said Marker, impatience about to replace caution.

"And, of course," the man went on, "except for the occasional irritability of my principals. They do have reason, however. Are you not warm?"

"No, I'm comfortable enough."

"Please turn on the air condition," said the man, altering neither his tone nor his smile.

Marker did so.

"And the radio. Some music. A bit louder. Very good. Thank you very much." He shook out a cigarette. "You do not smoke, I think? Very good. I wish I did not also." He lit up, cracking the window to let the smoke out.

"Well, now, Mr. . . . ah. . ." Marker began.

"Carlos, amigo. Just Carlos."

"Right. Carlos. I got a bunch of things I got to be doin'. And I'm beat. Can we. . . ?"

"Certainly, my friend. Here, we come to the point. I keep forgetting. Old habits die hard." Carlos cleared his throat. "It is a small difficulty."

"Oh?" Marker managed.

"I regret that my principals have come to second thoughts. They are not so sure they wish to wait so long."

"But that can't be what they said!" Marker's heart hammered. "You agreed! They agreed!"

"Tranquil, my friend, tranquil," Carlos replied, waving his hands, palms down. "I can hear. And I regret. My principals have no want to be unreasonable. Perhaps if you can give me information that will make them feel better."

"Such as what?"

"The fishing contest. It is all arranged?"

"Last Saturday. This was the first night."

"The wagers have been made? The money is in hand?"

"The bets and the money. Both."

"Amigo, be good enough to explain to me again how we know you will win."

"For Christ sake, man. . ."

Carlos clucked his tongue and wagged a forefinger. Marker took a deep breath.

"Okay,' he said. "I got the best boat. The best equipment. A great record."

"All that is very good, amigo. But this is still a game of luck, no? What if the fish do not like your bait? What then?"

"They will."

"But if they do not?"

"Then there are other ways. I'm takin' precautions. I'll win. Count on it."

Carlos shifted around, placing his hands on the steering wheel. "Ah, *amigo*," he said, exhaling and shaking his head, "I do not know. I do not know."

"But this ain't fair! You got to stick to your . . ."

"Amigo. What is not fair is that you have a very great obligation to us and you are not satisfying it."

"I would've paid off long ago, if it wasn't for your. . ."

"Our interest rates are not the issue. You came to us. You agreed. And amigo, we want the balance."

"I'll have it in October, after I win."

"Too long. Now."

"But how?" Marker was shouting again. Carlos put his hands over his ears. Marker lowered his voice. "But how? You've checked, I'm sure. You know I don't have it. Dammit, man, we're talking about almost half a million dollars"

"You have three expensive houses, two boats, cars. Sell something. You will not even notice. And we are talking about six hundred thousand, not five."

"It can't be done. You can't sell quarter-million-dollar houses and boats overnight. By the time I got it all together, it would be next October anyway."

"But it is certain."

"No it isn't. Besides. . ." Marker hesitated.

"Yes?"

"The boat here, and the house . . ."

Tell me, amigo," Carlos said.

"They ain't mine."

"Who, then?"

"A corporation. Some people I know."

"They own them? You have nothing?"

"Nothin'. All tax write-offs. They let me . . . use them."

"Wait, wait," Carlos said, fumbling for his wallet. He pulled out a smudged piece of paper, unfolded it, stabbed a finger. "Here! Right here! Your Florida boat, *Redemption.* It costs sixty thousand dollars a year to run it, no? Fuel, supplies, crew? Is that not right?"

"More or less."

"And the house. Worth $200,000, correct? Payments for the mortgage of $22,320 every year? And the servants, expenses? Perhaps another $30,000 each year, no?"

"Probably."

"You are saying that this corporation pays all of this? Over $210,000 for each year?"

Marker confirmed with a nod.

"And you? You have nothing that is yours?"

No answer. Carlos slapped Marker on the back of his head.

"YOU!" he bellowed, grabbing Marker by the shirt and yanking him close. "You have nothing?"

"I got royalties and residuals of maybe ten thousand dollars every month. It varies."

"That is all? But you told us . . ." Carlos stopped, scanning the face in disbelief. Then he thrust Marker away in disgust.

A voice from the radio lamented the loss of its mother. The air was frigid. Neither man spoke for several minutes.

"Amigo, amigo," said Carlos finally. "This is a very big mistake you have made."

"What'll they do?"

"Your wife. She is a movie star. What of her?"

"If she found out, she'd cut me dead."

The last word lingered. Suddenly, Carlos opened the door and swung out.

"I will call you."

"When?"

Carlos slammed the door and returned to his car without answering. Marker did not move for a long time.

Montgomery Childs was, at that moment, sitting on the couch in his living room. He was on the telephone, talking to his wife.

"Lustful thoughts, sweetheart," he was saying. "Foul weather for days, and I get hornier by the hour. If you walked in right now, I'd take you,right on the lanai. That's for starters. Then we'd. . . was that a gasp of horror or a moan of passion, dear?"

"Both, but mine was the moan," came the thin voice from New York. "I had you on the desk speaker and Margaret walked in at that very moment. You know what a straitlaced old dear she is. She just threw some reports down and bolted out of the office, beet red."

"What Margaret needs is a good. . . ."

"Yes, I know, dear. You think we all just need a good lay. In this case, I expect you're right. About both Margaret and me."

Childs decided to take the risk. "Then why don't you get down here on the next plane," he said, with a mute prayer that his calculations were correct, "and we'll have at it. Seriously, darling, I really do miss you. This cold snap is bound to let up soon, and I'll only be fishing nights. We haven't really had much time together lately."

The line was quiet for a moment. Childs held his breath.

"You don't make it easy for a girl," his wife said at last. "Darling, I'd truly love to be with you. You know I would. But I have this dreadful exposition coming up, and the place will be swarming with buyers-even one from Kuwait, did I tell you?-and there's no way I could possibly get away for---oh-days and days."

"I was afraid you'd say that," Childs answered, breathing again. "I warn you, though, if I must keep abusing myself much longer, I'll break out and grow hair on my palms. Max may take it into his head to give up and drop off. I notice he's looking a little peaked."

Childs shifted so he could see himself in the mirror on the opposite wall. He waved at his image, flashed his teeth, and relished his sinewy brown nakedness. Not at all bad for a man in his middle years, he thought.

". . . tell Max I am devastated at the lack of attention I've given him lately," Laraine was saying, her voice lilting, "and that I promise to make up for the neglect at the earliest moment."

Childs bent over and talked to his penis. "You hear that, Max?" he said loudly enough for Laraine's benefit. "Mother's going to come and make you all better."

Laraine snorted when she was amused, not one of her endearing traits. "Poor little fella," she said.

"He's not that little!"

"How well I know," Laraine replied, snorts subsiding.

"Darling, I do miss you so. I am positively desolate that I can't be there. You do understand, don't you, love?"

She also emphasized every fifth word, especially when she was being earnest.

"I suppose," Childs answered with a careful mingling of petulance and remorse.

"Promise to call every day," she said.

"Maybe."

"Now don't be peevish, dear. Promise."

"Okay."

"I really must be off, darling. Is there anything I can take care of for you up here?"

"No, nothing I can . . . oh, did Margaret make that deposit?"

"I think so. Wait a sec."

Childs heard his wife call to her assistant. He held his breath. There was a pause. A door closing.

"She did, yes," Laraine said finally. "Twenty thousand in the Lauderdale account. Is that right?"

"I told her forty."

"Did you?" Laraine attempted to sound mystified. "Well, she must have made a mistake when she wrote out the check. I'll look into it. Was there anything else, dear?"

"But I. . ." Childs bit his lip. "No, nothing."

"Okay, then. Much, much love, dearest. Catch a lot of fish."

"I will. Love you."

"Ciao, love," she said, and made a string of kissing noises.

Childs grimaced and hung up. Only twenty, he thought. That bitch. She's pulling in the leash. He pounded the cushion with his fist.

This, on top of losing that swordfish last night. But then, she had put up the million with surprisingly little protest After a while, he sighed and got up, preening for a moment in the mirror. He patted his flat stomach, turned sideways, flexed a bicep. Very early middle years, he corrected himself.

He padded across the carpeting to the other room. The girl was lying in the exact center of the bed, the sheet primly drawn to her chin. Her big eyes followed him as he walked to the foot of the bed. Childs leaned over and gathered the end of the sheet in his hands, drawing it down her body. Freckles dusted her shoulders, the upper slopes of her breasts, her sturdy thighs. Childs cast the sheet aside and parted her legs. As he bent between them, he wondered if Bunny Haskell could make it to Cozumel.

Lichine finally reached his brother at his home in Larchmont. Jason, as was his habit, managed to sound both angry and preoccupied.

"You did what?" he demanded.

"I'm sure you understood," said Lichine with a serenity he did not feel.

"I don't believe this," Jason said, before lapsing into an ostentatiously pregnant silence.

Lichine waited.

"Jesus," his brother said finally, "a million. One million! Ernie, you okay? All your systems on go? What could've given you the idea we could afford this?"

"It's my money, Jason."

"Ours, baby brother. Ours."

"My half. And what I do with it is my business."

"Ernie, I don't know whether you remember last summer. When you got those fish?"

"Jason. . ."

"Well, I do, old son. Those swords were a fluke. A freak! We were out there for a little harmless bottom fishing, maybe a school tuna or two. Figured to drink some brew, shoot the breeze. It was supposed to be R-and-R, not the Olympics. You'd been looking like a slug, and I felt a little sun and spray might bring you around. Or maybe I have a distorted memory of the event"

"No, I'm not pretending that. . ."

"Ernie, you're out of your league. Way out. And you're telling me you're putting in ten weeks at this!"

"I'll be back at the bench in between. We won't lose any. . ."

"Could you extend me the courtesy of letting me finish, little brother? I have listened to you, haven't I? Right. The thing is, you obviously haven't thought this out. It isn't just that bet, although God knows it's mind-boggling enough. It's all the rest. Gas, salaries, food, motels, airfares. And the way those guys use those three-buck baits, you could keep Lutece in filet of sole for a year. Altogether, a thousand a day, minimum. Am I right?"

Jason didn't wait for an answer.

"And what about a boat? You haven't even given that a thought, have you? A bare-boat charter will set us back--what?-at least two hundred dollars a day."

"I bought one."

Lichine heard a sharp noise, a hand slapping a desktop.

"Ernie," Jason said with manufactured reasonableness, "you already got a record. There are men who'd give a hand for what you've done. What's the point of pushing it?"

"No good, Jason."

"Maybe you get some masochistic boot out of breaking your ass dragging in half-dead fish that you're gonna, throw back anyway. . ."

"I'm not quitting."

"Why should now be different?" Jason replied with heavy irony.

The remark hung in the air. Lichine did not respond.

"Look. I have a lot of calls to make," Jason said finally. "Somebody has to think about the business, and I've got a squad of Jap engineers about to fly in. You let me know when rationality returns."

He hung up.

New Yorkers eagerly anticipated the first supple days of May, but it was not a happy month for the Lichines of Brooklyn Heights. Ernest was born on his brother's twelfth birthday. Although Jason made jokes about how their parents might have come up with a better present, he never entirely suppressed his underlying resentment at the dramatic loss of his status as the only son of Dr. and Mrs. Peter D. Lichine.

In another May, Ernest watched from his bedroom in early morning as their sister crept out the door and got into a car heading for a commune in New Mexico. Less than two weeks later Gail was committed to a sanitarium. Her confinement was expected to be permanent. And in the May of Ernest's eleventh year, Dr. Peter D. Lichine died after a brief illness. He was fifty-four.

On a night some weeks after the funeral, Jason and Ernest were in the rear parlor of the double brownstone on Joralemon Street in which they had lived all their lives. The large room with twenty-foot ceilings and intricately carved moldings was originally designated as a play area, adjacent to the kitchen so that their mother and her housekeeper could supervise the children. But the Lichine tradition of obsessive achievement quickly transformed it into a work studio, with books and easels and kilns and racks of tools competing for space.

Jason turned from his favored station at the desk beneath the sloping bank of windows that overlooked the garden.

"Just what the fuck are you doing?"

Ernest was bent over the bench against the opposite wall. Its surface of tidily arranged boxes of electrical parts was cleared in the middle to permit work on his project of the moment.

"It's my generator," he replied, startled. "The Van de Graaf? Just came today. Wait till you see, Jason. It actually makes St. Elmo's Fire! You believe that? I'm only trying to figure out why they set it at only 5,000 rpms. Seems kind of funny, when you. . ."

Jason irritably waved aside the explanation. "I don't give a damn if you're hand-forging a Rolls-Royce. Keep it quiet."

"But if I can dope this out. . ."

"Little brother mine," Jason said evenly, "I am two days away from an econ final and if I do not get this stuff down, they will be very reluctant to hand over that piece of parchment I've been chasing for six years. *Comprende*? Anyway, it's time you took dinner up to Mom."

"That's Wanetta's job."

"She had to go home early. She left the food in the oven. Just trot it up, will you? Not that Mom's any more likely to eat it than she was yesterday."

"How is she?" Ernest asked softly, fighting the welling sorrow.

Jason leaned over his books. "Sitting there like always. Shredding Kleenex one at a time. Jeff's with her."

Ernest assembled the meal on a tray, walked through the hushed center hall and very carefully up the, carpeted steps. The master bedroom was at the front of the house, on the second floor. He tapped lightly on the door, but he hadn't heard his mother speak since they returned from the cemetery, so he shoved the door open.

For as far back as Ernest could remember, Dr. Jeff Donaldson had been their guest for Sunday dinner. He and his father fished for brook trout in the Catskills, and took Jason and Ernest to Giants games to cheer Y.A. Tittle. The only light in the room came through the gap in the nearly closed drapes, but Ernest made out Dr. Donaldson. His father's friend was sitting on the edge of the bed. The blankets were rolled back. His Mother was sitting up, propped against pillows. Her nightgown was bunched around her waist. Dr. Donaldson's hand was on her thigh.

5

Patrick Fowler slept on his boat. When he awakened, dawn was only a sallow smudge on the horizon. He made coffee and went to the bridge. A light went on in the diner as he peered into the shadows of the parking lot at the end of the inlet. The flag above the tackle shop hung limply on its vertical standard. A windless day. He scanned the figures picking their way between the cars, hoping that his clients were among them. Instead, there were Arnie Rumfeld, and the long-haired musclebound ex-Marine he kept in constant attendance. Fowler considered casting off and getting out fast, but there was no point. When the broker waddled up, Fowler was hosing down his deck. Rumfeld watched him, slapping a roll of paper in his palm. He said nothing until Fowler climbed wearily to the dock.

"The keys, Pat," Rumfeld said, extending a chubby pink hand. The other man stepped to the right, placing himself in Fowler's path. With only that movement, his arms and torso swelled impressively beneath his sleeveless shirt. Fowler looked up at the hoop earring in the man's pierced right ear, then followed a pulsing vein running down over the ropey muscle of his neck. The clavicle was at Fowler's eye level.

"I'll have your money in an hour, Rumfeld," he said, without looking away. "My clients'll be here. They owe me for three days."

Rumfeld snorted. "I've heard that before. Hell, I've heard it for five months. Wouldn't be near enough, anyway. It's over, Pat. I'm taking the boat. This here's the court order. Now let's have the keys."

Fowler took a long breath, sighed. His shoulders slumped, but his eyes did not leave the hollow below the ex-Marine's pointed Adam's apple.

"They're in the ignition," he said.

"That's good, Palo" said Rumfeld. "Make it easy on yourself. You know how I hate to do this. . ."

"I know, Rumfeld. Appreciate you giving me as much time as you have."

"I gave you all I could, Pat. You know that."

"'Course," said Fowler. "We're all just tryin' to make a buck."

"Glad you see it that way."

"That's the way I see it," said Fowler. The ex-Marine was smiling. He did not move aside. "Good-lookin' boy you got here, Rumfeld. Served in 'Nam, didn't you, kid?"

The man nodded, showing his teeth.

"Hey, Rumfeld," said Fowler, as if he had made a discovery. "When a guy wears an earring, does that mean he's a fag?"

The grin disappeared. The man unfolded his arms.

"Or is that only when he has it on the left ear?" asked Fowler, reaching up as if to touch the gold hoop.

The man brushed Fowler's hand away. "Don't touch," he warned. His voice was incongruously tinny, as if it came from far away. He inhaled, huffing his back muscles to full breadth. This thrust his arms away from his sides, where they bounced slightly, in readiness.

"Nice lats," said Fowler in admiration. "Saw a banty rooster could do that. But, no shit, Rumfeld, what do you two do all day while I'm out busting my ass?"

"Pat. . . ."

"Fifty bucks says I know, Rumfeld. Most of that time, Cupcake here has your dick in his mouth."

The bodyguard puffed, began to color. He glanced over the captain's head for direction from his employer. Fowler's left hand flashed to the big man's head, stabbing a finger through the gold hoop and yanking it away through the earlobe.

The blood didn't start for a second, about as long as it took the man to realize what had happened. When he did, he howled, put his right hand to the ear, and reared back with his balled left fist, all at the same time.

Fowler slipped the blow. As the bodyguard's arm brushed past, he grabbed the massive bicep with both hands and pulled, spinning the man around. He placed his foot in the small of the exposed back and straightened his leg with all the force he had.

The bodyguard stumbled to the edge of the dock, arms flapping wildly. He teetered. And fell in. His hair streamed over his face when he burst to the surface. He tried to say something, but there was water in his mouth.

"Catch," said Fowler. He tossed the earring.

After a glance at Rumfeld, whose head was swiveling from Fowler to his sputtering bodyguard and back, the former owner and captain of the *All Wrong* walked quickly away. He withdrew a cigarette from its pack, but it shook from his fingers. Fowler expected he might have a drink.

The waitress brought another bourbon. Fowler stroked her arm mechanically.

"You game for a toss, Ginnie?"

She brought her eyes down, chewed her gum loudly, and left.

"That's my day," he said to no one. "Can't score Ginnie, you might's well pull the dirt over."

He got up and walked unsteadily to the bar. Ginnie took his money and poured his drink into a plastic tumbler. Outside, the night was thick and smelled of low tide in the bay. He approached his battered Bonneville with stately care.

Fowler drove automatically, without plan. When only ice rattled in his cup, he peered out and found he was in front of Wink Andros' house. There were six cars in the driveway and lights behind the drawn curtains. Fowler parked under the palm in the middle of the untended lawn. His nephew had bought the house a year before. Fowler had not asked how a mate's pay might cover the down payment.

He walked in without knocking. There were nine people in the living room. Most of them he knew, boatmen and their current women.

"Sumbitch," said Wink Andros, rousing himself from the other end of the couch. "It is Captain Uncle Pat, valiant seaman and intrepid defender of the rights of the impecunious, be they even himself."

"Siddown," said Fowler, "before you take off."

"Good thinking," Wink said, collapsing and throwing his arm around the nearest blonde. "You know everybody, I believe." Nods, murmurs. "Uncle Captain, you are in demand. Triga called. Wants to talk to you. He find you?"

"Nope."

"Figured. Fetch yourself a line or two, Captain Uncle. Clear your head."

He waved in the direction of the small room next to the flickering television set no one was watching. There was a girl kneeling by a glass-topped desk. She was diligently chopping with a razor blade at a mound of white powder culled from a larger heap next to it.

"I don't use that shit," said Fowler.

"Well I know, and I appreciate it," said his nephew. "More for us. But I thought you kicked the sauce, too." He indicated Fowler's empty plastic cup.

"Look. . . ."

Wink raised his palms. "I can dig it, Captain Uncle. To each his own trip according to his needs. The booze is in the kitchen."

When Fowler returned, the girl from the den was sitting cross legged in the middle of the scarlet carpet. She thrummed a finger against first one nostril and then the other as she inhaled deeply, her head thrown back. She passed a silvery object to Wink.

"What's that?" Fowler asked, his eyes on the girl. She tossed her head so her straight black hair fell down her back.

"You might ask," said Wink, holding up a machined piece of metal the shape and size of a .45 caliber cartridge. "That, Uncle, is the latest advance in man's unending quest for tight pussy and a wind-proof tooter."

"That right?" said Fowler without interest. The girl sat erect, her wrists on her knees, her level gaze on Wink. The corners of her mouth turned up slightly.

"In truth, Uncle," Wink continued. "Say you're on the bridge out in the middle of the Stream. You're doing eight knots, trolling for an uptight wealthy person, and there's a twenty-mile wind. Now you can't hardly pour out a quarter-ounce of nose candy and inhale a couple a lines, can you? You following this, Uncle? Three bills worth of goodies would just blowout over the waves. You understand the implications of such an event, do you not? We'd have twenty cubic fathoms of stoned dolphins."

Fowler did not answer. The girl was looking at him, now. If she wore makeup, it could only be on the tips of her sooty eyelashes.

"Uncle," said Wink, "the splendid lady you are contemplating is Pia Cippola. Pia, this is Captain Patrick Fowler, noted wastrel."

"Hi," said the girl.

"Pleasure," said Fowler.

"Now permit me to continue," said Wink. "With the wondrous windproof tooter, one unscrews the bottom, like so, and fills it with snow. One then replaces the top, in which there is this little hole. By twisting this knob on the side, so, the top fills. It is then brought to the nose, one snorts a substantial hit, and one is made happy." Wink demonstrated.

"And one gets busted for paraphernalia," said Fowler.

"An ever-present possibility. But I see your mind is elsewhere, Captain Uncle. Do you want to take Pia and dip your wick now, or shall we talk about our new venture?"

"Excuse him, Pia," said Fowler. "Two years of college in New York, and he not only talks like a flit, he forgets his manners."

"True," said Wink. "*Mea culpa.* But I should note, Pia, that you have here an artifact of a forgotten epoch. Although he is a lifelong juicer, a martinet with his crews, a runaway husband and father, and a fiscally irresponsible brawler, he does lug around this one piece of atavistic baggage. Ladies, he feels, must be protected from rough language and lascivious innuendo. Unless, of course, he decides they are cunts, which he usually does, eventually."

"Not funny, Wink," Fowler said.

"Come again?" said Wink, who heard the first time.

"I didn't stutter."

His nephew blinked, and his face went slack. "You working up to punching me out, too, Pat? 'Cause. . ."

The front door was thrown open. It bounced off the wall. Jeeter Doakes plunged through, drawing a heavy-lidded girl along with him. Her pendulous breasts quivered beneath a tee shirt that didn't quite cover her stomach. She was no more than sixteen. Jeeter gave her a nudge.

"Bedroom's back there, sweet taste," he said.

"But I'd like a drink or a toke or somethin', Jeeter."

"I'll bring somethin', honey . You just get on back there."

She complied, buttocks rolling.

"Sheee-it," said Jeeter softly, watching her.

"Little old for you, ain't she, Jeet?" said Wink.

"Best I could do this time of night," Doakes answered, already on his way to the den and the heap of cocaine.

"Don't suck it all up in one blow, Jellynose. The junk you already got in your mustache could buy an Eldorado."

"Be cool, Wink," whispered a man sitting with his ear to the stereo console. "He's been meaner 'n a two-headed snake."

"It's my house and my dope," said Wink. He turned to Fowler. "That's the second jailbait split-tail he's brought in here tonight. Bedroom looks like he went after the last one with an ax."

Jeeter came out, grabbed a reefer from one of the girls, and puffed on it as he went to the kitchen. He returned with both a bottle and a glass of bourbon. No water, no ice. He sat on the sofa, alternately dragging on the cigarette and gulping the drink.

"My nose is like crepe paper," he said. "Gimme an inhaler, Wink."

"I don't hardly wonder," said Wink, handing him a plastic squeeze bottle. "The way you snort, you're gonna have to wear a couple Tampax up your nose."

Doakes used the bottle, handed it back. Then he noticed Fowler for the first time. "Captain Hook!" He pounded Fowler on the thigh. "Christ, Wink lets anybody in here. Ain't seen you in a while, turkey. Heard about your hee-roic exploits this mornin'. You hear about the two swords we got? Ain't nobody else even hooked up since. How you doin'? You look like shit."

"Nice to see you, too, Jeet," said Fowler.

"Yeah," said Doakes, rising. "We'll talk. Soon's I take care that little honey." He started taking off his shirt. "Spread 'em wide, sweet taste," he thundered. "Jeeter's comin'!"

He picked up the bottle and glass and charged down the corridor.

No one spoke.

"Kinda leaves a hole in the air, don't he?" Wink said finally.

"How long's he been out?" asked Fowler.

"Since Tuesday week. Two years' probation," said Wink. "Been wired up and fucking ever since."

The others began to talk among themselves.

Fowler sipped. "Tell me about this tournament."

"Sure, Pat," Wink answered. "Look. Sorry about your boat. We heard. And about that tad of hostility before. I'm a little strung out."

"It's forgotten."

"Appreciate it," Wink said. He selected a joint from the pile on the table. "How much do you know?"

"Five million. Five anglers. Five places."

"That's most of it. A high-rent fish-off. Ho Triga, Cat Nettles, Theo Marker, Monty Childs, Ernie Lichine. Most of them've won a hatful of contests, and all of them have at least one IAA record apiece. They think they're gonna show who's number one honcho. Doesn't figure to prove anything, but who gives a damn? The bread's good."

"I've fished four of them one time or other," said Fowler. "Rather be a wart on a dog's ass than captain for Cat or Triga or Childs again. Marker's cool. . . ."

"Even considering he canned you?"

"Even considerin'. We was pretty tight once, it happens."

Pia was following the conversation, her black eyes swinging back and forth with interest. Fowler wrenched his attention back to his nephew.

"But who's this kid you'n Jeet are fishin'? Lichine?"

"Heard of Lichine Radio?" Wink said, massaging the blonde's back.

"The hi-fi stores?"

"Hundreds of them. He's a boy genius. Made his own amplifier when he was nine. From scratch. Switched to pocket calculators and CBs before his first wet dream. Had his own company by nineteen. Worth thirty million, I hear."

"What's he like?" Fowler said. "He know his way to the head?"

"He ain't exactly prepossessing. He was here earlier. Sat there for three hours, quivering like a goat that had broken glass for dinner. I believe our leisure time pursuits deviate from what he's used to."

"How'd he get in with them other heavy-duty dudes?"

"Happened to be there at the time." Wink slipped his hand over the blonde's shoulder and idly cupped her breast. She snuggled closer. "He may not be in Triga's league, but he ain't low-bore, either. Year ago he took a record broadbill off Montauk."

"Sounds like a fluke."

"Captain Uncle, you always told me the difference between luck and skill is human error. There are top-line anglers who haven't caught two swords in a lifetime."

"I have said that."

"And you wouldn't believe what happened the first night. Like to take that swordie apart with his bare hands. All I got was three separated ribs."

"What's the bread?"

"Don't know about the other crews. We're getting four hundred for every day on the water."

Fowler raised his eyebrows in mild surprise. "Plus room and board and travel?"

"Everything. Nothing out of our pockets. Do I detect more than passing interest?"

The blonde's nipple was erect under Wink's fingers. Fowler glanced away without answering. At Pia.

"Honey?" he said. "Would you mind too much sitting up here next to me?"

Pia rose effortlessly and straight-backed from her semi-lotus position. She tucked in her blouse. Fowler watched the navy fabric stretch taut, gaping between the buttons. She watched him watch, and waited for the man next to him to move. Then she walked around the coffee table and sat, her thigh lightly touching his.

"Honey . . ."

"Pia."

"Pia, you are . . ."

She touched a finger to his lips.

"Right," he said. He was going to say something easy.

"He's a one-woman man, Pia," said Wink, who was taking this in. "One woman at a time."

"Wink. . ."

"Says he has to get into a chick's head before he can get off on her."

"Wink.. . ."

"Serial monogamy, it's called. Or sequential polygamy. I forget."

"Wink, I'm about to kick your ass so high bluebirds will nest in it."

"Very colorful, Uncle. Trouble is, Pia, he's the only guy I know who couldn't make out in a woman's prison with a pocketful of pardons. You are demonstrating a shocking lack of taste."

Fowler didn't mind the byplay. It quieted the tingling at his temples.

Jeeter Doakes came back into the room. His hair was damp and plastered to the sides of his head. Sweat coursed through the matted curls on his chest. He leaned against the wall. He was naked. Except for his hat.

One of the girls giggled. Another chose to adjust the television set.

"Don't be shy, Jeet," said Wink. "Come right in."

"I can't get it up," said Doakes, cradling his genitals in one big hand.

"Don't pick at it, Jeet. It won't heal."

"It wouldn't do nothin'," said Doakes, staring down.

"She turned me ever' way but loose, and it wouldn't do nothin'."

"That's truly unfortunate, Jeet. But I did tell you she was somebody's grand-mamma."

"You go do it, Hook. She's ready. Jesus fuckin' Christ, is she ready! Do it for me, Hook."

Fowler put his hand to his face. "Can't do it, Jeet," he managed, choking. Doakes' penis looked like a wrinkled toadstool. "I'm savin' myself."

"You, then, Wink. She's ready, I tell you. Wrigglin' like a hooked eel."

"Me?" Wink looked at his blonde. "Couldn't do it, Jeet. I'm spoken for."

"Please, Wink."

"Jeez, I wish you wouldn't put it that way. I try to do what I can for a friend, but. . ."

"Wink," said Doakes, almost pleading.

"Shit, Jeet, if it means that much to you. . ." Wink stood, pulling the blonde with him. "But I want an observer. For later testimony."

"Right," said Doakes. "Just don't let me down."

"All I can do is my best," Wink said with solemnity.

"Coming, honey?"

The blonde made a show of reluctance but permitted herself to be drawn along. Doakes went to the vacated seat and fell into the cushions. Everyone watched the toadstool bob.

"One thing," he bellowed at Wink, now disappearing down the hall.

"Yeah, Jeet?"

"Afterward," said Doakes, reaching for a glass, "you gotta tell me about it."

6

Horst Triga peered glumly through the rivulets of rain coursing down the salon windows. The wind was lashing the water of the boat basin into spume-topped swells, and even *Highlander* rocked at its berth.

Saturday morning. After fishing through five nights, the standings remained unchanged. Apart from Lichine's two broadbills, only two undersized fish had been caught. Neither of them were Triga's, and he seethed with impotence. To be bested by a rank amateur was intolerable!

That situation would soon be altered. The two meetings yesterday, and the call now being placed, would put the stopper in that particular bottle. Very shortly, the imbalance would be redressed.

A light was blinking on the communications console at the end of a sofa covered in antelope skin. He strode to it and picked up the handset.

"Yes?"

"I have your call to New York, sir. The gentleman's secretary is looking for him."

"If she is still looking, Jerry," Triga said irritably, "then you don't have my call yet, do you?"

"I guess not, Mr. Triga, but. . . ."

"Then be good enough to buzz me when you have Mr. McNally on the line, and not before," Triga snapped, slamming the receiver into its cradle.

"Mr. Triga?" One of his stewards was at the door. It was the older one, employed only a week before. He had come highly recommended.

"What is it?"

"About luncheon, sir. I'm afraid we have no Meursault on hand. Would a Montrachet do?"

"Why don't we?"

"Sir?"

"Meursault. Why don't we have any?"

"I'm sure I don't know, sir. I have not yet had time to take proper stock of the cellar, nor, sir, have I been apprised of your preferences in these matters. If you'll recall, I have tried on several occasions to. . ."

"All right! The Montrachet, then, and get on with it!"

The steward drew himself up, flesh corrugating beneath his chin, and took a step toward the door. He hesitated, then turned back.

"Mr. Triga," he said.

"What is it?"

"Sir, I have been in private service for nearly twenty-five years. Over that time, I have grown accustomed to the eccentricities of my employers and have grown a thick skin, as well. Never, however, have I been as shabbily treated as by you these last eight days. You have snarled and yapped at me like a cur, and have not even taken the trouble to learn my name. I do not intend to tolerate these indignities another instant."

Triga was startled at the display. He considered his alternative responses and settled for appeasement. Skilled servants were nearly impossible to find.

"Now. . . ah. . ." he began.

"It's Duncan," said the man stonily.

"Of course," Triga said, forcing a smile. "Duncan, Ido apologize. You are quite correct to bring your feelings to my attention, and I assure you there will be a change for the better. Please understand that I have been suffering some anxiety since you joined us, and now this weather. Can we rub the slate clean and try again?"

"As you wish," said the steward, partially mollified. "And might I look forward to an early meeting to discuss certain household necessities and delineations of responsibilities?"

The buzzer on the console sounded. Triga reached for it, "Yes, you may, Duncan," he said, covering the mouthpiece.

"The Montrachet, then, sir?"

"Yes, Duncan, the Montrachet."

"Puligny or Chassagne?"

"Whichever." Triga's smile was crumblirig.

"The Puligny is overchilled."

"The Chassagne, Duncan," Triga said, holding the instrument to his ear.

"Very well, sir." The steward executed a crisp about-face and left. He paused outside the closed door, as was his custom, especially after the engineered confrontations with new employers that he had found were necessary to the establishment of satisfactory working relationships.

Triga's voice was muffled, but Duncan made out the words.

"Julius? How are you, old man? . . . Fine, just fine. Could do with a little sun. . . . Yes, you might do that. Julius, this line is not secure, if you understand me . . . good, good. About the matter of our recent conversation. You've taken the first steps? About when do you. . . I see . . . And there is no danger of premature disclosure? Timing, as you know, is of primary concern. . . ."

There was a long pause as Triga listened, so Duncan slipped away to attend to the wine. When he returned, Triga was on the sofa, a look of overweening satisfaction on his face.

"Ah, Duncan, there you are," he beamed. "Why not run back for another glass? I don't have to go out for another hour. We can have that conversation you wanted right away."

"Very good, sir. I took the precaution of bringing two."

Pia's cheek was still pink and creased with sleep, but her lips nonetheless now encircled his nipple, tongue flicking. Fowler opened his other eye. She looked up at his slight stirring, touched his chin, then nuzzled into his chest again and continued.

"Helluvaway t'wakeup," he croaked, his hand in the silky spill of black hair.

"Complaints?" she murmured, not stopping.

"Beats a ice pick in the ear."

She began to trace a path of light nips and kisses and flickers of eyelash across his chest. There was a pale puckered groove that ran from his armpit to his elbow, and she hesitated.

"This?" she asked.

"Marlin," he said. "Bill slashed me when I was tryin' t'get the gaff in him."

"Bill? You mean that sword-thing on their nose?"

"Yeah."

"Hmm." She examined it with the tip of her tongue. And continued, moving her body to reach his hand, her breasts pivoting his stomach. She came to the fingers, the last two on the right hand. They ended at the first joint.

"And these?"

"Another marlin."

"How?"

"I was a mate. Just a dumb kid. Grabbed the wire leader wrong. He jumped. Wire tightened, sliced off the fingers."

She was looking at them. With curiosity, he thought, not distaste.

"And these are the reason for that nickname."

"Yeah."

"You landed both fish, of course."

"'Course," he said, fully awake. "Now, where were you?"

"I like them," she said, as if she hadn't heard. "I especially" - she sucked one stump between her lips - "liked them when they were" - she did the same with the other - "inside me."

"Well, now," he said, reaching.

She pulled away. "Wait," she said.

And continued. She left not a part of him untouched, and whenever his flesh jumped or she heard his intake of air, she lingered. It took a long time, this exploration. She was very, very gently drawing his right testicle into her mouth when the doorbell rang.

It kept ringing, and whoever it was would not go away. Pia released Fowler. He swung to the floor, cursing, pulling on cut-off jeans. As he was about to zip the fly, Pia reached over and kissed the tip of his penis.

"Hurry back," she said.

It wasn't a large apartment, just the bedroom, the kitchenette, the dining-sitting room. Fowler was at the door in ten strides from his bed. There was a curtain of rain behind the dapper man with snowy hair.

"Fuck off," said Fowler. He slammed the door. The bell rang again.

"Just a few minutes, Pat," said Horst Triga when Fowler stood once more in the doorway.

"Make it a New York second," said Fowler, making no move to step aside.

"Can I come in?" asked Triga.

Fowler withdrew into the room. He did not offer a chair. Triga blinked in the dim light, but his smile did not waver.

"You aren't going to make this easy, are you, Pat?"

No answer.

"Very well. I'd like you to work for me, Pat. I'm sure you know the situation."

"The five-million-dollar ego trip. I heard."

Fowler walked to the kitchenette, poured a cup of water, put it in the microwave oven and pushed buttons. He tapped out a Marlboro and lit it by the flame of a stove burner.

"I don't want to work for you," he said finally, exhaling.

"Why not?"

Fowler stared at his maddeningly composed visitor for a moment, then lifted his fist. "Your boat's too big, one," he said, snapping out his forefinger. "You're cheap, two." Index finger. "You play with guns, three." The first stump. "I don't like you, four." The other. He used his thumb. "And you cheat."

"If you mean that time in Cat Cay. . ."

"I mean that time and a hunnert others I seen for my own self or heard about. I mean that you got more money than God, that there ain't no one nowhere spends more time on the water than you do or who needs less to, and you keep cheatin' anyway."

"You are a man of myriad contradictions, Pat. Your own code of morality leaves something to be desired, and yet you. . ."

"I been told my faults, Triga. By people who got more right."

The microwave buzzed. Fowler removed the cup and spooned instant coffee. For himself.

"In any event," Triga continued, "you admit, in a backhanded way, that I'm the best. I know that, and so do you." When he pressed his lips together, they disappeared.

"I'm going to win this tournament, Pat."

"Maybe. Don't mean nothin' to me one way or other."

"I'll give you a thousand dollars a day."

Fowler didn't permit his expression to change, but he delayed his response a fraction too long. Triga walked to a chair and sat down, carefully crossing his legs in a way intended to do the least damage to the creases in his trousers. Fowler sipped, his heart racing.

"That's. . ."

"Double what anyone else is paying. About sixty thousand dollars for perhaps sixty days' work over the next nine months."

"For me and my crew, you mean."

"No," said Triga, pressing the advantage. "I mean you alone. All of it. I'll take care of the crew separately."

Fowler stubbed out the cigarette and lit another. The hook was set and he was being reeled in.

"Why me?" he stalled, resisting.

"Come now, Pat. Don't turn bashful and unassuming." Fowler was silent. Triga sighed. "Very well," he said. "I have not done well this first week. I require more knowledgeable assistance than I am receiving from my regular crew. There are four or five top captains in the world. You're one, or at least you are when you're off the bottle."

Triga held up a hand. "Don't get excited. I know you have it under control, or at least you did until yesterday. Let's assume that that was a temporary aberration brought on by a personal setback. In any event, you captain better dead drunk than most men stone sober.

"One of those other captains is Chick Murphy. But he was boating a hammerhead off San Salvador three weeks ago and it broke his leg. Jeeter Doakes is excellent, when he's at the helm. Everywhere else, he has an awesome penchant for trouble, which makes him unreliable. Catherine Nettles has signed up Allie Cronski permanently, and Monty Childs has Steve Grubbs. That leaves you, Pat."

"Meaning you got around to me last," said Fowler, irrationally irritated at the slight.

Triga shrugged. "I had no reason to believe your assessment of my character had undergone a transformation."

"It ain't."

"Indeed," Triga said, pursing his lips and steepling his fingers. "And there was that other problem. Of yours, I mean."

"You take me as I am."

"Certainly," Triga said, slapping his hands on the arms of the chair and rising. "You're a professional, Pat. As am I, in my way. And I'm sure you will behave accordingly. I gather, then, that we have an agreement."

It was not a question.

"A couple things, Triga."

"Yes?"

"You still got the Merritt and the two Ryboviches?"

Triga nodded.

"We use the forty-three-footer for everything but tuna, right?"

"Very well."

"I want the small one for them."

"Agreed. And?"

"And I got a boat that's in hock. I want an advance."

"Ah, yes. The *All Wrong*." Triga put his thumb to his chin. "I have made a certain arrangement with the Rumfeld concern. Your account is no longer in arrears, and the boat will be returned to you" - Triga raised a finger as Fowler was about to speak - "when we have won the tournament."

"Bastard. What if we don't?"

"We will, Pat, we will. I'm certain that you will make every effort to insure that we do."

"I won't cheat for you, Triga."

"No, no," Triga soothed. "Of course you won't. Anyway, there will be an IAA umpire on every boat. But your boat is my condition, Pat. And your bonus, when we win."

"I bought that boat so I wouldn't have to work for none of you shitheads no more," Fowler muttered, not really to Triga.

"But you no longer have the boat, Pat. And no other prospects, as far as I know."

They held each other's eyes. Triga broke off first.

"Pat," he said at the door. "Please be on the *Adroit* by four tomorrow afternoon. My regular crew will have been informed. Select your own mate, but I'm fond of Wink Andros. He's amusing. And quite competent. I'd like to have him again. Until then."

He opened the door and left.

Fowler felt the bile of self-loathing rise in his throat. He fought it back down with the usual justifications. The boat was his only income, he told himself, and fishing was what he knew. He'd never be able to settle for a seafood store or a rundown beer-boats-bait marina on the beach like so many of the men he broke in with years ago. There was back alimony and child support, and the black-suited lawyer Alma sent around every month to remind him of his obligations. And there were the familiar stirrings he felt for the woman in the other room, something his forty-two years told him was more than sex. He wanted her around for a while. He'd have been crazy to pass up Triga's offer.

The sour taste didn't go away.

"I'm all empty," Pia said from the bedroom door.

Fowler started. "What? Oh. Coffee? Juice? Think I got some Sara Lee whatsis. . . ."

The corners of her mouth turned up. "Wasn't what I meant. But coffee, please."

Fowler watched her as he poured more water and reached for another cup. She was still naked, except for the thin gold chain looped around her waist. She walked slowly around the room, touching the mounted fish on the walls, the trophies on the tables. It was a model's walk, one foot directly in front of the other, learned so well it appeared unaffected. There was a faintly olive duskiness to her skin that didn't come from the sun. No bikini outline around the dark triangle beneath the flat stomach. Long-waisted, so the hips had to hurry their flare and sweep into tapering columns of thigh. Sheets of practiced responsive muscle beneath the sheen of flesh.

Pia stopped at the bulletin board on the wall at the end of the counter that separated the kitchen from the larger room. It was covered with color snapshots of boats and dead fish and parties. Beneath it, two neat piles of photographs awaited display.

"Wink seems to be in every other shot," she said, bending closer.

"He jumps in front of every camera he sees," Fowler answered, pouring water into the cup and stirring the coffee.

"Is he really your nephew?"

"Yeah. Sister's kid. He's mated for me, off'n on."

"You like him a lot, don't you?"

"We've had a lot of seas run over us."

"How is he going to feel about working for that man who was just here? Isn't he already hired by someone else?"

Fowler looked sharply at her.

"I couldn't help overhearing," she said, perching on one of the stools and reaching for the cup. "At least not once I had my ear to the crack in the door."

"It ain't gonna tickle him much, but he'll go along."

Fowler wasn't at all sure that was true.

"You're not too thrilled about it, either, I gather.'

"Look, honey. . ."

"Pia," she said. "Okay. Subject closed." She spun on the stool, breasts shimmering, stepped to the floor, and walked toward the bedroom with a deliberate sway to the sleek round hips.

Fowler put the cups in the sink, the urgency of the hours before returning. His eye fell upon the bulletin board. Wink probably wasn't even up yet, Fowler thought. He could call later.

Wink came out of his house right away, the flat-topped leather Stetson jammed down to his ears, his shirt-tails fluttering. He squeezed into the front seat with Fowler and Pia.

"You should never ever take that hat off," Pia said, admiringly.

" 'Cause it makes me look like Clint Eastwood?"

"No, turkey," said Fowler. "Because it covers your bald spot."

"Look how he jumps on my case so early in the day," Wink said, pulling Pia toward him. "Now that you've seen what the pits of middle-aged sexual inadequacy can be, Pia, you ready for youthful vitality and wonderment?"

"Not until he has nothing else to show me," Pia said, sliding her hand along Fowler's thigh.

Wink groaned. Fowler grinned, and wondered how he was going to tell Wink what he wanted to do.

"Did you believe that scene last night, Uncle?" Wink said. "Jeeter coming out like that?"

"That's Jeet."

"You missed the best part," said Wink. "When I came out, you'd taken this delectable lady off to ply her with strong spirits and soulful looks. Jeet wanted to know what happened. Expressed a forceful interest, you might say. As I do not pleasure myself by frustrating people of Jeet's dimensions, I told him. Quick and euphemistic, considering the company."

"Euphe-what?" Fowler asked.

"Just listen," said Wink. "Maybe you'll learn something. It is a bitch, Pia, baby, acclimatizing the elderly illiterate to your everyday four-syllable words. Anyway. Captain Doakes found my narrative in some way arousing. He stood up and that little bitty shrunken-up thing was all of a sudden big as a brick. All those honeys drooled more than a little, but Jeet was back down that hallway before they had a chance to get damp. You would not believe the uproar from down the hall."

They drove north, joking, laughing. Pia and Wink shared a joint. When Fowler turned onto the Interstate. Wink asked why.

" 'Cause this takes us where we're goin'. . ." Fowler said, staring straight ahead.

"We were going to the *Frog*. I thought." Wink said, distracted by his last sally at Pia.

"We're goin' to Palm Beach," Fowler said, trying to ignore the growing lump in his chest. "We got work."

"Captain Uncle, sir," Wink said, clipping off the end of a dying chuckle. "You may not recall that I am already employed. Is there some other fact of which you have yet to apprise me?"

"I been offered a job."

Wink cocked his head to see past Pia. "I believe I did miss something." he said. "And I didn't bring enough changes of underwear to figure it all out by myself. Gimme a hint, Uncle."

"Client asked for you special," said Fowler through teeth clenched so hard they hurt.

"Who? Marker?"

"No."

"Who then?" Wink was leaning across Pia, his voice getting sharper. "Tell me what I'm thinking isn't so. Tell me you aren't going back to work for a man we agreed we wouldn't take the time to piss on."

"I can't do that."

Wink didn't respond. Fowler knew that Wink's eyes had gone dull, his face slack. Pia pressed back into the seat, making herself small.

"It is," said Wink in a whisper. "It is."

"Wait'll you hear the bread I got out of him."

Wink didn't seem to hear. "Triga," he said to himself, nodding his head in confirmation. "That lying, low-rent, motherless, two-faced cheechbug."

"I said wait'll you hear about what he's payin', before you get in an uproar. Listen up, now, Wink. He . . ."

"Stop the car," Wink said quietly.

"Say what?"

Traffic thrummed past them, a line of roaring tractor-trailers to the right, blurs of overtaking sedans to the left.

"Stop the fucking car!"

"We're in the middle of the highway!"

Wink reached across Pia, yanked the key from the ignition, and threw it out the open window. Fowler pumped the brakes and waved his arm frantically at the cars behind. Before he came to a complete halt, Wink opened the door and leaped out. He tumbled to the blacktop, but tucked his shoulder under in time to roll to his feet. Brakes screamed.

Cars rocketed past, buffeting the Bonneville. Fists were shaken, faces contorted in soundless epithets. Horns howled and faded.

Wink slapped his hat against his leg and strode purposefully but without haste across the inside lane. A panel truck smeared to a stop inches away. The enraged driver started to get out, but Wink kept walking.

By the time Fowler had located his key, Wink was clambering over the top of an embankment.

7

Since he had arrived in Palm Beach, Ernest Lichine was destined, it seemed, to spend half his time in alien encounters and the other half in dismayed recapitulation. The killing of the swordfish. The party at Wink's house. Jeeter Doakes. This weekend with Catherine. Never had he known such people. Never had he experienced such a turmoil of emotions - pride, rage, terror, ecstasy, remorse, euphoria - at times, simultaneously. Even night had become day.

He was determined to recover a measure of order, if only through familiar ritual. On the car seat beside him was a bag of sweet rolls and the Sunday edition of the New York Times. After dropping off his car, he took his usual route around the clubhouse. The pennants on the flagpole stood flat out, crackling in the wind. Only one or two boats were out, and if members and their employees were around, they were not in sight. That suited Lichine perfectly. It was four hours until the second week of the tournament began. He stepped into *Brain Soup*, shut the salon door firmly behind him, and put water on to boil. Coffee made, juice drunk, and the plate of rolls beside him, he settled into a corner of the couch with a gratified sigh and began with section A, page one.

Few of his new compatriots seemed to care about the events of the day in the world beyond their own. Lichine, however, felt adrift without his daily dosage of guerrilla attacks, Pentagon overruns, and rising cost-of-living indices. He read ravenously. He was deep into a critique of the new Stoppard play when he heard a thump out in the cockpit.

Wink Andros dropped to the deck. The comforting interlude was over. Lichine shoved the glass door aside.

Wink was bent over a large canvas bag, loosening buckles.

"Afternoon, Mr. Lichine," he said, without his customary smile. "It's a parachute, in case you're wondering."

"A parachute? What for?"

"Jeeter's idea. We're going to use it for a sea anchor. Otherwise, with the wind as high as it is, we'd drift too fast."

Doakes came down the dock. "You see who's captaining *Adroit* now?" he asked.

Wink nodded grimly, hefted the bag, and started walking forward.

"Hook must be hard to it," Doakes went on, "working for Triga. I'd sooner eat a turd. Where you goin' with that chute?"

"To set it up."

"From the bow?" Doakes said, incredulous. "Wink, for a man that's s'posed to be smart, you are a puzzlement sometimes."

"Meaning?"

"Think on it," the captain replied. "We're out there driftin', right? Chute's out, current's pushin' it, boat's followin''. Got that so far?" Wink didn't respond. "Now you put your lines out. If you got the sea anchor running from the bow, what happens to the lines?"

Wink understood. He returned to the cockpit.

"What happens is," Doakes continued, "the baits drift under the boat. . ."

"I got it," Wink said.

". . . which makes it kind a hard for Mr. Lichine to catch hisself another swordie. Meanin' we got to run the chute from the stern."

"Picture's all drawn and colored, Jeet," said Wink wearily.

Doakes climbed to the bridge on the new metal ladder. "I want to go fishin' with you again someday, turkey," he said over his shoulder. "Once you learn how."

Wink didn't reply. After a while, Lichine tentatively asked if the mate had something on his mind. Maybe he could help?

"Something, yeah," said Wink, busying himself with rods and baits. "But no, nothing you can do, thanks."

Oscar Farrington had replaced the still-hospitalized Sparky Thomas as their umpire. In order to end the daily race to be first out of the basin, it was agreed by the anglers that the five boats could leave at any time but that baits would not be put in the water until a radio countdown. This also permitted more fishing time.

It was a steep, rolling sea, with a twenty-five-knot wind shredding the crests of the waves. Lichine was unable to keep his balance, so he went into the lounge and sat at the table to ride out the run. Reading the newspaper made him queasy, so he put it aside and began to mentally calculate costs. It was an exercise he had avoided.

The twelve rods and reels racked in graduated sizes across the ceiling of the lounge: $11,000. Baitfish: $2.50 to $3.00 each. For average daily use: $60. Asked why he changed baits so often, Wink had said that scent was very important, and that meant fresh bait. Diesel fuel: About $1.10 a gallon here, but $1.30 and more in Caribbean ports they were to visit. And the powerful twin engines burned two gallons per mile. Once they left Palm Beach: airfares, room and board, uniforms, laundry, repairs, dockage and customs fees. Eventually, an additional mate. Salaries at double the normal rates.

Not counting the bet itself, Lichine saw no way that expenses for his participation in the tournament could be trimmed to less than four hundred thousand dollars. Plus the loss of time at work and the need to sell assets adequate to cover initial expenditures. For a change, Jason had a right to be angry.

There were other costs. He felt adrift. The touchstones of his carefully constructed identity were submerged, perhaps even lost. The most harrowing of his experiences these last ten days was the party at Wink's house. Lichine attended few social gatherings, and they were invariably genteel affairs, with talk of neighborhood politics and foreign films, lubricated by judicious measures of wine. It was not merely the lavish use of cocaine and the offhanded sexuality that Lichine found discomfiting that Friday night. There was, as well, an undercurrent of violence about to happen and his recognition that many of the people in the house were, by his standards, criminals. Only once before had he felt such confusion and vulnerability.

His mother and his father's friend did not hear him. In the gloom of the bedroom, Ernest watched as Dr. Jeff Donaldson slipped the bedjacket from his mother's unresisting shoulders. As he drew the straps of her nightgown down her arms. As his hands began to move over her body.

Ernest backed from the room, placed the tray on the floor, and ran down the stairs and out the door and through lengthening shadows toward the waterfront. He was still running when he reached the Esplanade, facing across the East River to the lower Manhattan skyline that was backlighted now by a vermilion and rust sunset. He ran north, unseeing, past women with strollers and young men walking hand-in-hand with other young men, colliding with some, running on. He slowed on the steps leading up to the broad wooden walkway of the Brooklyn Bridge, his throat raw, lungs afire, dodging bicycles and other people running. Beyond the crest of the bridge, he accelerated once more. At City Hall Plaza, he was deflected northward by traffic. Trotting past telephone booths decorated by pagoda roofs, weaving through crowds smelling of fish and cooking oil and wet paper, moving without plan as obstacles real and imagined shunted him in other directions.

Finally, he tripped, sprawled. Got up. Walked. Figures hunched in doorways and darted between buildings of grimy brick and cast iron. On other blocks, farther on, radios blared from open windows, stoops were crowded with people shrieking words he didn't understand, drums were played, children hurtled past.

Ernest kept on. Walking, running, walking. He followed Park Avenue all the way to 125th Street, where he turned west, then south again when he encountered Riverside Drive. He reached the house on Joralemon Street as the sun was coming up.

His mother was sitting on the steps leading to the second floor. She caught him as he tried to brush past. Slapped him. Shook him. Embraced him. He said nothing, and he didn't cry.

The next day, his mother and Dr. Donaldson came to his room. His father's friend was a doctor, she said. Didn't he know that? Mother was ill. Dr. Donaldson was examining her that night. Didn't he know that, silly? His father's friend smiled in benevolent understanding. Ernest couldn't speak, and they left finally, looking relieved.

He wanted to believe them, but he never really did. Then on a day in early Fall, Dr. Donaldson came to talk to Ernest about his mother. This was something Ernest did *not* want to believe. But he did.

The night wore on. Captains watched the compressed seismic tracings of their fathometers and squinted at lines, waiting for tremors. Mates changed baits, their eyes straying from the rod tips only seconds at a stretch. Anglers held themselves in their fighting chairs, muscles straining against the rhythmic lurchings of the boats. Nothing happened. Some baits were taken, and lost. A few people were sick. No fish were caught.

It was the same the next night. The weather did not worsen, but it didn't improve, either. The anglers decided to declare a lay day.

Carlos called at 6:30 A.M. He cut off Theo Marker's protest with the curt instruction to be at their meeting place in one hour.

The procedure was the same, but Carlos' attitude was not.

"Mr. Marker," he said as soon as he was in the car, "you are a man of much luck. My principals have agreed to wait until the end of your contest for full payment of your debt."

Marker exhaled. "That's very. . ."

"However," Carlos continued, staring directly ahead, "we have arranged a down payment."

"But. . ."

"You will be using the boat called *Redemption* for the contest, we understand. The one that is the property of the corporation."

"That's right, but also. . ."

"The California fishing boat is the down payment."

"But it ain't even paid yet, and I was. . ."

"Arrangements were made. We have it."

"You've. . ."

"What we have done or will do is of no matter. It is the bargain we have made. You now owe us four hundred thousand dollars."

"That boat is worth at least two hundred fifty!"

"Not to my principals. Give thanks, amigo. You have nine months."

"Well, I suppose. . ."

"Full payment. We will be watching. One thing more. My principals want to make certain your victory. If you need assistance, you will call me at this number."

Carlos handed Marker a slip of paper, and left.

Something Rumfeld, the broker, was keeping up a hearty patter while riffling through a sheaf of papers and a box of index cards.

"Mr. Lichine?"

Ernest wrenched himself back. "Pardon?"

"I was just wondering," said the broker, reaffixing the professional smile, "how soon you needed to complete the closing?"

"Excuse my inattention, Mr. Rumfeld. I. . ."

"Make it Arnie."

"Thank you, ah, Arnie," said Lichine, trying to recall his purpose. "By Friday, I think. I must return home then."

Rumfeld leaned back in his chair and puffed his cheeks. "That's not a great deal of time. As I told you last week. . ."

"You said it could be done by today. That's why I'm here."

"That's true, but I also mentioned the possibility of complications. And I'm afraid, Mr. Lichine, that we've got 'em. The boat is registered under a foreign flag, as you know, and we're having some unexpected hassles over duty and federal approvals of the principals and such. You'll recall that I did make mention of these matters. We rely heavily here on referrals and repeats and I surely wouldn't want to think you were unhappy because we hadn't given you the whole story. Now if you could see your way clear to wait a little longer. . ."

"I can't," Lichine interrupted, weary of the broker's procrastination. "But if it will help, I'm prepared to pay the full purchase price. In cash."

Rumfeld exposed another inch of teeth. "Well, now," he said, "that does cut a corner or two. Let me make a call and see if we can get this off dead center."

Lichine nodded, astonished with himself for his calculation. He knew that the broker was at that moment reckoning the extra commission that a cash payment would permit. Rumfeld was not even finished talking on the telephone when he began placing papers in front of Lichine, indicating the places to sign.

". . . and he'll apply the cost of the lease to date," he was saying. "Should be all wrapped up by Friday."

He escorted Lichine through the outer office. "And how is the tournament going? You still hold the lead?"

"As of this morning, yes."

"May I ask, Mr. Lichine, are the stakes as high as I've heard?"

"Probably."

"I understand that Horst Triga has hired a new captain."

"Yes," Lichine replied distractedly. "Pat Fowler. Do you know him?"

There was a big man with a lantern jaw sitting on the edge of a desk, apparently waiting for the broker. A muscle in his cheek knotted at the mention of Fowler. Lichine did not notice Rumfeld's warning glance.

"Why, yes, I do," the broker said. "Pat Fowler's a fine captain. And quite an amusing storyteller. Have you spent much time with him?"

"Not really. There is a dinner, though, for owners and crews. Saturday night."

"Really? Where is that?"

"A place called The Old House. Do you know it?"

"Yes indeed," said Rumfeld, ushering Lichine to the door with a flourish. "Good groceries, as they say. Please forgive my inquisitiveness, Mr. Lichine. This tournament has aroused a great deal of interest in our circles."

Behind him, the big man touched his bandaged right ear.

On his way to the car, Lichine realized that there was more to the exchange than small talk. But Catherine was waiting.

The Palm Beach Observer printed its weekly Gold Coast Gaffer column that Saturday.

A few flakes of queer-looking white stuff descended on the Beaches yesterday. Were it not for this meteorological curiosity, reliable sources claimed that it was something called s-n-o-w, there would be little to report on the final outing of that widely-discussed Challenge Match over at the Floridian. Truth to tell, the swordfish phase of the tourney started with a bang and ended with a whimper. As was reported on every electronic happy news outlet on the Coast, Ernest Lichine of New York City boated two finny behemoths the first night out. After that, only Catherine Nettles and Montgomery Childs, both of West Palm, were fortunate enough to tie into broadbills that exceeded the weight limit. Theodore Marker of Bel Air, California and our own Horst Triga had to settle for two releases each. According to the admirably environmentally-minded scoring system, the heretofore unknown Mr. Lichine enjoys the commanding lead of 476 points! Runnerup is Ms. Nettles, with 226.

But the other contenders are far from out of it, with four upcoming segments in ports as far afield as Cairns, Australia, and Cozumel, Mexico. Given the rumored multi-million dollar stakes riding on the outcome, it's a certainty that all five competitors will be casting and cranking to the very end.

That night, the anglers took their captains and mates to dinner. Only Horst Triga was absent. By ten o'clock, they had yet to order food. After laborious tallying, however, it was determined that there were eighty-seven empty highball glasses on the table. Jeeter Doakes had dropped his pants twice and Allie Cronski, in rebuttal, had flopped his flaccid penis on his plate. When Patrick Fowler arrived with Pia, Wink Andros immediately left. Doakes asked if Fowler had eaten yet. Fowler shook his head. Doakes grabbed a T-bone off a tray held aloft by a passing waitress and slapped it, juices spraying, on the table in front of Fowler. Ernest Lichine left with a reluctant Catherine when Doakes challenged Cronski to a competition of more exacting and creative proportions. But I want to see, said Catherine, resisting.

On their way through the parking lot, neither Catherine nor Lichine noticed the unusually muscular man with a lantern jaw sitting in a dark blue Ford facing the entrance of the restaurant, waiting.

COZUMEL

ATLANTIC SAILFISH
(Istiophorus platypterus)

Partly due to its limited commercial desirability, the "sail" is plentiful on both sides of the Atlantic, occurring from Brazil to Cape Cod and from England to Angola. Its elongated body is distinctive for its splendid fan-like dorsal fin, which begins above the forehead, runs all the way to a point above the anal fin, and is three times the height of the slender body. Sailfish are short-lived. Few exceed six years. Although their migration and spawning habits were once believed predictable, conflicting declarations of marine biologists and charter captains have clouded these perceptions of late. Some assert, for example, that the primary breeding ground is the Yucatan Channel. Others are as insistent upon Sicily or the coastal shallows of Florida. And while commonly thought to be surface feeders, sails have been proven to be as voracious at middle and lower depths. In any event, sailfish are spectacular fighters known to greyhound and tailwalk across a hundred yards of open water. They are customarily played from a standing position, employing a waist belt with a socket for the rod butt. On occasion, they leap as high as twelve feet. They are most active when seas are turbulent, and can swim as fast as seventy miles an hour. Average weight is around forty pounds, but the current sporting record is 141 pounds, nine feet. That might be bested at any time. Because they sometimes school, daily catches of a dozen and more are not unusual.

-THE IAA HANDBOOK

8

The five fishing boats left Palm Beach early in the morning of the first Thursday in April, headed for the Keys and the first and only anchorage on the trip to Cozumel.

Highlander weighed anchor as well, but Horst Triga was not aboard. He informed the captain of his yacht and Patrick Fowler, on *Adroit*, that he would fly to Cozumel on Saturday. At noon, Triga drove alone to a roadside steakhouse near Fort Lauderdale where he met and talked with a recently employed associate who had already proven useful in the initial segment of the tournament.

Childs and Marker were to travel by plane too. At dusk that Thursday, however, Ernest Lichine was pacing the docks at the Faro Blanco Marine Resort in Marathon, impatiently awaiting the arrival of Catherine Nettles on *Aphrodite*. They had not seen each other for five weeks.

Brain Soup was already at dock. Wink and Doakes had washed down the decks and attended to a minor generator malfunction that cropped up on the ten-hour trip. Then they went off to eat and drink the evening hours away. The crews of the other boats did the same. Finally, Catherine was there, pressing against him and whispering urgently in his ear. They went immediately to his cabin. Afterward, they drove to the Turkey Roost for dinner, where the hostess guided them through the Pecky-cypress dining room to the terrace. Catherine insisted on margaritas for both of them - "They're immense!" she said - and they nibbled at toothpicked chunks of smoked lemonfish and touched fingertips across the table. Candles guttered in glass pots. Lichine hadn't seen a night so clear since summer camp in the Catskills. The waitress brought conch chowder - "It's pronounced 'conk,' dear" - and pale, icy wine. Stone crabs and pompano came, with hashbrowns and cole slaw. Later, over espresso and cognac, they watched the tide rip through Vaca Cut immediately below. The Atlantic rushed to meet the Gulf of Mexico in an anxious, phosphorescent tumble that lasted less than an hour before melding in glassy stillness. Dark figures on the bridge sent weighted nets on long tethers drifting down into the water, minutes later retrieving them and their unknown bounty. When Catherine remarked that she couldn't remember the last words they had spoken, Ernest called for the bill and they left.

The launch from *Aphrodite* dropped Lichine at the Faro Blanco docks at seven-thirty the next morning. "Stay with me, darling," Catherine had said. "It's a tediously long way to Cozumel, possibly even dangerous in a boat the size of his. We can play," she said. Lichine wanted to ride his boat. He didn't say, and barely admitted to himself, that he needed the rest.

His crew was already aboard. Jeeter Doakes was red-eyed, but Lichine noted no weariness in his beefy shoulders or slowness in his step. They made preparations he didn't understand with what looked to be efficiency and coordination. There was a rectangular collapsible plastic tank lashed in place across the rear of the cockpit It looked like a water-bed mattress. Wink said that was what it was, only now it was filled with diesel fuel. They needed the extra supply to make the second leg of the trip, which was forty hours long, with no ports. Lichine stowed his luggage in the master stateroom, adjacent to the galley.

The sun was clear of the low band of palms behind them. The scurryings of the crews slowed. On the bridge, Doakes went through the unwritten checklist, calling down to Wink. Lichine watched from a position near the bait table. Satisfied, Doakes started up the twin engines. They grumbled to life. He leaned out and peered along the bridges of the other boats. Lichine and Wink followed his gaze. All three saw Allie Cronski, captain of *Zodiac Arrest*, lock eyes with Doakes. With pointed deliberation, Cronski spat.

Doakes reddened, cut the engines, and plunged down the ladder. Wink intercepted him. "Not now, Jeet," he said softly, "not here. You ain't been out even two months. Let it go."

"It was him put me there," Doakes said, reaching to push Wink aside.

"You don't know that," said Wink, louder. "You don't! Let it go. We'll find out for sure. I'll help. But pick your spot. Not here. Not so soon."

"You saw him just now," Doakes said, still angry.

"You heard him last night. He's askin' to get bent."

But he relaxed slightly, and he didn't brush the hand away. Wink kept talking as he guided Doakes back to the boat.

At eight o'clock, *Brain Soup* eased out of the slip, following in the wakes of the other boats.

Adroit was in the lead as the fleet of sportfishermen streamed west, then south, beneath the Seven Mile Bridge. It was a luminous day, the water gin-clear and calm. Patrick Fowler had a good start and intended to stay there, for his mate had promoted a pool with the other crews. A thousand dollars each, the kitty to go to the first boat in Cozumel. Fowler smiled. Boots Dupree would bet on three moons rising if the odds were right. The mate climbed to the bridge, finished with his chores below. He sat on one of the seats bracketing the steering console.

"Cronski is runnin' that Merritt balls to the walls," he said, squinting at the trailing boats. "Says he's gonna polish your doors, Pat."

Fowler snorted. "Cronski's six feet of mouth. He lays on that shit, it just makes me bow up a little snugger. Last time we raced, I dusted him off good. And I was full fuel and he was light."

"I 'member. But jam those throttles right up to the go ahead anyway, son. I could purely employ an extra bone or two."

"Chili," said Fowler.

"What're you sayin', son? It's gettin' hotter'n a June bride in a featherbed."

"I mean to eat. Got a need for chili. You stocked up proper?"

"Top round, cumin, stock, coriander. . ."

"I don't wanna write a cookbook, Boots.'"

". . . woodruff, oil, garlic. . ."

"Shit, Boots. I'm a eater, not a French chef."

"Even got the makin's of three-bean salad 'n biscuits."

"Boots!"

Dupree got up. "I hear you, Cap'n, sir. Aye, aye. Comin' right up, sir." He kept muttering as he descended to the cockpit. "Got no more couth than a goat been raised up on bobbed wire and beer bottles."

Fowler was pleased to have Boots with him. Most of the other mates were kids, cocky and brash and only half as knowledgeable about the business as they thought. After a few years, they would find something else to do with their lives. Boots was different.

Fowler quit high school the day before Thanksgiving of his junior year. He informed no one of the decision. It took four days to hitchhike from West Texas to the green warm edges of the ocean. The night he arrived in Miami, he sought out a bowling alley.

The amplified clatter of balls rolling and pins flying comforted him. Things were not so different here. He walked slowly behind the lanes, noting lumpy family groups and teenagers on dates and industrial-league teams in matching polyester shirts. In the very far lane, he found his target. An angular, thread-thin man bowled alone. Fowler watched awhile. The man's movements were fluid, practiced, apparently unchanging. While Fowler stood there, the man made five consecutive strikes. When he finally spared, Fowler approached him.

"Feel like a game?" he asked.

Dupree looked him over. "Ain't you got school tomorrow?"

"Don't go to school."

"So you say." Dupree hesitated. "Okay, son. You're on."

After six full games, five of them won by Dupree, Fowler proposed a wager.

"You a hustler, son?" Dupree asked. But he agreed to $100 per game. Fowler had $6.73 in his pocket. He took the next four games. They introduced themselves then, and went on. The other lanes emptied. The bar closed. Apart from the desk attendant, only one spectator remained. He said nothing, but watched through thick round spectacles as Dupree and Fowler continued. After ten hours, the skin on Fowler's thumb was raw and bleeding. But he was young, only three games behind, and averaging 219. He was certain his rival was tiring.

And after four more games, they were even. The lanes were filling again.

"Mind a bit of advice, son?"

Fowler waited.

"What it is," Dupree continued, "is that you just rear up and toss the ball. No offense, son, but you got no style at all, and you ain't never gonna catch that pocket regular if you don't work on the hook."

"Seems like I done all right so far."

Dupree grinned for the first time. "There's that, yeah. Lookit here, son. Our fingers is too swoll up to fit the holes. What say we call a draw?"

Fowler agreed, with a mixture of relief and regret. When they emptied their pockets, they found that there wasn't enough money to cover the bill for drinks and shoes, let alone the wagers they had made over the last night and day.

The owlish spectator with the vivid latticework of broken facial capillaries picked up the tab. When he offered to bankroll both Dupree and Fowler on what he called "the tour," they warily accepted. By Christmas, they had won twenty-four thousand dollars between them, in alleys as far west as New Orleans and as far north as Louisville. They returned to Miami and rented a trailer in a court where they could hear, but not see, the ocean. Three weeks later, the manager locked them out for nonpayment of rent and called the police when Dupree tried to beat down the door with a propane tank. After a night in the county lockup, the judge let them off with costs and a tongue-lashing. On the courthouse steps, Boots allowed as how it was time to bite the bullet and beg his old job back. He had been mate on a forty-six-foot Bertram owned by a Wall Street brokerage house. The captain, it turned out, had specific orders not to rehire Boots, but was nevertheless sympathetic. He referred Dupree and his companion to the Rybovich yard. They were fitting out a forty-two-footer just purchased by a man described as a hot young Hollywood director. The next day, Boots Dupree related his qualifications to the new owner and Fowler lied about his. Theodore Marker hired them both.

It was a good life. Marker showed up infrequently, and only for a week or two. He was making one film after another. The rest of the time, Dupree chartered the boat and kept the tips and part of the fee for himself and Fowler. Then, on the last day of the 1956 Morgan Cay tuna tournament, Marker accused his captain of sleeping with his wife.

For the first few hours, Lichine reveled in renewed pride of ownership. He faced into the wind, his hair stinging his forehead, watching the water change from creamy green to emerald to blue to indigo. He sat in the fighting chair and scrambled up the tuna tower and delighted in the flocks of flying fish skimming the crests. He had, he thought, a great many reasons to be pleased with the way things were going. His boat was less than perfect, it was true. But he thought it beautiful - clean-lined, creamy yellow hull, white topsides. More, the boat represented an irrevocable commitment and therefore repressed the nagging pragmatism that threatened to lose him this chance for what, he was yet to identify. His signature on Rumfeld's contract bound him not just to an expensive piece of property, but to a determination to test himself against champions.

And there was Jason. When Lichine finally returned to New York, the expected tirade was not forthcoming. His brother did not approve, but he did not rant and condemn, either. Jason was distracted, his mind on other matters. Just the usual, he said. A possible walkout at the Jersey plant, the tax reform bill in Albany.

Catherine. Each new night was a homecoming, with enough known and enough forgotten to retain the excitement but to temper the fumblings. They fit. Elbows and knees didn't get in the way. Catherine no longer pulled him to her, she presented herself. It was a sharing, a mutual learning of scents and hollows and tremors. Lichine was troubled that Catherine donned the pebbly hide of her outside personality with her clothes, but he knew she could shed it as readily, and he chose to believe that this morning's transformation was reluctant. Her 'dears' and 'darlings' were no longer the venomous quills of the night they first met. With him, in those rooms, the words were delighted punctuations and drowsy, sated sighs.

By noon, the five boats were out of sight of land. The sun stabbed at his shoulders. When Lichine pressed a fingertip into his pink forearm, the indentation stayed white a long moment. He went below to the salon. The air conditioning hummed. Lichine traced their course on the large chart. He had the Northerner's indistinct picture of the West Indies and the Caribbean, of the specific locations of the island colonies and nations.

Doakes was running through the Straits of Florida, Lichine surmised, then easing into a long southwestern ellipse along the coast of Cuba to Cabo San Antonio, the westernmost landfall. A slight course adjustment, and they would head straight for Cozumel, an island which appeared to be about twice the size of Manhattan. He imagined that their fishing would be done on the leeward side of the island, in the nine-mile-wide channel separating Cozumel from the Yucatan Peninsula.

Wink Andros walked through the salon and down the two steps into the galley to make lunch. After a time, he handed his employer a bologna and cheese on white. Lichine wished it were pastrami. Wink returned with two cans of beer and plopped into the sofa.

"Cheers, Mr. Boss," he said. They drank.

"Could I ask that you make that. . ."

"Ernie?" Wink interrupted. "Right you are, Mr. Lichine."

"What was that about this morning?"

"With Jeet?" Wink said around a mouthful of food. "Don't know whether I should say. Oh, hell. I guess you heard that our captain spent a few months in the slammer. Little bit of smuggling, so it was said. Hard to believe, now. Anyway, we were out hoisting a few last night when Cronski said something that persuaded Jeet that Allie was responsible for his incarceration. Who knows? Cronski is a braggadocious mother even on his down days."

"I see," said Lichine. He groped for a different topic. "Another question?"

"I can take it," Wink said.

"Don't be offended, but I notice that sometimes you talk like a. . ."

". . . redneck," Wink supplied.

"Yes. But other times, like. . ."

"A college grad-joo-ate."

"Yes. And I've wondered ."

"You've wondered why."

Lichine nodded.

"Straight or quick?"

"Whichever is right. Both, I guess."

"Both," Wink repeated thoughtfully. He looked out the window at the purple sea. "Because I'm like the guy who said he wandered between two worlds--one dead, the other powerless to be born. And because I don't know what I want."

"I see," said Lichine.

"No, you don't. But then, neither do I."

The mate left to take a sandwich to the captain. Lichine flipped through the Yachtsman's Guides, full of caveats and entreaties that meant little to him. Another beer. He pulled his legs up on the sofa and stared at the water. There was no land in sight, no other boats, no clouds. Just a washed-out sky. He dozed.

The afternoon, night, and entire next day passed with more naps and sandwiches and beers and coffee. The autopilot was on most of the time. Wink and Doakes spelled each other at the wheel and talked of men and women and fish they had known.

They arrived after dusk Thursday night. An official party composed of the captain of the port, a customs officer, a doctor, and an immigration officer boarded as the crew was finishing its cleanup.

Papers were signed, money was passed, courtesy drinks were shared. The rental car was waiting. In fifteen minutes they were in their rooms at the Cabanas del Caribe. Lichine stood under a painfully hot shower for as long as he could. Wink told him it was the best cure for a new sunburn. Afterward, Lichine sprayed himself with an antiseptic. It helped. He stretched out, very gingerly, on the bed. Just for a few minutes, he told himself, then he'd call to see where *Aphrodite* was moored. He closed his eyes.

He awoke shivering, still atop the bed cover, the towel tangled around his legs. A shaft of sunlight fell across his thighs through the gap in the drapes. Every part of his body stung. He retrieved his watch from the heap of coins, bills, sunglasses, pens, and index cards on the side table. Eight-fifteen. He had slept through the night.

Cold water revived him partially. The desk put him through to Wink's room. *Aphrodite* was expected around noon, Wink said.

Relieved, Lichine pressed the button on the telephone and ordered dos huevos, melon, jugo de naranja, cafe, y un periodico, por favor. He showered, shaved, sprayed. The burn was deepest on the tops of his thighs, so he chose to stay in his bathrobe, the cloth parted. A small brown waiter in an embroidered guayabera set out breakfast on the terrace. Lichine signed the check and knew from the flash of teeth that the tip he added was too much. As usual.

The newspaper folded by the plate was the previous day's Miami Herald, and he read it as eagerly as he consumed the eggs and melon. Normally he skimmed the business and finance section, pausing only to check the market quotation for Lich Elec. Now, however, he scanned each headline, reluctant to surrender even one word. He poured another cup of coffee.

The pot slipped from his fingers, smashing the plate and flinging glasses and silverware to the floor. Coffee splashed on his thighs. Lichine didn't notice. His breath had stopped as if a great fist pressed against his chest. The item was at the bottom of column six. Succinct, objective, remote.

LICHINE ELECTRONICS RUMORED TAKEOVER TARGET

A direct tender offer of $24.60 per share will be made for the stock of Lichine Electronics, Inc. by an as-yet unidentified holding company, according to a highly placed executive within the company. The takeover proposal is to be made privately

to the firm's seven directors on Friday. As the Lichine shares were trading at only $13.35 at the close of business Wednesday, the size of the premium was believed to be unprecedented. The move was interpreted as a classic "Bear Hug" maneuver, designed to panic directors and shareholders over the weekend, when the stock exchange is closed and information is difficult to obtain. It was not known what effect early disclosure might have on the holding company's plans. Speculation over the development centered on both the magnitude of the bid and the fact of Lichine's relatively recent listing on the Big Board. A partner at a prominent Wall Street brokerage house observed that while Lichine Electronics is "generally viewed as a well-managed company with excellent long-range prospects, its aggressive expansion of its retail operations prompts a cautious investment stance at this time."
Lichine Electronics recently reported a first-quarter rise of 38.6 percent in consolidated sales of its consumer product line, largely high-fidelity stereo equipment. Jason Lichine, executive vice-president of the company, and his brother Ernest, president and chairman, were not available for comment.

Lichine read the article again while he attempted to place a call to Jason's house in Larchmont. He ground the palm of his hand against his temple, but the pounding would not stop.

It was an hour before the hotel operator called back. Senor Jason Lichine did not answer. Ernest gave her the office number. That took only twenty minutes. Erest snatched up the phone. Jason's voice sounded as if he was speaking from the bathroom, hollow, but near.

"Ernie, that you? How goes it? Catch any lunkers?"

Ernest fought to control his voice. "Jason," he said, "tell me quickly and simply what is going on."

Ernest listened to the evasions, to the angry denunciations of the executive who leaked the news, to the assurances that there was nothing to worry about, to the defensive assertions that Ernest never paid any attention to the business anyhow, to the demands to know why he cared now. He waited until his brother had trotted out and exhausted every weapon in his extensive arsenal of persuasion and cajolery.

Then he told Jason that he was taking the next plane to New York. Invoking his rarely used prerogative as president and chairman, he instructed Jason to call a meeting of the full board for twelve o'clock Monday. With a steeliness he hadn't known he possessed, he cautioned Jason that no decisions were to be made until he arrived. He hung up in the middle of his brother's protest.

Lichine pulled on the first set of shirt and jeans that came to hand. The hotel was laid out in single-story wings, with expanses of powdery sand and luxuriant plantings between. At the reception desk, the manager informed him that there were not to be any flights from the island to the States before the next day, and perhaps not even then. A strike of the air-traffic controllers in Miami, senor, and there was no expectation of early settlement. Yes, he would be happy to inquire if a charter plane was available. He would inform the senor.

Doakes and Wink were still on *Brain Soup.* Wink accepted the news stoically. Doakes was outraged. Lichine was too preoccupied to remember to be afraid. He had to leave the tournament, he told them. They would be paid for one month, and could stay in Cozumel as long as they wished. He asked only that they return the boat to Palm Beach within four weeks. Doakes fury intensified when he realized that Lichine was not intimidated. Lichine said he was sorry his captain felt that way, and left.

There was a flight leaving Merida the next day, with a plane change in Houston. He could reach New York Sunday night. A charter was available to make the connection. Lichine requested the necessary arrangements. That gave him twenty-four hours with Catherine.

9

"I've decided something," Lichine said, breaking the silence. It was midday, and he and Catherine were on the spacious fantail of *Aphrodite*. They lay next to each other on a wide chaise, a single bath towel stretched across their hips. The steward arrived to clear away the remains of their lunch. In concession to Lichine, Catherine held her bikini top in place while her steward was there.

"Mmm?" Catherine drowsed.

"I've decided something," Lichine repeated.

"Oh."

"Could you remove your hand from right there, please?"

She lifted one eyelid, but kept her hand where it was. "You've decided that?" she said.

"No, something else. But I can't concentrate."

"Tough," she said, wiggling her fingers. The steward, a lithe, dark-haired boy of eighteen, made greater haste in stacking the dishes.

"Will there be anything else, Miz Nettles?" he said, his eyes riveted on a point several inches above her head.

"No, dear," she said. "Just bring the pitcher and two glasses over here, please." The boy did as he was told.

"Right here, dear. That's fine," she said, smiling brightly and letting the bra fall away just as the boy straightened up. "Thank you. I'll ring if we need anything."

"Catherine!" Lichine hissed as the boy went down the starboard companionway.

"Must be losing my grip," she mused.

"Why do you do things like that?" Lichine persisted.

"Am I getting droopy?" she said, looking down.

"Catherine! Why?"

"Why did the first Cro-Magnon eat the first oyster?" she asked, as if she had just detected his indignation.

"That's no answer."

"I can't think of another one right off."

"It cheapens you, doing that sort of thing. It's something I. . ."

"Are we having our first fight, darling?" She rolled over, throwing one leg across his thighs.

He yelped and doubled over, pushing her leg away.

"Darling! What on earth. . . ?"

"Sunburn," he whistled through his teeth, rubbing the skin that had turned nearly purple. "I never knew so much of me could hurt so bad at the same time."

She plucked two ice cubes from the pitcher and swirled them over the inflamed flesh. He settled back and closed his eyes and waited for the stinging to subside. The ice cubes melted away and she nestled against him. They listened to the water flap against the hull.

"Better?" she asked finally, idly curling a finger in his chest hair.

"I guess," he breathed. "Be ready to sit up and take nourishment in another week or so."

"Don't say that," she said, rapping his breastbone with her fist. "Three days of enforced celibacy was bad enough. I expect you to fuck my brains out before you get on the plane tomorrow. Excuse me," she added quickly as he started to protest, "I mean, 'make love'."

"Those aren't bad words, Catherine."

"Neither is 'fuck,' my darling. You have a Calvinistic streak as broad as a barn."

"I came by it honestly. Mayflower antecedents and all that."

"Someday I'll tell you how I came to be me."

"Why not now?"

"Someday," she said. "Now what is it you've decided?"

"What? Oh, yes. Well. I've been thinking, which is a fresh experience, since I haven't had my head screwed on straight for two months. I'm really not the boob I must seem to you and everyone else down here, you know, although God knows I haven't given anyone much reason to think otherwise."

"I know you're not."

"Thank you, but I have no illusions. I might as well have been dropped by a UFO that night at the awards dinner, and I've been tripping over myself ever since. Nothing I believe or have known seems to fit. All my cherished assumptions have flopped over, to the point I don't even know what's right for me anymore. I just can't seem to, damn, I'm not saying it. . . do you understand?"

Catherine nodded.

"I hope so," he continued. "Anyway. Up to the moment I saw that story in the paper, I thought all this was just an interlude, a funny sort of hiccup in an otherwise ordered life. I'd sow my oat and go back to my bench and stuff wires in boxes so they'd make pretty sounds and do what my brother told me to do and keep the doors locked.

"Then that story, and Jason on the phone trying to crawl out of it, and the realization that not only was somebody trying to steal my company, but my. . ."

He searched for the word.

"Go on," Catherine said.

"Life, I guess. Although that's not really the word. Anyway, it made me mad. Me, do you believe it? I don't get mad. Never. I also don't get drunk, or cry, or argue, or see how far I can push myself, or demand my rights. I just toe the carpet and sweat a lot and hide in my workshop. But things have happened. You. The tournament. Catching those broadbills. It took everything I had, but I did it. And later, those men were happy for me, and they showed it, because they don't know how not to." He paused again. Catherine waited. "I'm going home. I am going to take my company back. Then I'm coming back here. I plan to win this tournament."

"Settle for a close second?" Catherine said, at length.

"Only to you," he said, coloring at his display of bravado.

"It won't be to anyone else."

She poured from the pitcher and handed a glass to Lichine. The drink tasted uncommonly good. He pulled her close.

"Catherine," he said, "if it hadn't been for. . ."

She pulled his face down to hers and shut off the rest of the sentence.

"Darling," she said after the long kiss, sitting up and twisting to face him.

"Yes?"

"I'm not getting droopy, am I?"

The next morning, Catherine drove Lichine to the hotel. He packed his bags, carried them to the desk, and paid his bill. In a show of confidence, he made a reservation for three days later. He went to Wink's room and knocked until the puffy-eyed mate pulled open the door. Lichine announced his plans quickly, without preamble. Wink blinked, spun away, got in the shower in his shorts, and stood under the spray for two minutes. Toweling off, he demanded that his employer repeat his words. Lichine did so. Wink, still dripping, roughly hugged the startled man, who, after a beat, returned the embrace. Then Wink rushed down the hall to pound on the door of Jeeter Doakes' room. Lichine waved good-bye.

Catherine drove him to the airport. The pilot of the charter plane was waiting, visibly anxious. He took the bags through the gate to a four-place Cessna parked thirty feet beyond. Lichine and Catherine held each other and kissed, many times. The pilot returned, shifting from one foot to the other. They had to leave, he said finally. There was an unusually broad and fast-moving front over Yucatan, he said, coming right at them. If they didn't leave right away, they might be grounded for hours, even a day or more. Catherine translated this from Spanish. Yet another skill, Lichine said in surprise. She made a vulgar reference to an experiment of the night before. He chuckled, and replied in kind. She pushed him on his way.

Catherine was not there when he looked back. There was a freshening in the sodden air, and the sky to the west was dark.

His father's friend took a long time telling Ernest about his mother. First, Dr. Jeff Donaldson asked what the boy was doing. Ernest crouched over his bench and dully pointed out the connections on his schematic, waiting. Finally, Dr. Donaldson told Ernest that just a few hours before, his mother had passed on. Very quickly, and without pain, Dr. Donaldson said. Ernest believed only that his mother was dead. He was thirteen. She was buried between stones dated 1857 and 1902 in an overgrown place near a school in a town upstate called Larchmont. It was the family plot, according to an aunt Ernest saw only at Christmas, although his father was not there. Ernest was sad for a while, but mostly he felt betrayed. Twice. It was May, of course.

Ernest finished his first amplifier. It had no cover, for he gave little thought to aesthetics. But it had a separate transformer for each channel, an overload level of nearly three hundred millivolts, and was a third smaller than comparable units.

There was nothing like it on the commercial market. When he hooked it up to the Bose speakers, even Jason was impressed. The Dorati version of the 1812 Overture sounded as if it were being performed right I there in the rear parlor, cannon booming, bells clanging.

Jason still worked at the desk by the windows overlooking the garden, although his MBA was behind him and he now spent his days in the offices of a brokerage house in lower Manhattan. They were alone in the house on Joralemon Street, only Wanetta attending to them. Relatives and Dr. Donaldson confined themselves to mailed notes and holiday telephone calls. Ernest knew that his brother labored over checking accounts and taxes and arrangements for household repairs, but his assistance was neither requested nor offered. He hardly noticed when Jason went off one day with his amplifier and the neatly diagramed specifications.

On a day some weeks later, there was a package on his workbench when he returned from school. The unit inside had a face of brushed steel and sides and top of walnut-stained wood. When he slid the chassis out, he recognized it as his own amplifier. Jason later explained that he had found a designer and a small assembly plant in New Jersey interested in working with them. Ernest was momentarily flattered. Over the next three years, he constructed tuners and receivers and pre-amps, most of them elaborations upon existing equipment he purchased and dissected. His brother took each of them away and returned with finished prototypes. Ernest paid little attention, even though Jason had quit his job and was home most days, writing letters and talking on the telephone.

Ernest did not return to school the day after his sixteenth birthday. When a man from the Board of Education came to the house, Jason talked to him. Ernest continued work on the citizen's-band radio, a new interest. It was 1966, and very few people cared about such things. As soon as he was done, Jason took it away. From time to time, papers were placed in front of him. Ernest signed them on the lines his brother indicated.

He was walking along Fulton Street one Saturday when he saw workmen lifting a sign into place above a newly refurbished store. LICHINE RADIO, it read. When he returned to the house, he asked his brother what was going on. Only then did he discover that the store on Fulton Street was the third retail enterprise of Lichine Electronics, Incorporated. Others were planned.

"You have your talents," Jason said, unaccountably angry. "I have mine. Between us we can make a bundle. Don't give me that look. You saw all the papers. I didn't put anything over on you. Straight down the middle. Fifty-fifty."

Ernest said nothing.

"It wasn't easy, y' know," Jason went on. "Being mother and father. You never cared about what I've had to do. And since we're at it, baby brother, it's time to share some guilt."

He hesitated. Ernest said nothing.

"Mom didn't die of what we said," Jason continued. "That night, in Jeff's house, she put a gun in her mouth and pulled the trigger."

Ernest left the house and circled the block three times and returned to his workbench.

Adroit lay as immobile in the water as in setting concrete. No detectable surge. Still, Pat Fowler was uneasy. He squinted at the narrow gap between the breakwaters. The palms on the jetty to the left were in silhouette, their trunks swaying, but not bending.

Horst Triga was walking along the pier, barrel-chested and spindly-legged in pale-blue polo shirt and shorts. He paused at the stern of his boat, hands on hips.

"Good morning, Pat," he called up to the bridge. "Are we ready?"

Fowler kept his eyes on the western horizon. "We are," he said. "Don't know about the weather though."

Triga glanced over his shoulder. "Indeed," he intoned. "The reports didn't promise a salubrious beginning."

He waved at Catherine Nettles, who was boarding her boat in the adjacent berth. She ignored him. Unperturbed, he stepped into his cockpit.

"However," he continued, "we may eke out a full day. Good morning, Sparky. How's the leg?" He shook hands with the umpire assigned to his boat for this phase of the tournament. Thomas was using a cane after his injuries on the first day in Palm Beach. "Shall we be off, Pat?"

"Now you're here," Fowler replied. He made certain that Boots Dupree was aboard, and then turned to the console and eased the right throttle forward.

He idled at the mouth of the harbor until the klaxon sounded. Eight-thirty. They were first away. Three miles out, he was driving straight at the mainland and into a cross-chop. The hull smacked the surface, rose up, pounded down again. Triga was at his side.

"It doesn't look promising, does it?" Triga asked after a while.

"No, it don't." Fowler made himself reply. He flicked the knob to channel nine on the VHF transceiver. Oscar Farrington's voice sputtered over the speaker.

"Five minutes to start. Five minutes. Are all boats reading?"

Fowler picked up the mike and confirmed reception. The captains of Marker's *Redemption*, Nettles' *Zodiac Arrest*, and Childs' *Crystal Ball* followed, in prescribed order. *Brain Soup* had not left the harbor, for reasons known to everyone.

At the drop-off, Fowler turned south, two hundred yards from the mainland and paralleling the sliver of pale beach crested by tangled blue-green vegetation. It was rough, even worse than usual.

"Do we have to go directly upsea, Pat?" Triga asked, grabbing for a handhold against the violent lurching.

"We do if you want to catch sailfish," Fowler replied testily. "They swim northeast, so we got to run southwest, against their flow."

He bent over and yelled down to Dupree. "Get set to put those strings out! Sixty seconds to kickoff!"

Boots Dupree positioned himself at the stern and craned around to await Fowler's signal.

The radio crackled. "All boats. We begin the countdown. . . now. Ten, nine, eight, seven, six, five, four, three, two, now! Good luck."

Dupree lowered the outriggers into position, then put the rod butts into the gunnel holders, and dropped the baits over the side. When the lines were one hundred feet out, he clipped them in the outrigger pins and ran them up. Triga scrambled down the ladder from the bridge and took his place in the fighting chair. The baits took up their skittering paths on opposite sides of the wake.

The edgy anticipation of the first minutes dissipated quickly. The radio was silent. A gray canopy slid across the sky toward the sun, and the troughs between the waves deepened. At 10:06, Allie Cronski on *Zodiac Arrest* advised Oscar Farrington on *Crystal Ball* that they had a sailfish "in the air." Less than five mirlutes later, he confirmed the release.

Fowler was monitoring, as were all the captains. He reached for the mike and called Cronski.

"What'd you pull?" he asked.

"Nothin' to write home about," Cronski replied. "But it still counts for fifty."

"They won't look so big by the end of the week," Fowler answered. "But that gives you first blood, *Zodiac.* Come back."

"It also lightens your jeans," Cronski said.

By eleven, there were ten-foot seas and the sun was lost. Every boat caught fish, but by mid-afternoon, all action ceased. Oscar Farrington consulted with the four contestants over the radio, and it was agreed to terminate the day's competition at three. The boats trolled the drop-off until the specified hour. Farrington was about to commence the countdown when Steve Grubbs broke in. Montgomery Childs had hooked up. A big one, he said. The other boats turned toward port.

The storm assaulted the island minutes later. Extra lines were secured, and as there were no pilings alongside, the crews sank double anchors on pelican hooks off the bows. Antennae and outriggers vibrated in the wind. Crew members and anglers crouched and ran to their cars. After a last look around, Pat Fowler was about to leave as well, but Triga summoned him into the salon. Fowler lifted the teak lid of the wet bar and poured a bourbon over ice.

"Something?" he said, glancing at Triga.

His employer was leafing through a sheaf of papers. "Rather a letdown, isn't it?" he asked conversationally, without looking up. "After all this preparation, to have the first day come a cropper?"

"Yeah," said Fowler, waiting.

"Pour me a glass of that chablis, will you, Pat? With a spritz, if you would."

Fowler glared at the top of the scrupulously barbered head of white hair. After a moment, he did as asked and placed the drink on the table. Only then did Triga sit back, slipping off his black-rimmed, half-lensed reading glasses.

"Hits the spot," he said. "Think we'll be able to go out tomorrow, Pat? I've always trusted that animal instinct of yours over the guesses of meteorologists."

"No, I don't," Fowler replied, keeping his tone even. "This weather's gonna stay awhile."

"Hmm. In that event, I'd better speak to the other anglers. Perhaps we should move the Wednesday lay day up. No adverse effects on anyone."

"Don't you have to wait for Lichine? Ain't he comin' back?"

"I'm certain not. I gather that his problems back home will require all of his attention for a long while."

"No difference to me," said Fowler, reaching for a refill.

Triga watched the liquor rise to the brim, but resisted comment. He picked up one of the sheets of paper.

"Pat," he said, "there is one other matter I want to discuss. It may appear minor, but I wouldn't want to get off on the wrong foot. I've been looking over our bills for Palm Beach, and find that some rather startling expenditures have been incurred."

"Like what?" Fowler was expecting this.

"Well, here," Triga said, tapping the paper. "Clothing. Ten sets of tee shirts and trousers, four pairs of shoes, four windbreakers. Nearly eight hundred dollars!"

"So?"

"Come now, Pat. Surely you agree that's excessive."

"How?"

"Fifteen ninety-five per tee shirt! Why so much?"

"It was you who wanted them made up special," Fowler said, pointing at the one he wore. "This sunrise with the name of the boat. You wanna trick your crew out like movie ushers, you gotta pay the freight. And the guy gave me a discount, too." *And a kickback.* "You want four colors and a custom design, you pay. I could care less."

"But why so many? Five sets for each of you?"

Fowler set his glass down. " 'Cause I figured we'd like to get 'em washed every now 'n' then and still have somethin' to wear. Laundry takes two or three days down here."

"Very well, put that aside for the moment. Why two pairs of shoes each, and why Topsiders, the most expensive?"

"One pair might just get wet, y' think? And Topsiders, 'cause they're the best an' I don't want us slidin' all over the deck while we're tryin' to land a fish. Look, Triga, what is this crap? You spend more'n this just gassin' up for a day's cruise. I told you up front that I wasn't gonna listen to you squeezin' nickels, and I ain't no more ready to hear it now than I was then."

"And I am not prepared to approve your profligacy," Triga replied sharply. "Look at this! Over fifteen hundred dollars for bait fish! Why did you have to purchase them in Florida? Why didn't you wait until we got here, where it would have been at least two hundred less?"

"One, I wasn't sure we could get 'em here. They been short before. Two, they ain't neither cheaper here. They're more. Have been since last year." Fowler wiped his hand across his face. "I ain't goin' on with this. You keep right on talkin', if you want, but I ain't listenin'."

He started to leave.

"I have a right to expect you to keep expenses down," Triga persisted.

Fowler turned at the door. "You got a right," he said, "to expect me to find fish an' put you over 'em an' bring 'em in. You got a right to expect that I won't do nothin' t' keep me from givin' my best when I'm at that wheel. But you want an accountant, you best buy yourself one."

They locked eyes. Both men were on the verge of delivering ultimata. For their own reasons, both were holding back. It was Triga who retreated.

"Perhaps you're right," he said, visibly bringing himself under control. "We'll put this aside. In the future, however, please present expenditures to my assistant, Russell. That should prevent this matter from becoming an issue of contention."

Fowler made a noncommittal sound and pulled open the glass door. A heavy, squall-driven rain had begun, ripping the water.

"I'll send Dupree to stay with the boat," he said over his shoulder.

"Fine," Triga answered, riffling his papers. "And, Pat, I look forward to witnessing your sober best in the morning."

Fowler stepped out on the deck and slid the door shut behind him.

Boots was waiting in the car at the end of the dock. He was not happy with the assignment, but he got out and jogged back to the *Adroit* with a minimum of grousing. Fowler drove to the Cabanas del Caribe and trotted across the parking lot through the open entrance. He went to his room and flicked the switch. It took a moment before he realized that it really was Pia Cipolla sitting in the pool of light thrown by the floor lamp.

10

The participants in the tournament disposed of the remainder of the afternoon of that first day in predictable fashion. The members of the crews napped or drank. The anglers made or received telephone calls.

"Mel? Theo," said Marker to his agent and business manager in Bel Air. The connection was a poor one, fading away, coming back. "Theo Marker!"

"Who? Oh. I thought it was . . . How's it going, Theo? Where are you?"

"Cozumel. I'm fine. You?"

"What? Oh. Me, too. Look, Theo, I can barely hear you. Maybe you should. . ."

"No, I won't try again, Mel. I've had too much trouble getting in touch with you. This'll be a quickie." It was difficult to both shout and sound nonchalant at the same time. "We got an off-day here, and I was wonderin' if you heard anything from UA yet. I said, any word from Myers at UA yet!"

". . . a little better now. Sorry you couldn't reach me. Been busier'n a one-armed paperhanger . . . was it you wanted again?"

"United! Myers! You hear anything?"

". . . can hardly . . . Myers, did you say? No, nothing, Theo."

"Why not, for crissake? It's been four months!"

"It's a big project, Theo. Really big. Every director in town wants it. I've been trying to . . . can you still hear me?"

"YES! *I can hear you!!* For Godsake, why are you. . . look, Mel. I really want that project. It was practically made for me. I know the writer, I done two treatments already. What's holdin' it up?"

"Isn't that, Theo. I'm not even sure what's causing the delay. Grapevine says they're trying to pull off a co-production deal with Metro, but Myers says not. All I can do is keep pushing. Carefully, of course."

"Are you pushin'?"

"What do you mean by that? You should know by now that. . ."

"Okay, okay. Don't get yourself in an uproar. I'm only. . . it's just. . . shit, Mel, who's kiddin' who? I don't just want that movie, I need it."

"It's not as though I had the strongest hand, Theo. Your last few projects. . . well. . ."

"Three bombs in a row. You ain't tellin' me nothin', Mel. But what about the eighteen before that? Ain't no studio has lost money on me, not if they count the total."

"They don't count the total.'

Marker twisted the telephone cord in his fingers and counted to five.

"Theo?"

"Yeah, Mel. Look. Give them another nudge, will you? I'd appreciate it. I have to be makin' other plans."

"Sure, Theo, sure."

"Don't you want my number here?"

"What? Oh, right. Shoot."

Marker recited the number, twice. "I'll be here about ten more days, Mel, but try to get back to me sooner than that, okay?"

"Sure, Theo." The agent's tone was placating.

Marker's fragile construction of reasonableness collapsed. "Don't put me off like that, you bloodsucker!" he screamed. "I ain't no pimple-assed film-school dropout and it's time you started earnin' that percentage you been skimmin' for twenty-eight years! You readin' me loud'n clear?"

The line was dead. Marker threw the instrument at the bureau mirror. It stopped in midair at the end of its cord, fell on the bed, bounced, and hit him in the shin. He cursed, grabbed his shin, and hurled a convenient liquor bottle at the sliding window. It ricocheted into an arm-chair. Both window and bottle remained intact.

Marker glared dumbly at the telephone, bottle, and window. He felt a giggle, choked it back, but then started to chuckle. And then he laughed and laughed and laughed until tears ran down his cheeks into his beard.

Triga spoke to Julius McNally again, in an intentionally elliptical conversation that the steward Duncan could not decipher. Something about "early disclosure" and "right on track" and "no problems." His employer appeared pleased.

The four anglers and five umpires met on *Highlander* that evening. Duncan filled requests. When Catherine eventually tired of the banter with her rivals, she asked what business was to be conducted. In light of the weather, they agreed to take Tuesday off. Oscar Farrington raised minor points about communication procedures. Monty Childs complained about delays at the scales. Sparky Thomas proposed that released fish first be tagged.

And Triga suggested that Ernest Lichine be considered withdrawn from the contest.

"Oops!" said Theo Marker under his breath, glancing at Catherine. Everyone waited.

Catherine set her glass down and focused on Triga, as if to determine whether be was serious. She decided be was.

"Prick," she said.

"Now, Catherine. . ."

"Low-grade gutless mealymouthed backstabbing hypocrite,!"

"Now really, Catherine," Triga attempted, "You know that none of us here want. . ."

"Pompous supercilious no-balled freak."

"Careful, Ho," said Childs. "I think she's going to get mad in a minute."

". . . really want to do this," Triga continued. "But we all agreed to the three-day condition, and we must face facts. Ernest will not return."

"We don't know that. He hasn't been gone even one day, and he promised me he'd be back. With the lay day, that gives him until Friday morning. But you couldn't wait to whittle down your competition, could you? Snake. Worm."

"The simple fact of the takeover bid for his company certifies problems which will compel his presence in New York for a long time to come," Triga replied. "Possibly he did not realize that when he made his valiant pledge to you."

"He could just accept the offer and be done with it," Catherine said, knowing Lichine would do no such thing.

"I doubt you are that naive, Catherine. In any event, I was simply bringing the matter to everyone's attention. If Ernest is not here by nine o'clock Friday morning. . ."

Catherine did not accept the capitulation gracefully. She kicked Triga in the kneecap.

"Damn," she said. "I missed."

Duncan, the steward, moved aside to let Catherine leave. He placed discreet fingertips over his mouth to mask his amusement as he watched his employer hop to the sofa holding his knee.

While she was waiting for Lichine to come on the line, Catherine had a moment of panic. For that instant, she could not remember his face. There she sat, fluttery as a schoolgirl, and she could not. . .

"Hello? Catherine, is that you?"

Then it was all right. "Yes, darling. Can you hear me? Did I disturb you?"

"No, no, of course not," he said. "There isn't anyone I'd rather speak to, believe me. It's been a madhouse ever since I got here. Haven't had more than two hours of sleep. . . Catherine! Are you all right? Is anything wrong?"

"No, darling. Apart from a desperate need for extensive fondling, I'm fine."

She heard him exhale. "Thank God," he said. "I've been having these eerie premonitions ever since I left. I guess that happens when you. . ." He paused. "Was that as fondlee or fondler?"

"I'll take what I can get," she said. "When are you coming back to give it to me?"

"I wish I knew," he said. "Catherine, you can't believe how complicated and nasty it all is. Down there , with you, I had these simple little notions of charging up here, laying waste to the bad guys with my singing sword, and scooting back on the return flight. Trouble is, I'm beginning to think I'm the heavy. It's just an incredibly tangled rat's nest, and I don't know how long it's going to take."

"But you are coming back? By Friday?"

"Well, I . . . yes, yes, I am. Sure. 'When' is another question."

"I see."

"Catherine, are you sure nothing's wrong? You sound. . . not the same."

She did not answer.

"Catherine?"

"Do what you must, darling, for as long as you must," she said finally. "But come back to me."

Very quietly, she replaced the receiver in its cradle.

Wednesday morning was hot and still, the air washed clean. The crews, all on their boats earlier than necessary, found tasks to fill the time until the first signal. The anglers paced their cockpits, waiting. Engines grumbled to life. *Brain Soup* wasn't going out, but Wink Andros was aboard anyway. Pia Cipolla strolled over to speak with him. He was obviously happy to see her. Fowler noticed Pia glancing in his direction. Fowler drew a breath, went down the ladder, and hopped to the dock.

Wink spotted his uncle approaching. He stepped back from Pia, his expression suddenly flat. When Fowler was ten feet away, Wink pointedly disappeared into the cabin. Fowler stalked back to *Adroit*. He knew Pia was coming after him, but he reached the boat and had Dupree cast off before she got there. *Adroit* was, again, the first boat out of the harbor.

In the lee of the island, the water was unruffled. But three miles out, the impatient northeasterly rush of the current through the strait goaded the surface into bellying, precipitous folds. Often, as the boats toppled over the peaks of the waves, the screws rolled into the air, whining in frustration.

The captains quartered the swells, knowing that the maneuver could only partially moderate the bucking of their vessels. Toes clutched at heaving decks and fingers, ached with the strain of constant gripping. After a while, muscles adapted, as they always did. Balance was less precariously maintained and steps were less consciously considered.

Sparky Thomas struggled up the ladder and dropped onto the cushioned bench. Once he regarded Fowler's malevolent glower, he suppressed his intention of initiating conversation.

Many things made Sparky Thomas uneasy. Among these were elevators, bench saws, bridges, and groups of three or more teen-agers. He regarded these as wholly rational phobias, no doubt shared by many others. But Fowler and . . . his kind . . . quite simply terrified Thomas.

A life of privilege and the patina of years served to mask these dreads, though, as did the cloak of avuncularity he drew around himself.

Thomas retreated into what he hoped was interpreted as profound reverie.

He sucked on the unlit pipe, rubbing his healing leg and stealing a peek at Fowler. It was the captain's physical appearance, partly. Heavy brows over deep-set eyes. Red-brown flesh, scored by seams that infrequently followed the underlying bone structure. A slight but permanent curl in the right comer of the upper lip. Thomas conceded that women, given their endemic perversity, might find Fowler attractive. All he saw was the threat of unpredictable savagery.

Fowler continued to scowl, snarling orders at Boots when they reached the drop-off. Within five minutes of the countdown, both *Crystal Ball* and *Zodiac Arrest* called in their first hookups. Fowler and Thomas had visual contact with *Redemption*. Theo Marker stood at the transom, the rod bucking in his hands, a sailfish pinwheeling in the air fifty yards astern. *Redemption* was dead in the water.

"That stupid fucker Curry," Fowler said aloud.

"The captain of *Redemption*?" Sparky Thomas heard himself ask.

"If you want to call what he does that," Fowler said contemptuously. "Look at him!"

"What should he be doing?"

"He should be backin' up, is what he should be doin'. He should be keepin' the fish astern. He should get that port line in. Better still, he should get out of the business."

"Ah hah," said Thomas, as if grateful for this edification. In fact, as a member of the IAA for three decades, the deficiencies of technique on the part of the *Redemption* captain were as apparent to him as to Fowler. "I see, I see," he said nonetheless, feigning enlightenment. "Now that you point it out, I do agree. No doubt at all. Yes. Mmm."

The radio crackled. Five fish, brought to the sides and released. Two more gaffed and boated. Not an hour gone and *Adroit* was in last place. Fowler decided. He shoved the throttles forward and turned in a wide arc downsea. There were dismayed shouts from below, but no one came to the bridge. It took over a half an hour, running on plane at thirty-two knots, to reach the area he had in mind.

"Maybe somethin' will happen now," he said.

"What can we expect?" Thomas said, his first words since the burst of sycophancy over which he had been brooding ever since.

"A lot of action, usually," Fowler replied. "Most times, this channel is so thick with fish you could get out and walk to the beach on their backs. Marlin, dolphin, skipjacks, makos, bluefin. Even swords. Down here, you can get any kind of trash on the line."

"Really, now, Captain," said Thomas. " 'Trash'? Living creatures? Don't you think that such terms are inappropriate to. . ."

"Thomas," Fowler angrily interrupted. "Leave off the ecology crap. I'm already a believer. I release nine out of ten fish my clients catch. The keepers go to smokehouses or get mounted. I make my livin' on fish, and I don't kill any more than I have to. But right now, right here, we're sailfishin', and anythin' else is trash. A month from now, we go for tuna. Then sailfish will be trash. You gettin' me?"

"Steady, old man," said Thomas, alarmed by the outburst. "I quite understand. Yes, indeed. Quite right."

The rod in the port holder bounced. Triga lunged for it. Dupree looped the strap around the angler's waist and buckled it in place, then snatched up the other rod and cranked furiously. Triga fit the butt in the socket at the front of the strap and continued to work the rod, his thighs braced against the covering board. He had the sailfish at the side in seven minutes, full of fight. It was by no means certain that it was over the limit, but the angler ordered the gaff. The fish was his first, and he was behind in the standings.

At 10 points per fish, and one point per excess pound, Triga's total at day's end was 109. Theodore Marker posted 114 and Montgomery Childs, 136.

Catherine Nettles hooked twenty-two sailfish, all but two of which she released. Her score was 259.

Anglers and crews rarely came together socially. At many of the clubs and resorts at which they docked, crews were denied entrance to certain restaurants, bars, game rooms, golf courses, buildings, and even sections of islands set aside for the exclusive use of member anglers.

It was customary during tournaments, however, for owners to invite their crews once or twice a week to cocktails and dinner. As a rule, these affairs were strained and awkward for all in attendance. They groped for conversational topics of common interest but never strayed far from boats and fishing. Given the inherent gaps in age, education, income, and attendant interests and convictions, this was to be expected. Crews accepted the events as occasions for free food and liquor. Owners endured them as exercises in employee relations. The dinner arranged for that night bore additional burdens. Seating, for one.

There were two large tables in the private dining room of the Mayan Plaza. Umpires, friends, and spouses were deployed as buffers between those anglers and captains currently at odds with each other over matters personal and professional. Wink Andros, for example, got up and moved when Fowler and Pia sat at his table. Festivities proceeded in an atmosphere of brittle restraint and unctuous solicitude. That facade cracked when Jeeter Doakes chose to squeeze the ample left buttock of the Mexican waitress. The act inspired a dry rebuke from Oscar Farrington and a machine-gun burst of Spanish from the waitress. Asked to translate, Catherine explained to Doakes that the waitress asserted that he was a person of dubious masculinity who had carnal knowledge of his mother, the village priest, and a variety of domesticated beasts. What was more, Doakes could regard himself as fortunate if the waitress deigned to serve him donkey excrement on a communion wafer.

To the relief of at least half the people in the room, Doakes found this hilarious. Sparky Thomas made himself very small. Pat Fowler brooded over the latest slight by his nephew. Bunny Haskell bubbled brightly at Monty Childs.

"You haven't introduced the playmate-of-the-week, Monty, dear," Catherine reminded Childs.

"Bunny Haskell," Childs replied, "this is Catherine Nettles, ball breaker of the seven seas."

"Truly?" Catherine asked. "It's 'Bunny'? How adorable."

"Isn't it dreadful?" said the girl ingenuously. "I've never really forgiven Daddy. It's a cross to bear."

"Not at all," Catherine said. "I think it's very . . . fitting."

Bunny smiled uneasily and pulled at the top of her pink halter, which was proving inadequate to its task. The clatter of the dozen golden bracelets on her wrists attracted eager contemplation of her struggle to contain her breasts.

"Body language in action," mused Catherine. "They're lovely, dear."

"Amen to that!" breathed Doakes, who rose to his feet, swept his hat from his head and held it reverentially over his heart.

"I meant the bracelets," said Catherine, although she didn't. "Does Monty give you one every time he can't get it up?"

The menus came, and Childs used the interruption to avoid constructing a reply. He was already dtunk. He patted Bunny on the hand and ordered another round for the table. The new waiter delivered them and asked for their dinner selections.

"The salad, please," said Bunny, nibbling her lip."And could I have a plate of just broccoli carrots, and rice? Thank you so much."

"I see just the thing for you, Monty," Catherine said, scanning the menu.

"Prolly hate myself for asking, Cat, but what?"

"Pork tartare."

The remark eluded Bunny. "0oo, that sounds terrible," she said with a pretty crinkle of her nose.

"Really, dear?" said Catherine. "I would have thought you were fond of pig."

"Oh, no. I'm a vegetarian."

"What on earth for?

"I don't want my body to be a graveyard for rotting flesh," Bunny answered. "I absolutely shudder at the thought of putting what used to be living things in my stomach."

"How compassionate of you, love. For your sake, I do hope broccoli doesn't learn how to scream."

"We are ignoring this delectable lady over here," Childs said, indicating Pia Cipolla. "What might your name be, honey?"

Pia didn't respond.

"Honey?" Childs persisted. His eyelids were drooping, his hand wavering. "You gonna keep mysterious?"

She told him her name with a frostiness she hoped would deter further attention.

"A beauty, innit she?" Childs appealed to Doakes.

"Innit she?"

"Damn straight," Doakes replied, raising his glass in salute.

"That long black hair. Juicy lips. Great jugs."

Fowler glared at Childs, his lip curling more than usual. That was usually enough to deflect any line of conversation which displeased him, but Childs did not heed the warning.

"Jeeter," he said. "I ask you, are those not great jugs? Look how those nipples pucker up like little cherry pits. Stan' up, honey, an' give us a look at the rest of it."

Pia did not move, blush, avert her eyes, or speak.

"Bet she can suck the chrome off a trailer hitch. C'mon and tell us, Hook, what's her technique?"

"Put a lid on it, Childs," said Fowler.

"Damn sure would like to stick it to her," Childs continued. "I think she's got a wide-on for me already."

"That girl don't want you in her pants, Monty," Doakes said.

Childs feigned indignation. "Why the hell not?"

" 'Cause she's already got an asshole in there."

Childs groped for his drink and a properly acerbic reply, but the heel of his hand caught the rim of the glass, spilling its contents across the tabletop.

"You're all style, Monty," said Catherine, sopping up the liquid with her napkin. "Why don't you and Bunny go chew on a root?"

"Rather chew on Pia's button," Childs said. "How 'bout it, baby? Unload that ugly fucker so we can go do the old in-out."

"That's it, Childs," Fowler said.

"Opps! Cap' Hook is pissed. I am shaking all over."

The waiter chose that moment to deliver their meals. Sparky Thomas excused himself. Doakes was enjoying himself enormously, his head swiveling from Fowler to Childs. The angler had his hands up and was shaking his head in simulated fear.

"No, no," Childs said. "Please don't strike me, Cap'n Fowler, sir. I'll be good."

Fowler snorted, picked up his fork, and skewered a chunk of fish.

"Pia, honey," Childs said after a long moment. The diners fell quiet. Silverware was placed carefully on plates.

"No more, Childs," Fowler growled. "You've run out your string."

"Pia, honey," the angler pressed on. "I can eat my way out of a barrel of shark chum. C'mon and let me show you."

Fowler reached across the table and flipped the plate of enchiladas verdes into Childs' lap. The angler did not move. He simply watched the mass of chopped chicken, tortillas, and chili-tomato sauce seep into the raw silk of his trousers. Fowler got up and leaned on his fists. He spoke very slowly, one word at a time. "Was there any part of what I been sayin' that you did not understand?"

Childs looked up, glassy-eyed. He opened his mouth once. Then he shook his head and looked back at his lap. Catherine and Doakes nearly doubled over. Bunny fluttered. Oscar Farrington hurried to join Sparky Thomas. Waiters dashed about with rags and pitchers of water. Fowler lifted Pia by one arm and they walked from the room. The crew members, anglers, and remaining guests watched them leave, and then erupted into a babble which was equal parts consternation, glee, and approbation. No one noticed Wink Andros leaving.

11

Pia followed Fowler as he stalked through the lobby and across the terrace and down to the beach. He went through the line of palms, past a flamboyant in full fiery bloom, past the row of open-sided thatched-roofed shelters. He didn't stop until his shoes were in water. A stunning gold and mauve sunset was in progress. The air was a fragrant sigh. Fowler didn't notice.

Pia waited. After a long while, Fowler sucked in a deep breath and let his shoulders sag.

"Feel better?" she said.

"No."

"You could go back in and throw Triga out a window," she suggested. "Or ravish your prize damsel."

He looked at her. She was not making a joke. "You got a problem I ain't heard about, honey?"

"Pia," she corrected, her face pinched. "And yes, I do. I've waited you out as long as I care to. I thought maybe if I was patient, you'd pull out of it. Now I think you're probably just naturally a sour, mean son of a bitch and whatever we had was a short-term fluke."

Fowler was astonished, the incident in the dining room forgotten. "What the hell is this all about?"

"It's about how I'm up to here with having to watch you feel sorry for yourself. It's about how I have better things to do than sit around holding your hand while you get madder and madder at the world. Life is too short."

"If you mean about back there. . ."

"And that's another thing! Who appointed you my owner?"

" 'Owner'? That rich fucker was insultin' you! I was just. . ."

"Doing what any good, chivalrous, hairy-chested redneck does. Protecting your property." She was saying this evenly, without tears or gestures.

"I don't fuckin' believe this."

"No doubt," she said. "But believe it. I'm full grown, and I made it all the way without bodyguards."

She swung around and trudged away as quickly as the tug of the sand permitted. Fowler watched her, his mouth open, flabbergasted. When she had reached the shelters, he pulled himself together and ran after her. He caught her under the flamboyant, spun her around, and gripped her shoulders. The black eyes snapped, but she didn't struggle.

"Pia. . ."

"Yes?" Ice. Steel.

"You got it," he said, an unfamiliar ache in his throat. "Your rules. And mine. Down the middle. Just let me know."

She surveyed his face. "I have," she said at length and slipped her arms around him.

They held each other a long time, without moving, listening to the combers collapsing on the packed sand.

"Pat," she murmured against his neck.

"Yeah?"

"Wanna screw?"

"Smooth talker."

They didn't leave the beach. They walked to a wooden bench beneath one of the shelters, sat, and watched the sky change from wisps of waning pink to dark blue. Before they did anything else, there was a voice behind them.

"That seat taken?"

Wink was managing to hold two bottles, three glasses, and an ice bucket. Fowler looked up and down the empty bench.

"It ain't hardly crowded," he said, his anger with his nephew blunted by the moment and by Wink's apparent conciliatory intentions.

"Your timing could be better," Pia said. She made space on the bench.

"But I brought my tickets," Wink countered, handing them glasses. He distributed ice cubes, poured rum, splashed cola, and talked the whole time. Finally, he ran out of things to say.

"Thought you wouldn't never run down," said Fowler. "Always did have an LP tongue, even when you was a kid."

Wink leaned over and squinted at his uncle. He detected no rancor, only wariness.

"I heard about your boat," Wink said. "About what Triga did."

Fowler glanced at Pia.

"Yes, I told him," she said, a defiant tilt to her chin.

"This morning, after you went out."

Fowler grunted.

"It explained some things, Pat," Wink put in. "Don't get mad at her. I know what your boat means, but I didn't know Triga was holding it over your head."

"I ain't pissed."

They finished the bottle of rum. It didn't take long.

"We're down to Co-Cola, good buddies," Wink said, reaching into his pocket. "And reefer."

"Gimme some that," Fowler said.

"You don't do this shit, Captain Uncle."

"Tonight I do."

"Well, lemme get it lit, least."

"What was Childs doin' when you left?"

"First, he was outlining the destruction he was gonna bring down on your ass," Wink said through his teeth, passing the cigarette to Pia. "Then that little honey with the lungs started wiping dinner off his lap and Monty lost his pique all of a sudden. Man was drunker than a cooter brown and hornier than a two-peckered billy goat."

"And worthless as a cup of chicken shit." Fowler drew on the joint and immediately started coughing.

"That too. Told you you didn't do this, Uncle Captain."

"Whadda you kids see in that?" Fowler asked, still choking.

"Periwinkles, moonbeams, and sugar cones," Wink answered.

"Glad I asked. Let's go get somethin' makes me see things." He started to get up.

"One thing, Pat," said Wink, staying him. "I dig why you're working for Triga."

"That's cool."

"But me and Jeeter and Lichine are gonna whip you. No hard feelings."

Thursday, the boats approached the drop-off and the countdown in the same air of palpable tournament day. The sea was uncommonly smooth. Repeatedly, the clips on the outriggers snicked open, loosing their looping lines and setting crews and anglers into frenzies of activity. Nearly every time, it was for nothing. The anglers reeled in half eaten baits or barracuda, which were torn from the hooks and flung contemptuously into the water.

Allie Cronski on *Zodiac Arrest* was so furious when his mate hauled in their tenth barracuda that he put the boat on automatic, scrambled down to the cockpit, snatched the offending fish away, and ripped its belly open with his knife before hurling it fifty feet astern. Catherine and the umpire protested. "Shit-eating bait-robbers" was the mildest expletive Cronski uttered as he returned to the helm.

Shortly before noon, even the barracuda stopped biting. Anglers and umpires sought refuge from the heat in their air-conditioned salons, and mates found tasks for themselves in the galleys. Only Triga stayed in his fighting chair, relentlessly scanning the water to locate the brown smudge that meant a sailfish was rising. Boots Dupree joined Fowler in the shade of the bridge.

"He's some kinda fisherman," Boots observed. "You got to give him that."

"That's all I'll give him," Fowler replied.

"Yeah. These last few days, I'd sooner stick a corncob up a wildcat's ass than talk to him. What's eatin' him? He was always an uppity mother, but least you could pass some lies with him to make the time go. Now you look at him crossways and he tears your head off."

"He ain't used to losin'," Fowler said, his back to the wheel and his eyes on the baits. "I ain't neither, come to that."

"We ain't losin', we just ain't in first place yet. And we been behind afore. It ain't the money, Christ knows. He couldn't spend all he's got if he lived to three hunnert."

"You ain't got it yet, have you, Boots? This here is the big one. The four best crews and the four best anglers in the world. There ain't never gonna be a fish-off like this again, ever. Ain't nothin' he could buy that would get him off like takin' this. He could pull his pud over that even after he was chin-deep in his grave."

"I reckon," Dupree said, nodding. He looked out over the bulge of lime water drawn behind the boat. Before the thought was gone, he swung back to Fowler. "It don't mean all that to you, does it, Pat?"

"Shit, you know better'n that, Boots. All this is eatin' money. I got too much else goin'."

"Sure 'nough, Pat?" asked Dupree, not unkindly. "What else you got goin'?"

Fowler touched the throttles and bent to check the fathometer. The stylus traced an uninterrupted path across the slowly rolling paper.

He was dismayed to realize that he couldn't think of an answer.

"Whyn't you make yourself useful," he said, "and go fix us a couple sandwiches."

"Sure, Pat," Dupree said. "I'll do that. A beer, too?"

"You know I don't do nothin' more'n coffee when I'm workin'."

"Dr. Pepper? Co-Cola?"

"Just get it, will you?"

Boots returned in ten minutes with two sandwiches and soft drinks.

"Some boat," he said, passing Fowler his lunch. "Thomas sittin' and puffin' and makin' like a Supreme Court judge with piles. Triga down there fryin' what littte brains he got waitin' for a strike that don't look like it's com in' . And two rickety-ass boatmen who shoulda found them a Pecos Valley hog farm ten years ago."

"*You* say," Fowler snorted. "I wouldn't go back there to eat dust again if a nymphomaniac with a liquor store held a shotgun to my head. If you can't think of nothin' else to talk about, get the fuck off my bridge."

Dupree shrugged and began to unwrap his sandwich. His expression remained morosely contemplative.

"Got an idea," Fowler said eventually, breaking their silence. "We ain't gettin' no action at all. Triga's hoppin' around down there like a bug on a griddle. I think he'll let us try anythin' if there's a chance to land a fish. Even this."

"So?" Dupree was indifferent.

"So, up till now, we've tried mullet, bonito belly, ballyhoo, even a couple of lures, and we ain't had nothin' but 'cudas. Sails like a lot of surface action, and I ain't never seen it so calm as today. Am I right?"

The mate nodded.

"So I'm gonna take us over to the windward side of the island."

"We'll lose an hour gettin' there. And ain't nobody ever fishes there."

"There's lots of current rips and it's bound to be clean."

"Be rough as hell, too. We'll get our asses kicked all day."

"We'll also get fish. Go down and get the lines in."

"You're the captain," Dupree said, skeptical. "I don't believe it'll work, though."

" 'Cause nobody ever does it? Well, were goin' to. Doin' doughnuts out here all day ain't my idea of fishin'. We got to stir things up. And, Boots, when you got to wire a sail, leave off your gloves. I told you that before."

"Ain't no need."

"You hear me?"

"Okay, okay." Boots descended to the cockpit and did what he was told.

Triga clambered to the bridge and demanded to know where Fowler was going.

"Tryin' somethin'," Fowler replied. "And don't work yourself up. We're goin' over east of the island. No one's called in a catch for four hours. We got to shake things up."

"But nobody ever fishes there," said Triga. "It isn't done."

"That ain't true. It is, but not often. Look, Triga. I don't know whether it'll work, but the fishin' can't get no worse. If you wanted a captain who didn't use his head once in a while, you coulda just throwed a rock in the Frog and hit one."

"Very well, Pat," said the millionaire dubiously. He was caught offguard by Fowler's mild tone.

It did work. At 2:36 in the afternoon, the *Adroit* called in its first sailfish of the day. Fifteen minutes later, another was on the line. That was no sooner held fast against the hull and recorded by Sparky Thomas than a third had jumped on the other bait. Triga barely reached the pole in time. And at 3:20, both lines went taut-a double strike. Triga shouted to Boots to let the fish on the left line run. In the shortest battle umpire and crew had ever seen, Triga brought the sailfish on the starboard rod to the side, Dupree touched the leader and affected the release, and Triga was at the other rod, playing the second fish.

Triga was exultant. He fairly leaped to the flybridge to pump Fowler's hand and was back in the cockpit just as quickly, urging the mate to get the new baits in the water.

The radio came to life. The other captains were all calling to find out where *Adroit* was. Fowler evaded their demands to know what he was doing that they were not.

Again, the clip on the outrigger clacked and the line drifted lazily out. Triga braced his feet and set the drag. With a sudden force that nearly yanked him to his knees, the rod bent into an inverted "U," throbbed, and twanged straight. He cranked as fast as he could until tension was restored.

"It's a big 'un!" Dupree yelped, crouching at Triga's side. The fish hadn't shown itself yet, unusuall behavior for the species. It was worth the wait.

The fish broke the surface in a breathtaking leap and then walked on its tail across open water. Finally, it dropped with a head-shaking crash, erupting seconds later in a series of porpoiselike leaps that carried it even farther in the opposite direction. The great sweep of its purple-black dorsal fin was three times as high as its body was wide. It folded into the ridge along its back when the fish threw itself into the air, but fanned erect on each descent. Its hide pulsated with unearthly blues and greens. It was big, for the breed. At least one hundred pounds, Fowler judged. With the bonus for the extra pounds over the tournament minimum, Triga would easily pass Childs in the standings. Catherine Nettles' lead had appeared insurmountable only hours before, but was now within reach.

Everyone was doing his job. Fowler backed the boat, all-out for a time, then barely moving, then thumping into the low swells once again. Triga smoothly wound in line with each lunge of the fish. Dupree was ready to grab the leader as soon as the connecting swivel touched the eyelet on the rod tip. After twenty-five minutes, a long time for it to persevere against such odds, the sailfish was yielding, its splendid dorsal slicing toward the boat.

Dupree leaned over the side, reaching for the line. Triga stepped inboard to make the leader more accessible. When the swivel hit the rod tip, Dupree grabbed the leader and took two quick wraps. In the excitement he had forgotten to remove his gloves. The light plastic monofilament snagged in the cloth. It bunched. Tangled. The fish jerked its head.

The leader parted. The sailfish dropped back from the gunnel and swam away.

Sparky Thomas groaned. Triga threw the rod to the deck and stamped his feet and bellowed at Dupree until his face purpled. Patrick Fowler, at first disbelieving, exploded from the bridge, swooping down the ladder backward with only his hands on the railings. He clawed for a fistful of Dupree's shirt.

"The gloves!" he snarled, their noses not two inches apart. "The fuckin' gloves! I told you!"

"Pat . . ." There was pain in the ruined face and Dupree's skin was the color of dead ashes.

Fowler released his grip as if he had grasped harbor muck.

"Maybe you was right, Boots," he said. "Maybe you ain't got nothin' left."

Wink and Pia went down to the dock at six-thirty that night. Their mood was festive, anticipating the night ahead. "We gonna party, now," Wink said as he handed Pia into the cockpit of the *Adroit*. He shoved the glass door aside, and they stepped into an atmosphere of tangible gloom.

Fowler and Dupree sat facing each other, elbows on knees, staring at the drinks in their hands. There were no words of greeting, although Fowler managed a bleak smile for Pia.

"Man, is this a downer," said Wink., "Is somebody going to elucidate on the cause of this here unrestrained joyfulness?"

"Build yourselves a couple jolts," Fowler replied, waving at the bar.

Wink did so, his brow furrowed. He handed a drink to Pia and stood in the middle of the room, swiveling to survey the two men.

"So?" he said when no explanation was forthcoming."Nobody talking?"

"It ain't nothin'," Fowler said finally. "We lost a big one, is all."

"I blew it," Dupree finally said to the beer can in his scarred knotted hands. "We didn't lose that fish. I did."

More silence.

"Is that it?" said Wink, turning the palm of his hand up in exasperation. "Pia and me has been invited to a wake 'cause somebody lost a fish? Nobody here ever lost a fish before?"

"Pat told me a hunnert times," Dupree continued. "Told me not to take any wraps. Told me to keep my gloves off. But I got all twitterpatted and forgot. Like some green kid. Or a old man. Seein' I been a wire man for near thirty years, there ain't no question which."

"The action was heavy," said Fowler, his fury of two hours before now diminished to disappointment. "Anybody could've forgot."

" 'Course they could," Wink said. "Ease up on yourself, Boots."

Dupree looked up, and they were stunned by the anguish in the leathery face. He spoke then, only to Fowler. The others might not have been there. The despairing words spewed out, unstoppable.

"Wasn't nobody else, it was me, Boots Dupree, and I was the best wire man there was. Wasn't no excuse. There can't be no forgettin'. But that ain't it, Pat. You'n me been at this near our whole lives, the part that counts, leastways. I brought you in, taught you, an' ever since you learnt you been carryin' me on your back, one way or 'nother. 'But it ain't even that I let you down when it counted. I done that afore.

"It's me. It's you, too. It's what we got. What we ain't got, more 'xactly. I'm fifty-three, an' you're-what, Pat? forty-two? I had me four wives. You had two. Six wives between us an' only two kids, neither of which we seen more'n three times apiece since they was born.

"Nothin' else. After all that drinkin', whorin', fish killin', and gettin' our brains scrambled by shrimpers 'n' cops meaner'n us, we got nothin'. You look around, Pat. There ain't nothin' but kids in this business. Ain't no one in this tournament nearer'n ten years of you, Pat, not to mention me. We're like pitchers with dead arms waitin' to be called up again from the bottom of the Texas league. But we still make mock of guys our age who put themselves on the beach.

"So mebbe they ain't as happy as they was. Mebbe they got passels of snot-noses hangin' on their belts 'n' they don't never get laid or wet a line no more. But they got more'n we do, Pat. And that ain't difficult, too bad for us."

Wink spoke. "Experience counts for something, Boots."

Dupree exhaled in a stuttering sigh. "I learnt most every thin' I needed to know my first year on the boats. I ain't got any better, I got older. Think on it, Pat."

He placed his hands on his knees, pushed himself erect, and went to the door.

"If you can't find no one down here, Pat," he said, "I'll stick until we get back to West Palm. Lot of boys there be pleasured to get in on this."

Pia thought one of them - or all of them - should go after Boots. No one moved.

"Ain't nothin' we can say to him," Fowler said.

"Intimations of mortality do not suffer placation," Wink added.

"What?"

"Something I heard once in Death and Dying 102," Wink glumly answered. " 'In perpetual fear, labor, and anguish do we run from one plague, one burden, to another.' "

"What?"

"Same place."

"I ain't got the sorriest notion what you're talkin' about."

"Me, neither," Wink allowed. He went into the bar. "So we gonna sit here and get shitfaced? Or we going somewhere else and get shitfaced?"

They went to Wink's hotel room. He pulled a hand mirror from his suitcase and a small plastic bag of cocaine from behind the second drawer in the bureau. Within fifteen minutes, there were ten people in the room.

As it happened, Theo Marker was only half correct in accusing Boots Dupree of bedding his wife. The third Mrs. Marker had accepted Fowler immediately afterward. And, on subsequent occasions, simultaneously. This was the not unnatural result of leaving a bored young woman on an island inhabited at the time only by families and strictly segregated crew members. What could Marker expect, Boots placidly replied when confronted. If Marker insisted upon flying off to Hollywood after every telephone call and abandoning his women, Boots reasoned that it was his responsibility to keep them entertained. Marker sent his ex-captain home on the next seaplane. After he calmed down, he asked Fowler if he could run the boat. The mate was not yet twenty and had never handled the controls. He said of course he could. Then you're my captain, Marker said, and left once again for California.

Fowler was alone, eighty miles from West Palm Beach, with a forty-two-foot boat and the Gulf Stream to cross. His only protection was ignorance. He didn't know enough to be afraid. The four-hour trip took ten. All the way, he battled toppling, ragged seas beneath deceptively clear skies. Since the navigational devices were indecipherable to him and the compass later proved to have a ten-degree error, he recognized nothing when he made landfall. It was necessary to steam up, then down the coast hunting the entrance to Lake Worth.

Once he reached it, he infuriated the skippers of other craft by persisting in running on the wrong sides of channel markers. In docking, he gouged a four-foot long groove in the hull. He went to find Boots.

"Hell, no, son. I ain't mad," said Dupree. "You gotta take hold of your chances. Don't know why I took that captain's job in the first place. Always said I'd sooner kiss a cottonmouth. Responsibility gives me hives. Tell you what, now. Siddown there, We'll kill us a couple six-packs, talk about it. First thing tomorrow, we'll go out. Monday week, you'll know everything I do."

By the time Theo Marker returned to Florida, another woman in tow, Fowler knew more than that. About navigation and boat handling, at least. Marker wanted to go to St. Thomas for marlin. Fowler correctly interpreted his employer's mellow mood, and persuaded him to take Dupree back, this time as a mate.

On the way to the fishing ground north of the island, Boots went to the bridge.

"You ain't done marlin afore," he said softly, so Marker couldn't hear. "And we only got the two of us. If the boss hangs a big one, I'll be needin' help. So when I'm ready to wire him, you chop the engines, get down fast, and grab the gaff. Y' hear?"

The starboard bait was taken within minutes after they began trolling. It was a large marlin, but sluggish. Marker worked it quickly and efficiently to the stern. Fowler cut the engines and slid to the cockpit. He could not account for his actions later, but instead of going for the gaff, he reached for the wire leader. He took two twists around his gloved right hand. In the wrong direction.

The fish lunged away with a mighty splash. The leader twanged tight. Fowler felt nothing at first, but when he looked at his hand, parts of the last two fingers were gone. The stumps gushed red.

Boots dived into the water with the marlin. He retrieved one severed stub as it floated down.

Catherine ate dinner alone on the afterdeck of *Aphrodite.* Afterward, she put Paul Mitchell and Paco Ibanez on the stereo, poured a snifter of armagnac, and read the first page of a novel three times. She threw the book aside, jumped to her feet, refilled her glass. And paced. She missed Lichine, she admitted to herself it was no more complicated than that. Her suspicions about Triga were supported by nothing but speculation and her distaste for the man.

The last note faded away and the tone arm of the record player clicked back onto its bracket. Catherine went out the door, leaving the lights and the decanter of brandy. In her stateroom, she stripped off her shirt and slacks, brushed her teeth, swallowed two of the white capsules from the bottle in the cabinet, and took a leisurely shower. When she finished drying herself, she hesitated, then streaked drops of cologne behind her ears, on her wrists, on the insides of her knees, around her navel and on each pelvic crest.

In bed, she plumped both pillows behind her and folded the covers to her waist. There was a blemish on the apricot wall covering over the vanity, she noticed, and a loose screw on the right curtain-rod bracket. She was scrutinizing a spot in one corner of the Clave print when her hand floated to the bedside call button.

12

After the cocaine was gone and the hotel bar had closed, eight of them packed into Fowler's car And drove to the far side of the island to watch the sun come up. The group was comprised of Fowler and Pia, Wink and a waitress, Jeeter Doakes and a whore of perhaps fourteen years, her Mexican pimp and his pet iguana, and Steve Grubbs, the captain of Crystal Ball.

They settled on the beach, facing the brightening sky and passing bottles and joints. Doakes commenced to drag the whore's blouse over her head while the pimp looked on through hooded, indifferent eyes.

"Jellynose," said Wink, "if you insist on getting it on with that scabby infant, would you either get a little more ruly about it or get your hairy ass over behind those rocks somewhere? I got a queasy stomach."

Doakes ignored the request, so the others moved a hundred yards down the beach, past a rock outcropping and beneath a stand of coconut palms. The surf was higher there, driven by the unhindered trade winds.

"Anyone up to a swim?" Pia asked.

"I'll pass," said Fowler.

"Later, maybe," said Wink.

"Why not now?" Pia persisted, on her feet now.

"Sharks come in next to the beach at night and don't go out till the sun is up."

"Good thinking," Pia said, collapsing next to Fowler.

"What we need, Wink," Steve Grubbs said as he rolled a cigarette on his thigh, "is a little Buffettizin'."

"You sing?" the waitress from the bar asked.

"In addition," said Wink.

They wheedled and nagged until Wink agreed to go back to the car and get his guitar. When he returned, Fowler and Grubbs were telling fish stories. The waitress was asleep in a fetal curl. Their clothes and their flesh and the beach and the trunks of the palms were shades of pink from the sun that was nudging the sky.

". . . jumped over the cockpit twice," Grubbs was saying, "and then right into the lap of the captain."

"What was it was doing this?" Wink asked, squatting.

"Sailfish," said Grubbs. "Over off Bimini a couple years ago. A guy told me."

"Told you he got a sailfish in his lap while he was on the bridge?"

"Way he told it to me."

"That," said Wink, sitting and wriggling a hollow in the sand, "is the fourth biggest lie I ever heard."

No one spoke.

"Ain't nobody gonna ask?" Wink peered into each face.

"Okay," Pia said. "What were the other three biggest lies you ever heard?"

Wink strummed the strings of the guitar. "One is," he said, "'The check's in the mail.' Two is, 'I got a bite'."

"And three?"

Strum. " 'I won't come in your mouth'."

"You fixin' to play that box," Fowler said, "or you gonna keep the gooney birds holdin' their sides?"

"You do get surly of a new morning, Uncle Pat. That was just what us entertainers call a 'warm-up'. Gets the paying customers in the mood."

Fowler reached in his pocket and slapped a ten-peso note on the sand in front of his nephew. "I"m in the mood already."

"You don't have to get huffy," Wink said, adjusting keys. "This one's written about you, Captain Uncle." He tipped his hat over his forehead and played a verse without singing, tilting over the guitar to hear the sound and watch his fingers. The waitress rolled over, still asleep. Jeeter Doakes stumbled toward them, dragging his shirt and pants, alone. The pimp appeared unconcerned. Wink finished the wordless verse and started singing Jimmy Buffett's "A Pirate Looks at Forty."

When he finished, Pia applauded. Fowler looked at waves spreading and retreating over the hard sand. The pimp bobbed his head in appreciation. His iguana stalked in slow motion toward the grass. Grubbs went for a walk along the water's edge. Doakes rolled a cigarette.

"I'm whelmed," Wink said, glancing around. "Pia, honey, you are obviously the onliest person of taste and discernment in this gathering."

"I had no idea you could sing so well," she said.

"Was you singin'?" Doakes asked. "I thought it was a pig on a pointy stick."

Wink poked the waitress. "Honey? Is it true that persons of the female persuasion most 'specially dig making it on the beach?"

"'He ain't never gone to bed with an ugly woman," Fowler said to Pia, "but he's woke up with a whole bunch."

"Sing another," Pia urged. "A sad one."

"Do that, nephew. It feels so good feelin' so bad."

Wink was halfway into another song when they saw Steve Grubbs pounding through the sand toward them.

"You come all the way back at the sound of my golden voice?" Wink shouted. But there was urgency, panic, in the way the man ran.

He stopped several feet away, pointing off in the direction from which he came and trying to catch his breath.

"Pat. . . back there. . . body. . . lotta blood. . ."

"Hold it, Steve. Easy," Fowler said. "Get a breath."

"Can't . . . gotta come . . ." He punched his chest, sucking in. "Man down there . . . in the sand . . . blood all over. . . a gun."

They were all on their feet. Fowler had his hand on Grubbs' shoulder. Doakes and Wink were already sprinting off.

"Was he dead?" Fowler demanded. "You sure?"

"Think so," Grubbs gasped. There was anguish in the cherubic face. "Pat. . ."

Fowler wanted to choke off the next words before the man uttered them.

"It's Boots."

No matter how hard she willed it, Catherine could not get back to sleep. She shifted her hips off the large stiff spot of dried semen. The boy had compensated in prodigality for what he lacked in sensitivity. She glanced about at the other leavings of the night. Overflowing ashtrays, half empty glasses, a tipped-over bottle, crumpled wads of toilet paper, flecks of tobacco and ash powdering the sheets and end tables, damp towels and underwear and shoes scattered in a ring about the bed. A miasma of stale smoke eddied before the air conditioning vent. There was one black sock.

The steward did not knock. He simply came into the stateroom, tray in hand, and closed the door. Barefoot and bare-chested. He placed the tray on the small table and turned to look at her. Not at her face, but at the part of her between chin and sheet.

"I'm not hungry," she said.

The boy stood hands on hips, weight on one leg, a possessive smirk on his lips.

"I don't want breakfast," she said.

"I do," he said, walking toward her.

Afterward, she thought as the rough, knuckly hands poked and squeezed and probed, *afterward I will take a very long shower and sluice my insides out and give my hair one hundred strokes and take two biphetamine twenties. Then I believe I will throw up for a while.*

Theodore Marker had two tequila sunrises and one English muffin on his terrace to accompany his week-old *Variety* and *Los Angeles Times*. Six days gone, and his agent was yet to call. Marker put aside both his newspaper and his resolve not to initiate further communication. He went to the phone and placed a call to Bel Air. But Mel wasn't there, or so the hotel operator said. Marker couldn't think why he shouldn't order another breakfast.

"Mr. Triga," Duncan announced from the door to the companionway, "there is a communication on the - ah - single sideband. From New York. The captain has put it through here."

"Ah, yes," said the millionaire, lowering his coffee cup and patting his lips with his napkin. "I've been expecting it."

"Will you be having anything else, sir?"

"A little coffee, perhaps. Take the rest away, please." Triga pressed button four and lifted the receiver.

"I believe it is the elder Mr. Triga, sir," Duncan said as he poured, glancing out of the corner of his eye.

The receiver stopped halfway to Horst Triga's ear. That was not who he expected. His mind raced through the possible implications. He did not receive six calls in a year from his father, and the occasions were never benign or frivolous. There were hollow little hellos issuing from the receiver.

"Good morning, B.K.," Triga said heartily. "A pleasure to hear from you. How are you?"

"In robust good health, you'll be pleased to know." The voice was glacial. "And you?"

"Can't complain, B.K. Apart from a contretemps or two with the help. . ."

"And the tournament? Prevailing over all with your customary alacrity and dispatch?"

"Modesty forbids me to say, B.K."

"That's understandable. From what I hear, you have much to be modest about. That little blond girl Nettles is leading, is she not?"

Horst tried to decipher his father's intent. Filial joshing? Censure? Something else?

"Horst?"

"I'm here, B.K. Catherine Nettles is a highly competent angler. But sailfish are her speciality. A woman's prey. Once we move along to tuna and marlin, where far greater skill and physical strength are required, there should be no difficulty in overcoming her lead."

"I hope that shall be the case, since I have placed a small wager in that expectation. On your nose. With Julius McNally. I believe you know him?"

Horst tried to swallow, his mouth suddenly dry. "Why, yes, I believe so. Superficially. One of your headquarters staff, as I recall."

"Quite so. Julius is our VP for acquisitions. But you know him rather better than that, don't you?" B.K. was inept at portraying lack of guile." I believe he mentioned that he had been with you on *Highlander*."

"Really? To be frank, I don't know. Perhaps he was among one of the executive parties. I never have been good at names, as you know."

"No, I didn't know that, Horst. But you must be right, else I can't imagine why he would bet against you, even considering the highly favorable odds he extracted from me."

"Indeed. That would be curious," said Horst. He glanced at his watch. Only a half hour until starting time. *Will he ever get to the point?*

"But then, as I don't really know him, it isn't surprising. What odds did you give?"

"Five to one."

"Thank you for the vote of confidence."

"Not at all. I think he might have pressed for ten to one if he hadn't been preoccupied at the time."

"Oh? And why was that?"

There was a measured pause.

"He had just confessed that he had made a tender offer for control of Lichine Electronics."

Horst managed not to croak. " 'Confessed'? But I thought you said that acquisitions were his function?"

"I cannot rid myself of a failing of my youth," said his father. "I want to know what's going on in my organization. These B-school types keep telling me I must delegate, shepherd my energies. But I persist in poking around. During one of my explorations of desk tops and wastepaper baskets, I found that Triga Associates, Inc., was engaged in an ill-conceived effort to take over a nickel-and-dime outfit that peddles electric music boxes."

"It was my impression that Lichine Electronics was an attractive candidate. A 'sleeping beauty,' I believe is the phrase."

"Hardly, Horst, although it is gratifying to learn that you keep up with current jargon. They do have a relatively limited number of shares and an acceptable price-earnings ratio, but that is the extent of the positive factors. They are overextended on virtually every critical front, the company is controlled by only three men - if you count Ernest Lichine, which is moot - and the market share price is perilously close to book value."

"I see," said Horst, impatience replacing caution. "But B.K., I really don't understand why you're going into all this. It's well beyond my ken."

"There is more to it than that," his father continued as if he hadn't heard. "Two very large considerations, in fact. One, I do not now, nor have I ever had, any interest in acquiring companies engaged primarily in the manufacturing of consumer products. One simply becomes visible to all those assorted regulatory agencies run by hippies and liberals, and too little profit. But the second reason is the big one."

"All right, B.K. I'll bite. What is that?"

"A corporation known as Praga-Sunset Industries owns 8.6 percent of Lichine Electronics. Another organization, by the name of Whitney Group, made a bid of $20.60. Very generous, considering the shares were trading at $13.35 at the time."

"B.K., this is getting past me."

"Pay attention. Praga-Sunset was distressed by the bid. They thought they could squeeze out a higher bid for their Lichine shares. So they made an offer of $22.50 per share, almost two dollars more than the original players, Whitney Group. Whitney countered with $24.60. That was their top, they said, although they didn't mean it."

"So the insiders were bidding against the outsiders," Horst said, warming to his bluff. "So?"

"As you may know, Horst, Whitney Group is a wholly-owned subsidiary of Triga Associates. Julius McNally was captaining the takeover team."

"It's your company, you mean."

"That's very good, Horst. You get one more guess."

"I give up."

"I also own Praga-Sunset."

Horst groped for a neutral comment. He failed.

"You do grasp the implications, don't you, Horst?"

"Why. . . I. . ."

"Permit me. This distressingly uncoordinated activity meant, not to put too fine a point on it, that I was bidding against myself."

Duncan chose that moment to enter the room. Horst waved him away.

"Horst?" said the father. "You are there?"

The younger Triga made a strangled sound intended as affirmation. .

"You'll remember, I trust, that at the end of your brief tenure with Triga Associates, I vowed to insure your eternal subsistence in the style to which you were accustomed. In exchange, you were never, ever, to darken our corporate threshold again."

"That was, to put it brutally, our agreement," Horst stiffly replied.

"That was, to put it precisely, our agreement. You violated it."

"I didn't, BK."

"You did. I don't yet know what favors you called in on Julius McNally, but there is no question in my mind that you somehow contrived to gain his cooperation in your scheme."

"Scheme? B.K.! It isn't true! You can't really believe it."

"I can. I do. And I know why."

"B.K., I swear to you. . ."

"Certainly you do. Nonetheless, my very own son, you will have to win this game of yours on your own. I will not be a party to any intrigues you might devise to eliminate your competition."

"BK.! What are you saying?"

"I had hoped that my meaning would be clear." There was, Horst thought, a small sigh. "Very well. The tender offers were withdrawn. And you, my son, had best come up with some excellent reasons why I should not terminate your personal support."

"BK.! What can I say to convince you that I didn't. . ."

"Absolutely nothing. Good-bye, Horst."

"Dad! Listen! It isn't. . ."

There was a click, then a steady hum. Beyond the closed door to the afterdeck, Duncan straightened and walked soundlessly to the wheelhouse.

By the time the doctor arrived, Wink and Pia had washed away the caked black blood from the face and arms. The doctor examined the nearly lifeless form on the bed. Then he administered a hypodermic, took three stitches to close a gash across the right forearm, and left with a series of nods of the head.

"Anybody know what he was sayin'?" Jeeter Doakes asked.

" 'Fraid he said I was gonna live," Boots Dupree said from the bed. "Can't say I'm all that perky about it. Somebody gonna tell me?"

"Steve found you," said Wink, who was sitting on the side of the bed. "Jellynose picked you up and put you in the car. We brought you to your room, and Pia cleaned you up. Boots, you look like dog shit."

"Don't feel that good."

"Good enough to bring us up to date?" Fowler asked.

"Whatever that bitty Mex medic give me feels better'n a quart of bourbon," Dupree said drowsily, "but it don't make me no more talky."

"Give it a try," said Fowler. "You scared hell out of us."

Dupree touched his cheek. The right eye was swollen shut, the skin on his nose was split, his jaw was scraped raw. He flinched as he explored the egg-sized bubble on his forehead with his fingertips.

"Goddam, that smarts," he said.

"Don't hardly wonder," Wink said. "What happened, Boots?"

"Hafta be quick," was the answer. "What was that stuff? They oughta sell it in the Mini-Mart."

"What happened, Boots?" Fowler insisted.

"Yeah. Lemme see." Dupree closed the other eye. "Left you folks after my speechifyin'. Found a bar. Raised a few. Picked a fight with a couple fellas. Little buggers. Figgered I could take 'em."

"Or maybe you didn't," Wink said quietly.

"Or maybe I didn't," Dupree agreed. "Anyways, they proceeded to kick my wrinkled ass from one side of the room to the other. Dumped me out back when their arms and legs got tired."

Dupree looked as if he was asleep.

"And?" Fowler prodded.

"Leave him be, Pat," Wink said.

"And," Dupree continued, "I figured, after a while, that I oughta get up. Went to the boat. Broke the lock on Triga's gun case. In his stateroom. Took me a Colt Python. That big mother? Went to find a beach and some water to listen to."

"You were all over sea grass when we found you," Doakes said.

"I got cold. Pulled it over me like a blanket."

"Why the gun, Boots?" Fowler asked.

Dupree opened the undamaged eye. "Wonder why I imagined you wouldn't ask that, Pat?" He closed the eye. "Tired. Think I'll cut a little slack."

Grubbs lingered after the others left. He turned off the lights and drew the drapes.

"Kid," Boots whispered from the bed. "There any drinkin' stuff around?"

The tournament resumed. Pia sat on the dock box while Fowler and his new mate readied *Adroit.* Fowler had found a local man until Boots was well enough to resume his duties. Triga was in a black mood, rendered no lighter by the news that his mate had damaged himself in a brawl. With a comment that "perhaps it was just as well, considering how Dupree botched the last fish," Triga closeted himself in his stateroom. Fowler had replaced the revolver taken by Boots and hoped his employer wouldn't notice the broken lock on the gun case. Pia waved as *Adroit* pulled away, and watched as the boat slid up to the fuel dock over by the harbor entrance.

"Feeling abandoned?"

It was Catherine Nettles, speaking from the cockpit of *Zodiac Arrest,* which had yet to leave. Although they had been at the same table that one night, she and Catherine had never spoken to each other.

"A little," Pia answered. "There isn't much to do here but fish, and I've never been much for sunning and swimming."

"Come along with me, then," Catherine said. "It's been weeks since I talked to anyone who doesn't think with a pecker.

Pia hesitated.

"Come on, dear," Catherine insisted. "Contrary to the evidence of the other night, I can be downright agreeable at times. In fact, I feel an uncontrollable surge of niceness coming on at this very moment."

"You talked me into it," Pia said, picking up her small canvas tote and going aboard.

It was an unremarkable day. No boat caught more than ten sailfish, nor fewer than five. There would be no stories to tell that night - no records, no special streak of luck, good or bad. Standings were destined to remain unchanged - Catherine far ahead, Triga and Childs within one fish of each other for second place, Marker a distant fourth.

The director brooded in frustration over his inability to narrow the gulf. There was nothing he or his crew was doing wrong, as far as he could see. They just weren't getting the breaks. It was more than just losing. The fact that his agent continued to avoid him meant only one thing: Marker was not going to get the film assignment. And that meant that he had to win the tournament. Not only could he not afford to throwaway the one million dollars, he had to have the entire prize to ward off bankruptcy, not to mention Carlos and his friends. With care, there might even be enough left to finance his own picture and end-run the bastards who now dismissed him as a has-been. That would be sweet. Marker resolved to extract more information from his contact on *Highlander.*

Montgomery Childs irritably instructed Bunny Haskell that if she felt driven to remove her bra, she could damn well stay out of sight of his crew. They were out there to fish, not whack off, he said. Bunny pouted. This wasn't all that much fun for her, she wanted him to know, and she'd just as soon stay in bed as watch him destroy all these poor helpless fish who hadn't done anything to him.

Horst Triga, although by no means moved to ebullience, was at least gratified by the evident competence of the Mexican mate. He ventured the suggestion that Fowler engage the new man for the remainder of the tournament. The captain furiously rejected the proposal and was in the process of elaborating when a sailfish took the port bait.

During the midday pause in action, Catherine and Pia learned, to their mutual surprise, that they liked each other. In the face of Pia's assurance and calm intelligence, Catherine gradually lowered her bristly defenses. Catherine admitted to Pia that competition in a sport dominated by men sharpened her protective instincts. The choice dictated by those men, she asserted, was between presenting oneself as a simpering package of buns and boobs awaiting its preordained fate or as a lady shot-putter on the verge of an unnecessary sex-change operation. Catherine rejected both options, she said, in favor of unflagging attack. In doing so, she cheerfully conceded she was merely following the natural bend of her tree. About the time the fish started biting again, she realized she had done most of the talking and that her monologue had included confessions she had never made aloud. As she went out into the cockpit, Cathbrine said Pia was a world-class listener. Pia said that she just happened to be there.

They talked again on the run back to port at the end of the day. Catherine did, anyway. She felt better, the episode with the steward now at arm's length. There remained, however, a vague emptiness. She didn't identify it until *Zodiac Arrest* decelerated to a low chug as it passed into the harbor. Someone was pacing the dock. It was Ernest Lichine.

13

"Now tell me." Catherine put both her hands on Lichine's forearm and squeezed. "You cut it awfully close. They were going to throw you out tomorrow."

The waiter was walking away, and there were no people at the nearby tables. They were on the terrace of the Cabanas del Caribe because Catherine, for some unstated reason, did not want to go to *Aphrodite.*

"I'm a little dazed," Lichine answered. "Flying back and forth between temperate and tropic zones addles your brains."

"You don't look addled."

"Really? How do I look?"

"Marvelous. More later. Now what happened?"

"I'm not sure." He leaned over and kissed her. "Except that I've never missed anyone like I have. . . ."

"Me too," she said. "Darling, speak."

"Okay. Let's see." He drank automatically, without tasting. "There is either an awful lot to tell or nothing at all. I haven't really sorted it out yet." He paused, gathering his thoughts. "It goes back to when we got ourselves listed on the big board. My brother, Jason, wanted to go public in order to finance expansion of our retail outlets beyond the northeast. We were standing still, was his argument. I on the other hand, wanted to keep the company exclusively in our hands, and saw no reason why we couldn't go on simply selling our products through the few stores we already had, peddling the rest through distributors. He said that we were at the start of a boom in pocket calculators and c.b. radios and that we could maximize profits more efficiently through our own chain. We'd developed a startup line, he said, and were among the first to be able to bring prices down to reasonable levels. So I went along with it, with the condition that we retain absolute majority control between us. We did, sixty per cent. Half his, half mine. Then we got ourselves a real live board of directors, I was made chairman, and Jason was executive vice-president All that bored me - the glad-handing and subterfuges - so I just snuck back to my lab. As long as sufficient funds were budgeted for research and development, I didn't pay much attention. Then came the takeover bid."

"Who made the offer?" Catherine asked.

"An outfit called Whitney Group, not that that meant anything. It's a holding company. Just the tip of the spear for some conglomerate. Never did find out who was behind them."

"Go on." Catherine signaled the waiter.

"I arrived in New York Monday morning. No one met me. When I finally got to Jason's inner sanctum, he was in a huddle with the other directors. Three of them trying to pressure the other three into accepting the offer, as it turned out. We proceeded to run the whole thing around the table: After ten hours of threats and screaming, nothing had really changed. Jason and two directors were on one side, me and two others in the opposite corner. And one fence-sitter."

"So at least you had two friends."

"Not really. One of those was the Praga-Sunset Industries rep. It turned out that he was stalling while his superiors were framing a counter-offer. That came the next morning. The other director was the lawyer for an estate with explicit directions not to sell under any circumstances for reasons yet to be determined. And the one in the middle was just plain ambivalent, and getting whipsawed by both groups. .Anyway, the Whitney Group raised their bid over Praga-Sunset. I demanded that the proposal be presented to the shareholders for a vote. Jason and the Whitney Group insisted that we had a fiduciary responsibility to the shareholders to accept the bid before it was withdrawn. It went on and on. Wrangles. Blackmail, polite and not-very. Outside attorneys, irrelevant issues, hedging, attacking. Unbelievable. One of the directors even threw a coffee percolator at one of the others. Then on Wednesday it all just collapsed, like a hot-air balloon."

"How? What happened?"

"Whitney and Praga-Sunset withdrew their offers. Almost simultaneously. Just like that. Poof! No explanations. Nothing."

"And now what?"

"Jason and I spent last night scraping a fragile truce together. He agreed never to entertain any future offers without consulting me. I agreed to keep an open mind. When neither of us could stand to look at each other another minute I got on a plane and came back here. Slept all the way."

"Sounds like everything worked out as you hoped."

"I suppose."

"It doesn't sound as though you're too happy about it, love."

"No, I am. It's just. . . I guess it's something of a letdown. I went galloping up there on my white horse, took on men I didn't dare contradict a month ago, wheeled and dealed as I never have before, absorbed vast quantities of information. . ."

". . . and then had the whole thing fizzle," Catherine completed.

"Yes, that's it," he agreed. "I went through all that, and I got what I wanted in the end, but it wasn't my doing. I don't know if I would have won on my own."

"But you did fight it," she said. "And you did learn, and you got what you wanted."

"Not everything," he said, taking her hands in his. "Catherine, I want to talk about where we go from here. You and me."

She pulled away. "No," she said.

"Don't stop me," he said. "I've got it all rehearsed."

"I can't let you."

"Catherine, please. . ."

"Sorry, darling," she said, looking over his shoulder. "But right now, you have a whole new challenge to work on." She made a pointing gesture with her chin. "Your troops approach."

Lichine twisted around. Wink was striding toward them, a broad grin flashing in the shadow of his broad-brimmed hat. Jeeter Doakes was right behind.

"I'm all over fish-stink and sweat," Catherine said, rising. "I'll go on back and dunk myself in fragrant ointments and essence of musk. Show up anytime after eight o'clock and I may let you have your way with me. No, wait," she said, remembering something. "I'll come back here, to your room. Order up a dinner of oysters and rhinoceros horn."

She brushed his lips with hers and walked quickly away. Lichine was torn between watching her departure and his crew's approach.

"Ernie, baby," Wink said, wrapping Lichine in a rough embrace. "Good t'see you, mother."

"Good to be seen," said Lichine, warmth washing over him. "Captain, how are you? Sit down and tell me everything. What are the standings so far? What are my chances?"

"Our chances ain't shit," said Doakes. He handed Lichine a folded paper. It was a score sheet, updated to include that day's catch. "Nettles has 672 points, total. Even Marker's got 376, and he was so far back he couldn't hit the others with a guided missile."

"Until I got back," Lichine said ruefully. He stared at the figures. His lead from Palm Beach had evaporated. He fixed his jaw in a pose of determination that exceeded his conviction. "So what's our strategy?"

Doakes squinted at him. "Same as before. You all are gonna do what I say, only faster and without no argument."

"That's not very constructive, Captain," Lichine said evenly. "Your authority is already established. Now just what are we going to do?"

If Doakes was startled by his employer's mild reproach, he didn't show it. "First," he said, "we look at where we are and what's comin' up. Nettles figured to do well here. Sailfish are her number. She's good at them, and she's been lucky. And her captain, Cronski, may be looser than a snake's asshole, but he's fished these waters more'n any of us. Right from the start, they figured to be ahead at this point."

"I thought everyone believed that anyone could catch sailfish," Lichine said.

"Anyone can," Wink said. "I've seen ten-year-olds pull in fifty-pounders."

"That ain't the point," Doakes said. "Anybody can throw a ball, too, 'cept some throw it higher and farther and more accurate. Right here, Nettles 'n' Cronski got the edge."

"So what do we do?"

"We play catch-up," Doakes continued. "Couple ways. Nettles is catchin' so many fish and is so soft-hearted that she's only bringin' in the biggest ones. Meanin' she's givin' up bonus points, mebbe as much as a hunnert so far. She releases anything that ain't least ten pounds over the minimum. That's like throwin' away a whole extra fish."

"And we're not going to do that," Lichine said in half question.

"We ain't, no," Doakes replied. "We're boatin' anything that has a fair chance of weighin' out at seventy-six pounds. We're squeezin' out every extra point we can."

"That's awfully risky," Lichine said. "I'm not that good at estimating weight, not of a fish in the water that I haven't even had a good look at."

"I am," said Doakes. "From here on, you ain't sayin' when we boat a sail or not. I am."

"That's normally the angler's prerogative, as I understand it," Lichine said. "But okay. I defer to your judgment."

"Yeah. You'd best do that. Also. I want you to bust your ass gettin' those fish in, fast as you can. No restin', no complainin' about how you're tired. When the action gets heavy, I want those fish at the side like that!" His finger snap sounded like a firecracker. "And we hang any double-headers, you're gonna bring 'em both in. We ain't cuttin' one fish loose."

"Two fish simultaneously? I've never done that," Lichine said dubiously. "Even when I had help. And the rules are that I have to do it all unassisted."

"Mr. Lichine, you're fightin' me."

"No, I'm not. It was just an observation. Actually, I was thinking that it's too bad we can't put three or four lines out."

"More like it." Doakes paused, considering other tactics. "Other than that, I'm gonna take us where they are and feed 'em what they're eatin'. We'll be first out, last back, and we ain't cuttin' no slack in between. By Saturday, we're gonna have some points on the rack. One thing, Wink."

"I am at your command, Cap'n Jellynose, sir."

"I wanna know what Hook was doin' Saturday."

"What do you mean?" asked Lichine.

"There wasn't anything happening on the drop-off," Wink explained. "Hardly any fish at all. Then Pat drove off somewhere and dragged in a cockpitful. We don't know whether he just found another spot, or changed his bait, or took up deep-trolling, or what."

"Find out," Doakes ordered.

"Find out what?" Wink asked. "It was a fluke. He was back with the rest of them today, doing the same things."

"It was good enough today not to bother," Doakes persisted.

"Find out."

"Who from? Pat won't tell me."

"Try Boots."

"Boots? Shit, Jeet, if I held my hand in my ass waitin' for him to spill, I'd wind up with a skin graft."

"Maybe not," said Doakes. "He can talk the paint off a wall. Could be he'll slip. Prob'ly needs company, anyway."

"Meanin' I should take advantage of him being all busted up," said Wink. "You bastard."

"I ain't hardly started."

Lichine broke the ensuing silence by standing and saying, "I guess I'd better get some dinner and a lot of rest. It sounds like I'm in for a bit of work tomorrow."

"Do it in your own bed, Mr. Lichine," Doakes said, peering up from beneath the low brim of his hat.

Lichine flushed. "I'm not sure what that means."

"It ain't smart to fight someone all day and fuck 'em all night."

"That's one step too far over the line, Captain," Lichine said.

"I want you ready," said Doakes. "That cunt'll suck the life outa you."

"That's enough!" Lichine said, trying not to shout.

"Ease off, Jeet," Wink said. "Ernie ain't no boxer, and you ain't his manager."

Doakes regarded both of them coldly. "No offense," he said finally. "Just keep in mind, Mr. Lichine you need everything you got the next ten days, and in those other three places, too."

"I'll determine the course of my own life," Lichine answered, anger and triumph warring within him. "And I'll see you at eight on the dot tomorrow morning. Make certain that you're as clearheaded as I will be."

Once *Brain Soup* was in the channel, running at trolling speed, there was no time to think. The rods were set, the lines in the outriggers.

Wink stood at the stern, baits at he ready, watching Doakes on the bridge. Oscar Farrington was counting off over the VHF. The instant he finished, Wink flung the mullets into the wake. A sailfish ate the right bait before the line straightened, and Lichine started cranking.

By noon, they had hauled five fish aboard - three of them perilously close to the minimum weight - and released four others. There was little time for exultation or self-congratulation, but they all knew that they were on the way to an exceptional day. Unfortunately, the unceasing stream of transmissions over the radio meant the other boats were at least as busy.

The fish stopped biting at noon, almost as if a whistle had blown. Lichine and his crew waited nearly an hour to be sure. Then Wink made sandwiches and distributed them. Their umpire, Hugh Casper, withdrew to the salon. Doakes used the pause to turn and run north, turn again, and troll south. Wink rigged baits. Lichine began another sandwich.

"Left 'rigger!" Doakes bellowed, breaking the quiet.

"Get on it!"

Lichine dropped the sandwich in the chair and jumped for the rod. He was starting to get the knack of fishing while standing up, the rod butt in the socket of the belt strapped around his waist. But the fish was strong. It leaped and pinwheeled and kept Lichine constantly off balance. The fishes already in the boat were piled out of the way, but blood from them oozed across the deck and he kept skidding in it. His thighs were pressed for support against the transom when three things happened.

Doakes eased the throttles forward to realign the stern to the fish. The fish chose that moment to undertake a ferocious lunge in the opposite direction. And Lichine slipped and went over the side.

He held onto the rod. Doakes cut the engines and let the waves push the boat sideways to his angler. Wink leaned over, reaching.

"Gimme the rod, Ernie," he yelled.

"No," Lichine said, spitting water.

"He must land the fish unassisted,' said the umpire, hovering nearby.

"He ain't gonna land this fish, for God' sake," Wink said. "He's just getting out."

"No," Lichine said again. "I'm bringing him in."

A wave broke over him and slammed him against the side of the boat.

"Get back, Wink," he shouted. Then he grabbed for the covering board with his left hand, still hanging onto the rod. "Where's the holder?"

Wink pointed at the socket. Lichine kicked and propelled himself from the water. With his arm over the transom for support, he thrust the rod butt into the hole and pushed the drag lever on the side of the reel to the rear. The line whizzed off the spool as he pulled himself aboard. Once in the cockpit, he retrieved the rod, adjusted the drag, and started pumping and cranking. In ten minutes, the fish was gaffed and hauled aboard. Once it was stacked with the others, Wink turned to Lichine.

"You some kind of fanatic, Ernie?" he ask .

"Didn't want Captain Doakes to think I was lying down on the job," Lichine replied, without humor.

"Even Jellynose don't expect you to swim after them."

"I will, if that's what it takes."

Horst Triga stopped Fowler as the captain was leaving the galley with his first food of the day. Boots Dupree was at the helm. He had shown up that morning at the dock, his face a rainbow of bruises. No broken bones, he had said, except maybe a cracked rib, and the doctor had taped him up. He insisted that he was ready to go back to work. Through the morning of heavy action, both men functioned well. Triga had no cause for complaint, but Fowler was certain he was about to make one anyway.

"Pat," said Triga, his eyes on the baits, "maybe we should go back over to the other side of the island."

"Why? The fishin's good right here."

"We haven't had a strike in over an hour."

"Christ, Triga, give us a break. We already got more sails than we had any other day out here. It'll pick up again soon."

"As you say," Triga reluctantly agreed. Fowler moved toward the ladder. "One other thing, Pat, before you go."

"Yeah?"

"Why are you having Dupree bring aboard the trash fish we're hooking?"

"That ain't slowin' us down."

"Debatable," Triga said. "But that wasn't my question."

Fowler sighed. "You been at the weighin' station every night."

"Certainly. So what?"

"You seen those twenty, thirty little Mexican kids waitin' there."

"The point, Pat."

"They're hungry, Triga. They eat everything we give 'em. You and me wouldn't eat these sails, but they do, and every one of them's got ten people waitin' for 'em back in town. Don't hurt us none to bring in what we catch."

"That's admirable, Pat," Triga said. "You are a source of constant amazement. However, I trust you will not lose your sense of proportion and forget why we're here."

"It don't take even five minutes out of he day to boat these here dolphins and kingfish and such and toss 'em in the icebox. The lines gotta be brung in anyway."

"Nevertheless, Pat, I will not have your altruism get in the way of our mission. If you don't. . ."

"Mission? What in the pluperfect hell are you talkin' about? We ain't carryin' a bomb into the Kremlin! We're killin' fish!"

"Irregardless, we shall not permit your otherwise commendable

compassion to divert us from our primary . . . task, if that word is more acceptable. Shall we."

"You never been hungry, Triga," Fowler said, his voice once again under control. When Triga started to reply, Fowler waved him silent. "Lemme put it a way might make you happier. Them Mexicans is dirt-poor, but if we keep bringin' these fish back for 'em, we're gonna be the last ones they steal from and the last ones to get harassed, because the people are gonna like us."

"Perhaps."

"No 'perhaps' about it," Fowler said. "Now I ain't talkin' about it no more. We're gonna keep doin' it whether you like it or not. And it ain't gonna stop us from takin' this tournament."

His employer did not answer right away. "That," he said finally, "is a consummation devoutly to be wished."

"Ain't a wish."

"Very well, Pat. We'll put the issue on the back burner." He gestured dismissal, but Fowler didn't leave.

"While we're ventilatin', Triga, I got some 'n' to tell you."

"Could we take it up later, Pat?"

"No. It's about the electrical wiring. You let it go too long. There's shorts all over the boat. Lights, radio, fathometer - they're all flickerin' and poppin' like flashbulbs."

"I'm sure you and Dupree can take care of it," Triga said wearily.

"We done as much as we can," Fowler replied. "Whole wiring system is shot. Just held together with Scotch tape and chewin' tobacco. It's all gotta be ripped out and replaced. Only a matter of time before a spark meets a fuel leak. I ain't even sure we can make it back to Florida next week, and I sure as hell don't feature driftin' all over the Gulf with nothin' between us and the bottom but Cuban gunboats."

Triga was aghast. "Replace the entire system? Great heavens, man, that would cost twenty thousand dollars!"

"More like thirty, I figure."

"I'll think about it."

"You'll do it. Soon's we get it back to West Palm. *If* we get back. You call ahead to Rybovich. They can do the job in the time we got until Morgan Cay."

"I said I'll think about it," Triga said. Petulantly.

"If it ain't done by then, you can think about findin' another captain, while you're at it The only reason I ain't sayin' it's got to be done sooner is there ain't no one here can do it."

"Threats are inappropriate. I'll remind you. . ."

". . . about how you're danglin' my own boat over my head." Fowler completed. "My boat won't do me no good if I'm feedin' the crabs."

"Very well, Pat. I'll call Rybovich."

"Good."

"But this friendly warning, Pat," Triga said "Don't persist in believing you are irreplaceable."

"Ain't no belief," Fowler said, moving against the ladder. "It's a fact."

The day was Lichine's. He released twelve and boated nine. One of the nine was underweight by three pounds, but his score was 262.

14

Catherine persuaded Lichine to charter a plane to Merida, the Yucatecan capital. A chauffeured car drove them to the ruins at Chichen Itza. They strolled through the ancient city hand in hand and ate cold chicken and drank beer on the steps of the Temple of the Warriors, listening to the ghosts.

When the sailfish totals were tallied at the end of the second week, nothing had changed. Catherine was still well in the lead, followed by Childs, Triga, Lichine, and Marker.

Most of the anglers, captains, and crews found reasons to celebrate, in groups contrived to avoid inflammation of persisting animosities. Pia Cipolla and Pat Fowler argued over Pia's acceptance of an offer to return to Florida with Catherine on *Aphrodite.* Fowler eventually conceded selfishness. Pia would be more comfortable - and safer - on the big yacht than on *Adroit,* with him. After much tequila, Fowler decided that he would not wait until Monday. He and Boots left at four-thirty Sunday afternoon.

They had not slept the night before, and it was at least thirty hours to Key West.

Midway between Puerto Juarez and Cabo San Antonio, Fowler summoned Boots to take the wheel. He opened a chart and spread it across the console.

"You straight yet?" Dupree asked.

"Halfway," Fowler answered. "Wink gave me a couple beauties. I won't never learn not to pop speed. My teeth are ground down to stubs."

"He chews 'em like gum," Boots said. "Kid'll never see forty, the way he does."

"Least he ain't on borrowed time yet." Fowler concentrated on the charts. "Look. You're gonna hafta spell me. I'm halfway asleep, beauty and all. Here's how I want to go."

His finger traced a path that bent around the Archipelago de los Colorados. The reef ordered the northern edge of the western end of Cuba.

"We gonna cut so close?" Dupree asked."Why not keep straight on to the Tortugas, then east to Key West, like usual?"

"One," said Fowler, " 'cause I don't want to be out in the middle of the Gulf with that low-pressure area comin' up. At least a Cuban jail is half a step up on dead. Two, it'll add five hours, and I ain't even sure this bucket will make it another ten minutes, the wiring the way it is."

"But the Colorado, Pat. It is somethin' else' now. Remember Manny Turbo? And Kit? Never saw Kit again."

"They didn't stay sharp. Ain't no trick to the Colorado. We stay at least fifteen miles out, never closer. We keep on a forty-four-degree heading to here, then forty-eight to Bahia Honda, then straight up to Key West. Onliest thing to remember is the current. It flows from where we are now direct to the Keys, but there's a reverse wash right through here that can drive you toward shore without you hardly knowin'. We just got to pay attention."

"That's the way you want it, Pat."

"Boots," Fowler said, folding the chart. "You still fixin' to split when we get back?"

"I am."

"There ain't no need, y'know. Triga ain't said nothin'."

"I don't need him to tell me when to get out." He checked the compass reading. "I woke up last Thursday mornin' and a voice said 'Strike Two!' I may be dumb, but I ain't stupid."

"Get off it, Boots. You ain't got to. . ."

"Yeah, I do."

Fowler remained on the bridge until the first course correction off Cabo San Antonio. It was dark, the moon sliding behind high luminous clouds. The sea was fairly calm, the wind negligible. Fowler's head dropped on his chest, snapped up.

"Boots," he said, "I can't cut it no more. Goin' below for awhile."

"You got it," Boots answered. "When you want up?"

"Two hours. We'll take the next loran bearing about then if the skywaves ain't screwin' us up. Remember, you gotta compensate for the backwash. Keep fifteen miles out. Three miles south, there's coral heads everywhere."

"I ain't hardly seen no lights at all over there."

"Don't matter," Fowler said from the ladder. "Can't trust 'em anyway. I hear they run lights back and forth on shore to draw boats onto the rocks. Commies or not, they still dig all these American goodies we got on board. Just keep on that heading."

Fowler decided to use Triga's stateroom. He kicked off his shoes and crawled across the bed and collapsed onto the mink throw. Sleep took him immediately.

Something woke him. Fowler squinted at his watch. Less than an hour had passed. Then there was a horrific grinding scream beneath him and the boat heeled sharply over. Fowler tumbled from the bed, cracking his right knee and both elbows against the bulkhead. Bottles and canisters crashed to the galley floor. The boat righted as he pushed to his feet, then heeled again, although less precipitously this time.

Fowler stumbled down the companionway, up the stairs, across the salon, out into the cockpit. The deck reared up, flinging him against the bait table. He couldn't protect his head this time as it slammed into the cabinet door. The bow went under, then lifted, sending water rushing back along the side decks, soaking him. He crawled over and grasped the hand rail of the ladder, making sure of his grip before pulling himself erect.

Their situation was clear enough. Amidship, the keel was hard atop a rock or coral head, the boat seesawing stem to bow and back. At the same time, six-foot waves were pounding the port side at a quartering angle, tipping the starboard gunnel very nearly under with each new wave. They were rocking forward and back and heeling to the side at the same time. No boat could long withstand it.

Fowler struggled up the ladder, bracing against the vicious motion and the sheets of water crashing over him. Boots was shouting into the microphone, his face yellow in the light of the gauges. Fowler grabbed him by the shoulder and spun him around.

"*What the fuck have you done?*" he yelled. "*Where are we? Where's Cuba?*"

"Over there!" Boots pointed behind him. His bloody lips were drawn tight across his teeth, the illumination from the console throwing the shadows of his cheek bones into his eye sockets. "Way back there!"

Fowler looked back. "That's San Antone Light! We're in too close! We ain't even five miles offshore!"

"I know! Don't you think I know? An' I can't raise the Coast Guard."

"Get off the radio." Fowler made his voice calm. Boots' skin was stretched taut from jaw to hairline, his neck muscles leaping. "*Boots*! I said get off!"

"But Pat, we ain't gonna last an hour!"

"You're wrong. But our Coast Guard won't get here for five hours, anyway. *If* they come. We're in Cuban waters. And if your call is monitored, we'll have Cubans all over us."

"What, then?"

"You think we put a hole in the hull?"

"Don't think so. Didn't sound like nothin' more'n us scrapin' bottom."

"We're bangin' against somethin' on the right. Get out that big hand light."

He leaned over both sides. On the left, the waves continued to break against the hull, sometimes pouring over the gunnel into the cockpit.

"If that keeps up," he said, "the transom'll be toothpicks."

On the right, the water flattened into a broad blue-white boil over an oblong area eighty feet long and twenty feet wide. Beyond, the waves gathered themselves and swelled up again, rolling toward the low, silhouetted shore. When the boat heeled over, there was a noise like tree branches snapping in a high wind.

"We're up against the edge of an elkhorn coral patch. Can't have ripped a hole or we'd be talkin' to shrimp right now. Shine the light down there."

The mate flicked the light on, changing the water within its halo to a milky, translucent green and startling a small red-eyed manta ray into a panicked departure. At a point directly below Fowler and Boots, the light caught the tip of a coral head, four feet off the side. When *Adroit* rocked over, it came within inches of the jagged protuberance. All around it, deeper, were clusters of fanning elkhorn formations. While they watched, a splintered length of board popped to the surface. It was part of the keel.

"We will be soon if we can't stop this teeter-totterin'," Boots said. "Keel's gonna crack off. Maybe we oughta just get out the raft and paddle like hell to the beach."

"I told you I ain't spendin' no time in jail. Besides, there's coral heads stickin' up all over out there. They'd tear the raft to ribbons."

The boat made a wracking forward-sideward lurch, the bow wallowing a long moment before lifting once again. They clung to the railing with mounting desperation.

"When did the weather turn?" Fowler asked.

"Didn't," Boots answered. "Wind's up a little, a thicker cloud cover, is all. The tide just changed on us. Out north there, it's probably near as flat-calm as when we set out. Pat, what're we gonna do?"

Fowler thought out loud. "We got to turn the bow into the sea. We can't wait to get floated off."

"I hear you, Pat. But how? We're hung up, we ain't sure the engines are operational since I stopped down and we'd hafta bring her about more'n ninety degrees to get the bow right."

"Try the engines. In neutral."

The port engine started up. The other didn't. The men glared at the instrument panel.

"Might be a cable pulled loose," Dupree said.

"Or another short in the fuckin' wiring," Fowler said .

"No difference. We take that chance when we have to. Okay, let's go."

"What're we doin'?"

"I'm gonna take an anchor and walk it out from the bow," Fowler said, his jaw set to dissuade protest. "Then I'm gonna take in the chain and crank us off here and get the boat headin' into the sea."

"Jesus Christ Almighty, Pat. . ."

"This ain't a debate," Fowler snapped. "Just do what I tell you. Think you can, this time?"

Boots looked as if he had been slapped.

There was no alternative, Fowler told himself. He fetched his shoes, then edged toward the bow, clinging, slipping. Normally, the captain stayed at the helm. A mate would do this. But he couldn't bring himself to trust Boots. It was, in the end, his responsibility, and this was no time for recriminations. Or delay.

He reached the foredeck and curled his fingers under the lip of the forward hatch cover while the bow dipped and water tumbled over his legs. On the uplift, he rapped his knuckles on the hatch cover. Boots shoved it open from below and pushed up the grappling anchor. It took three more plunges and ascents of the bow to get the chain, the rope, and Boots out. Fowler made loops in the twenty-foot chain and swung it over his shoulder. He held the anchor in his right hand.

"That stuff's too heavy," Boots said.

"No, it ain't," said Fowler. "Tie off the end of the rope."

"Why don't we take off the chain and just use the rope?"

"The rope'd fray too easy on this coral."

Fowler sat poised on the rim of the deck, bending forward, his free hand on the safety rail. He intend to slip over with the next dip of the bow, but paused a second too long.

"How do you know it's shallow enough?" Boots shouted.

"I don't," said Fowler before he let himself be carried off the side.

The water was warm at the top, cooler below. Fowler hit the bottom straight-legged, the weight of chain and anchor taking him down faster than he anticipated. A wave caught him immediately and sent him tumbling. The chain slipped from his shoulder. He got his feet under him and stood, gathering up the chain. In the troughs, the water came to his chest. At the crests, it was over his head. He managed four sluggish steps, the coral crunching and breaking against his legs, before he was lifted off the bottom by another wave and toppled once more. Again the chain fell off. Again, he retrieved it. Again, he walked. A link of chain caught on an obstruction. He was dragged under. When his head was clear of the surface, he spat water and shouted back at Boots. The boat reared up, the prow obliterating the moon. The mate was hanging on the bow rail.

"Say again?" he cried.

"Get that small plastic garbage can. From the forward rope locker!"

Fowler walked back to the side, struggling to keep his balance just beyond the plunging bow. Boots finally returned with the plastic container.

"You got your knife?" Fowler shouted. Boots nodded vigorously.

"Then cut a hole in the lid. Just big enough to feed the rope through."

When Boots had done so, Fowler passed the anchor and chain back aboard, timing his move to the plunging of the deck.

"Now put those in the bottom," he ordered, "coil the rope on top, and feed the end of the line out the hole."

Boots did as instructed. At that moment, a particularly powerful wave hit the far side of the boat. Fowler was nearly pinned between hull and coral. Boots almost slid off, but grabbed the rail in time. The boat shifted on its perch with a groan, but was held.

"Secure the rope again. Good. Now clamp the lid down and hand me the bucket. Okay, got it. Go back to the bridge. Monitor the radio. See if you can pick up *Brain Soup* or *Redemption* or one of them others. Maybe one of them's close. But don't transmit! You read me? Just try to get a fix on them."

It worked. The pail floated, the rope paid out behind. Fowler guided the pail, trying to keep the top above the surface. The coral crunched beneath his feet and pierced his clothes and lacerated his flesh. He stepped off into depressions and went under and the waves continued to all over him. His throat was raw with swallowed water. Creatures bumped against him and squirmed past. But it worked.

On the bridge, Boots strained to follow Fowler. When the captain was thirty feet off, though, Boots caught only the occasional flash of the bobbing yellow pail. He continued listening to the radio, turning the dial to all likely channels. Voices squawked landing instructions to planes and gossiped about catches of shrimp, but none of them seemed close, and none were recognizable.

Boots beat the wheel with his fist and urged the unseen Fowler on. He tried very hard not to think the thoughts that pressed in upon him, the harsh reproaches he knew were true. He willed his senses to work.

Perhaps he did not hear it, but beneath the thunder of the sea and the moans of the keel on its perch, there was a muffled . . . sloshing. Inside the hull, below deck. He imagined a plank torn loose, water rushing through. He squinted into the night, caught sight of what must be the yellow pail. It - and Pat? - was fifty feet out, at eleven o'clock of the bow. Boots could bear the anguish of waiting no longer. He had to do something. Anything. He went down to the cockpit. The glass salon door was rolling back and forth in its groove with the movement of the boat. Boots locked it open and flipped back the rug covering the salon floor. Then he raised the engine-room hatch and peered in.

There was water in there. Not enough to indicate a gash in the hull, but more than there should be. He found the light and played it carefully over every comer. There was no visible hull damage. Fuel lines were apparently intact. He lowered himself into the narrow space between the engines.

It was necessary to crouch. There were only four feet of clearance forward beyond the hatch opening. The water was to his waist, washing side to side with the boat. A few inches were acceptable. This was not. They would not have use of the flooded right engine until the water was out, and they would need it to get free.

As he suspected, the bilge pump wasn't working. He squatted, leaning against the port engine and bracing one foot against the other. The plastic top of the pump came off easily. Boots held the bolts between his teeth and craned to look inside. The rotating vanes at the bottom were clogged. He picked out the stringy black mass and replaced the cover. The outstretched leg cramped. He brought it back under him and rubbed the knotted muscle.

Above his head, a cable carrying 110 volts was affixed to the floor timber. It ran to the generator. Right there, the cable drooped. Over many months, the staple holding it had scraped the crumbling rubber insulation away, exposing three inches of bare copper wire.

At the moment Boots was massaging the sharp ache in his calf, a wave much higher than the others caught the boat broadside. Boots was thrown to starboard. He flailed out to break his fall and his hand found the three inches of bare copper wire. The hatch cover broke its catch and banged shut.

Fowler looked back. Sixty feet from the boat, he estimated. The bottom started to slope up. When it leveled off, he was waist-deep. After ten more slogging paces, he stepped off into nothing.

It was the brink of the patch. He swam a few strokes, kicking his feet to be sure. Nothing. It might be four hundred feet straight down, or twenty. Enough, either way. He rolled on his back and pulled back to firm footing, dragging the pail. With some difficulty, he wrenched off the lid and tipped out the anchor and chain. After yanking several times on the chain to make sure the hooks were firmly embedded, he rested a moment.

He looked left, right, and over the vastness to the place where the black sky met the blacker sea. He shivered. Never had he felt so alone. Something nudged its way between his thighs. Fowler turned and started back, guiding himself along the rope.

At this distance, the boat was a defenseless toy. It was rocking less savagely, though, as the tide continued to fill in beneath it. Fowler permitted himself hope at the same time he admitted the lack of it an hour before. Humps of water rose up in front of him and he speeded his half-walk, half-swim until he could see the boat again. It was easier, for he was no longer fighting the current.

Boots was not at the wheel. Fowler cursed.

As he watched, all the lights but those in the instrument panel went out. It took several tries to get back aboard, since the boat was more stable than before and the foredeck was riding higher. Boots did not answer his shouts. Fowler hauled in the slack rope, then wrapped the end around drum of the power windlass mounted behind the juncture of the toe rail. He decided that he would not start the engines, because they could be damaged when they churned.

The rope stretched across the waves. After a deep breath, he pressed the button on the windlass with the heel of his hand. The motor hummed. The rope thrummed taut. The pitch of the motor sound fell as the drum slowed under the strain. Drops of water sprayed from the rope. The boat rose and fell, but did not budge from its fulcrum. Fowler mashed the button flat. The windlass stalled, started up again, stalled. He waited for the next high wave, his lungs aching.

When it came, it brought an extra inch of water cushion. Fowler anticipated it, and mashed the button again. The motor roared. *Adroit* lurched forward less than a foot, stopped for an instant, and then kept coming. The entire boat shuddered as it ground across the ridge, the nerve-wracking sound diminishing as the hull beneath the cockpit slid over the obstruction.

Then there was a different noise, a long, painful screech of metal against rock like that of rusted spike slowly drawn from ancient timber. The noise ended with a clatter as the stem glided free.

He didn't rejoice, for it was not over. The current caught the boat and swept it along in a wide arc, helpless as a cork on a string. Fowler felt and heard the crumbling of coral, fragments of which popped to the surface off port, but the jarring impact of wood against unyielding rock did not happen.

The bow was upsea, prow cleaving the waves, in under a minute. Fowler recovered more of the anchor rope and released the windlass button. He sucked for air, and walked shakily toward the stem. That last noise as *Adroit* slid free was probably just what he hoped it was not. All things considered, the boat appeared to be sound topside. But it was quiet, and Boots was not there.

Fowler lifted the door to the engine compartment. The water was two feet deep and rising. There was a detectable gurgling right below him, but he could barely see it. He found a flashlight in the salon cabinet and some rags and a stick in the forward locker. On the way back, he threw off the main power switch in the galley.

He clicked the light on and pointed it at the gurgling sound. It was as he suspected. When the boat came off the ridge, the propeller shaft was yanked from the coupling and shaft log. There was a neat one-and-three-quarter-inch hole in the bottom. Fowler lowered himself into the compartment, facing the stern. Stuffing the rags into the hole did not take long.

Finally, he made himself turn around, flashing the beam forward, over the engines. Toward the bilge pump.

Boots was sitting at the far end of the engines. He was twisted toward Fowler, legs bent beneath him. The fingers of his left hand were wrapped around the cable, fused together. The skin flaked in places, revealing patches of pink underflesh. Fowler tried not to look at Boots' face. One eye merely bulged. The other one was on his cheek.

The fingers peeled off the wire easily enough. It was harder to straighten the body out. To do it, Fowler had to push the trunk and face down into the water while he sat on the thighs. He felt bad about having to do that.

Eventually, he managed to drag the body over to the hatch opening, lift it through, and lay it on the the flooring beneath the fighting chair. He covered it with the mink throw from the master stateroom. Then Fowler closed the trap door and sat on the back step, looking off at Cuba.

The lightening sky stirred him. "Got to start thinkin' about gettin' outa here," he said aloud. "Cubans'll find us. Call the Coast Guard? No. We'll get a loran fix."

He went to the receiver, switched it on, and fine-tuned the stations. When the coordinates appeared on the viewscreen, he decided to try to raise one of the other boats. After an hour of fruitless transmission, he was ready to send an all-channel Mayday. But then there was a response.

"*Adroit*, this is *Brain Soup*. Come back, turkey."

It was Wink Andros.

Fowler made first visual contact with *Brain Soup* an hour later. Shortly after, a helicopter with military markings beat toward him from the shore and hovered overhead, flattening the water. The pilot called down on his radio in Spanish. Fowler explained his circumstances in English. He expected to be out of Cuban territorial waters within two hours, he said. There was no way to tell if he was understood. The helicopter left.

Brain Soup arrived. Doakes stood off beyond the rim of the reef, and Wink and Ernest Lichine swam a towline to *Adroit*. Fowler pulled them aboard. Wink's first words drifted off when he saw the bundle beneath the fighting chair. Lichine carried the towline forward and secured it. He asked instructions and began to winch in the anchor.

"You got power?" Wink said, staring at the blanketed object.

"Port engine," Fowler said, his eyes on the shoreline. "But the propeller's gone."

"And you?"

Fowler didn't answer.

"You want to transfer to the other boat?" Wink asked.

"Guess not."

"Okay if we stay with you, then?"

Fowler nodded. Wink went to the radio.

"Let's get outa here, Jeet," he said into the microphone. "Gonna have a mess of Cubans crawling over us soon."

Doakes asked what had happened, but Wink cut him off. The towline came out of the water and tightened. The screws on *Brain Soup* churned ineffectually for a moment, then bit in. Doakes moved slowly off, shoving the throttles to three-quarters full when *Adroit* was clear of the reef. When they were twenty miles out, Doakes veered to the northeast and ran for Key West.

Lichine mixed a highball for Fowler and drew the captain into the salon to drink, away from the covered heap on the deck beneath the fighting chair. Wimk went below to complete repair of the bilge pump. Lichite monitored the radio, getting up from time to time to refill Fowler's glass. The captain didn't talk and Lichine didn't press him.

Redemption, *Crystal Ball*, and *Zodiac Arrest* caught up with them at noon. By then, Wink had pieced together what had happened during the night. He made a suggestion to Fowler, who agreed. Wink called the Coast Guard for the permission they needed. At a point thirty miles east of Sandy Key, the five boats closed in a tight box formation and cut their engines. Wink and Lichine tied the mink throw around the body. In a ceremony without words, they lowered Boots Dupree over the side.

Back at West Palm Beach, the anglers and crews separated. Lichine flew to New York, Theo Marker to Los Angeles. Wink drove to Marathon, declaring he needed a week of conch fritters and bonefishing. Jeeter Doakes and Steve Grubbs heard that a nine-foot Florida skunk ape was seen raping a stable full of horses up near Okeechobee and decided they would try to catch it. Montgomery Childs settled in with Bunny Haskell at his duplex. Horst Triga arranged for the repair of *Adroit* and then continued on to Morgan Cay in *Highlander*. His father was there. Horst was not eager to see him.

Aphrodite arrived a day later. No one could tell Pia Cippola where Fowler was. She went to his apartment, persuaded the manager to let her in, and waited.

MORGAN CAY

BLUEFIN TUNA

(Thunnus thynnus)

Imagine a fish so large that an individual of routine dimension can fill 1500 of those six-ounce supermarket cans. Or one known to school in such vast numbers that ancient warships had to proceed in battle formation to break through. Ignobly reduced to sandwich filling, the bluefin is stripped of its heroic attributes in life. The giant tuna (as it is also known) is the largest member of the aptly named horse mackerel family. Having one crash a bait is not unlike attempting to persuade a Percheron to go in a direction he does not wish. Decidedly pelagic, the bluefin is worldwide in distribution, although debate continues over subspecific relationships. The female broadcasts up to six million eggs during spawning times. It is royal blue on the back, as a rule, shading to silver underneath. The small-scaled, mucus-sheathed body is imprecisely described as torpedo-shaped, swelling from a pointed snout and narrowing to an unusually narrow juncture with the crescent tail. Tactics require finely tuned teamwork between captain and angler. Average sizes caught on sportfishing equipment are in the 200 to 400 pound range, but the present record is 1,496, and specimens exceeding 1,600 pounds reportedly have been taken by commercial methods. The prime Atlantic area during late April and May is the Bahamian side of the Florida Passage, when the bluefin is spurred into its annual northward journey. Reliable hot spots since Hemingway's time are Bimini, Cat Cay, and Morgan Cay.

-THE IAA HANDBOOK

15

There were four categories of human life on Morgan Cay: Members, Guests, Staff, and Visitors. These classifications were promulgated when Commodore Whitney Triga Somerset purchased the island in 1933 as a refuge for himself and a handful of meticulously selected friends. B.K. Triga initiated numerous innovations when the island passed into his hands following the death of his uncle. But the original designations of caste persisted.

Morgan Cay was an L-shaped sand bar, the last in the broken strand dangling from the two Biminis and paralleling the Gulf Stream. Unrelievedly featureless at the time of its acquisition by the Commodore, its highest point was now a man-made twenty-three feet above sea-level fourteenth green of the golf course that covered one quarter of the total land surface.

A strip of beach running from tip to tip along the leeward shore was parceled out to those regarded as worthy intimates of the founder. They built modest cottages in which they only slept and bathed. Days were spent on the water, the skeet range, the white sand beach, the course, or the tennis courts. Evenings were passed in the eating and entertainment complex centered around the expanded twenty-room manor house built by the Commodore. There were shipwreck parties, first-run films, and luaus that were not unusually lavish, considering their auspices. Six times a year, the Morgan Cay Club sponsored one-week fishing tournaments. On these occasions, movie stars and ex-Presidents visited the island. The thirty-two families who owned property were Members. The others were Guests, who were presented laminated badges certifying that status. Members and Guests had access to all facilities and all sections of the island. They were assured of expeditious and courteous treatment by the lone Bahamian customs and immigration inspector. He manned the open-sided shed next to the concrete apron which received the vintage seaplanes of Chaulk's International Airline on its commuter flights from Miami.

Members and Guests were served by a permanent Staff quartered in clapboard cabins bordering the mangrove of the southeastern quadrant of the island. As they were year-round residents and their employers merely transients, the Staff people conducted themselves with the hauteur of Maine lobstermen confronted by vacationers from Yonkers.

Members and Guests were white. Staff were, with the exception of the social director and harbormaster, black. Staff endeavored to ensure that Members and Guests did not come into contact with Visitors.

Yachtsmen running for shelter from weather or "clearing in" at the customs shed were Visitors. They were infrequent callers, for the exclusivity of Morgan Cay was well-known. The crews of the boats owned by Members and Guests were also Visitors.

It was the night before the first day of the tuna phase of the tournament, and Catherine Nettles was describing this pecking order to Ernest Lichine. They were sitting at a painted metal table with green placemats on the marble terrace of the clubhouse. All the other tables were filled. The five-piece steel band imported from Nassau played pop tunes of the forties transformed to reggae and calypso. Dinner was nearly over.

"I'm sorry, darling," Catherine said. "I've been prattling at you ever since you got off the plane. It's just that I'm so glad to see you." She twined her fingers through his. "I haven't given you three seconds. How did it go in New York?"

"Quite well, I thought. I learned quite a bit. There's someone heading toward us. Isn't that Pia whatsername? The one attached to Captain Fowler?"

Pia Cippola glided between the tables, flipping her long black hair over her shoulder, chin up, back straight, knowing but not acknowledging the eyes that followed her.

"Yes, it is," Catherine said. "I asked her to join us."

Staff were clearing dishes and bringing coffee. The combo blared a fanfare, and the leader undertook an excessive introduction of the "genuine live Bahamian" entertainment to follow. A muscular young black man in loincloth and braided fright wig leaped into the center of the dance floor with a bloodcurdling scream. He held a sword in each hand, with which he sliced the air over his dodging head and those of the ringside Members and Guests.The man glistened and writhed for a while and then pretended to thrust the sword into his chest.

Lichine faced back at Catherine.

"I know we have a kind of tacit agreement not to discuss the tournament," he said, "but could you give me an idea what to expect or watch out for the next two weeks? I've fished tuna a few times, but never down here."

"It isn't that different," she said. "It's not like sailfish, of course. Giant tuna are hard to tease onto the bait. You have to put it right on their snouts. Sails will take anything in a hundred yards."

"How big are they?" Pia asked.

"Four, five hundred pounds. One of them makes a big sailfish look like a sardine."

"What test line do we use?"

"The heaviest one-thirty. In every way, it's the exact opposite of what we were doing in Cozumel."

"How, for example?" Pia asked.

"Sails fight on the surface, with all that jumping and greyhounding. They tire themselves out faster that way and come in faster, so we use the lightest reasonable tackle. Tuna, though, go right to the bottom and stay there. The angler doesn't even see one until it's nearly to the gaff. And they're ten times as heavy, so it's like hauling a piano up the face of a forty-story building. Quite literally."

"Doesn't that require a great deal of strength?" Pia said. "And you're only. . ."

"A hundred-pound weakling," Catherine supplied.

"Look, darling, that whole number about how this is a man's sport is a crock. I once saw an absolutely mountainous pro fullback give up after fifteen minutes with an only average tuna. It isn't strength, it's finesse."

"And Catherine has an excess of that," said a modulated voice behind them. It was Montgomery Childs. "Now don't start dipping your darts in acid, Cat. I meant that as a sincere compliment." Childs looked at Pia. "And I come in peace."

He indicated the empty chair. "May I?"

Catherine and Pia returned only frosty stares, so Lichine said, "Of course. Please join us."

"Thank you." Childs sat, and gestured at a waiter. He adjusted his smile and absently touched his flawlessly groomed hair. "Cat, as you may not know, Pia, holds the Morgan Cay Club record for bluefin tuna. The - ah - women's record, that is."

"What Monty is so genteelly thumping his chest about," Catherine said, "is that he holds the club all-tackle record, male or female. At the moment. What he isn't mentioning is the fact that Theo Marker holds the *world* record."

"Let's not fight," Childs said. "I really came over to apologize to this lovely lady."

Pia neither looked away nor replied.

"Don't let him off the hook, Pia," Catherine said. "I am fascinated by this display of contrition."

The dancer concluded his act by rolling his nearly naked body over a bed of broken glass. The social director took pictures and the master of ceremonies milked applause. The band launched a reggae version of "Some Enchanted Evening." Catherine nudged Lichine.

"Horst is going to get his nose stuck," she said, nodding at a nearby table.

"Who's the pale person with him?" Pia asked.

"B. K. Triga himself," Catherine answered.

In white suit, snowy hair, and urban pallor, the elderly billionaire was a perversely riveting figure amid the flowered silks and voiles. His son leaned toward him, the crinkles around his eyes as deeply etched as the cleft in his chin.

"Horst looks like he's pitching hard," Childs said, without interest. "Wonder what he's selling?" He shifted closer to Pia.

"Asking Daddy for a bail-out, I imagine," Catherine said.

"What do you mean?" asked Lichine.

"I hear that Triga the younger is overdrawn on his allowance," Catherine replied, draining her glass. "And that B.K. has chastised him."

"You 'hear'?" Childs said, intrigued. "Where? Who from?"

Catherine noticed Lichine's frown.

"The usual," she said, attempting to dismiss the remark. "In this snake pit of good buddies, you hear whatever tickles your libido, about whoever you want. And take your pick of what to believe."

"Gossip, you mean," Lichine said, thin-lipped. "Triga isn't my favorite person, but I don't see any point in circulating that sort of. . ."

"Forget I said it, darling. It's just that I'd dearly love to think that Horst was about to have his gears stripped."

Childs had returned his attention to Pia. ". . . really, honey," he was saying, "I was drunk that night in Cozumel. I know that's no excuse, but I don't make a habit of it. Give me another chance."

"At what?" Pia said, rising. She smiled, but at Catherine and Lichine. ""Thank you for dinner, Cat, Mr. Lichine. I have to go find Pat. He was going to ask Mr. Triga if I could go out with them tomorrow. Good night." She left without a glance at Childs.

"Monty, dear," Catherine said after Pia had gone, "I don't believe I've ever seen you so crushed. You really must accommodate yourself to the fact that some women are immune to whatever it is that the Bunnys of the world regard as your charms. How is that sweet bovine little thing, by the way? Contentedly chewing her organic cud, trust."

"Don't think it hasn't been grand, Cat," Childs said, pushing back his chair and standing. "Good luck tomorrow."

Childs threaded his way back to his table where a girl of age and configuration similar to Bunny Haskell awaited him. The Trigas were joined by some other Members. Horst excused himself. His father did not acknowledge his departure.

"Monty is trying to screw his way through all the stews and porn-porn girls between here and Manitoba," Catherine said.

"I think you hit the marrow this time," Lichine said. "He really looked hurt. I don't see why you have to attack everyone in sight."

"Now that reminds me . . ." she replied, snuggling against him.

Pia Cippola paused in the shadow of the passageway leading from the terrace to the docks. Satisfied she was no longer being observed, she continued on out to the docks, along the path to the Visitors and Staff Lounge.

Aphrodite and *Highlander* were moored lengthwise, bow to stern, along the third dock. Pia left the shell path and walked past the first yacht. She paused at the foot of the wooden steps that led to the fantail of the second boat and looked around once again. No one, except the steward, Duncan. He touched the bill of his cap as Pia mounted the steps to *Highlander*. She walked quickly toward the light spilling from the enclosed afterdeck.

The next morning, *Brain Soup* ran over dappled green shallows toward Dagger Key Light. Doakes told Wink to take the wheel and gestured for Lichine to go below. Doakes followed. They slid into opposite sides of the dinette.

"You been doin' those exercises these last two weeks like I told you?" Doakes asked without preamble.

"Yes. I was sore all over at first, but I feel pretty good now."

"You keep 'em up for the rest of the tournament. From here on out, muscle starts countin'. We ain't playin' no more."

"You've made your point."

"And I'm gonna keep makin' it. You keep doin' what I tell you, we won't have no problems." Doakes inhaled, let it out. "Now. We got a bad start in Cozumel, but we come on strong at the end."

"We're still in fourth place."

"I know where we are, Ernie. Now listen up, and we'll make it third by the end of the week. Okay. Your competition is Triga and Childs. Forget the others."

"Catherine Nettles is in first."

"Excuse me for talkin' while you was interruptin'."

"Sorry."

"Nettles is good, damn good," Doakes said. "But she's a woman."

"So?" Lichine remembered Catherine's comments of the night before.

"Goddamit, Ernie! Pay attention to what I'm tellin you!" Doakes rubbed his face in exasperation. "Nettles is a woman, a small woman. Got no strength at all. There ain't no fish we'll be goin' after where strength and endurance are more important than giant tuna. Now that don't mean you can just reel 'em in. You still gotta remember to fight the fish, not yourself. But I seen her with tuna. She takes too long. She lets the fish rest. Way she does, she can't hardly boat two tuna a day. You gotta do twice that. You gotta get the fish in fast. No restin' for you or it. You readin' me?"

Lichine nodded.

"Good, 'cause you ain't never gonna bust your ass like the next two weeks. Quantity counts here. The fleabrains who made up the rules put the minimum for boatin' tuna at six hundred, when chances are we won't see two like that the whole time. Okay, so we live with that. We do like we did in Cozumel. We get 'em in fast and we keep every one of 'em that looks like two pounds over the weight. Nettles caught eighty-three sails down there. She won't get twenty tuna here.

"We're gonna do like Childs and Triga will. Soon's I put you over Mo, you get in the chair and set the drag to fifty pounds."

"Fifty? That's awfully risky, isn't it? With that much drag, it'll break off."

"At fifty, you're stickin' it to the fish. He knows youre giving it all you got. He gives up faster 'cause he cant get no slack to run with. But you gotta feel him, keep the pressure on. Every half turn on the reel is important. They ain't like sails that all you hafta do is hang on. With a big fish, the longer the fight, the longer the odds in the fish's favor."

"I'll do my best."

"You'll do better than that. I'll let you know how when I see you workin'. Only other thing is weather."

"How do you mean?"

"We want heavy water action and we want a wind from the south."

"Why?"

"The tuna are migratin' now. They follow the Gulf Stream, which runs north. The tuna we miss here in May are the ones that they'll be haulin' in up north off Montauk come July. We want a wind from the south to hurry 'em along. Nettles, now, she'll be prayin' for dead-calm seas or a wind from the east or no wind at all."

"Because the tuna don't move or feed under those conditions?"

"You got it. The fewer the rest of us catch here, the better her lead from the sailfish holds up. And once we get to blue marlin in St. Thomas, she's got a species she's better with."

"How does it look today?"

Doakes studied the water. "Like her prayers ain't gonna be answered," he said finally. "Them tuna are gonna be movin' today."

Fowler put *Adroit* on automatic pilot and climbed the narrow ladder from the bridge up the tuna tower. Once he had squeezed under the railing and taken position at the controls, he called down to Pia.

"Tell Chuck I'm takin' it from here," he said. "And come on up. Hang on tight. It's slippery."

"Whoo!" she exclaimed as she crawled onto the platform. "You weren't kidding. I almost took a header."

Fowler soaked up the sight of her and felt the familiar longing. Pia examined her surroundings: a platform beneath her feet, the padded railing all around supported by struts, the station for wheel and throttles and radio that overrode those below, a flat awning above their heads, room for three people, all standing, for there were no seats. It felt as if they would surely capsize. They were higher above the water than the boat was long, and it was like standing in the greased saddle of a mechanical arcade bucking horse, over forty feet up. The platform heaved forward and back, side to side, the movement of the boat itself accentuated threefold.

And it soon became cold, despite the tropical warmth back on the dock. Pia wore only a bikini. She hugged herself and almost lost her footing. Fowler grabbed her, sliding his arm around her waist.

"Careful," he said. "Water gets hard from this high up." He slipped out of his windbreaker. "I purely hate to cover all that good stuff up, but put this on. You're one big goosebump."

"Thanks." The platform heaved as she was pulling the jacket on, throwing her into the rail and knocking the breath from her. After a few minutes, she adjusted to the motion. The trick was bracing the legs and keeping at least one hand always locked around the rail or a strut.

That technique mastered, she surveyed this different world. It was enchanting. Colors were so much clearer and deeper, the distances so much greater. It almost seemed as if she could see the curvature of the earth. A shoal of flying fish erupted from the water and skimmed through the white caps.

"Oh, look!" she squealed. "Aren't they adorable?"

"You took the word right outa my mouth." Fowler grinned at her childlike delight. "Easy, honey, you don't wanna lose your cool." He knew she was happy. She let the "honey" pass.

"Look, look! What's that? 0oo, and that" She pointed at one flash of silver and another of cobalt.

"The first was a 'cuda, the second was a shark, maybe even a white. Don't see those much. Water changes the color. Like, in the water, the tuna are a tobacco brown. Out of it, they're sort of bluish purple. And, Pia, once we start fishin', don't point no more unless you see tuna. It's confusin'."

The two-minute warning came over the radio. Fowler shouted to the mates to get ready. "See that?" He indicated a broad sapphire strip along the bottom, its hue in vibrant contrast to the deep indigo surrounding it. "They call it 'Tuna Alley.' Fifty feet wide, hunnert feet deep. Drops right off to six hunnert. Runs for miles, north-south. Bluefins follow it like an expressway sometimes. We'll hold on this course awhile to see if they're doin' it today."

"Okay," said Pia. "Tell what's going to happen and then I'll shut up."

"We put just one line out," Fowler said. He was leaning far over the wheel, searching the water. "Flat line. No outrigger, 'cause we don't need no drop-back time with tuna. We'll troll, but we won't catch 'em that way. We got to hunt them. That's why we're on top this ten-thousand dollar jungle gym. I can see better. When I spot a school I circle the boat and put the bait right over the fish. If I don't lose sight of the fish when I turn and he decides he's pissed off or hungry, he eats the bait. Triga wheels him in. We lid that all day.

"My legs turn to rubber tryin' to hang onto this tower. I don't eat nothin' or drink much, 'cause there ain't time. And I got to stare so hard for eight hours, my eyes pop outa my head."

As soon as he said it, the image rushed back: the thing in the bilge that used to be Boots. He blinked and tried to think of something else.

Steve Grubbs was a good man. Captain of *Crystal Ball* in Cozumel, he was fired two days after returning to West Palm Beach. Monty Childs changed his crews as often as his women. Grubbs, a cheerily phlegmatic man with a cap of ropy blond hair, was perfectly content to replace Boots as first mate. Chuck Timmins was the new second mate. All the owners had hired additional crew members, for the last three phases of the tournament involved fish reaching weights of one thousand pounds or more. Timmins was not yet twenty and uncommonly laconic in this company, but he was quick, wiry, and responsive to orders. Triga, although parsimonious in most things, paid his crews well. In this case, the angler was gratified to have a man of Grubbs' recognized skill aboard, but had the grace not to rejoice over the replacement of the mate he felt was inept. Fowler had not discussed the death with Triga. He intended a final accounting, nonetheless.

"Get ready" Fowler hollered down. Grubbs and Timmins poised at the transom, looking up. The countdown ended. "Get it out!"

Immediately, he jammed the right throttle forward and spun the wheel in a tight left turn, sending Pia sprawling against the railing.

"What? What?" she cried, shaken.

He did not answer. He was bent far over the wheel, every muscle tense, pressing her head down when she interfered with his line of sight. The boat reversed its direction and Fowler ran it at full speed. His expression went from intensity to dismay.

"Where'd the fuckers go?" he muttered.

"What? Where?"

"Four, five bluefins," he answered distractedly. "About two hunnert yards off port. Where'd they go?" He cut speed, his eyes still sweeping the water. "Wait! There they are!"

The engines roared again and the boat heeled as he spun the wheel once more. His excitement was contagious, and Pia's heart pounded, although she couldn't understand why. She looked where Pat looked, but saw nothing. The two mates were in readiness at the sides of the fighting chair, Timmins watching the single bait, Grubbs awaiting information from Fowler. Triga snapped the harness clasps in the eyelets on the side of the reel and waited, shoulders hunched.

"Five of 'em!" Fowler shouted. "Fifty yards! One o'clock!" He was facing the stern, but his right hand remained on the wheel. The sun glinted off the surface in the area he indicated, sparkling, prismatic.

"You see 'em?"he asked Pia.

"No. What do I look for? Oh, there! Oh, look!"

Mossy brown smudges dimpled the surface, submerged, rolled again. The first-four disdained the bait, but the last one charged the mackerel, swallowed it, and dived. Triga raised back hard, three times, setting the hook.

Grubbs lowered the seat back until it was horizontal to the deck. Triga placed his hands on the armrests and pushed back, the harness bearing the strain of the bending fiberglass rod. The line faded swiftly from the reel, so fast that Grubbs poured a bucket of seawater over it to keep it from overheating.

"Let's go!" Fowler said to Pia. "Go! Down!"

She scrambled down the slippery ladder as fast as she could. Fowler was right behind. He jumped to the bridge controls. The wheel was turning and the throttles were moving by themselves. He took them and faced the cockpit, deftly manipulating the controls behind his back.

The fish slowed, and Triga tilted farther back, bringing the rod straight up. Without a break in the motion, he then swayed forward, his left hand on the back of the reel, his right cranking smoothly. At the farthest point of the arc, the rod was parallel with the deck and Triga permitted the harness attached to it to lift him off the chair. And, again without jerk or pause, he straightened his legs and eased back once more, the rod raising as he did, his left hand still on the reel. Then forward, cranking. And back.

"Will you look at that bastard?" Fowler said to Pia. "There ain't no one better at this than him. Don't make move one that don't inch that fish closer."

Brain Soup had pulled up fifty yards off, its passengers and crew watching the battle. Fowler reached for the microphone.

"I thought you didn't like him," Pia said.

"I hate the bastard," Fowler said as he brought the mike to his lips. "Don't mean I don't know class." He depressed the button, and called in the hookup to the committee boat. Once a fish was on the line, there wasn't much for the captain to do but keep the stern facing it - stopping down, adjusting course, or chasing after, as necessary. In this case, they were backing into a following sea. The stern plowed clumsily into the waves, which shattered, flooded the cockpit, and drenched the angler, mates, and umpire. Much of the time, Triga could not see. Yet not once did he falter, or crank when the fish was running, or fail to relieve line when the tension eased.

"Ain't this a bitch?" Fowler said to Pia. He was delighted to be where he was, and it showed. "That rich mother fucker actually pays me to drown him!"

At 9:26, the tuna was alongside. Grubbs touched the wire and the umpire declared the fish caught. Timmins reached over and snipped the leader as close to the hook as possible. The fish flicked its tail and drifted away.

"That's it?" Pia said, feeling somehow let down. "You go to all this trouble and expense, and Triga, through all this back-breaking drudgery, just to catch a fish and let him go?"

"Ain't nothin' either of us'd rather be doin'. Almost. We don't hardly ever keep the fish."

Pia shook her head in bafflement.

"Fishermen," she decided, "are weird."

That evening, the social director tacked two notices to the bulletin board at the entrance of the clubhouse. The first announced a cocktail party and dinner on Wednesday night for anglers and their crews.

The second listed the results of the day's fishing. It read:

Redemption (Marker+Curry). 135

Adroit (Triga+Fowler). 114

Crystal Ball (Childs+Mann). 112

Zodiac Arrest (Nettles+Cronski).. 38

Brain Soup (Lichine and Doakes) 0

16

Most of the captains and mates were in the Visitors and Staff Lounge, two hundred yards away on the other side of the harbor. Ernest Lichine was the only owner there. He was supposed to meet Catherine soon, but he delayed leaving.

These men continued to intrigue him. Before he was caught up in this tournament, he imagined them as grizzled old salts. Instead, most of them were lean, brown, young, handsome. Stereotypical beach boys, Lichine thought. All of them bore bands of white skin around their eyes from the wrap-around Polaroid glasses they wore to cut the glare on the water. All of them, without exception, wore expensive watches that were capable of withstanding water pressures to depths of two hundred feet. Most strung gold chains around their necks, usually with nuggets or shark teeth as pendants. Some had tee shirts with the names of their boats across front and back, provided by their employers. Wink's shirt front, though, featured a cartoon of a dyspeptic frog and the legend, "I'm So Happy I Could Just Shit. . ."

Silence was an abhorrent state for them. They talked to fill the void, devoting as many hours to discussion of banal topics regarded as unworthy of ten minutes in his own world as they did to recountings of fish and men and to arguments about techniques and equipment. Given the restrictions on their movements on Morgan Cay, there was little else they could do in their off hours. But there was a compulsive cadence to their imagery and conversation, and Lichine was reluctant to miss anything. More, he felt closer to these men than to the wealthy anglers and their friends, and he was no longer terrified of them. Only apprehensive.

"Don't let it get you down, Ernie," Wink was saying.

"Marker had the breaks today and we didn't."

"Right on," said Doakes. "Most times, Marker couldn't catch a turd in a dead eddy with a dip net." This was said less with the intent of comforting Lichine than to hector Earl Curry, Marker's captain. Curry was squatting on the floor, nursing a beer and picking his nose.

"Now, Jeet," he said, contemplating the residue of his exploration, "you ain't got call to come down like that. What it was before was bad luck. Today was just a sample of how we gonna whup the rest of you from here on out. Can't keep down a dynamite combination of good boat, good crew, and good angler."

"Even a blind hog can find a acorn-once in a while," said Doakes.

"And Earl," Wink added, "that boat don't roll all that wide. The plain fact is, it's ugly."

"Fish don't jump out of the water to see how pretty a boat is," Curry replied. "Makes no never mind, anyway. I'm just happy to get out from under. Marker's been meaner than a mad dog in a meathouse since this contest started up. Ain't never seen a man so uptight."

"He needs the money worse'n them others," said Lyle Scully, Curry's first mate. "Ain't had a movie in three years. I heard him on the radio yellin' at his agent twice already."

Pat Fowler arrived, picking his way through the mates and captains crowded around tables on the screened porch. He nodded at some, shook hands with others, and registered no surprise that Lichine was there.

"Jeet," he said, "'you do good today?"

"Hell, yes," Doakes replied. "Twelve more fish and we'd of had an even dozen. Baited ten, struck four, hung two. One busted the leader twelve inches before the swivel hit the rod tip. Other'un damn near pulled Mr. Lichine outa the chair before it threw the hook."

"Sorry to hear that, Mr. Lichine," Fowler said, tipping his glass slightly in acknowledgment. "Better luck tomorrow."

"Call him Ernie," Wink said. He put his hand on Lichine's shoulder and squeezed. "He's one of them, but he ain't too bad for a kind of rich professor."

Lichine flushed. He couldn't get used to displays of affection, or even approval, from men. Which was not to say he didn't like it

"That true about Marker's California boat, Earl?" Fowler asked.

Curry nodded.

"What about his boat?" Doakes asked.

"Hijacked. Before we left for Cozumel. Nobody even knew until we got back to West Palm."

"Couldn't happen to a sweeter guy," said Wink.

Allie Cronski burst in, threw a chair back and sat. "Crew ain't nothing but white niggers," he said, bringing his fist down on the table.

"You ain't that good," said Jeeter Doakes.

Cronski was caught up in his indignation and didn't hear.

"I'm comin' down the dock just now," he said. "First time I ever been here, so I go over there to that building that's got a sign on it. I'm about to go into the bar, the round one, when this big nigger dressed up like some kinda jive ass cop comes up and says to me, "You a Member, mon?" 'I'm with Nettles,' I says. 'You run Miz Nettles' boat for her?' he says. I tell him 'Yeah.' He says, 'then you can't be here. mon.' I start to tell him what he can do when the uppity tucker puts his hand on this humungus .44 magnum he's got on his belt. He tells me that 'Visitors' are confined to the docks and to the path from there up to here. And that's it, he says. None of us can go nowhere else. You believe that shit?

When a nigger can tell a white man how to do, somethin's bad wrong."

The others glanced quickly at the bar where four black Staff were watching television.

"Cool it, Allie." Fowler said. "We got two weeks here yet."

Cronski glowered. Fowler ordered another round. Lichine thought he noticed an exchange of conspiratorial glances between Wink and Jeeter.

"How's Cronski's wife, Jeeter?" Wink said after a moment.

"Better'n nothin'," Doakes said.

"She does think the world of her pussy, that's a fact." Wink said, thoughtfully smoothing his new mustache. "And she ain't too swift. But show Betty Ann what you like and she picks up on it right off."

"What're you sayin'?" Cronski asked, new rage building. "That better not be my old lady you're talkin' about."

"She *is* a juicer. though," Wink continued.

"Really," Doakes agreed. "I didn't know she drank until I saw her sober."

"Listen up, now, motherfucker," Cronski said, his voice rising. "You best. . ."

"You know that ol' Betty Ann is AC-DC, Jeet?" Wink went on, ignoring Cronski.

"That's cool. I got me an adapter. It's that she goes down on all them Cuban shrimpers that bothers me some."

"It's not like they try to take advantage of her, Jeet Point of fact, every time you try to get up, she pushes you right back down."

"You're about to get your hair mussed, boy," Cronski warned.

"Whatever's right," Wink calmly replied.

"Dumber'n a clam sometimes," Doakes persisted.

"Betty Ann keeps goin' to the laundromat and forgettin' what she's there for."

"Not in the sack, she don't," Wink replied. "Let's be fair."

"That's a fact," Doakes said. "Guy was tellin' me a couple nights ago at the Frog that she got him off so many times it felt like a flock of doves flyin' out his asshole."

Doakes turned to Cronski as if he had only now noticed him. "Big black buck nigger, he was."

Cronski bawled like a heifer and hurled himself across the table at Doakes, who twisted away. Cronski kept on going, right into the cement-block wall. His head made a pulpy sound on impact, and he dropped to the floor, taking table and glasses with him. Doakes had his foot poised over Cronski's neck when the security guard ran onto the porch, his hand on his holster.

Wink looked down at Cronski, who was not moving. "Allie never did care for black folks," he explained to Lichine. "Ever since he went to Haiti and they made him ride in the back of the bus."

A shaken Lichine left the lounge as soon as seemed practicable. The propensity for casual violence that he sensed in these men had finally shown itself, apparently ignited by no greater stimulus than boredom. But in fact, the origins of this seemingly random episode dated back two years, and neither Wink nor Doakes felt that their revenge was complete.

They were running on a northeasterly course, cutting diagonally across the Stream toward Little Bahama Bank. Doakes, at the wheel, squinted into the starlit, moonless dark.

"What kinda boat we lookin' for?" he asked Wink, who was standing beside him. "Longliner? Shrimper? Yacht? What?"

"Man didn't say. All he told me was to keep on this heading until we got a call on channel six on the CB. We answer on twelve, he comes back on eighteen, and so on, by sixes, until we run out, when we go back to the start. I expect he's got a plane up there coordinating the whole thing. Take it easy. It'll go down okay."

"I ain't never done this before. And I can't hardly see nothin' with the lights off."

"I don't make a habit of it, either. Just comfort yourself with thoughts of eighty thousand dollars for one night's work. Keep you in blow and fluff all the way to Saturday."

At midnight, someone came on the radio. "Mojo, this is Denise. Got your ears on?"

"That's us," Wink said, reaching for the microphone. "Denise, this is Mojo. Come back."

"Mojo, correct oh-four degrees north. You'll be meeting your party in about fifteen minutes. Out."

Soon, the mother ship loomed, blotting out the stars at the horizon. It was a low-lying coastal freighter of perhaps 120 feet. Doakes dropped the engines to neutral and let the current carry their boat to within a few yards of the rust-streaked patchy black hull.

"Stand off!" barked a voice from the railing twenty feet above the waterline. A flashlight beam swept over the sportfisherman and settled on the bridge. "What's your business?"

"Put that fuckin' light out!" Doakes bellowed.

"Easy, Jeet," Wink whispered. "We got half-a-dozen guns on us."

He held up the torn half of a Bahamian five-dollar note. A stone wrapped in the corresponding half fell to the cockpit, and the light was extinguished. They were plunged into darkness, left with only the rise and fall of the boat and the pervasive aroma of raw canabis.

"Get a contact high just standing here," Wink murmured.

Immediately, pillow-shaped bales wrapped in burlap began thudding on the deck. Wink went down and started carrying them into the cabin. Doakes remained at the helm, keeping as close to the ship as he dared.

They had stripped the forward cabins, galley, and salon of every movable piece of furniture and equipment. Wink worked quickly, shoving the fifty-pound bales into every available space. In less than an hour, the boat was packed floor to ceiling. One last bundle hit the deck, and the disembodied voice from ship told them that was it.

"Move out! Now!"

Doakes threw the throttles forward. Wink had drawn all the curtains in the salon. He closed the sliding door, concealing what he calculated to be three thousand pounds of marijuana. He struggled up the ladder, sweat-soaked, covered with dust, exhausted.

"What is it, you think?" Doakes asked.

"What we got, good buddy, is about one million dollars' worth of Jamaican ganga."

"Not Colombian?" Doakes sounded disappointed.

"We're selling it, not smoking it. But if the man's fair with us, our labors will be amply compensated. Say one hundred thousand dollars?"

They slapped hands in delight, but quickly sobered as the adrenalin drained away. The mother ship was out of sight.

"This wasn't the hard part," Doakes said.

"Easy for you to say," Wink replied, sprawling on the bench.

"What about that last bale?"

"Couldn't fit it in."

"Well, was you fixin' on leavin' it there?"

"Just waiting until we were out from under those guns. They wouldn't have been too pleasured by me dumping right there. Now if I can get up, I'm gonna go down, take us a sample, roll a couple of Texas joints, and heave the rest. That suit you, Cap'n Jellynose, sir?"

By the time they could pick out the lights of West Palm Beach, Denise had given and retracted three sets of instructions on their rendezvous. With dawn nearing, they were considering jettisoning the cargo. Denise called with directions to an area slightly north of Fort Lauderdale. The destination proved to be a canal bisecting an expensive residential neighborhood, lined on both sides with runabouts and small cabin cruisers. Their big boat was incongruously out of place. Two men were waiting behind the fifth house on the left.

Both of them stood. "Mojo?" asked one.

"Denise?" Wink replied.

"He sent us. Truck's on the side of the house. Let's get it loaded up."

They started walking away.

"Hold up," Doakes warned.

The men turned. "Yeah?"

"Money first."

"No way, man. In the truck. Then the money."

"Ain't no way to do." Doakes glanced at Wink, who shrugged. "How 'bout a hand, then?"

"We're drivers, not haulers."

Doakes watched their retreating backs. He was about to protest, but a light went on in the house next door.

"Town's waking up, Jeet. Let's get it done."

Sweating and grunting, they transported the bales across the springy lawn, past the screened Florida room, into the open truck. The drivers watched from either side of the rear door. There was no conversation. A half hour passed.

"How much more?" asked the first driver when Doakes was laboring up the slope with the fifty-ninth bale. "Other guy's gettin' the last one."

The second driver stepped quickly behind Doakes and pressed something hard against his back.

"Then you keep right on walkin', asshole," he snarled. "You're all ours."

Wink didn't see the gun, but he knew something was wrong as he watched the three figures. He slipped silently over the transom and stroked under water to the opposite side of the canal, emerging in the space between the seawall and the cruiser moored there. There was a commotion on the lawn. Lights flicked on in adjacent houses. Wink submerged again and swam to the next boat, and the next.

Doakes was driven in an unmarked car to a building in downtown Fort Lauderdale and thrust into an unfurnished, windowless room. Another man was sitting on the floor, his back against the wall.

"You too?" asked Allie Cronski, captain of the *Zodiac Arrest.*

Wink escaped. Cronski was released. Jeeter Doakes was sentenced to twelve months at the minimum-security facility at Eglund, in the Panhandle.

On the first day out of Morgan Cay, the wind had been out of the south. The anglers and crews believed that this sparked a compulsion in the bluefin tuna to resume their migration north. On the second day, the wind was from the east, cutting at right angles across the current. This condition, the participants concurred, confused the fish and sent them into deep or erratic swimming patterns. The radios, which had crackled constantly with calls about sightings, strikes, and landings on Monday, were quiet

Pia was riding in the tower with Fowler on *Adroit.* She was tired from resisting the endless motion of the platform. And she was bored. There had been a sand-colored saber-tooth barracuda to watch, and a huge sea turtle floating on the surface and sunning itself, but nothing else except the flying fish, which were no longer novel.

Fowler was irritable, his replies to her questions reduced to monosyllables.

"You need a break," she tried.

"No, I don't," he snapped. "What I need's a fish. Ain't seen two all mornin'."

"It could be worse."

"Not much."

The platform bucked and heeled and Fowler kept squinting at the water. You had to look into it, he had told her, not at the surface. The strain showed. Pia decided to go below, asking if she could bring him something. He didn't answer.

Even Triga had deserted his post. He was in the salon, making calls on the radio. Timmins was in the galley, assembling sandwiches. Steve Grubbs was rigging baits.

Pia watched him awhile, then asked, "Why do you take out the backbone?"

"Makes 'em wiggle in the water. Look more alive," he answered pleasantly. "Figured I'd get a few ahead. Don't look like we're goin' to use many today."

"Doesn't this inaction get you down?"

"Not really. I've seen it be quiet like this for hours," he said, "when all of a sudden, it really got dull."

"I just said that to Pat, even though I didn't know whether it could get worse. What might happen?"

"Could go dead-calm. Then we wouldn't even see the few we have. Or we could get a high wind from the north."

"Which does what?"

"Sets up what us nautical folks call a 'hobgobly' condition. Wind blows counter to the current. The seas start goin' every which way, mostly about twenty feet straight up. Makes it hard to hang on, let alone spot tuna."

"I think I'll stay home that day."

"Might have that tomorrow," he said, raising his eyes to watch the scudding clouds. "Good thing it's a lay day."

"Steve?"

"Yes, ma'am?"

"Pia. Tell me something. What is there in this for you? Where are the kicks?"

"For me?"

"You, or any of you, for that matter."

He cut open another mackerel. "Well, for the captain, it's the stalking, the hunt. Most kinds of deep-sea game fish, he just takes the boat out where they're supposed to be and hopes they are. Giant tuna, though, he has to find. Has to get actual sight of them, lock in, and put the bait over 'em'. He's like an African safari hunter. It isn't the killing that's kicks, it's the stalk. For the first mate, the biggest boot is grabbin' the wire on a green fish."

" 'Green'?"

"One that still has a lot of fight in him. Happens a lot with an angler as good as Triga, 'cause he gets 'em in so fast. When you take hold of that wire, you got to do it perfect. If you don't, the leader can break or you can lose your hand or even wind up in the water with a very mad fish four times as big as you."

"And Mr. Triga?" Pia glanced into the salon. Triga was still on the radio. Through the closed glass door, she heard him shout "Bel Air, operator! Bel Air! In California!"

"For him," Grubbs said, "I don't know. All he gets is just plain hard work. Testing himself, I guess. Maybe putting a little conflict in a life that doesn't have much. Suppose we all need that some. I'm here, and God knows I should have had enough."

"How's that? Where are you from?"

"Indiana, by way of Danang. Tractors and helicopters."

Timmins came out with sandwiches. Triga followed. Pia went inside, and was soon asleep on the couch.

The principal gathering that night was aboard *Brain Soup*. Lichine had left for dinner with the other anglers. Wink chopped three grams of cocaine on a mirror setup on an upper bunk of the crew cabin.

"Go take a look at yourself, Jeet," he said when he came out into the salon. "You look like your dick's draggin'."

"How long you been holdin', mother?" said Doakes, charging off through the galley. "Day like this, I could of used a couple dozen toots."

"Things go better with coke," Wink said after him.

"You have a bad day?" Fowler asked.

"We've had better," Wink replied. "Tuna were spooky and fading the whole time. All we saw was one at a time. No schools. Soon's Jeet'd turn the boat, he'd lose the fish in the sun. We'd bait 'em, but not raise strike one. You?"

"Same. Hung one about four-thirty. Pulled the hook before Triga took three cranks. It was a rat, anyway."

Doakes came back. Grubbs and Timmins walked in from the cockpit.

"It snowing yet?" said Grubbs.

Wink pointed forward. "Assuming Jellynose left any."

"Didn't no one catch nothin'?" Doakes asked as he chewed the top off a can of beer.

"They got a little bitty tab on the top there that opens it up, Jeet," Wink said.

"My finger don't fit."

"*Redemption* hung one just before five," Fowler said.

"They ain't back yet?"

"Marker's still fightin' it, last time I heard."

"That's a downer," Doakes said. "Don't look like we ever gonna get out from under."

"Doesn't sound like you, Jeet," Wink said. "Go take another hit."

"I will, but that won't do it. All we got us is a cherry New York Jew, a piss-poor boat, and about six months bad luck ahead."

"Is Lichine Jewish?" asked Grubbs, who was returning to the salon.

"He's from New York, ain't he?" said Doakes, tearing open another beer.

"Your logic is unassailable, Jeet," Wink said. "Not that it matters any, but I think he's Presbyterian."

"Well." said Doakes, "it's one of those."

When the cocaine was gone, they decided to go to the Visitors and Staff Lounge. They were walking beneath the palm trees lining the boat basin when Wink asked where Pia was.

" 'Fraid she's a little unhappy with me," Fowler replied. "Seems I wasn't too polite on the boat today."

"Told me she was going back to the *Aphrodite*," Grubbs said.

"Hey now, Hook," said Doakes, "how're you'n' The Snapper gettin' on?"

"Say what?" Fowler froze.

"You'n Pia," Doakes said, heedless of Wink's cautionary signal and of Fowler's stunned expression. "Let me tell you, bubba, I would purely love to take a header into that sweet thing. It is in-fuckin-credible what she does with that. . ."

Wink caught Fowler by the bicep. "Jeeter," he said, "why don't you get on up to the Lounge? We'll be along."

Doakes raised his eyebrows, shrugged, and walked off.

Fowler whirled on his nephew. "Why'd you stop me? Ain't no way I'm lettin' Doakes come down like that!"

"Let it go, Pat." Wink looked pained. "Jeet didn't mean anything. You know how he runs off at. . ."

"The 'Snapper'? What'd that signify?" Fowler started off after Doakes, but Wink stayed him again.

"Please, Pat. Don't push it. You don't know what. . . "

"You tell me, then," Fowler said, his anger building. "Right now. What'd he. . ."

"Don't ask."

"I am askin'. Now."

Wink searched Fowler's face, then his eyes slewed away, off into the shadows. The palm leaves ticked together in the scurrying puffs of air.

"Wink."

"Pat, don't make me."

Fowler stepped closer.

"Okay, Pat. She used to work at a club out by the Palmetto Expressway in Miami. Near the airport?"

"I know it," Fowler said impatiently. "A topless joint. So?"

"You ever go in there?"

"No."

"Pia was a dancer." Wink concentrated on a spot on the ground.

"That's it? She danced without a shirt?"

"That's it. Nothing more to it."

"There's more. What's that shit about 'The Snapper'?"

"Christ, Pat." Wink sighed, then spoke very quickly.

"She wasn't just topless, she was naked. And she didn't just dance, she had specialities. There's this low narrow bar around the dance floor, raised up so the customers' heads are about knee high to the girls. Pia would stand in front of them, put two beer cans end-to-end between her legs and crush them flat with just her thighs. Or she'd pick up folded dollar bills from the bar with her . . . without her hands. Or. . ."

"And that's it?" Fowler said, almost inaudibly. He knew it wasn't.

"No. There was a room in back. She'd pick out a dude every set, come off the dance floor and rub herself over him, and they'd go to the room."

Fowler expelled his breath and dropped his head back, staring unseeing at the sky.

"The club is where I met her, Pat. That's how come she was at my place that night. At first, I thought you knew about her. Then I wasn't sure, but didn't figure it was my place to say anything. Pat, it doesn't matter, you know that. We aren't any of us. . ."

Fowler didn't hear the last words. He was running down the shell path toward *Aphrodite.*

17

Lichine was on his way to Blackbeard's Table for lunch the next day, when he saw Wink and Pia Cipolla. They were off to one side of the customs shed. Wink was talking animatedly. Lichine was too far away to hear, but as Pia was shaking her head vigorously and often, it was clear that she was not being persuaded. Theo Marker was propped against the wall of the shed, preumably awaiting a delivery on the seaplane that was due in fifteen minutes. He was listening to the conversation, and pretending he wasn't.

Eventually, Pia turned away and Wink accepted defeat. He walked quickly away, toward Lichine.

"Problems?" Lichine said as Wink neared.

"Yeah, problems," Wink said unhappily. "My uncle has chicken fat between his ears. He's running Pia off, like he does to anyone who's any good for him. I'm going to find Pat and see if I can get him over here before she gets on that plane."

Lichine watched his mate hurry off.

Back at the shed, Pia was talking now to Theo Marker. Lichine hadn't realized they knew each other.

Catherine was waiting in the restaurant. Monty Childs was with her, Lichine was surprised to see. He remained baffied that people who clearly disliked each other continually placed themselves in such proximity, as did Cronski and Jeeter the night before. He took a seat and asked about Cronski's condition.

"Looks like death," she said, "but he didn't miss a beat out there today."

"They all have granite up there, anyway," said Childs, tapping his head. "Take them off their boats and they'd starve to death in a year."

"Ah, yes," said Catherine wearily, "it is tedious, having to deal with the nether classes. They are so like children. But it is our duty to nurture them, don't you think, Monty dear?"

"Okay, Cat, leave off," Childs replied. "I keep forgetting your prior incarnation as a professional bleeding-heart."

Marker bustled over to the table, his safari jacket flapping, his lips thin.

"You look like you were just served papers by your fourth, Theo," Childs said.

"Somethin's goin' down," Marker said with heat, "and I figure someone in this room knows about it. Maybe you, gigolo."

"Like what?" Childs asked."

Marker spun a chair around and straddled it.

"My alternator's gone," he said. "New one just come on the plane. Gonna take half the night to install, if I know Earl. Leak somewhere in the fuel tank. Little one, but we can't find it. Might have to drain it, and let it dry out before we can seal it. Lose a day or more, even if we can do it here."

"So?" Childs stifled a yawn.

"And this," Marker said, reaching into his pocket and slapping a small coil of monofilament on the table. "Cat, Ernie, you look at that end there."

They did, looking back at Marker for clarification. "It's been shaved, ain't it?"

"I don't know," said Lichine. "Why?"

" 'Cause this here's the line that I had that bluefin on yesterday afternoon," Marker replied. "Only it busted, just above the swivel, right as my mate was goin' to wire it."

Catherine examined it more closely. "Might have been shaved," she said.

"Ha!" said the director, smacking the back of his chair with the palm of his hand.

"Surely that could have been accidental," said Lichine. "Say when your mate was rigging the leader."

"By itself, maybe," said Marker.

"Come to think of it," Childs interjected, "I lost my first sailfish in Cozumel the same way."

"Theo," said Catherine, "if you're on the verge of accusations, you're at the wrong table."

The three men followed her gaze. On the far side of the room, the two Trigas were giving their orders to the waiter.

"He's done worse," Marker agreed. "And he wants this thing so bad he can taste it."

"You have no proof," Lichine protested. "Either that these things were deliberate, or that he did it, if they were."

"Didn't have to do it hisself,""Marker replied.

"Meaning conspirators?" Lichine said.

No one answered.

Wink found his uncle sitting on the seawall, dropping pebbles in the water. They talked through the serving hours of the restaurant, and past the cocktail party. They did the same thing after the next day's fishing. Finally, Fowler let himself be persuaded to take the Saturday night plane to Miami.

TOURNAMENT

The last flight from La Guardia arrived at West Palm Beach at 11:36 that night. Laraine Vernon-Childs had declined the champagne and the meal. She wished she had been able to sleep, but that was just as well, she thought, for it made her eyes puffy. If only she weren't so tired. She checked herself in her compact mirror as the cabin attendants urged the coach passengers to remain seated until the plane had come to a complete stop at the terminal.

Not bad, Laraine decided, touching her hair. She tweaked her cheeks and lifted the flesh from her jawline. Three or four more years before Dr. Becker would need to take another couple of tucks. Considering the dreadful month past, with the exposition and its aftermath, not bad at all.

She dropped the compact into her purse and saw the folded mailgram. It wasn't necessary to open it again. She knew the words:

"Darling, I miss you. Please join me Saturday at the apartment in Miami, if only for the weekend. Monty."

Laraine hadn't seen her husband in over a month, what with his tournament and her absolutely frantic schedule in New York. She imagined his expert hands upon her and recalled the incredible smoothness of his skin. It wasn't really fair that she had to practically drown herself in moisturizers and emollients, while he baked in the sun every day and still felt as soft as a baby's bottom. Those thoughts submerged the twinge of doubt about the words in the mailgram, which she had found, at first reading, somehow stilted. But letters and cables and postcards always sounded that way, especially from Monty, the dear love, who never put pen to paper if he could avoid it.

Laraine carried no luggage. There were clothes at the apartment. The doorman recognized her, of course, although she was in residence no more than three weeks a year. She swept past the security desk and its bank of television monitors, her heels clicking and echoing in the marble-lined lobby. In the elevator, she took a final glance at her mirror.

There were only two doors in the entryway on her floor, both leading to nine-room terrace suites. One was hers. And Monty's. She let herself in, gaily calling her husband's name. No answer. She checked all the rooms. He was out, apparently. At first disappointed, she decided that she could put the time to good use. After a careful shower and brushout, she reapplied as little makeup as she dared. Debating three nightgowns, she settled on the wispy slip of apricot silk. Then she arranged herself prettily in the bed, opened a book, and waited.

There was a voice from the front room, jerking Laraine out of half sleep. Then the door opened, and a woman was silhouetted in the hall light. Her blouse was undone and she was pulling it free of the waistband of her jeans. Monty's name trailed from her lips.

Fowler went to all the places they had been together. He drove to West Palm Beach and back to Miami. He forced himself to go into the nightclub where Wink said she worked. Pia hadn't been there for weeks, he was told. He did not look at the dancers when he left. He tried the Frog last. Pia wasn't there, either, and Ginnie the bartender said she wouldn't know her if she did come in. Some boatmen bought drinks for Fowler and pumped him about the tournament. He was not very talkative, so they drifted off.

"Last call, Hook," said Ginnie. It was past three in the morning.

"Bourbon, honey. Put it in a go-cup, okay?"

"Sure." She dawdled. "I'm goin' home soon."

"Thass nice. Sleep tight."

She chewed her gum a moment, but the response she expected didn't come, so she moved down the bar. Pia was nowhere to be found, which meant she didn't want to be. There was no place left to search. She would have to find him, he decided. After she thought about it awhile, Pia would come back.

Ginnie took his money and handed him his drink in a plastic tumbler. Fowler stuffed the change into her shirt pocket, patted her cheek, and walked unsteadily to the door. He was, again, the last customer. Outside, he stretched and yawned. After a moment of disorientation, he remembered where he had parked his car and went in that direction, carefully placing one foot in front of the other. A man watched from the shadows at the end of the row of bushes that concealed the garbage cans at the side of the building. He was very large, with a lantern jaw and shoulder-length hair. As Fowler walked past his waiting place, the man put his fingers to the nubby scab on his right earlobe.

Fowler heard the crunch of gravel behind him, and wheeled. The first blow arrived simultaneously with his recognition of the man in the striped tank top. After that, he was aware of nothing but sharp and unrelenting pain and the eventual welcome darkness that came up behind his eyes.

Every Sunday from seven to nine, the Staff served dinner on the terrace. By the time Lichine finished his first plate and was considering a refill, most of the other Members and Guests were off in the bar or at their bungalows. Theodore Marker was standing in the middle of the dance floor, plates in both hands, looking about. He spotted Lichine and walked to his table.

"Mind?" he said, indicating the empty chair.

"Not at all," said Lichine, without enthusiasm. He wondered where Catherine was.

Marker flicked open his rolled napkin, spilled out the silverware, and attacked his meal with noisy determination.

"Congratulations on your week," said Lichine. After five days in Morgan Cay, Marker had pulled even with Childs and Triga.

"Thanks," Marker said around a mouthful of melon and prosciutto. "Not that it probably matters."

"Oh? Why is that?" Lichine hoped he wasn't in for a confession.

"You stickin'?" Marker asked as he forked chicken between his teeth.

"In the tournament? Of course." Lichine thought about that, and decided to tell the truth. "Actually, I was thinking about dropping out if I haven't improved my position by the end of this week."

"Don't."

"Pardon?"

Marker threw his knife and fork down. "Shit. I gotta tell someone."

"Tell what?" Lichine asked. Catherine was an hour late.

"I feel like I'm watchin' my ex-wives go over a cliff in my new Maserati," Marker said as he stuffed a roll into his mouth. "Mixed feelin's. What it is, Ernie, is it looks like I'm about to get somethin' I wanted more'n anything. And it happens at the same time I'm startin' to close in on Triga and your lady friend."

"I don't believe I. . ."

"Ernie, there's a property I been wantin' to film. Didn't think I'd get it." Marker consumed half a martini.

"Got a call from my agent this mornin'. Said I'm a nose away from breakin' the tape."

"That's good news."

"Yeah. Then again, it ain't. 'Cause now I figure I got a shot at this here five-million pot, too."

"Really?"

"Don't look so surprised, Ernie. You 'n' me been tusslin' for last place, but we just improved our positions."

"Oh? How?"

"You ain't heard?" Marker studied Lichine's face to be certain.

"Heard?"

"Monty Childs is out of the contest."

"Really?" said Lichine. Marker had his attention. "Why?"

"Bound to happen sooner or later. Just did." Marker started eating again. "His old lady found him out. No one knows who the broad was. Shit, Childs prob'ly don't know who she was. Anyway, Laraine or whatever her name is has cut him off flat. No more bucks, no more broads, no more fishin', no more nothin'. This was one time too many."

"Can she do that?"

"Bet your ass. Monty ain't got no money. It's all hers. He fucks her, she pays. That's how he makes his livin'. Right now, he's up to New York kissin' her feet He won't be back." Marker shoveled artichoke hearts into his mouth. "As of next Saturday," he said around them, "I might hafta split, too. If so, that moves you up to third, baby."

Catherine was stalling. She paced the fantail of *Aphrodite*, thirty minutes late for her dinner with Lichine. A dozen times since the night Ernest returned to Cozumel, he had begun labored protestations of his feelings for her. On each occasion, Catherine had deflected him, with a touch or a joke or a statement calculated to violate his sense of propriety. But she was running out of diversions and he was growing more determined. Tonight, she was certain, he would not be denied. And Catherine was not prepared to respond to any such dec!arations. She just wasn't.

James Thackeray Nettles hired Catherine two days after her graduation from Barnard. It was a buoyantly idealistic time. The first President born in this century was in the sixth month of his first term, and he was persuading his countrymen that change was possible. Even Catherine, a surface cynic and emotional utopian, was convinced. And James was part of it. His paramount failing was an inability to turn away the representatives of any worthy cause. Late one night, weeks after her employment, Catherine counted. James Thackeray was serving on fifty-six committees, boards, and commissions at that moment, all but two involved with education, race relations, low-income housing, and international cooperation. Catherine's function was to keep it all sorted out. She made certain that he was not scheduled to speak in Spokane the same night he was in conference in Atlanta, and checked out the legitimacy of the organizations scrabbling for his attention. Catherine was with him five days a week, then six, then seven, and finally, nearly every waking hour. She relished every moment.

Catherine was never able to construct a succinct one-phrase description of her duties or her employer. People knew that James Nettles had money, a lot of it. But that wasn't what he was. It was in his family, generations of it. With hardly a thought, he quadrupled his share. Somewhere on the way to becoming vastly wealthy, he decided he bore responsibilities. Altruism, it was. James could be a little pompous about it, in an offhanded, patrician way. When she pressed him on why he did what he did, he sucked reflectively on his pipe a long time before answering. It was an idea, he said, that because he didn't have to scratch for a living, he was free to do things that needed doing. It had taken him forty-five years to recognize that duty. Service to others, he continued, is the only true satisfaction. He said it just that one time. Despite her devotion to him, she could not resist the observation that the road to perdition is paved with diabetic Teddy bears.

They were in Washington one of many times. James was invited to a dinner kicking off a Presidential Commission on Hunger, ruefully conceding the inherent contradiction. Only two hours before, James told Catherine she was to accompany him. He was bewildered by her reaction and then amused by her complaint that she had nothing to wear. On top of that, she said, he didn't even drive. How were they to get there? Rent a car, he said. Pick me up at the house in Georgetown. He went off in an unconcerned wreath of fragrant smoke. Somehow, Catherine managed. The night-desk man at her hotel braced at the mention of James Thackeray Nettles and promised to arrange appropriate transportation. Catherine found a chambermaid and bribed her into ironing a wholly unsatisfactory dress. By the time Catherine was behind the wheel of a twenty-foot Chrysler Imperial, her mother's ocelot jacket over her shoulders, she was no more collected. But her anxiety was transformed to delighted expectation. Tonight, she might meet the President. Actually hear him speak, even touch him!

She stopped at a traffic light at the comer of M Street and Wisconsin. Before she was able to react, a man - a boy - opened the door and got in the car. He put his arm around her and pressed the point of a knife into the gap of the ocelot jacket and told her to drive to a certain place. Rock Creek Park. Three of his friends were there. They were oddly solicitous, until she refused to remove her clothes.

Fowler kept his eyes closed. First, he moved his fingers. One. At. A. Time. Even the stubs worked. Then his toes. Then he raised a whole hand. That didn't hurt too badly, so he lifted the forearm. That did, so he stopped awhile. The right side of his face was warm. He turned his head in the other direction, and that made him gasp.

The sheets felt clean, ironed. There was a smell like his grandmother's house the day she died. He raised his right eyelid, just a bit. There were legs. Three of them. No, make that four.

"I hope he doesn't say it," said Wink.

"Where my?" Fowler managed.

"He said it."

"Watch?" This was taking a very long time.

"No, he didn't," said a woman's voice. "He wants to know where his watch and money are."

He felt a cool hand on his.

"They're here," said the voice. "He didn't take them."

"Nurse?"

"No, Pat."

"Don make guess."

"Try the other eye, Pat," said Wink. "It'll work better."

He did, and it really was Pia. It was not a good idea to grin. It made a warm salty taste.

"Hospittle?" he asked. His voice cracked.

"Gets sharper by the minute," said Wink.. "Sunday week, he ought to be running off whole sentences."

"Hush," said Pia.

"Hurt bad?" said Fowler.

"You ain't hurt good, Pat. A mouse big as a grapefruit, balls like watermelons, bruises the color of prunes. Maybe cracked ribs. You are a fruit salad. But the fuzzy-cheeked doc here expects you to live long enough to arrange for death by cirrhosis of the liver."

"How get here?"

"That's three. Outasight, Uncle. Pia called us in Morgan Cay. Ernie let us come over in the boat. Steve and Chuck are outside."

There was something right there that Fowler couldn't grasp, but he didn't try too hard.

"Looked ev'where," he said, turning his hand over to hold hers. "Found ev'one. 'cept you."

"It's all right now, Pat," she said. "Why don't you try to go back to sleep?"

"Wan'ed tell you. I wrong. Didin mean what said. Don care 'bout 'fore."

"Guess my presence isn't required," said Wink. Fowler thought his nephew's eyes looked blurry, but it was probably his own.

"Want out."

"You aren't going anywhere for a while, Pat."

"Yes. Am. Now. Tell 'em. Go back t'night."

"No way, Pat. The baby doctor says . . ."

"Where Jeet?"

"He went off to look for someone."

"Not p'lice?"

"Jeet? Police? Not hardly. Said he had in mind dropping in at Rumfeld's. Wanted to look somebody up. Said he can't stand hospitals."

"Get me out, Wink. Go. Please. Want to be back. T'night."

Eventually, Wink left the room to speak with the doctor and arrange payment.

Fowler raised his sheet. "Honey?"

"Pia," she corrected. But with a glance at the other bed, which was empty, she sat next to him, stretched out, pulled the sheet over her, and very carefully, put her arms around him.

Monday morning, all five boats left the docks on schedule, *Crystal Ball* kept on going, though, past Tuna Alley and on toward Florida. The rumor was thus confirmed. Montgomery Childs was out of the tournament.

The fishing was good. The wind was from the south, just heavy enough to galvanize the drifting tuna into resuming their run north.

Adroit baited three schools, and hooked and released one bluefin from each, all before noon. Fowler stayed in the tower through the midday hiatus, spurning offers of food. At three-thirty, he sighted another school. In five minutes, the bait was over it. The rod bounced and its reel whirred. Triga settled into his task.

It didn't go as the others had. The fish took nine hundred feet of line before Triga was able to stop him. He managed a half crank. Another. Then fifty more feet were lost. A half hour. An hour. Another twenty feet, and the reel would be stripped to the spool. Triga tightened the drag beyond the breaking point, raised up, and I pushed back. He recovered inches. A foot. A yard. The radio came to life. The day was ending in five minutes, it said.

By five-thirty, the other boats had returned to dock. *Adroit* remained. Fowler leaned against the console, Timmins guided the chair, Grubbs and the umpire stood ready. It was uncommonly quiet. The angler huffed and grunted, the engines roared and faded as Fowler followed the point where the slanting line entered the water. But no one spoke, and the boat was backing down sea, following the waves rather than pounding against them.

Neither fish nor angler conceded a second of rest, but by six o'clock, the reel was half full.

The rod jounced, and suddenly resistance ended. Triga wound in as fast as he could, but the five men registered dismay, not jubilation. Even before the swivel rose from the water and Grubbs prepared to reach for the leader, they knew what had happened.

The tuna was as large as they thought. It might have exceeded eight hundred pounds when it first swallowed the hook. But no longer. A half-moon of shredded red flesh was all that was left of its belly. The tail was gone, as well as a portion of its back behind the dorsal.

One of the sharks followed the tuna to the surface and lunged and clamped its jaws and shook its head. The men heard the crunch of bone and hide. Other shapes - larger appeared. Triga unhooked the belt, thrust the rod into the side holder, and leaped from the chair.

"Let it lay!" he shouted before he plunged into the salon, heading toward his stateroom. Captain and crew were mesmerized by the furious crimson boil of torn flesh. In less than a minute the tuna was nearly gone, and the sharks turned on each other Fowler snapped out of his trance in time to see Triga burst from the cabin. His neck puffed and purple, Triga began firing the Belgian automatic assault rifle into the whirlpool of swarming gray bodies. An arc of spent cartridges clattered to the deck as he hosed the water immediately offstern. Rows of tiny waterspouts swept over the thrashing mindless predators. When the hammer clacked against the empty chamber, Triga ejected the magazine and fumbled to insert a fresh one. Fowler dropped the eight feet from the bridge to deck and wrested the weapon away. He placed his left palm against the angler's chest and held the gun behind his back. Triga's eyes bulged and his lips drew back, but then he sucked air and stamped back inside.

Fowler flicked on the safety catch and watched with the others as the feeding orgy continued, and as it ended. In five minutes, there was nothing left to see.

"Call the dogs and piss on the fire," Fowler said quietly. "The hunt's over."

"I never seen anything like it," Grubbs said that night in the lounge. "Must of been thirty of 'em. Big, little, makos, tiger, threshers, porbeagles. A hammerhead big as a Jeep. Must of come from all over the Caribbean just to chomp on Triga's tuna. And him looking to wipe out the entire population singlehanded. That was nervous-making, Cappy. People that play with guns like he does, I try to keep a long way out of range."

"I hear you," Fowler agreed. "I never did see how someone can get to be fifty years old, accumulate a couple hunnert million dollars, fish all his life, and still be so fuckin' stupid."

"Ain't that bad," Jeeter Doakes said. "I hate sharks enough I'd like to use a machine gun on 'em myself sometimes."

"Them sharks was just doin' what it is they do," Fowler said. "Like we do what we do."

"Could've been a record, that tuna," said Timmins.

"That ain't what was buggin' Triga," Fowler replied. "What it was, he's still second. That fish wouldn't have changed nothin'."

"I can dig it," Doakes said. "I finally got Lichine to stop crankin' with both hands, we brung in four fish, all in under thirty minutes each, and then *Redemption* comes in with six tuna flags up. That is disheartenin', now."

"You best take care when you go to wire a fish," Wink said to Grubbs. "You screw up, Triga might not take it kindly."

"There's no part of that I don't understand," the mate replied. "I do wish you'd come more'n halfway closer to a joke, though, Wink. Out there today, I saw a man who'd kill more'n fish to win this contest."

Five days later, the social director of the Morgan Cay Club handed two stencils to the mimeograph operator. He wanted two hundred copies run off, he said, collated and stapled by dinnertime.

MORGAN CAY POOP SCOOP
Final Special Edition

The day started out splendiferously for this, the last battle in the Morgan Cay segment of the Sooper Dooper Brobdingnagian Bowl for the World Champeenship of Deep Sea Angling. The seas were under three feet in the lee, up to five outside. No wind to speak of. Mighty T. Marker, doyen of the tinsel set, radioed three tuna by noon. Delucious Cat and Handsome Ho were hangin' in there with two apiece. Newcomer Ernie Lichine (as in "Ma-sheen"), sorrowful to relate, added another bead to his string of goldurnawful luck. Brain Soup threw a prop blade while they were fightin' their first biggie of the day, and is, at this writing, limping back to port. Regrets, Ern.

Pat Fowler of Adroit is recovering swiftly from fearsome injuries inflicted by a cowardly attacker - as yet unidentified - in Miami last weekend. "Cap'n Hook" didn't miss a day on the water. He is what is called, boys and girls, a "pro." Not counting whatever they haul in before five peeyem, the standings for the two weeks in our azure corner of Eden look like this:

Redemption (Marker+Curry). 1026

Adroit (Triga+Fowler). 938

Zodiac Arrest (Nettles+Cronski). 843

Brain Soup (Lichine+Doakes). 797

The triumph of Redemption notwithstanding, the overall standings, counting the earlier segments in West Palm and Cozumel, daub a different picture: Delovely Cat clings seductively to first place, followed by Tenacious Ho Triga, Bulldog Theo, and

Pertinacious Ern. (For reasons before which Yours Truly will draw a discreet curtain, Marvelous Monty Childs decided to withdraw from the fray on Sunday past. Ply me with pina coladas at the limbo bash under the stars at nine tonight, and I might let a hint slip.)

Next stop for the Phabulous Phishcatorial Phoursome off to the sinful Virgins to beard the legendary marlin. Hang one up for your green-eyed reporter, gang!

ST. THOMAS

ATLATIC BLUE MARLIN
(Makaira nigricans ampla)

Many sportsmen feel that the blue combines all the laudable virtues of the billed istiophorids, for it joins great size with the strength of the whites and the spectacular surface combat of the sails. They are known to tailwalk across a football field of water without falling back, an unimaginable display when it is realized that average sizes are from 250 to 400 pounds. It is generally smaller than its Pacific cousin, but this is a relative differential. Together, they are circumglobal in non-Arctic waters. The record Atlantic blue was 1402 pounds, but reports of 2000-plus specimens are not uncommon. Their known range is from Uruguay to Georges Bank and from the Bay of Bistay to Capetown. In their adult form, they are metallic blue up top, shading to a ventral white. Vertical bars normally connect back and stomach, and they pulsate like neon during battle. The spear is semicircular in cross-section, less flat than the broadbill and seemingly longer, due to retarded development of the lower beak. Unlike the others, the dorsal peaks just beyond the forehead and then sweeps down in a low ridge to a point well behind the anal rudder. Females are invariably larger, with the males seldom exceeding 300 pounds. Data about reproduction is spotty, but it seems to take place all year, in one location or another. The blue is carnivorous and favors mollusks, bonito, and even small swordfish.

---THE IAA HANDBOOK

18

Lichine arrived in St. Thomas on the second Thursday in June, four days before the tournament was to resume. In part, this was to escape the office. After the takeover bid, Ernest had demanded that he be involved in all aspects of company operations. Jason Lichine petulantly complied, burying his brother's desk in complaints of distributors and shop stewards, HEW affirmative-action directives, cash-flow statements, computer printouts, and proposed revisions of billing and personnel procedures. Ernest had no option but to work through it all, although the only matter that genuinely provoked his interest was the suit filed by a group of stockholders disgruntled by the loss of the tender offers made in April.

Lichine missed Catherine, Wink, and even Jeeter Doakes. And he was anxious for the next round to begin. But those weren't the reasons. No one was due before Saturday.

His motive for the early arrival was ill defined, and important only to him. From the very first night at the awards dinner, his response to each new person and environment was shaped by the prejudices and past experiences of one or more of the other participants. This distorted his valuations, a fact he found unsettling. Of all the sites to be visited in the course of the contest, St. Thomas was likely to be the most engaging. Cozumel and Morgan Cay were topographically and culturally bland. At those times when the single-minded pursuits of his companions became so narrow and cramped as to bring on claustrophobia, Lichine had no place to run for relief. Fishing, drugs, endless talk, and copulation seemed enough for them. Occasionally, at least, he needed spaces that were not unrelievedly sterile, the touch of stones and wood and mortar that conceded age, the company of people who did not look like him, and encounters with fresh prides and assumptions.

St. Thomas promised all that, and Lichine wanted to form his impressions before they were ground through the mesh of biases of the others.

His preconceptions were satisfied. The Virgins were a jumble of verdant, humpbacked islands often as tall as they were long. The waters surrounding them were, if anything, even more dazzlingly clear and impossibly hued than those of Morgan Cay and Cozumel. He rented a dusty Maverick at the airport and decided to make a leisurely circuit of the island to his hotel. From the map on his lap, he identified Perseverance and Botany and Dorothea Bays. On a ridge overlooking Magens Bay, a broad square of turquoise and sapphire bracketed in creamy foam, he looked northwest to Inner Brass Island, north to Little Hans Lollik and Big Hans Lollik, and beyond, to the two Tobagos. He ignored the man with the decorated burro waiting to rent his presence to photographers, as he did the occasional heap of tin cans and bottles and the hulks of abandoned cars. He preferred to focus upon the effulgence of poinciana, flamboyant, hibiscus, bougainvillea, and crape myrtle. All of these he identified with one of the books heaped on the seat beside him. After a while, driving on the left came naturally and he was alert to the goats that trotted across the road and the trucks that rocked around the curves.

After many stops and detours, he reached his hotel, checked in, unpacked, washed up, and then left again, to spend the evening in Charlotte Amalie. On Palm Passage, one of the shopping alleys between the converted warehouses that lined the waterfront, Lichine bought more books. On Dronningens Gade, called Main Street, he found a small restaurant with dark wood and stained glass and ventured to order kallaloo, souse, and escabeche. He had no idea what any of the dishes were, and was little enlightened when he finished. He was, nevertheless, quite content. He strolled around the town, peeking into doorways from which music came. The rest of that night, and the next day and night, he was alone. He delighted in the accents and people and place names and the sorting out of local customs.

He saw her first, emerging from the corridor at the far end of the corrugated-iron hangar that served as the airline terminal. She was looking about, honey hair bouncing. Searching for him. His heart raced. They trotted toward each other and embraced.

"Again," Catherine said after they kissed. She tugged at his shirt.

As he bent to her mouth, he noticed Pia Cippola standing at a discreet distance, waiting.

"You're holding on very tight," Catherine said, wriggling against him, "and making me very horny."

"Wait'll I start using both lips," he replied.

"Bed, first, I thought," she said.

"Dinner, first."

"Dinner in bed, then."

"Nope. Dinner in a restaurant. My crew's getting in about now. I want to take them out. And I'm not letting you out of my sight."

"In that case," she said, "I will do maddening things to you under the table all night."

"I should certainly hope so."

L'Escargot was not the best choice, under the circumstances. But Lichine was happy to see Wink and Jeeter and Chris Havens, his new second mate. Feeling expansive, be decided that only the most elegant restaurant in St. Thomas would do.

His crew changed on the boat - from soiled tee shirts and jeans to clean tee shirts and jeans. Doakes retained his hat. Lichine wondered if island informality prevailed over dress regulations at L'Escargot. Pia Cippola and Pat Fowler and his mates joined them, similarly attired.

Adroit and *Brain Soup* had made the nearly 1,200-mile run from Palm Beach together. The trip was accomplished straight through, without stops. in less than three days. All the crew members talked swiftly and compulsively. Catherine asked Wink for a black beauty so she could keep up.

They were seated on the glassed-in terrace lounge overlooking the lights of the harbor. Illumination was by candlelight, and a man played the piano and sang obscure Rodgers and Hart tunes. There was a low buzz among the other patrons when the party of nine came in. Tables would be available in a few minutes, said the nervously smiling captain, and would they care to have a drink while they waited?

The captain distributed menus with the drinks. In the comer, a plump, balding man sat with his wife and young daughter. Doakes saluted the girl with his glass.

"How do, sweet taste," he said very loudly.

Lichine cringed.

That little girl ain't yet thirteen, Jeet," said Wink.

"I know that," said Doakes. "Don't I know that? She'll be ready in one more mango season, though."

The captain hovered. "Would m'sieur care to order dinner now?"

"What's your hurry, son?" Doakes said. "We ain't hardly drunk nothin' yet."

"There is no hurry, m'sieur," said the captain. "But fine food requires careful preparation and if you will be good enough to make your selections now, we will. . ."

Doakes shoved the menu at the man without glancing at it.

"Just bring me somethin' that'll make a turd," he said.

"And fill these up again."

The captain recoiled. Catherine drew him aside and ordered for all of them. No one objected. Doakes watched the man walk away, his posture very stiff.

"You dig that'un?" Doakes said in disbelief. "Ain't no part of him ain't queer."

"He's French, Jeeter," said Lichine, his face flaming with embarrassment.

Doakes looked at him. "Same thing."

Things did not improve, but with the repeated rounds of drinks and Catherine's not-very-circumspect caresses, Lichine found that he was able to regard his companions with somewhat less alarm, if not sanguineness. Eventually, they were seated at two adjacent tables. A waiter poured an inch of champagne into Doakes' glass and waited for judgment. Doakes glanced up at him.

"The wine, m'sieur?" prompted the waiter.

"Yeah?" said Doakes, perplexed.

"Would you care to taste it, m'sieur?"

"Why, sure 'nough, honey. Whyn't you say so?"

Doakes snatched the jeroboam from the startled waiter's hands, put it to his lips, and drank. Some of the wine dribbled out of the corner of his mouth and disappeared in his beard. "Damn fuckin' good," he pronounced after handing the bottle back. "Bring some more, honey."

The waiter scuttled away. When the snails came, Doakes sucked them from their shells in less than a minute. Wink asked if he liked them.

"They was okay. Wasn't hardly enough of them to bring up a memory, though."

When the pheasant and the wild rice were delivered, Doakes coated them with a thick layer of black pepper. Lichine watched in disbelief as his captain picked up the bird with his hands and devoured it, bones, gristle, and all. Espresso was served. Doakes poked uncertainly at the demitasse, but drank. It tasted a little like mud, he said, but it wasn't too bad. He asked the waiter for a real cup. The crewmen talked about the trip down, and the relative merits of alternative routes. Doakes liked the brandy, and ordered more as they discussed tactics for blue marlin. At ten o'clock, Horst Triga entered the restaurant. Theo Marker was with him. Lichine was stunned. "I thought Marker was out of this," Wink said.

"So did I," Lichine replied.

The two anglers nodded greetings as they were conducted to a small table on the opposite side of the room.

"Theo overestimated his desirability to the producers, I hear," Catherine said. "They're still wrangling over the director. Some hot young kid with a sure-fire hit just in release is being romanced to take on the project. Theo is not happy."

"So we're back to fourth again," said Doakes. He beckoned the captain.

"M'sieur?"

"Honey," Doakes said, "we gotta split now. We owe you anythin'?"

The captain dropped the check on the table as if it were afire. Lichine paid, adding a grossly extravagant tip.

"Wink," said Doakes, "what you was sayin' on the boat. 'Bout Triga? You still think you're right?"

"Yeah, Jeet."

"Good 'nough for me," Doakes said, standing.

"What was that?" Lichine asked.

"Tell you later," Wink replied.

On the way out, Doakes paused just beyond the table where Triga and Marker were sitting. There was a glass divider etched with Art Nouveau flowers between Doakes and the two anglers. He tapped a stubby finger against the panel. The glass rattled.

Triga looked up, a fork with a dangling oyster poised midway between his plate and his mouth.

Jeeter Doakes made a noise in his throat and propelled a globule of spittle at the glass. Triga's eyes followed its downward flow. He dropped his fork. Doakes wiggled his fingers in farewell.

Doakes insisted on driving. Under other circumstances, Lichine would have been terrified, for the captain was contemptuous of the local expectation that he drive on the left side of the road. Pedestrians and goats and cars scattered before them as they hurtled down the narrow streets of the old capital and then over the dips and curves of the road leading to the eastern end of the island.

But after cocktails, wine, brandy, and the helpless recognition that there was no way Doakes' behavior could be moderated, Lichine found himself giggling and hooting with the others. Poorly rolled cigarettes were passed, and Wink made Doakes slow down as he dipped cocaine from a plastic bag and held the tiny spoon to each nostril of each passenger.

"Shee-it!" said Doakes after inhaling his double ration.

"Now that there is the best stuff to come down the pike since tits!"

"We aim to please," said Wink. "Now will you endeavor to plunk me down 'midst some fluff? Watching Cat 'n' Ernie groping each other is getting me all twitterpated."

"Just keep your dick dry," said Doakes. Without warning, he yanked the wheel and the car left the pavement and landed with a screech of metal on an unlit dirt road Lichine hadn't known was there. After several hundred yards, Doakes propelled the Maverick through an opening in a high chain-link fence, braked, and spun around in a shower of gravel. The car rocked on its springs. Everyone breathed. "We is there," Doakes announced.

They walked past rows of shuttered sheds toward a glow of light and sound at the water's edge. A crudely constructed plywood bar stood at one end of a beached barge. There were metal tables arranged around it, and music came from a jukebox in the restaurant several steps beyond. Fowler and Doakes knew the bartender and waitresses and most of the customers. Lichine whispered to Catherine that they would leave as soon as it was tactful. But they didn't.

At four o'clock in the morning, the bartender wanted to close. The thirteen remaining patrons and two waitresses considered options.

"What it is, Jeet," said Fowler, who was no more drunk than anyone else, "is we oughta go fishin'."

"Question: What is it that professional fishermen do on their day off?" asked Pia, smiling.

"How come we ain't left yet?" said Doakes.

"Ain't no way we're gettin' all these people in one boat," said Fowler from the back seat of the Maverick as they rocketed down the road to the Lagoon Fishing Center.

"How many we got in this car?" said Doakes, veering around a slow-moving pickup. "Whoever's hand that is, I think I'm in love."

"Got twelve in here," said Wink.

"Ain't got no twelve in this car. Ain't possible."

"Is. Do."

"Ain't. Count noses, not tits."

"Oh," said Wink. "Make that nine, then. Honey, shift a tad to the right and I won't inflict myself upon you any further."

"Need another boat," Fowler said. "Is Lyle Scully in here?"

"Yo," said a muffled voice.

"Where's Theo stayin'?"

"Secret Harbor."

"His boat at Lagoon?"

"Yo."

"Jeeter, pull off there."

"You got it."

Theo Marker was not pleased to see them. He told them to go away and shut the door in their faces. He did not lock it, however, so Fowler and Doakes and Wink followed him back through the immense suite to his bed. They flipped back the sheet.

"Gruesome sight," said Doakes, looking down at the naked director. Marker was curled into a ball, attempting to reclaim sleep.

"Like a gray-haired embryo rhesus monkey," Wink agreed.

"Here's his bathin' suit," said Fowler.

He held the flowered briefs open while Wink and Doakes lifted Marker from the bed and guided his legs through the openings. When the director was standing, with Wink and Fowler pulling the bathing suit over his thighs, Marker opened one eye.

"I'll shove my own pecker in there, if you don't mind," he said.

He walked out on wobbly legs, supported between Wink and Doakes. Fowler scooped up his shirt, money clip, and watch as they went out.

"Where we goin'?" Marker asked, resigned.

"T'find Big Mo, Theo," Wink replied cheerfully.

"Need your boat."

"Whyn't you say so? Get me them Topsiders, Hook."

The others were assembled on the dock at the Lagoon Fishing Center. They milled around *Brain Soup* and *Redemption*, which were in adjacent berths.

"Okay, now!" shouted Fowler, clapping his hands. "Less get our act t'gether! We got all the necessaries aboard?"

"We do, Pat," said Chuck Timmins, who appeared to be sober. "Rods, fuel, baits, lures, gaffs. . ."

"Son, I'm about to give up on you. Them's luxuries. How 'bout vodka, Marlboros, beer, bourbon. . ."

"... ice, reefer, Buffett tapes?" Wink added.

"Ain't you got no sense at all, boy?" Fowler shook his head in despair.

"We got them things, too, Pat," said Timmins.

"Why ain't we gone yet?" said Doakes.

"Pick a boat," Fowler told them.

When they sorted themselves out, Pia, the three owners, and their captains and crews were all on the *Redemption.*

"Go skipper the other 'un," Fowler said to Steve Gnibbs. "Ain't nobody on there but bartenders and waitresses."

"Speakin' of which," Wink said, "we require a more equitable distribution of assets. Toss over one of them honeys. The one with the full-up shirt."

"You already got two," said a man from the cockpit of *Brain Soup.*

"Who is that turkey?" Wink asked. No one knew. "They're both taken," he shouted. "Get on over here, honey."

The waitress transferred, giggling, to *Redemption.* When Wink reached to lift her aboard, she jumped into his arms and locked her legs around his waist.

"All right!" he said, nuzzling into her chest. Neither of them let go. Wink walked to the transom with his burden and yelled, "Leave us haul ass outa here!"

"So to speak," said Catherine.

The boats set off down the channel at what Lichine regarded as excessive speed. Catherine put a drink in his hand and sat in his lap. Except for Wink and the waitress, both of whom disappeared into the cabin, everyone was on the bridge. Fowler was at the helm. A finger of mangrove passed on the right. Houses painted ocher, pink, and umber marched up the slope behind the marina. The sea was a rumpled blue blanket. It was, Lichine decided, an in-describably beautiful day.

"Keep them stakes around Sand Cay close to port," Doakes said. "It ain't no more'n five feet here."

"I been here before, Jeet," Fowler replied.

"And stay a hunnert yards off that next 'un."

"It's called Rotto Cay, Jeet."

"Whatever. Watch for them rocks. And why ain't we movin' hardly at all?"

"Watch out, slow down, speed up. Dammit, Jeet, I was drivin' sportsfishermen down here 'fore you stopped wettin' your pants."

"Don't hardly see how you survived. Do what I say, now, and you might make another mile or two."

That continued. As they were rounding Cowpet Head into Current Cut, there was a frantic cry from below.

"Pat! Pat!" Wink was out in the cockpit, shouting up to them.

"What's matter?"

"It's a terrible thing! Send a Mayday!"

"What? What?"

"We are all out of medicinal purposes alcohol!"

"Hang on," Fowler replied. "I will summon us 'sistance." He turned on the radio. "Braaaain Zoobp! BRAAAAin Suuuup!" he warbled into the microphone. "Come BAAA-ck, Braaain Sup. Sooopy, soopy, soo-eee."

"Cap'n Hook is smoked, now," Doakes said. "'Truly a shockin' thing t'witness."

"Bren Zup! Our situation is desperate, y'hear?"

"Get off the air long enough so's I can answer, Cappy," Grubbs interposed. "I can damn near hear you without this thing. What's your problem?"

"*Brain Soup*, we is in terrible need of . . . what was it? Oh, yeah. Grubbsie, you ain't gonna believe it."

"I won't have a chance, you don't say it soon."

"Grubbsie, we is out of medicinal purposes . . ." He groped for a word, gave up. "Medicine."

"Of what specification, Cappy?"

"Of whatever you got extra of, Grubbsie."

"I hear you, Cappy. Pull up alongside here and I'll float a supply over."

While Fowler maneuvered off the stem of *Brain Soup*, Grubbs and the bartender taped two fifths and two six- packs of beer to the inside of a life jacket. They wrapped it with rope and dropped it over the side. With painstaking care, Fowler adjusted to drift and wind, fingers light upon the controls. Wink stood ready, and at the proper moment, gaffed the life jacket and swept it aboard. He bowed to applause.

The boats traversed an erratic path northwest through Pillsbury Sound, then due north to the Drop-Off. At that point, over an hour from the marina, the shallows abruptly plunged six hundred feet into the Puerto Rican Trench. This was where the blue marlin lived.

"Hook," said Marker, his drink slopping, "you know what?"

"No, Theo."

"I got ninety-nine recorded blue marlin as of right this minute."

"That's great, Theo. Fill me up, will you, honey?"

"I caught the first fifty when you was workin' for me."

"I 'member." There was the tingling again.

"Hung number fifty right out here. You 'n' Boots was still with me. That was a night we had."

"It was that, Theo." Fowler drained the glass, but it didn't help.

"It'd be good to get one-oh-oh with you, Pat."

"That it would."

"There ain't been twenty anglers have done that," said Doakes.

"I still got Molly below. I caught most all them others on her." Marker slapped his thighs. "I'm gonna put her out."

"Whatever feels right."

Marker went down the ladder. He missed the last two steps.

"Molly?" Pia asked.

"His lucky rig," Fowler replied. "Some got a lucky hat, or lucky pants. Or lucky pipes, people, watches, shoes. Theo's got him a lucky rod 'n' reel."

"Hemingway use t' rub sprigs of mint on his line, hear," Wink said. "Pass the brownies."

"Know a cat that carries a silver spoon from the 1939 World's Fair everywhere he goes," Doakes said. "Ever since he hung a record white. Mother's so old 'n' weak I don't know how he picks it up."

"I thought you didn't like Marker," Pia said to Fowler.

"We been tight," Fowler answered. "We also had our differences."

"You said you'd tell about that sometime," Wink said.

"These?" Fowler held up his hand and wiggled the two stumps. "A long time back, when I was just startin' as his mate, I lost 'em wirin' a marlin. Spent a lot of time in the hospital. Theo paid for everything, even though he didn't have to. Kept my job open, too."

"And?" Pia prompted.

"That marlin of his?" Fowler said after a pause.

"Number fifty? I backed over it when Boots was wirin' it. Wasn't hardly no thin' left of it. I was drunk. Had been for two weeks. Theo fired me."

Marker was back out on the deck with his rod. He set the butt in the holder and selected a frozen mackerel from the tank. When he had it rigged and in the water, the bait didn't move, so he pulled it out and whacked it very hard against the covering board, several times more than necessary. Back bouncing in the wake, the bait wriggled more satisfactorily.

"You want the line on the 'rigger, Theo?" Fowler called down.

"No matter," the angler replied. "Ain't no reason for the 'riggers 'cept for drop-back. I can still count to ten." He. settled into the chair.

"Take a refill down to the old fart," Fowler said to no one in particular. Pia did it.

"Take a blow while you're there," Wink said. "Crystal's chopped out in the stateroom. And see if that honey with the lungs 'tends to sleep the day away."

"It is time for 'nother distress call, Hook," Doakes said, turning the bottle upside down.

"Speakin' of which, Ernie," Wink said, "if you 'n' Miz Nettles don't leave off what you're doin', I'm gonna start humpin' Jellynose."

Lichine and Catherine straightened up reluctantly. Pia returned to the bridge.

"You believe this, Captain Uncle?" Wink continued. "First night Ernie came to my house, he was so nervous he hugged his feet." Wink grabbed Lichine's shoulder and squeezed. "You remember the questions asked you that night, Ernie?"

Lichine grinned sheepishly. "Yes."

"You come up with answers yet, now you got some sand in your shoes and shook off some that smog?"

"Not sure."

"Ernie, what do you like?"

"Pardon?"

"Pay attention. You like speed, blondes, grass, thighs, redheads, coke, booze, inzies, outsies, what?"

"All of the above."

"Outasight. Now, Ernie, what don't you like?"

"Violence and exercise."

"Ernie, you still got any phobias?"

"One."

"What's that?"

"Fear of widths."

Wink grinned and clapped Lichine on the back of his head. "I told you," he said to Doakes, "that Ernie wasn't just another low-rent tourist. Can't hold it against him he's from New York."

"I allow as how you might be right," Doakes said.

"Mr. Lichine could overcome his upbringin' yet."

"I 'preciate it," said Lichine.

Catherine stood up with a groan. "If I have to listen to one more queasy second of this mawkish male bonding," she announced, "I will downgo and upthrow. Pat, stop down. I want to go swimming."

She pulled her white silk blouse over her head, kicked off her shoes, and pushed off her slacks. Her breasts bobbed as she did this, for she wore nothing underneath. The six others gawked.

"You do have a way 'bout you, Miz Nettles." said Wink. "What was we sayin', Ernie?"

"Hmm?"

"Me too."

"Are you joining me, dear?" Catherine said to Pia. She turned and dove directly from the bridge without waiting for an answer.

Pia stood, shrugged at Fowler, slipped out of her tee shirt and shorts, and followed. The splash jolted the men on the bridge into action. Wink,. Doakes,. and Timmins tore off their shirts and pants. The waitress came out of the cabin, saw what was happening, and joined the others in the water. Fowler picked up the microphone as he stepped out of his jeans.

"*Brain Soup*!" he said, louder than required. "Listen up. Grubbsie! Another infusion is needed. Wrap up another package and toss it over. We is sendin' messengers."

Fowler cut the engines. "Theo, you're up." he shouted before he dived in.

Lichine debated about staying aboard, stalled by a vision of fish with large teeth. He had lied to Wink. Deep water scared him. He emptied the remaining bottle, stripped off his clothes, and jumped in.

Brain Soup hove to about twenty yards away. Grubbs remained at the wheel, but all the others went into the water, one of them carrying another bound life jacket. One of the bottles was opened immediately and passed around. There was a great deal of squealing and splashing.

Right then, there was an accident. A marlin swallowed the bait on Marker's lucky hook.

Marker kicked open the tuna door in the transom while he cranked the reel. The swimmers dragged each other aboard. Somehow, Marker brought the marlin to the side. It was not large, and Wink, still naked, grabbed the leader and snipped it near the hook. The fish drifted away.

Marker was jubilant, and so were the others. They jumped around the cockpit, penises and breasts bouncing, embracing, pumping hands and whooping with delight. Wink went to the crew quarters and ripped a sheet from one of the bunks. Pia found a can of paint and a brush. They spread the sheet and painted a one and two zeros on it. Doakes and Fowler attached it to one of the outriggers.

When the celebrations quieted, Lichine stumbled back to the master stateroom to find a towel. His jaws ached with the residue of laughter. He punched the door open with the flat of his hand.

Pia was facing him. Droplets of water clung to her, glistening in the light of the bedside lamp. She was holding a towel around her hips, just below a thin gold waist chain.

Catherine's sleek tanned back was to the door. Lichine noticed for the first time the tiny downy triangle above the cleft of her buttocks. Catherine twisted her head around at the sound of his entry. He couldn't be sure, but he thought he saw her snatch her hand away from Pia as he entered.

There was a glassy brightness in her eyes he recognized from other moments at other times.

19

The two boats returned as the shadow of the hill behind the marina was reaching across the dock. The crews undertook disorganized housekeeping efforts. Some of the passengers lingered, but after an hour, all had gone off in their own directions. Catherine had left *Aphrodite* in Florida, for there was a favorite hotel on the eastern tip of the island she wanted to share with Lichine.

That now seemed a mistake. She and Lichine had not exchanged a word or touch since he had burst into the stateroom of *Redemption.* Now they found themselves alone in the Maverick. He drove to the hotel following her terse directions. She massaged her throat, but the ache would not go away.

They went about preparations for sleep. When she came out of the shower, he was on the far edge of the bed, facing the wall. She crawled under the sheet and tentatively brushed her lips across his shoulder. He drew away. Catherine rolled over and waited for the yellow pills to take effect.

There was no horn to signal the start of the third round of the tournament, since the four boats were berthed in two different harbors. Instead, Oscar Farrington informed the captains and anglers by radio that they would rendezvous off Water Point at 0800 hours.

The two mates joined Lichine and Doakes on the flybridge as the boats began their run to the Drop-Off. Wink did not look well, Lichine commented.

"Ernie, it is a bitch to know that this is the best I'm gonna feel all day. You, Jeet?"

"Can't hardly say I'm lookin' forward to eight hours trollin'," Doakes replied. "But I've felt worse."

"What speed are we doin' once we get the baits out?" Havens, the new second mate, asked.

"We'll try five to six knots for a while. Nothin' happens, we'll goose it to eight. Good water action today."

"Marker was tellin' me he sometimes trolls on plane."

"That's a crock," Doakes snorted. "You drive the boat that fast, you whip the baits right out of the marlin's mouth."

"If he catches it, though, you got him hung good."

"If I was a duck, I'd fly."

"Do you have advice for me, Captain?" Lichine asked.

"Always," said Wink.

"No, I ain't," Doakes said. "He's been doin' all right. Only Mr. Lichine, don't take an hour to get one of these in, like the tuna. It shouldn't be no problem. Around here, the marlin stay on the surface and most always swim downsea. They jump a lot and tire faster, and you won't have to work so hard. Things go right, there won't be one of them takes more'n thirty minutes to boat."

"Meantime," said Wink, "take it easy. Most of the time, blue marlin fishin' is about as excitin' as watchin' grass grow."

"'Cept when you hang one," said Doakes. "Marlin fishin' is hours of boredom punctuated by minutes of mass confusion," said Havens.

"Now we got all the appropriate cliches out of the way," said Wink, "let's talk about existential self-determination."

"Say what?" Doakes asked.

"About pussy, then."

The radio came on and Oscar Farrington said there were five minutes to countdown. Lichine went below for coffee. He lingered in the salon, surveying the inset panels of direction- and depth-finding equipment, transceivers, tape decks, television controls. Twenty thousand dollars worth of electronics. He was, he mused, an affluent child of the late twentieth century engaged in a prehistoric struggle for survival transformed through high technology into blood sport. Lichine wondered if he cared anymore.

After that weekend, the renewal of the tournament itself was bound to seem anticlimactic for most of the crews and anglers. All were grimly mechanical at their chores and the exuberance that normally marked the releasing or boating of a big fish approached indifference. At the end of the day, each boat flew two marlin flags. Nothing was changed. That night, even Wink and Doakes turned in early, and unaccompanied. Lichine and Catherine undertook a single act of mute, perfunctory sex and fell asleep on opposite sides of the bed. Fowler was snoring when Pia came out of their bathroom, a burning cigarette in one hand, a half-empty glass in the other. Theo Marker tried to concentrate on the script his agent had sent, but turned off the light when he realized he was reading the same line of dialogue for the fourth time. Only Horst Triga remained awake. He dismissed Duncan for the night after the steward had decanted the '58 Fonseca and poured the first glass. Then Triga put through another call to the number in Bel Air.

It was agreed at the owners' meeting Tuesday evening to switch the Wednesday lay day to Saturday. Triga initiated the suggestion, but did not profit from it. One of *Adroit's* generators malfunctioned on the way out and the boat had to return to port for repairs. He lost the day. Lichine and Marker, on the other hand, caught four marlin apiece. Since *Zodiac Arrest* failed to exploit the few strikes it had, the gap between frontrunners and followers narrowed. Thursday, Marker brought to the dock the only marlin captured by any of the boats.

"Need the towel?" Lichine asked.

Catherine, lighting a cigarette, shook her head. He balled it up and threw it in the direction of the bathroom. They reached simultaneously for the snifters on the end tables.

"That was better," she said, remaining on her back but moving closer to him.

"Yes." He kept his arms at his sides.

They sipped. He drew the sheet up to his chest. She expelled a plume of smoke and watched it drift to the ceiling. They listened to the palms dithering in the breeze beyond the open window.

"Catherine. . ." he said after a long moment.

She made a languid sound of curiosity, but he felt the tensing of her arm, her leg.

"I was wondering. . ." he said. He stopped. They had formulated a tacit truce, built of carefully considered teasings, scraps of affectionate murmurs, and no questions. It was too soon to test it, too few days since that moment in the stateroom of *Redemption*. But it was too late.

"Yes?" she prompted. Even-toned, guarded, with a trace of challenge.

"Nothing really," he said. What he was about to say was trivial, but it would lead to what was not. "Just. . .those pills in the bathroom. Are they for anything special?"

"No," she said, making a noise like the first syllable of a chuckle. "I am not about to expire of a rare, unnamed disease."

"Truly?"

"Yes, dear, truly."

"Then what are they for?"

She puffed her cheeks and let the air out with a breathy pop. "What they are for," she said, "is to make me work the way I want to when I want to."

"What does that mean? What are they?"

"Pertinacious Ern," she said. "That pooper scooper in Morgan Cay didn't know how close he came. The yellow ones, my persistent love, are mild Valiums. The blues are strong Valium. The whites are Quaaludes. The blacks are biphetamines, known as 'beauties.' The ones with brown tops that look like cold capsules are Dexedrine. The greenies are something like the brownies, only weaker. The pinks are. . ."

"Catherine! What do you need all those for?"

"To get my heart started in the morning. To make myself strong. To get mellow. To sleep. To get horny."

"It's dangerous, all that. I don't see why you have to. . ."

"I know you don't, but take a good look." She threw off the sheet

"You are beautiful," he said, glancing at her. "What does that have to do with what we're talking about?"

"Christ!" she said, and bounded off the bed. She came around to his side and raised the lampshade so the light fell on her as she stood inches away. "Look!" she commanded.

"Catherine, you are the loveliest woman I have ever known or ever expect to know," he said, very conscious of the swellings and concavities of her.

She hit the lampshade and he lunged for it, too late. It hit the wall and fell to the floor, carrying base and bulb with it.

"I am something else, if you'll just open your eyes," she said. "Look Herel And here, and here." She pointed at the comers of her eyes, the backs of her hands, beneath her buttocks.

He was baffled. He turned up his palms. "What?" he said.

"I am," she said, hands on hips and legs apart, "your very basic older woman."

Ernest did the wrong thing. He laughed. It was in disbelief, not mockery, but that didn't matter. She ran to the bathroom.

"Catherine, for heaven's sake," he called, swinging his feet to the floor.

She came out, carrying her overnight case. She tore it open and emptied the contents. Bottles and tubes and jars cascaded over him. He splayed his fingers over his crotch.

"And those," she said, "are some of the things that hold me together. Those, and the pills, and four weeks a year on a fat farm, and hairdressers, and two hours of situps and jogging every day, and. . ."

"I've never seen you do exercises," he said irrelevantly. "And what's all this about age? Two or three years, maybe."

"My dear sweet innocent," she said, clipping off each word. "You are twenty-eight. I am forty."

"I don't believe it," he said, and he didn't.

"Take a good look at yourself, then, if not at me," she went on. "Right about now in your life, you are noticing the first few tiny signs. You can't run as far or as fast as you used to, and you get out of breath a little sooner. Nothing much, and you can brush it off because you still think of yourself as fifteen. So you've lost half-a-step, what's that? You're young!"

She was pacing, to the window and back. "But, my dear sweet darling, it's just beginning. All of a sudden, you'll be a not-yet-old, but-no-longer-young full-fledged adult. And your flesh will start to sag and your wind will go and you will begin to deteriorate in a dozen little ways that won't disappear like they used to. And before you know it, you'll wake up one day and realize that you have twice as much life behind you as you have up ahead. You'll start to get desperate then. You'll do new things or go to new places or pop pills or dive into a bottle or learn to be vicious or dump your friends or start fucking girls half your age. Or, as you say, 'all of the above.' But you'll do it. All to keep on convincing yourself that you're everything you once were, when you know you aren't."

Catherine halted at the window and gathered a fistful of drape. "And then," she said, so softly he could barely hear, "you'll be as ridiculous a figure as I am."

He should have gone to her then, perhaps. But he was confused and full of his own unarticulated anger. He picked up the lamp and set it in its place. He pulled on his slacks and slipped on his shoes.

"None of that explains," he heard himself saying, "what you were doing with Pia that day, or why."

He found his shirt. Catherine did not move.

"Finally, you get to it," she said.

He filled his pockets with his wallet and change and walked to the door.

"Catherine," he said, stopping. "Do you know that you never used my name?"

There was no quaver in her voice and she did not turn around.

"Really?" she said. "I never really noticed. But it isn't an especially beguiling name, is it, darling?"

As the boat cleared the harbor, Chris Havens went to the bait well and selected two mackerel. He laid the trout-sized baitfish on the cutting board, sliced their bellies open, and gouged out the entrails. Then he inserted a hollow metal tube through each mouth to scoop out the backbones. After throwing the offal over the side, he pushed hooks through the mouths and commenced to sew up the stomachs with waxed twine.

"Is all that necessary?" asked Lichine, trying to take his mind off Catherine.

"This is the easy way," said Havens. "Some guys do a number that wraps up the bait like a Christmas package."

Wink placed the rods in the holders on the sides of the fighting chair. Havens lit a reefer and offered it to Lichine.

"No, thanks."

"Mind if we do?" he asked, passing it to Wink.

Lichine shook his head, the thoughts rushing back.

An hour later at the Drop-Off, the four boats took up their trolling. The mates threw the mackerels in the water and free-spooled until the baits trolled three hundred feet astern. Each line was clipped and run to one of the tips of the two outriggers, which were already in their gull-wing positions at the sides of the boat. This pulled the baits to the surface and out of the wake. The mackerels erupted from beneath the curl of one wave and burrowed into the back of the next.

Burrowing, erupting, burrowing. Lichine settled into the chair to watch, his eyes flicking from one bait to the other. But he couldn't concentrate. He asked if Wink had another reefer.

"How do I do it?" he asked when it was passed to him.

"Just take a long pull, get it down in your lungs, and hold it there as long as you can."

Lichine was grateful that no one laughed when he choked. He tried again, drawing more gently.

Nothing. He didn't know what he expected, but he felt nothing. He puffed again. And once more.

"It isn't a nipple, Ernie," Wink said.

"What?" said Lichine, concentrating on his analysis.

"Etiquette demands that you pass it around."

"What?" said Lichine.

"The joint, Ernie."

"Oh," said Ernie, observing the stub burning to his fingers. "Of course. Here."

Curious, he thought. I don't feel anything. Is that all there is to it?

"It isn't the same every time for everyone," Wink said, and Lichine realized he had spoken aloud.

"Curious," he said again.

Wink was standing next to the fighting chair, his hands resting on the arm.

"Ever think what boundless optimism we have to have?" Lichine mused aloud. "To believe that a good fish is going to pick our pathetic baits out of the millions down there?"

"I don't think about it, no," said Wink. "If I did, I'd be selling shoes for a living. Can I ask you something, Ernie?"

"Sure."

"How often you fished marlin?"

Lichine fixed on the mackerels. It was quite hypnotic, really, watching them dart through the water.

"Ernie?" Wink repeated.

"Never."

Wink digested that information for a moment. He was uncharacteristically speechless.

"You have never. . ."

"No," said Lichine. "Never."

"Like to get this straight," said Wink, as quietly as the roar of the engines permitted. "You got yourself into a contest with four of the top anglers in the entire world for a million-dollar nut . . . and you've never even wet a line for marlin?"

"Sailfish, either," said Lichine. He didn't interrupt his vigil on the mackerels. "I've read about them, though."

"Until this thing started, you have, in fact, never been south of Coney Island," said Wink with intended irony.

"That's right. Not fishing, anyway."

"What about those broadbills, for crissake? Two in one day!"

"I was lucky."

"Lucky?"

"I have done tuna, though," Lichine said. "In Maine."

"Lucky!" Wink said again. He stared at the intent Lichine. Wink's mouth opened and closed, but no words came out.

"Ernie," Wink said at last. "Can I offer a suggestion?"

"Sure."

"Get out of that chair and come sit at the back of the cockpit."

"But the rods. . ."

"If anything happens, Doakes will see it from where he is before either of us. Then when the bait gets taken, you strike the fish from behind the chair. While he's running, you get in the chair, bring over the rod, I strap you in, and you're set."

"I haven't heard of doing it that way."

"It isn't in your books, Ernie. Just trust me."

Lichine did as he was told.

Doakes stamped on the roof. "We've raised one! Right rigger! Get your asses in gear!"

By noon, *Zodiac Arrest* had boated one marlin and released two others. The first mate went to the bridge to raise the third flag.

"You see that bitch?" Carey snarled at Allie Cronski. He gestured down at Catherine, in her fighting chair. "Did you? Ain't nothin' me 'n' Billy have done right since she got on board this mornin', if you listen t' her."

"Don't get on me," Cronski replied, surveying the water ahead. "It ain't my doin'. Just keep thinkin' on the biggest paycheck any of us ever seen."

"Ain't nothin' enough to have to put up with what that cunt is layin' on us," Carey said.

"What's so bad? She's been pretty much okay."

"Next time she gets in that chair and spreads her legs to take the rod, I'm gonna stick it right up her."

"Yeah, yeah," Cronski said. "You're real likely to do that."

"Treats me like some kinda nigger retard. Gets in the chair 'n' sits there like the fuckin' Queen of England while I strap the rod on. Now she even holds her hands up and wiggles her fingers for me to pull her gloves on for her! Ain't no kinda money pays for that."

The clip on the port outrigger snapped.

"Tim!" Catherine yelled.

"Get on it, boy," Cronski said.

It was a big one. After the first flurry of shouts and scrambling, the angler, crew, and umpire of *Zodiac Arrest* settled in for what they anticipated would be a long battle. At one point, Catherine asked Carey to bring her two of the yellow pills in the bottle on the shelf above her bed. "Fetch" was the word she used.

Later, she asked him to bring her hat. And a Coke, which she told him to hold to her lips. All the while, she fought the fish. It had sounded immediately. She had not been able to bring it up, but this did not seem to trouble her.

"Tim," she said, bestowing a beatific smile, "be a dear and get that bottle of suntan oil."

He brought it to her. She glanced down at it.

"Tim, dear, I really am occupied, as you can see." She leaned back and wound in another foot of line. "Be a love and put some of that stuff on me."

Catherine was wearing a bikini. Carey squeezed some lotion into his hand, and hesitated.

"On the shoulders," she said, intent on her work. "Do get on with it. My friend out there is acting as if he plans to keep this up. I don't want to burn to a crisp while he's at it."

Carey applied the lotion to her back, her shoulders, her arms. His irritation was fading beneath his almost painful arousal. When he started to massage a second layer of the cream into her shoulders, she made a throaty sound of approval. Encouraged, he worked his fingers over the collar bones until they nudged the edges of her bra. He paused again.

"Thank you, dear," she said without looking at him. "You can play with my boobs later. Perhaps. Right now both of us must concentrate on that fish. He could be a big one, don't you think? Dear, my legs, would you?"

The digital clock in the cabin read 4:16. *Brain Soup* had yet to register a catch. Only false alarms, thrown hooks, and parted lines.

"Here comes another one. Right 'rigger!"

Lichine jumped for the chair, bracing himself against the lurching deck. Wink was beside him, to his left.

"Leave the rod in the holder, Ernie. Hit him when I tell you."

There wasn't anything to see at first. The mackerel continued skipping and planing. Then there was a shape behind it, darker than the water. It followed the bait for long seconds, then accelerated.

The clip on the outrigger snapped open and a long "U" of line drifted into the water. It straightened. Lichine's rod bowed. The big reel screamed as line was torn from the spindle, ripping through the water.

"Wait. . . wait. . ." said Wink. "Now! Hit him! Hit him!"

Lichine braked the speeding spool and pulled back the rod with a grunt. Wink was furiously retrieving line on the other rod to get it out of the way.

"Again. Ernie! Him again! Again! Okay! Get in the chair!"

Lichine scrambled around and lifted the rod, slamming the butt into the socket between his legs. Doakes throttled down so the boat was nearly dead in the water. The line kept whirling from the reel even though Lichine tightened the drag a little more and struggled to hold the rod back.

Wink strapped the harness across Lichine's lower back, snapping the ends to the reel, then dropped the seat back to its horizontal position.

"You think I got him?" Ernie asked. "Should I strike him again?"

"You got him, Ernie. Let him run."

The slanting line cut to starboard, so Doakes swung the boat to keep the fish astern. Then to port, then back again.

"He's taken five hundred yards," said Lichine, glancing with alarm at the whizzing reel and its disappearing reserve of line.

"He's coming up," said Wink.

The water boiled.

"Here he fuckin' comes!" said Wink.

"Oh, God!" said Lichine.

The fish exploded spear first through the surface in a perpendicular ascent that lasted until even its forked tail was clear of the water. It hung for a long instant at the twenty-foot apogee of its thrust, shaking its massive head in disbelieving rage. Its mouth opened and closed and its body glowed like blue-green neon, throwing off a vast cone of spray. Even a quarter-mile away, Lichine saw the monstrous eye roll back in cold fury.

After that interminable moment, the fish fell back on its side, sending up a wall of water nearly as high as it had jumped. Then it went up again. And again. Five times. Lichine was certain his heart had stopped beating. He prayed that the fish might cast off the hook. Then he prayed that it wouldn't.

There was no more time. With the final catapult and plunge, the fish turned and ran. Line sang from the reel, fading so quickly Lichine was sure it would run out. But Doakes had swung the boat and was following the fish at full speed. Wink turned Lichine's chair to reduce the dangerous angle of the line. Lichine eased the rod back whenever the pressure slackened, cranking the reel on the down thrust, then pulling back. He thought he recovered some line, but couldn't be sure.

Suddenly the fish stopped. Doakes threw the clutches to neutral at Wink's warning. Lichine tightened the drag as much as he dared and pumped.

"Don't jerk it, Ernie. Smooth, smooth. Feel him."

Lichine nodded, his mouth dry, his tongue swollen. He concentrated with more intensity than he had imagined possible. Pull back evenly. Flow into the downdrop, crank steadily. Pull back without yanking.

"Back it up, Jeet," Wink shouted. "Slow, now."

"I have him, Wink," Lichine gasped. "He's coming."

"Maybe, Ernie. Maybe. Just keep working." Wink stood behind Lichine, guiding the chair. His tone was calm.

The rod continued to bend, especially on the upstroke, but not alarmingly. And the pressure of the fish was steady but yielding. Lichine had recovered half the line. Once he saw the erect dorsal of the fish break the surface. It seemed a certain sign that the fish was surrendering.

Lichine glanced at the spool, now three-quarters full. It was almost over. The ache in his shoulders and arms was turning to pain, but it was almost over.

"How big is he, do you think?" Lichine said.

"Go over eight hundred, I'd guess," Wink answered, as if quoting the price of a used car.

"That's good, isn't it? Above average?"

"Real good, Ernie."

"Wink, is it a male?"

"Not likely. They don't get that big. Females get over a thousand pounds. I heard that a longliner pulled in one last year that was over sixteen hundred."

"That's hard to even imagine. What would something like that be? Fourteen, fifteen feet?"

"About that."

"I think he's a male."

"Why?"

"Because I want him to be. It wouldn't be the same otherwise."

Wink smiled. "You don't watch out, the Libbers'll get you."

"There are still some things they can't take away," Lichine replied, immediately wondering what made him say it. He had nearly forgotten Catherine in the excitement.

In the middle of the next upstroke, the rod whipped downward with such force Lichine was almost snatched from the chair. Line ripped away from the spindle and there was nothing he could do but hold on.

"Better ease off the drag, Ernie, or he'll bust the line."

Lichine did that, and watched in despair as he lost the gut-wrenching work of an hour. The fish sounded, heading for the bottom. Doakes slowed the boat, and the line dropped straight down.

"See if you can stop him,"said Wink.

Lichine eased back and managed one half crank. The rod tip quivered, then bounced with four violent jerks, as if the fish were throwing his head from side to side down there in the sunless depths. When that was over, Lichine recovered line. But not much.

The other boats were headed in. A string of six flags with marlin symbols flew from the *Zodiac Arrest* outrigger.

Allie Cronski watched Catherine climb to the bridge. She had changed to shorts and a blouse, which was unbuttoned, rolled up and knotted. Cronski hitched up his pants and concentrated on his course.

"Fantastic day," she said, grasping the handle at the side of the console with one hand, and the back of his swivel chair with the other.

Cronski slipped off the seat and stood. "Sure 'nough was, Miz Nettles," he said. "Few years ago, six blues would of been a record for one day."

"We have five more days to beat that," she said.

Cronski stole a glance at her. Her chin was up, face into the wind, hair snapping about. She was standing in profile to him, but as he watched, she adjusted her position slightly, and the fabric of her blouse bellied back in the wind. She turned her head, slowly, and looked - not down, but directly at him. She made no move to cover herself.

"You've done very well for me," she said, her eyes locked on his. "Five weeks gone, and I still hold the lead."

Cronski tore his eyes away and cleared his throat. "Tobago comin' up," he said.

"Bonus time," he heard her say.

She drew the other side of the blouse back. Then she kneeled on the deck. Put her hands on his hips. Turned him toward her. Reached for his belt buckle.

Chris Havens carried a beer up to Doakes.

"You want something else?" he asked the captain. "A bourbon, maybe?"

"No," he said. "Not until we've boated this mother."

"How big is it, you figure?"

"Six hundred, maybe seven."

"Looked over eight to me."

"It ain't."

"Okay." Havens didn't like to argue, especially with Doakes. "The kid's doin' all right, ain't he?"

"If he stops fightin' hisself harder'n the fish."

Wink told Ernie to start thinking about getting the fish in, because they should boat it before dark. Lichine found that an incredible remark. Just what did Wink think he was trying to do? Wink ignored the heat in Lichine's reply and observed that there was still time.

"Funny," Lichine said, pumping rhythmically. "It's like when you're driving a long way and your instincts take over. You kind of 'come to' when you get where you're going and can't even remember the last hundred miles. You know what I mean?"

"Yeah, Ernie."

"This is like that. I must be doing what I'm supposed to do with this fish because I've still got him, but I haven't been thinking about the mechanics. It seems an eternity since I hung him, but now I can't remember most of it. You know?"

"Yeah."

"What I'm doing is thinking about him. How we're connected now, how we're together, and I don't mean this line. Whatever happens, we're part of each other. Even when it's over."

Talking was taking the breath from him. He stopped. Ordinarily, he would feel awkward admitting such sentiments. Not now. He was sure Wink understood, perhaps even Doakes. He felt a bond with them, too. They were everything he was not, but they were with him, sharing this.

"How're you feeling?" Wink asked.

Lichine took an inventory, ticking off the elements of his condition as if standing outside himself. He was certain he could never again uncurl his fingers. There was no feeling in his arms. Across his back was the contrasting sharpness of a longitudinal welt rubbed raw by the sawing of the harness. His ankles and calves quivered from pushing for leverage against the footrest. His head felt twice its size. The skin on his face was taut with the dried salt of sweat and water. His jaws ached from gritting his teeth, and although Wink kept holding fluids to his lips, his mouth felt like cotton.

"I'd have to feel a whole lot better to die," he said finally.

In unintentional emphasis, he threw up. On the deck, because he couldn't leave the chair. Wink sluiced it away with a bucket of water and then wiped Lichine's mouth. Lichine was aware of Doakes' hulking form at his side.

"Want me to cut it loose, Mr. Lichine?"

"I can't," Lichine heard himself saying. He couldn't believe his own words. Here was his escape, and he was rejecting it.

"Your funeral," Doakes said at length. "Only you got to get it in before dark. That's no time to boat a fish that big, not if we don't have to."

"I almost have him. I can feel it."

"How big, you think?" Wink said to the captain.

"Under seven hundred."

"Fifty says it's over."

"You got it," said Doakes.

"And a hundred says it's over eight," said Wink.

"You're half a twist short of a full wrap," Doakes replied. "We ain't even seen the mother since we hooked him."

"You betting or flapping?"

"You got it."

The reel was half empty, and the fish began to bore toward bottom still another time. Doakes returned to the helm. Lichine responded automatically, waiting for the marlin to exhaust himself. He sagged with a fatigue beyond any he had ever known.

"You want a boost?" Wink asked, holding the silver bullet before Lichine's eyes.

"Anything," Lichine rasped.

Wink held the cartridge to each of the angler's nostrils, depressing the other as Lichine breathed in.

At first, Lichine felt only lightness. Then euphoria. Then certainty he could accomplish anything. He straightened.

"Now I can go till Monday," he said.

"Good. You might have to. That fish is about the meanest I've ever seen."

"No kidding? What time is it?"

"Almost eight-thirty."

"No shit?"

"Ernie, your language."

"No shit, Wink, how long is that?"

"Over four hours, Ernie."

"Isn't that fantastic, Wink? I mean, really?"

"Yeah, Ernie. That's the word I'd pick."

Unexpectedly, the line went slack again, but it wasn't the same as the other times. Lichine cranked as fast as his lifeless arms allowed but he couldn't recover tension.

"Wink!" he cried in dismay. "Have I lost him?"

"No, you haven't. Here he comes!"

The dorsal, high in front then curving low along the back, was plowing through the inky water. Straight at them.

Ten yards away the fish launched itself from the water with its mouth yawning wide as a barrel top and its back glistening and its awesome spear pointing directly at Lichine who was helpless in his chair. At the top of its leap Lichine could see through the mouth and out the flaring gills and the fish came down and the bill penetrated six inches of wood planking with a vicious jolt that sent Wink and Havens sprawling and then the marlin flung its flank against the boat and the bill broke off and the fish fell back into the water. And the hook stayed in its mouth and Lichine kept pumping.

The mates were back on their feet and Doakes put the boat in neutral and came down to the cockpit to get the gaff. Sixty feet away, the fish rolled slowly, its head out of the water and the eye almost spinning in its bony socket. Finally, the swivel connecting leader to line touched the rod tip. Wink reached out and grabbed the leader with gloved hands. He and Havens worked the fish around to starboard and grasped at the dorsal and what was left of the bill. Doakes raised the gaff and sent it home. It was done.

Lichine's legs gave away. Doakes lifted him to his feet and half-carried him to the cabin.

"I can do it. . ." Lichine muttered dreamily.

"You already did, Ernie," said Doakes, laying Lichine on the sofa.

Havens brought a cup of coffee. Wink held it to Lichine's lips because the man couldn't raise his hands.

"A question, Ernie?"

"Umm?"

"How'd you do it? How'd you keep up?"

Lichine was drifting off, but he managed to answer. "I've been resting up for twenty-eight years."

Wink pulled a blanket over him and lit a cigarette.

"C'mon, Jeet, you low-rent mother. I want to get myself around a quart or two of rum. Think you can manage without running us aground?"

Doakes started the engines and ran full bore for port.

20

Lichine awoke an hour later to the abruptly lowered pitch of the engines. The boat was being backed into the dock. After some experimentation, he found he could raise himself by dropping his feet to the floor and rocking into a sitting position. His arms were stiff and unresponsive, and he wasn't sure his legs would work. He waited, breathing deeply, until the lightheadedness passed. Then he stood and shuffled cautiously out into the cockpit.

A three-quarter moon was suspended above the long silver band of its own reflection. Havens was making the stern lines fast, Wink was scrubbing the bait table, and Doakes was dragging the dock hose to the bow to start washing down. Lichine reached the transom. It was three feet high but might as well have been twenty. He could not lift his foot even halfway, nor raise his arm to grasp the handrail Doakes had just locked in place. Lichine stood there helplessly, feeling foolish, until big hands slipped under his arms and lifted him like an infant to the dock.

Doakes pulled over a box and told Lichine to sit. Wink put a can of beer in his hands. Lichine couldn't bring it to his lips, so he leaned over and slurped little sips while he watched his crew continue their chores.

His eyes caught the splintered end of the marlin bill protruding from the stern. He whispered some words even he couldn't hear. He tried again.

"What'll we do with that?"

"The bill?" Wink asked, following Lichine's gaze. "If I were you, I'd cut it flush, sand it smooth, and get a brass circle made to put around it. With an inscription."

"Really?" Lichine asked. "Is that done?"

"All the time," Wink answered as he unrolled the canvas cockpit cover. "It could say something like, 'On this date, the year of our Lord so-and-so, intrepid Ernest Lichine purt' near got hisself made into fish-kabob."

"A stirring sentiment," said Lichine, grinning.

Finally, the cleaning-up was done. Doakes returned from the weighing scaffold, and the four men walked to the car at the end of the dock. Lichine managed to get into the front seat without assistance. Doakes slid behind the wheel and started up. Lichine asked to be dropped off at the hotel.

"No way, Ernie," Wink replied. "We got some heavy partying to do. And Jellynose is buying."

"Say what?" Doakes asked, already going fifty in second gear. "I'm doin' what?"

"Picking up a tab for a change. Was that mother over eight hundred or not?"

"Hell, no, it wasn't no eight hundred. Scales was off."

"You lying douche bag," Wink shouted. "That was a horse, now, and you damn well know it."

"Fish was a rat," Doakes said.

"Rat?" Wink was outraged. "What we just done was catch us a rat? Ernie's half-dead from catchin' a rat?"

"Shit, my granmammy could a reeled that bitty fish in," said

Doakes. "In fifteen minutes. An' she was so weak she couldn't pull a greased string from a cat's ass."

Wink shrieked in disbelief and launched a stream of invective remarkable for its ripeness of imagery. The others listened, impressed. He did not sputter to silence until they were outside their apparent destination, a nightclub called the Cinnamon Balloon. At that point, Doakes did two things Lichine never expected to see. Cocking his head slightly, he bared his teeth in what was intended to be a smile. Then he winked at Lichine.

Wink saw the exchange. "I been skizzled," he said.

"How big was the fish, grasshopper?"

"Eight hunnert six pounds," Doakes replied. He put his arm across Lichine's shoulders. "Let's go get some braggin' done."

The Cinnamon Balloon was a bilevel bar and discotheque on a corner of Crystal Gade in the center of Charlotte Amalie. There was a narrow, aquarium in the vestibule, under a shelf of abundant ferns. In the tank was a catfish as long as a forearm, charcoal gray, with an orange topfin and tail and a white stripe down its side. It liked to be stroked behind its fins, and if fingers were dangled before its eyes, the catfish nudged them to demand attention.

Lichine watched Wink do this while Doakes talked to the doorman. The man was very thin and very short and wore a glittering shirt open to the waist to display a tangle of gold chains.

"I really do not believe you will enjoy yourself here," he was saying to Doakes. "Our interests are, I suspect, rather opposite to yours."

"Goddam, son," said Doakes. "That ain't hardly what I think on as friendly. I was here last year and enjoyed the shit out of myself."

"That may be, sir," said the doorman, palms raised, "but the management and clientele have undergone transformation since then."

Lichine flashed a bill behind his captain's back.

"Of course, sir," said the doorman to Doakes, suddenly displaying his teeth, "as long as you understand, I'm certain you do, I take pleasure in welcoming you to our establishment."

He waved Doakes through the door. The bill was plucked from Lichine's fingers as he followed Doakes.

"Ain't hardly nothin' that beats an appeal to reason," Wink said to Lichine.

"It bothers me that I'm getting good at bribery," Lichine replied.

"But not much," Wink said.

"No," Lichine said. "That's what bothers me most."

There was a massive mahogany bar in the first room. Behind it, backing the rows of bottles, was a series of ceiling-high mirrors in ornately carved frames. The light from a street lamp angled through the banks of plants set in the large front window and reached across the checkerboard marble floor. That was the only illumination, apart from a dozen candles set in small pots along the back bar and on the tables. Five step up, in the other room, customers danced to music by a costumed six-piece band. A revolving mirrored ball cast fragments of crimson and green light over the floor and walls and swaying bodies.

Doakes pushed through to the bar. A slender, pasty-faced young man was stroking an equally slender, chocolate-faced young man. The first one craned around at the intrusion, intending to protest the jostling. When he looked up at Doakes, however, he contented himself with a toss of his head.

They were given their drinks and Doakes led the way to a just vacated table by the window. Lichine laid his hand on Wink's arm.

"Do you think we should sit there?" he asked as quietly as the din of music permitted.

"Why not?"

Lichine nodded at the adjacent table. Allie Cronski and his two mates, Carey and Hatch, were sitting there.

"Ernie," Wink said, "if you don't anticipate trouble, most times you don't get it. At the same time, you don't hide, 'cause that's when it comes to find you."

"Reassuring." Lichine took the chair between Cronski and Wink.

"No, it don't," Tim Carey was saying to Cronski. "It tastes like a mouthful of copper pennies."

"Don't neither," said Cronski. "Tastes like shrimp in hot sauce."

Wink heard the exchange and apparently knew what they were talking about. "No, no. What it tastes like," he said patiently, "is artichokes vinaigrette."

"Wonder what we taste like t'them?" Cronski said.

"I'll have t'ask Miz Cat." He smirked. Lichine failed to respond, so Cronski shrugged. "Think I'll go find me some nigger poon. That's like peach-flavored battery acid, I hear."

Cronski got up and shouldered his way toward the dance floor.

"What did he mean about Catherine?" Lichine asked Wink.

"Beats me," said Wink. "But I don't think either of us wants to know."

Carey scooted his chair closer.

"You ain't heard?" he said, displaying the gap where his left front incisor used to be.

"No, Tim," said Wink, "and I'd just as leave not. Why don't you go up there and make sure Cap'n Allie doesn't start eating his foot? He does have this problem relating to black folks."

"He's full-growed," Carey said. "Don't see why he cares, anyway, after his reward for good work this afternoon."

"You want another drink?" Wink pointedly asked Carey, nodding surreptitiously at Lichine.

Cronski returned, livid.

"Strike out, Allie?" Wink asked.

Cronski slapped the glasses off his table and sat. "These ain't only niggers, they's queer."

"These people live here, Allie," Wink said. "We're just visiting. They don't have to get within breathing distance of you if they don't want to."

"This here is still part of America, ain't it?" Cronski glowered at the dancers in the far room. "Since when is niggers the same as people?"

"Don't think nothin' of it, man," Wink said to the muscular black waiter who came to clean up the broken glass. "He's just got a case of the Master Race Wobblies. Only afflicts him when the stars come out."

The waiter was not amused. Eyes blazing, he opened his hand and let the fragments shower on the table in front of Cronski. He brushed his hands with deliberation and walked away.

"Allie, old son," Wink said, "you was doin' good just before you fucked up. I do believe I would endeavor not to annoy that man, regardless of pigmentation or sexual proclivity."

The arrival of Pat Fowler, Pia Cipolla, and Steve Grubbs shut off Cronski's reply.

"Captain Uncle! Pia, baby!" said Wink. "Sit yourselves. We were about to make merry, if she shows up."

"Don't pay him no mind, Pia," Fowler said. "Allie, you must be buyin', what with them six marlin today."

Wink made a face. "Pat. . ."

"Sooner talk about my ree-ward," Cronski said.

"Just what does that mean?" Lichine angrily asked. "You've been. . ."

"Leave it, Ernie," Wink cautioned.

"I won't!"

"Do what Wink tells you," Doakes said over the blaring music. "Cronski ain't never said nothin' that was worth attendin' to."

Cronski threw his shoulders back and stood. "You comin' up on somethin', Doakes? If you is, let's get it out."

"You're a lyin' sack of shit," said Doakes calmly.

"Ain't no swingin' dick calls me that," said Cronski.

"You feelin' froggy, then, you best go ahead 'n' hop."

Cronski made a noise in his chest, coiled, and began to edge to the left of the table. Nearby patrons edged away.

"Allie, park it," said Fowler. "Have a drink."

Cronski shook off the restraining hand. "You got nothin' left but seeds and stems, Doakes. You been comin' at me for months. Time to get this done."

The marble eyes rolled toward the door. By reflex, Cronski followed the glance. Doakes came up from his chair. With the table.

He rammed it into Cronski and held it there and kept pumping his legs, a terrifying bellow bursting from him. Cronski clawed at the table, backpedaling as fast as be could. Chairs and people toppled in their wake. Cronski kept his feet under him, finally coming to a crashing halt against the wall. The back bar swayed, sending mirrors and bottles flying. Doakes cast the table aside and proceeded to club Cronski with his forearms.

The music had stopped. Shards of glass crunched beneath their feet. Someone cried "Get the honkies!" as satellite fights broke out. One of the bartenders vaulted the bar behind Doakes, raised a billy, and brought it down into the angle between Doakes' neck and shoulder. The captain wheeled and buried his fist to the wrist in the bartender's stomach. The man made a hooshing sound and doubled over. Doakes caught him by hair and belt and hurled him into a rank of brass plant stands. Cronski escaped, caroming blindly along the bar and knocking aside stools and imprudent customers.

"We gotta stop this," Wink said to Fowler.

"I'd sooner stop a truck."

Doakes pounced on Cronski again and resumed the measured pummeling. When Wink caught him by the arm, he was flung into the knot of people trying to get out the door. Other men set upon him. Lichine found himself shoving at them, trying to protect his mate, but he took a blow on his temple and went down.

The crowd filled in behind Cronski as he reeled up the steps to the dance floor. Doakes waded through, but as he reached Cronski, the tiny doorman and the remaining bartender jumped on his back. He sent the bartender sprawling and then took the doorman by shirtfront and crotch and threw him into the band.

Six policemen arrived. Doakes was at the center of a tangle of flailing arms and legs that was surging from one side of the room to the other. The police peeled off combatants, clubs high, until they reached Doakes.

After a final flurry, Doakes was subdued and manacled. The crowd parted as he was carried out, roaring. His face was an unrecognizable pulp, his clothes shredded and soaked in blood, patches of beard and hair missing. Worst was the large scrap of skin torn from the corner of his mouth and flapping against his jaw.

He was shoved into the back of the first of two squad cars waiting outside. Then the police set to sorting out grievances and attempting to quiet the crowd that milled around the cars. There were two dull thumps and a splintering of glass on the far side of the first squad car. Doakes was kicking the window out.

One of the policemen stabbed at Doakes through the shattered window with the end of his truncheon. Another emptied the contents of an aerosol can in Doakes' face. They added straps around his arms and ankles, and he seemed, finally, to be quiet.

The shaken officers got in the cars, abandoning their efforts to obtain names and addresses. As the cars moved off, Doakes shouted something from the open window.

Lichine was standing next to Wink and Fowler, dazedly watching.

"What's Jeeter saying?" he asked Fowler.

"He's sayin'," Fowler replied, "that this is the most fun he ever had with his clothes on."

21

It was the next afternoon, Saturday, before Lichine returned to the hotel. The time had been spent with lawyers, policemen and doctors. He had not slept, even when he was in front of her door, he was not certain he could carry it through.

Eventually, Catherine answered his repeated knocks. It took her a moment to focus, then her mouth formed an "O." She swayed, and her hand pawed the air.

"Go 'way," she said.

Lichine caught the door before it shut. There was no resistance. Catherine was walking back into the room, exaggeratedly straight backed, but hobbling. Only one foot had a shoe.

"Catherine," he said.

She was at the bureau, poking through a pile of bottles and tubes and jewelry. "Can't find it," she mumbled. "One shoe, one eyelash." She looked in the mirror. "You still here? Said go away."

"I must talk to you," he said. "Please."

"A-ha!" she said, plucking something out of the pile and holding it aloft. "Other eyelass. Lash. Looks like dead caterpillar." She threw it aside, peeled off the one already affixed to her eyelid, and limped over to the chair by the window.

The room was a shambles. The bed was unmade. Newspapers, damp towels, and clothes were scattered about. Pictures were askew. An upset breakfast tray. A red stain on the wall.

Lichine stood in the middle, rigid, looking helplessly about. "Catherine, what is all this? Was someone . . .what happened?"

"Hmm?" she said, uninterested. "Oh. Maid didn't come. Or I sent her away. Or something. You, too. Go."

She reached for a bottle but tipped it over. She picked it up and drank what was left.

"Stop," he said. "I don't want to see you like this. Let me help." He started picking up clothes and papers.

"Leave," she said. "Out."

She got up and pushed at him. Then her eyes widened and she pressed her lips together and pushed past him to the bathroom. His stomach churned at the retching sounds. After a while, she closed the door. After a longer while, he grew alarmed at the quiet. He moved toward the bathroom, but then he heard water running in the sink and he went back and sat on a corner of the bed.

She came out, supporting herself against the wall. Her hair was brushed straight back, her pallid face scrubbed clean. She walked deliberately to the bureau, ignoring him. There was a fresh bottle of brandy. She slit the seal with some difficulty and went to the chair. She poured a glass.

Now she looked at him. "Okay," she said evenly, "you won't go. Get it over with."

He reached for the bottle. "No more, please, Catherine. . ."

She snatched it away. *"Hands off."*

She drained the glass and refilled it.

"Talk fast," she said. "I just took a blue, I'm about to bliss out, and I don't want you around messing it up."

He shrugged, for lack of a more appropriate gesture, and concentrated on his hands.

"Someone said something last night," he said, the words catching. "About you. I want to hear your answer."

No response. He glanced up. She was staring at him.

"What were you doing out there yesterday? With Cronski?"

Catherine was grinding her teeth. He waited.

"I was doing to Cronski what I've done to you fifty times."

"Catherine. . ."

"I was sucking his dick."

". . . please. . ."

"Just like I sucked the hundred dicks before that."

"All right." Lichine stared at her. She stared back. He ground the palms of his hands into his cheeks, fingers over his eyes.

"That day," he continued, forcing the words, "that day I found. . . saw you with Pia. Was that what. . ."

"Yes."

"Then you are. . ."

"Bilingual. Yes, in point of fact, I am." She giggled into her glass. "Yes, indeed. Certainly am."

"But why?" he asked helplessly.

"This is getting tedious."

"All this. Why all this? It can't be just that age business. There has to be something else."

"No there doesn't."

"There must be."

"I'm very oral." She sighed. "Now do please get out of here. Go on. Give me a ring in a year or so. Maybe I'll give you a break."

"Not until I understand."

"Now!" she shrieked, and threw the glass at him. "Now, you simple bastard, now!"

She jumped up and ran to the bureau, hurling everything that came to hand. He shielded himself against the barrage, but otherwise did not move. She flew at him, striking him with her fists. When she stopped, exhausted, he simply looked up at her, a trickle of blood on his cheek and tears welling in his eyes.

The sight triggered some deeper, hidden fury in her. She slapped him, with all her strength.

He stood, then, and slapped her back. With all his strength.

She fell. He did not touch her. After several minutes, she crept unassisted to the chair and pulled herself into it.

"Sooner or later it comes to that." She bent her legs up and hugged them and rested her chin on her knees. "Sooner or later."

"I suppose it does," he said quietly. There was an unexpected firmness in his voice. "It does, when nothing else is left."

"So now what?"

"So now I want to know. You said that some day you'd tell me how you got to be you. A man has a right to know."

"Man?" She snorted. "What in God's name do you know about manhood?"

"I'm learning," he said. "And I'm still waiting."

"You'll leave then?"

He did not answer.

"James Thackeray Nettles," she said. Lichine leaned forward to hear. "A man." She took a long shuddering breath.

One of the four boys pinned her wrists to the ground and clamped a hand over her mouth. Two of them held her legs. The fourth pushed the ocelot jacket aside, paused, gathered the fabric of her dress in one fist, and ripped it from bodice to hem in one stroke. Catherine screamed against the hand, so they stuffed her panties in her mouth and tied it fast with her shredded slip.

When the four were done with her, they took her purse, the Chrysler, the strand of pearls from her throat, the ring from her finger, the ocelot jacket, and her shoes. They left, and after a long while, she struggled up the slope of the ravine through underbrush and patches of snow. Cars on the parkway at the top either slowed or speeded up at the sight of her, but none of them stopped. Finally, the police came and permitted James to take her away from the station when she proved unwilling or unable to speak.

James flew her back to New York in a chartered jet to his house. For a month, he stayed with her, a housekeeper or a nurse in constant attendance. He reduced his obligations to those that could be met within the sound of her voice. Catherine was not, she conceded in lucid moments, a wonderful person to be around. James was patient, withstanding her outbursts and scorn and days of despair. When she found she was pregnant - not by James, for he had touched her only to comfort - he arranged for the operation. That was possible and relatively safe for those with money, although disclosure might have ruined him.

Afterward, he buried her in work. Every time she looked up, James was there with another stack of folders. Every time she tried to retreat, James was there.

"Catherine, please," said Lichine, pained. "I didn't know. . ."

"Shut up! You wanted to hear this!" She filled her glass again, absently swirling the cognac and staring out the window. "Just shut up. James was there, always. It was all of a piece, from I-wish-I-could-die to I-wish-I-could-live-forever. Hardly a seam, except for a few dozen jags. Eventually, we wound up doing exactly what you think. You were about nine at the time."

She learned more from him than she thought there was to learn, but he did not instruct. He shared. Catherine agreed with every word he uttered and was incensed at the ways in which other people used him. She felt fiercely protective and utterly dependent, at the same time. Eventually, the happy moments outnumbered the depressive ones. One night, in her apartment in Greenwich Village, Catherine was attempting veal piccata. There was a noise in the other room. James was on the floor, clutching at himself.

A massive coronary occlusion, the doctor intoned. James recovered, part way. They were married in the hospital room. A formal wedding at a later time would satisfy the social and familial niceties, they both agreed. But James knew something that Catherine wouldn't let herself believe. One night, as she was about to leave his room, he started to cry. He had never done that. Tiny, choked little sobs. He said he was sorry. He said he wished he was dead. A week later, he was.

Lichine went to her. She was rigid, her fists and forearms against his chest.

"Don't say it," she said. "I know it was a long time ago. That doesn't matter. Older is only older. Not grown-up. I miss him. I haven't stopped missing him."

"I understand," Lichine said, because he couldn't think of anything else.

"Don't understand me too well."

After a long time, he guided her to the bed. They held each other. Later still, he shifted, saying he was just going to pick up a bit. She said that the maid would come again in the next twelve hours, so he stayed.

Triga glanced at his watch. Nearly five o'clock.. He could break his rule. He buzzed for Duncan and read once again the note handed him upon his return to *Highlander*. The words were few, and ambiguous to anyone not privy to the essential elements of the matter.

"Assignment definitely confirmed. Subject to receive notification coming week. His return to competition virtually impossible. M.S."

Duncan made a discreet cough.

"Ah, yes, Duncan," Triga said. "I believe I'll have my cassis now, if you'll be so kind."

The steward nodded, and left.

Horst Triga had every reason to be satisfied with the course of events. By the end of the week, the field would be reduced to three boats and anglers. More, the captains of *Brain Soup* and *Zodiac Arrest* were incapacitated for at least the duration of the St. Thomas segment. Allie Cronski might not be able to return even two months hence, in Cairns. Jeeter Doakes would probably be in jail.

It was useful to have the disputatious Doakes out of the way, Triga allowed, but that fact was unlikely to influence the final standings. Although Lichine had proven an abler competitor than Triga expected, the newcomer's lost time in Cozumel left him well behind. Much more significant was the loss to Catherine Nettles of her captain, Cronski. They were on a damnably persistent streak of luck. Every time he managed to pull closer in the competition, Catherine Nettles had a day like Friday. Six marlin! In all his years, five was the best Triga had managed in a single day.

Without Cronski, that critical rhythm would be broken, in Triga's favor, he hoped. Even if Catherine was able to find a replacement, it would take some time to build the kind of coordinated teamwork Cronski and his mates had developed over their years of working together.

But Triga still wasn't satisfied. He decided to make a list of every top captain in St. Thomas. It would be useful to know if any of them were available for hire. And if so, whether they might be persuaded to accept tasks - lucrative tasks - prior to possible contact by Catherine Nettles.

Duncan returned and placed the small silver tray with the single fluted glass on the end table.

"Thank you, Duncan," Triga said distractedly.

The steward inclined his head and pivoted to leave.

"Oh, by the way, Duncan. Do you find that your circumstances are now to your liking?"

"Why, yes, thank you, sir."

"No further confusion over duties or such?"

"None at all, sir. All is quite gratifyingly satisfactory."

"I'm pleased to hear that." Triga picked up the glass. "I will be staying aboard this evening. An old friend is arriving. I won't be needing you tonight. I've advised the chef and crew."

"I *would* like to see a little of the island, sir."

"You must, then," Triga agreed. "It's really quite charming."

"Thank you, sir. I will. I'll just go below to change clothes and be on my way." The steward dipped at the waist and withdrew.

He stopped in the galley. Only he and Triga possessed keys to the temperature-controlled, humidified wine closet. Duncan opened it, and after careful deliberation and some hesitation, selected a Chateau Petrus. It was a '71, and he ruefully conceded, two years short of its maturity. But for that very reason, Triga would never notice its absence. Duncan placed the bottle on a tray with a glass, a knife, a broad wedge of brie, and a small basket of unsalted wheat crackers. He carried this to the door, looked both ways, and walked quickly down the companionway to his stateroom.

Duncan was compelled to share the cabin with the chef, an emaciated Basque with an inadequate command of English. The chef had been persuaded-by Duncan to visit Charlotte Amalie that night. Duncan carefully stripped the foil from the neck of the bottle, wiped away the residue, removed the cork, and poured.

The bulkhead against which his bunk abutted separated the master stateroom from his own. When he heard voices on the other side, he looked at his watch. It was 6:38, Saturday evening. He was able to hear quite clearly, apart from the words understandable only when the moving lips could be seen.

"I don't have long," said the woman. "I'm supposed to meet him at eight."

"How does he seem?" Triga asked.

"A little itchy. He doesn't like you, but you haven't given him a reason to quit. Yet. He's in line."

"You've done very well, so far. I shall have to punish you."

"Games again?"

"You'll find the things in that drawer."

"No marks this time," said the woman.

"No promises."

"Yes you will. It was very awkward the last time."

"Very well. I'll be careful."

"Be sure. The ribbons okay?"

"I'd rather the other."

"They make burns," the woman said.

"Very well." Triga sighed. "But leave those on. And put your hands up here. No, the other way around."

"I hope this will be worth it!"

"This time, you mean?"

"I didn't say that."

Another pause.

"Too tight," she said. "The right one."

"Better?"

"I suppose."

"Ah," he said. "Magnificent. Say it, please."

"I'd rather not." Muffled.

"You will."

Another sigh. Hers. "Do what you will with me," she said finally.

Duncan filled his glass and spread another cracker. Similar, previous encounters in the room beyond that wall had been diverting, even stimulating. And once transcribed in suitably titillating form, they had proven fairly profitable, as well. The steward sipped, and settled into his pillow.

Lichine and Catherine drove to each of the several marinas on Sunday. Catherine was subdued, but not waspish, as Ernest half expected. It was not so much that he dreaded her mockery as that he did not want reasons to be reminded of her actions. While he felt that he now understood why she was the way she was, he was not yet able to deal with the results. His nerve ends were too frayed, his confusion too great over whatever future they might have together.

No licensed captains were available for the coming week. One of them said he wished he had known Lichine and Catherine might be interested in his services. He surely would have been interested he said, but had just that morning accepted a reservation from an old client from New York. Another said they were ten minutes too late, that he was booked for the next month. The gentleman had just left he said, after leaving a very generous retainer. When Catherine pressed him for a description of the client the captain claimed that he did not have much of a memory for that kind of thing. Just your average sort, he said.

Calls to St. John and St. Croix were no more productive. At the end of the fruitless day, they decided that they would compete with only their remaining crews for the rest of the week. Lichine believed that Wink could be persuaded to take over. Tim Carey had captaining experience. Catherine had no doubt he would accept the position. She and Ernest carefully avoided the implications of that conviction. They returned to his boat.

"Why not?" Lichine asked after Wink refused his request. "You have a license, don't you?"

"But not the inclination," the mate replied. He was checking equipment and mopping up in preparation for Monday. "Authority makes my hair fall out. Professor, admiral, executive secretary, olive drab, gold braid, oakleaf clusters, titles on the door, all that shit gives me shingles. I'll mate for you any time, Ernie, but I won't captain.""

"Then I don't know what to do." He glanced at Catherine, but she offered no advice.

"No problem," Wink said, motioning at the doc." Our leader approaches."

Doakes was striding down the dock. Most of the bandages had been removed. Scarlet flesh bulged around his eyes and mouth. There were two rows of ugly black stitches from the comer of his mouth to his jaw and back again. His left arm was in a sling. Without the beard, his chin receded more than Lichine had imagined.

"We ready to go fishin'?" he asked.

"What're you doing here?" Wink asked.

"Where else? Got dull in that hospital. They would've let me out in another day or two, even without me hollerin'. And from what I hear, you boys need me."

Lichine wanted to know if the captain could work effectively with the arm. He was deciding something. Doakes slipped the arm out of the sling and waggled his hand in demonstration. No sweat, he said, but he wasn't able to suppress a tightening around his eyes. Wink wanted to know why they let Doakes out.

"Why the fuck wouldn't they?" Doakes replied, mystified.

"Ernie," Wink said, "I do believe that Jellynose isn't carrying a full seabag. He appears to be genuinely mystified that certain folks might be harboring a touch of pique over his evening's frolicment. Jeet, old buddy, lackadaisical attitude isn't hardly fitting to the situation."

"Run it down," Doakes said.

"Christ. Don't worry about it any. Shouldn't cost you more'n three years and fifty thousand dollars up to the point where they stick you in the bottom of a well and pour in the cement."

"Ernie?" Doakes asked. "You tell me."

"Okay," Lichine said. "Back there. On the dock."

"Ain't there coffee?" Doakes asked, stepping jauntily into the cockpit. "Come on aboard. We'll talk."

"No. We'll talk out here. On the dock."

Doakes looked at his mate and Catherine.

"You heard, Jeet," Wink said, backing away. "I do believe it goes back to the first conversation you two ever had."

"What's that mean?"

"Think about it. Miz Nettles? Join me for a little lunch?"

Lichine walked down the dock to the table outside the snack bar. Doakes followed, perplexed.

"Ernie," he said, "we got some things to do these last few days"

"I'll be very interested to hear what you have in mind," Lichine answered. "Later."

Doakes cocked his head and stared at his employer.

"If you got some thin' stuck in your. . ."

"I do," Lichine interrupted. "And I'd appreciate it if you paid attention."

The captain's eyebrows bobbed, but he was silent.

"First," Lichine began after clearing his throat, "there's your bail. It was twenty-five thousand dollars. I paid it. If you default, I lose it all. Even if you don't, the bondsman's cut is twenty-five percent. My money."

"I can dig it, Ernie, but. . ."

"Let me finish, please. Your lawyer has given me a preliminary estimate of ten thousand dollars for his fee. That will depend, of course, on a great many variables. Court costs, for example, should litigation be required."

"Lawyer?" Doakes asked. "I got a lawyer?"

"How do you think you got out of the police station and into that hospital bed? I had to go through the entire Bar Association before I could find someone who'd touch this mess. Anyway, it's his guess that the other participants will settle out of court. Apparently most of them are as leery of suits and trials as you must be. He tells me that these arrangements will total at least twenty-five thousand dollars. Allowing for buy-offs and medical expenses, the total could go as high as forty thousand dollars."

"*Forty?* Those eggsuckers will say different when I. . ."

"I asked you to let me finish. Three of your opponents are still in the hospital. Seven others required treatment. They have to wait for the swelling to go down before they can decide how to go about rebuilding Cronski's face.

"They don't know yet the amount of damages to the nightclub," Lichine went on. "Furniture, the band instruments, glassware, stock. The owner is one of the patients. We don't know when he'll be able to give an estimate."

"What else?"

"Destruction of government property, for one. The squad car. Resisting arrest. Assault and battery. But there's some hope there. The police may accept damages and drop their charges. And they found a lot of drugs and under-age customers at the club. The owner has a criminal record, I understand. That won't stop him from taking legal action, necessarily, but probably he'll settle."

"Fuck that!" Doakes bellowed. "Ain't no way I'm gonna. . ."

"Be quiet!"

Doakes closed his mouth after a moment. Lichine waited.

"I ain't gonna listen to no more of this," Doakes said.

"You are. You will. You owe me."

"You're usin' your bucks, Ernie."

"We use what we have."

"You'll get every cent back."

"I expect to. If everything works out in your favor, your debt will be somewhere around forty-five thousand dollars. With bad luck, it could be twice that. So, then. For the rest of our time in St. Thomas, you will remain on the boat. I will withhold all future compensation apart from room and board. You will give me a binder of ten thousand dollars as soon as we return to Miami. I assume you have that from prior payments. When the entire matter is resolved, I will return the balance to you. If there is any."

Doakes placed the palms of his hands on the table.

"That it?"

"No, Jeeter, it isn't. It is possible that your total final expenses will exceed the amount I owe you for your services. If it does, I shall forgive the debt - wipe the slate clean - on only one condition. Should that not occur, I will expect full compensation."

"I'm listenin'."

"It's straight forward enough. I must win this tournament. You will make certain I do."

Doakes leaned back and regarded his employer. His expression revealed nothing.

"Count on it." he said finally. "Long as you do like I say."

"You're still the boss. On the boat."

"Let's get at it then."

22

The tournament resumed. At the rendezvous point, Lichine saw that Pia Cipolla was aboard *Zodiac Arrest.* She waved at Pat Fowler. Catherine was not in sight.

There was little action at the Drop-Off. Porpoises broke the surface a hundred yards aft. Doakes turned the boat to troll over the spot. Nothing happened.

Wink was at the table preparing additional baits. Lichine was in the chair, head in hand, glumly watching the baits.

"You see Curry and Scully out on the dock this morning?" Wink asked.

"No," said Lichine. "Why?"

"They're sitting there looking up at some birds flying over, when one of the gulls shits right in Curry's eye. Scully says he'll go get some toilet paper. But Curry says 'Never mind. The bird'll be gone by then'."

Lichine made a wan smile.

"That was meant to be funny, Ernie."

"It was."

"Well then, when you stop rolling around on the deck holding your sides, I'll tell another one." He was quiet for a moment.

"Ernie, you mind if I ask you something?"

"No."

"Can't you afford to lose the money?"

"No one can afford to lose a million dollars. But it doesn't represent an irretrievable loss. Why?"

"An observation?"

"Okay."

"This thing is beginning to mean more to you than it should."

Lichine thought about that. "How about you?" he asked. "Why are you here?"

"I'm a whore, Ernie. I do this for the money."

"I see."

"Asked you a question, Ernie."

Lichine took a deep breath and leaned back in the chair.

"I've discovered two things about myself," he said. "They conflict. One is that I'm basically a weekend fisherman. The other is, I want to take this tournament more than anything ever before in my entire life."

"But you've done good, Ernie. Real good. You stayed with them. Anyone else in your case would've been eliminated halfway through. You're still in it."

"To be good is nothing. What counts is being the best."

"I hope you don' believe that, Ernie."

"I didn't. I do now."

Wink deboned another mackerel and thrust the hook through.

"You were a little rough on Jeet," he said, stitching up the stomach.

"I didn't think so," Lichine replied, unmoving.

"He only got it on with Cronski so you wouldn't find out about. . . so you wouldn't have to know. Partly, anyway."

"Doakes had his own reasons."

"Nothing's that simple, Ernie."

Lichine stiffened, and the pent-up words tumbled out.

"It is for you people," he said. "Doakes thinks beating people to a pulp is fun. You avoid responsibility of any kind, despite your intelligence and education. The other anglers are bad children. All of you elevate a sport, a game, to the reason for existence, whoring and drinking and doping in between. But the world can't function that way. Someone has to learn how to patch you up and feed us and stop you from killing each other. Fuck you all. I'm going to win, and then I'm going home and try to make up for wasting nine months of my life."

Wink let the outburst hang. He went to the table to prepare more baits. He was working on the second mackerel when he spoke again.

"You're a good man, Mr. Lichine," he said. "In the worst sense."

Their joining that night was tentative, as if they had been long apart. Nuances were imperfectly performed, or even recalled.

"We must meet again like this," Catherine said, attempting lightness.

"Unbelievable," Lichine said. "The last three months, I mean."

"That's a judicious choice of word, darling."

"I can't even believe that was me that first night."

"It wasn't. This is you." She pressed her lips to his neck. "This is you, right now. Here." She paused. "You are what you eat."

"You are incurable."

"That's incorrigible.'"

"That too." He pulled her closer. "Catherine. . ."

"Don't."

"What?"

"You have that seeking-after-revelation pitch in your voice."

"Just a small revelation."

She breathed against his chest and rolled away.

"What?"

"Why did you pick me? That night?"

No answer.

"More important, why did you let me stick around?"

No answer.

"Catherine?"

"You don't want to know."

"Maybe not. Tell me anyway."

"Because you were a virgin."

"I wasn't."

"You were. For all practical purposes."

"Say I was. Why did it matter?"

"I liked it. I liked watching your Adam's apple bobbing up and down, and the way you walked, all pitched over as if you couldn't wait to get where you were going and not at all sure you wanted to get there."

"You picked me because of how I looked?"

"Of course I did. How else would I? You didn't say three words."

"It sounds very superficial."

"Does it now?" Her voice flattened. "And how do you pick bed partners? By their bright, burning intellects and perspicacity?"

"Something like that."

"Bullshit. You look at the shape of their boobs and whether they have bee-stung lips."

"That's not true."

"It is. And just because I do what *you* do. . ."

"That's not what I do."

"*You.* Collective. *All* of you. A woman does it, and you can't deal with it."

"I'm not like that. I won't be treated as a stand-in for my sex. And you are . . . the way you are because that's the way you protect yourself. By keeping everyone off balance, by being as brutal as you think they might be."

She got up suddenly and went to the bathroom.

"Please don't take anything," he said. "Talk to me."

He heard the cabinet slide open, a bottle cap popping. When she came back into the room, she was pulling on a robe.

"Do please change the subject, darling," she said, trying to smile. "I don't want this."

"What was it you really liked, Catherine? This?"

"Your skin. You don't know that about us. Skin's the thing."

"Collective 'you'?"

"And specific." She sat on the bed and took his hand. "Please, Ernest, please. Don't pick at the scab. Not again."

He withdrew his hand. "So," he said. "You've anesthetized yourself. You hold everyone at arm's length by cutting them to little chunks before they do it to you."

"Come off it. We all have our defenses. You, for example. You cloak yourself in this stiff-necked naivete and self-righteous innocence. Really, darling, it does get just a bit cloying. Especially since you've started showing signs of incipient flintiness."

"I do not, at least, try to neutralize my life."

She faced the other way. "Not bad, darling. Don't slam the door."

"I wasn't leaving."

"Yes, you were."

At ten minutes after three the next afternoon, Lichine hooked his fourth blue marlin of the day. Fifty minutes later, his crew was wrestling the fish through the transom door. It was not yet spent, so Doakes beat it with the billy until it was still. Lichine stood to one side, teetering with exhaustion, and then went to his stateroom. Doakes turned on the radio.

"*Highlander*, this here's *Brain Soup*! Y'all asleep already? *Highlander!* Come on back, fuckers!"

Eventually, a voice answered and asked Doakes to keep the channel open. There was a long wait.

"*Brain Soup*, this is *Highlander*. Is that you, Captain Doakes? Over."

"Damn straight it's Doakes. Who's that?"

"Oscar Farrington. Captain, is Mr. Lichine listening?"

"He's below. Beat. He just caught him a big one. Six hunnert if it's an ounce."

"Good. That he isn't there, I mean. Something has.". . . Farrington's voice trailed off.

"Oscar? You was cut off there. Say again."

"Please return immediately."

"What's up?"

"I'd rather not say. Return right away, please."

"Dammit, Oscar, what's goin' on? I ain't goin' where till you loosen up."

There was a hiss of dead air.

"Very well," Farrington said finally. "There has be a most unfortunate occurrence."

Doakes waited for Farrington to continue. When the words came over the speaker, he had to strain to hear.

"Catherine Nettles is dead."

Theo Marker rocked back, bringing the rod up. The marlin was giving him a great deal of trouble. Over two hours so far. A large brown sea bird banked over the point where his line entered the water. It was a blue-billed boobie, an appellation Marker normally found amusing.

Not now. It came down to this, he was thinking. Thirty-six days on the water, spread over nearly six months. The wager itself. Four hundred thousand dollars in out-of-pocket expenses. A brand-new mortgage on the house that was paid off only two years before. Carlos snapping at his heels.

All that, and the other things he had done, were rendered meaningless by the phone call last night from Bel Air. The project was his. Absolutely, irretrievably. In two years - less - he would be back on top. The property was that foolproof. The central condition was straightforward: he must begin now, this week. That. Or this. Just when he was closing the gap.

Curry monitored the conversation between Doakes and Farrington and relayed the information to his employer. Marker watched his fish break the surface. It put him in second place.

With a sigh, Marker slid the drag lever all the way to the front. The line didn't break, so he held the spool stationary until it did.

Lichine did not awaken until the engines stopped. He sat up from the sofa bench where he had collapsed after the marlin was boated. They were back at the Lagoon Marina. Jeeter, Wink, and Havens were standing in the cockpit, talking to Oscar Farrington, above them on the dock. Marker and Triga hovered. The other boats were there, in rank. Farther off, two strangers moved among the waiting knots of people. The one in uniform scribbled in a notebook. Lichine went to the door and slid it open. The faces turned toward him at the sound, and talking stopped. Wink walked quickly to Lichine, backed him into the cabin, closed the door, made Lichine sit, and then told him.

Someone had straightened up the master stateroom of *Zodiac Arrest.* Clothes were put away, ashtrays emptied, table surfaces wiped clean. Catherine was in the middle of the bed, the covers drawn to her throat and folded neatly back. She appeared to be sleeping. Only that.

The door opened. Lichine was sitting on the edge of the bed.

"They got to go now," Wink said after a moment.

"Why don't you come out? Farrington's here, if you want to ask him anything."

Lichine raised his head, parted his lips.

"Come on out." Wink gently insisted when Lichine failed to speak. "You been here a long time. Let's go."

Wink followed Lichine out. When they mounted the stairs to the salon, Farrington jumped up from his perch on the couch.

"Mr. Lichine," he said. "I am most dreadfully sorry. You were very close, I know."

"How?" Lichine asked.

"How? Well, just that I . . . I was given to understand. . ."

"Oscar," Wink said as he guided Lichine to a seat, "he means he wants to know how it happened."

"Ah. Yes," said Farrington. He sounded relieved. "An immense tragedy. Most harrowing for all of us. Very unfortunate. But, ah, mightn't it be best to defer discussion until some later time?"

"How?" Lichine asked, ignoring the cup of coffee Wink held out to him.

Farrington glanced nervously at Wink, who nodded. "As you wish. Please stop me when. . . I'm dreadfully sorry, Mr. Lichine. I'm not handling this very well. Words do not come easily."

"I know. Please tell me."

"Well," Farrington said, steeling himself, "it is all rather straightforward. Uncomplicated, that is. This boat left on schedule this morning, as you may know. Tim Carey radioed a release at about eleven in the morning, and added that they were returning right away. He gave no reason. They arrived here an hour later. The crew washed down and returned to their lodgings. Miss Nettles chose to stay aboard."

"Why?"

Farrington darted a look at Wink. "That is uncertain, he continued. "The mate alleges that she was in poor spirits, that she had not been herself for the past day or two. According to his description, her behavior was what is customarily labeled manic-depressive."

"You said 'alleges', Lichine said.

"Another poor choice of words, I'm afraid. I merely meant that that was what he told us. And the police."

"Go on."

"She was found late this afternoon, about four."

"Who by?"

"Her captain, Carey." Farrington rubbed a bony hand over his forehead and cheek. "There was a brandy bottle. Nearly empty. And another bottle, for prescription drugs. Also nearly empty. The label indicated tranquilizers. Judging from the size of the two remaining capsules, the bottle originally held perhaps twenty-five. There is no way to know, of course, how many she might have taken. Carey recalls being asked to bring her pills from a similar container, but those were yellow. These were blue. I really don't know much about these things, but. . ."

"The yellows are five milligrams," Wink said. "The blues are ten."

"That may be. In any event, it is conjectured that Miss Nettles ingested at least six of the more potent pills, perhaps as many as twenty. I am told that even the smaller amount is sufficient in itself to be. . . very dangerous. But in combination with apparently large amounts of alcohol . . ."

The unspoken words hung in the air.

"And?" Lichine said finally.

"Beg pardon?"

"What else?"

"I fear I don't understand. The conclusions of all concerned were clear. The majority view, including that of the police, I gather, is that it was accidental. Miss Nettles was known to consume both substances with some frequency. When under the influence of alcohol, it is not difficult to imagine an inadvertent miscalculation as to the number of capsules taken. It takes so few, really, to be . . . excessive."

"And the minority view?"

"I do wish you wouldn't ask that I articulate what must be obvious. This whole affair is really most. . ."

"Harrowing. So you said."

"Forgive me. The alternative is, of course, the possibility that the massive intake of capsules was intentional. But it hardly matters, does it?"

"No, Oscar," Wink said. "It doesn't. Ernie, we got to go. They're ready to leave."

"Have to . . ." Lichine stopped. What was it he was going to say? "Make arrangements." That was it.

"It's done, Ernie. Her father's coming down for her. A plane's been chartered. The calls are made. It's done."

Lichine let his mate take his elbow. The people waiting and watching outside parted for them. When the two men reached their own boat, Lichine froze at the lip of deck, staring down into the cockpit.

"What is it, Ernie?"

"Fish is still there."

"We'll get rid of it."

"No."

"What, then?"

"Weigh it."

Theo Marker arranged for a room at his motel. Lichine slept. Whenever he woke up, Wink was there. At dusk the next day, they decided to go to dinner.

The hum of conversation in the restaurant by the beach halted as they entered, and stumblingly resumed almost immediately. Most of the other crew members were there. Triga huddled with Farrington and the other umpires at the far table. Wink and Lichine joined Doakes and Havens. Food came, but Lichine didn't even lift his fork. After a time, he was aware of the silence of his companions, and tried to think of something to say.

"How much was the fish?" he asked Doakes.

"Six hunnert ten."

That was that. The plates were emptied and the glasses were drained. They made the motions of leaving, without knowing their destination or purpose.

"A word, Ernest?" It was Triga, with the umpires.

"Okay."

"We are cognizant of your distress," Triga said, "and do not wish to impose."

"That's right nice," said Wink.

"We have been deliberating." Triga gestured at the men beside him. "We have decided that - after a suitable period of respect - we would like to proceed unto the conclusion of the tournament."

Wink rocked back in his chair and surveyed the men with incredulity.

"Okay," Lichine said very quietly. "But there's no need to let any more time pass."

"Ernie!" Wink said in disbelief. "What the hell?"

Triga turned to Farrington, who nodded, his eyebrows bobbing.

"As you wish," he said. "We will resume tomorrow morning, then, and continue through Saturday. After that, it will be over two months until we meet again in Cairns. Is that acceptable?"

"Yes," said Lichine.

Wink leaped to his feet, his chair clattering to the tiled floor. "I don't fucking believe this!" He thrust his face at Triga. "Two people are dead! You going for a grand slam?" Triga was impassive. "Ernie! What are you thinking?" Lichine blankly returned his mate's furious gaze.

Wink stormed off. After a pause to express ritualistic regrets, the others left, too.

Marker announced his withdrawal from his tournament the next day. By the end of the week, Lichine was five hundred and twenty-six points behind Triga.

CAIRNS

BLACK MARLIN
(Makaira indica)

One approaches the subject of this mythic fish with humility. There is its size, of course. Although the longstanding mark on rod-and-reel is 1560 pounds, it is assumed that individuals exist that are twice as large. With the exception of certain sharks, no gamefish achieves greater weight or girth. And there is the fact of its speed: Blacks have been clocked at 57 miles per hour. Admittedly less scientific are the claims that locomotives would be easier to land. As far as can be determined, blacks are an Indo-Pacific marine species with incidental strays past the Cape of Good Hope into the Atlantic. Evidence indicates that they are markedly less pelagic than other billfish, confining themselves to localized habitats. In the Pacific, they are found from northern Chile to southern California and from New Zealand to Japan. Concentrated populations are notable off Peru, Panama, and Taiwan. The current focus for anglers is the Great Barrier Reef. It resembles the blue marlin, with which it is often confused, but is distinguished by rigid, unfoldable pectorals and a more pronounced shoulder hump. Despite the name, "blacks" are highly variable in coloration. Frequent albinos prompt the Japanese description, shirokajiki. Normally, though, they are slate-toned topside, changing abruptly to silver grey below the midlateral demarcation. The flesh is basic to Oriental cuisines, but is rarely consumed by Westerners. The black is itself indiscriminately carnivorous, and while cephalopods are a favorite dietary item, reported stomach contents have included the Portuguese Man O' War and 200 pound tunas.

-THE IAA HANDBOOK

23

Ten weeks later, Lichine flew to Australia, and then from Sydney to Cairns. He had little impression of the town other than that of broad verandas on white clapboard houses shaded and bordered by frangipani, palms, cassias, and poinciana. For no good reason, he had expected semidetached brick houses and rose gardens. His crew was quartered at the Reef House. They greeted him with reserve. Wink did observe that it was by no means certain that their full complement would arrive. Jeeter Doakes, as it happened, was afraid of flying.

Although grainy-eyed and lightheaded from twenty-two hours in the air, Lichine agreed to a planning meeting after dinner. In addition to the two owners, two umpires and six crewmen, there was the Australian captain and first mate of the mother ship engaged after St. Thomas. Lichine attempted to will away the memory of those not in attendance. It didn't work.

Oscar Farrington assumed the chair, consulting his notes and waited for the men to quiet down.

"As you all know," he began, "there are a variety of unique challenges pertaining to the final segment of the - ah - contest. And since the black marlin is of special interest to me, I have devoted some thought to these considerations."

Doakes slumped in his chair and groaned at the prospect of another lecture. Farrington eyed him nervously and pressed on.

"I shall be brief," he said. "Now then, the two contestant anglers have engaged the services of a mother ship, as well as the charter of their own fishing craft. The costs for such vessels are not inconsiderable. In addition, of course, the anglers have provided for our transportation, salaries, food, and lodging. And the like. All of this becomes most expensive, needless to say. Mr. Triga has proposed, therefore, that for this phase, we do away with scheduled lay days and fish for ten consecutive days. This should prove no hardship. There is, as most of you know, very little in the way of diversion on the northeastern Australia coast."

"They got a traffic light now," said Wink.

"Yes, indeed," Farrington replied. "Very amusing. May I ask if this proposal meets with your approval?"

The anglers nodded; the crewmen shrugged.

"Just so. May I also suggest that we retain the same boat names as in the earlier segments in order to avoid confusion?"

Nods, shuffling.

"Very well," Farrington continued. "Now while I have my own notions about this next subject, may I ask for opinions about the minimum boating weight?"

"It seems to me that it would be best to boat only granders," Triga said.

"That figures," said Doakes. "It means we don't have the chance of a one-legged man in an ass-kickin' contest."

"And how is that, Captain?"

"I guess you know, Mr. Triga. Our only shot is to pile up extra points on pounds over the limit. We'll be lucky if we see ten granders and catch two in the whole ten days."

"Granders?" Lichine asked.

"A thousand pounds or over," Wink explained.

"There ain't twenty anglers in the world who've caught more'n two."

"The record is 1,560 pounds," Triga said.

"Yeah," Doakes shot back. "In 1953. Off Peru. That ain't happenin' no more."

"Japanese longliners haul in double-granders all the time."

"Once in a while, not all the time," said Doakes. He looked at Lichine. "Give you an idea, Mr. Lichine. There's a standin' prize of a hundred thousand dollars for the first person who ever lands a two-thousand-pounder on sportfishin' equipment. Ain't nobody's even come close."

The two anglers could not agree, so they asked the umpires to resolve the issue. They voted for the one-thousand-pound limit on environmental grounds. Farrington asked if there was other business.

"One item," said Lichine. "What hours do we fish?"

"Noon to six is customary," Triga replied.

"Why?"

Triga sighed. "Because, Ernest, black marlin in this area do not feed in the morning. And because we need those hours to catch our bait."

"No good," Lichine said. "I am far behind you. Reducing the number of hours from eight to six a day also reduces my chances of catching up."

"But as we have said."

"As *you* have said."

". . . there is really no chance of catching blacks before noon."

"Maybe," said Lichine, "but I have no intention of cutting my chances from eighty hours to sixty."

"Have you a counterproposal?"

"This is the last phase," Lichine answered. "You have a prohibitive edge in both points and experience. I've never gone for black marlin. Since we are doing this straight through, without a break, I think we should also remove the restrictions on hours to be fished. The ultimate result would then be conclusive, and the loser couldn't pretend that he didn't have every opportunity to win."

"There would be no point," Triga said. No one ever catches blacks in the morning or at night. Really, Ernest, I'm certain that if you give this just a bit more thought, you'll recognize its impracticality."

"There is no requirement that either of us be out the entire time."

"Very well," Triga said, pursing his lips and lifting his eyes to the ceiling. "I see you will not be dissuaded, so I shall yield."

Farrington cleared his throat. "It is therefore stipulated that from midnight of the first day, either boat may fish at any time it chooses, even if that be every hour of the full ten days. The tournament will end at six o'clock in the evening of the last day."

Triga sniffed. Lichine knew that it mattered little to the others. His chances of catching up were remote, at best.

After the meeting, Doakes drew his employer aside.

"Mr. Lichine, we just got ourselves an edg e. I don't know whether you knew what you was doin', but you got it."

"What do you mean?"

"That business about fishin' anytime," Doakes replied conspiratorily. "Thing is, all the American anglers that've come down here have been brainwashed. They think that since the blacks don't feed in the mornin', they ain't losin' time by catchin' bait instead."

"Isn't bait available for sale here?"

"Nope. And there's where what you done tied in with what I done." Doakes glanced around. "What it is, I shipped five hundred processed Spanish mackerel down. Comes the first mornin', and every other mornin', we'll be fishin'. Triga won't. If we don't sleep too much, we'll have 160 hours with the lines out. He won't have half that."

"Sounds good. Shall we go get a drink?"

At the bar, Wink and Havens joined them over schooners of Swan Lager. Their talk was solemn and desultory. At one point, Wink observed that despite the presence of the best crews, anglers, and boats, not one record fish had been caught since the tournament began.

"That's gonna change," Doakes announced. "I'm puttin' Mr. Lichine over Super Mo. He's gonna be the first fisherman in the history of the world who boats a double-grander. Hear me?"

"I do," said Lichine.

"And believe it."

"That's the hard part."

The fishing boats followed the chartered mother ship out of Cairns at noon on Sunday. They ran north behind the Great Barrier Reef, which formed a natural breakwater undulating at distances from ten to one hundred miles off the Queensland coast.

Mother was eighty feet long and twenty-four feet wide, with eight staterooms, three showers and heads, a galley, and a dining cabin. The Australian crew of three, the anglers, and the umpires were to sleep aboard Mother, and the crews aboard their boats.

These arrangements were necessary because optimum marlin conditions were to be found one hundred miles north, off a largely uninhabited coast. Straight east from Cairns, it was a two and a half hour run to the lip of the continental shelf. When Lichine asked why they didn't go there, Wink explained that the Reef in that area stopped three miles short of the edge. What they wanted, he said, was the point of closest confluence between the Reef and the drop-off. The marlin preferred those places where they could stay in deep water and yet be close to their food. As the Reef sheltered vast quantities of baitfish, the blacks congregated in greatest numbers where it came right to the hundred-fathom edge. They would be in places where it was only eighty feet deep off one side of the boat and six hundred off the other.

It took nearly six hours to reach Linden Bank. The mother ship anchored. The two fishing boats moored off the stern. The men settled in to their tasks.

After five days, Lichine thought he might go mad. Partly, it was frustration. He and his crew were up each day before first light and were trolling the edge by the time the sun was up. They returned to the mother ship after dark. *Adroit*, on the other hand, rarely left before midday, and was always back at the scheduled dinner hour. *Brain Soup* did catch more fish, but none of them was any larger than the blues of St. Thomas and thus far short of the minimum and the bonus points Lichine had to have.

More, he felt caged. It was never once having solid ground beneath his feet, never once being able to walk fifteen feet in a straight line without ducking his head, and never once being able to look out and see anything but the wine-dark vastness of ocean. Even the weather was static.

The mood of the participants was one of grim resolution. There was little joking, and even the occasional episodes of short-tempered confrontation were quickly squelched. They fished and ate and slept and fished again. And talked. That was one advantage. Out of proximity and long hours of tedium, Wink and Lichine found themselves growing friendly again. Neither of them mentioned the days in St. Thomas, nor formally apologized, but it was better.

Havens was making sandwiches. The others were at their usual stations - helm, bait table, fighting chair.

"All we need's one big one," Wink was saying.

"And all it has to be is a world record."

"It's gotta be somebody. Mo is out there. You hear about that pointer shark some Aussie caught on rod and reel over off the other side of the continent?"

"No."

"Three thousand, three hundred and eighty pounds. That is over one and one half tons now."

"That's nearly impossible to conceive."

"Ernie, somewhere out there is a three-thousand-pound black marlin. Maybe sitting right under us right now."

"I wish he'd take an interest in one of those mackerels."

They watched the baits.

"I also wish," Lichine said, forcing himself to sustain conversation, "that I could be somewhere where I could kick some dirt for a day or so. Or that I could look out there and see one little building or hear a car horn."

"You can take the boy out of the city but. . ."

"Yeah."

"This hasn't been bad, Ernie. That cook on Mother has laid some good tucker on us and the weather's been great."

"I'm beginning to hope for a typhoon."

"There's more to it than that, ain't there?"

Lichine did not reply.

"Ernie? Maybe that's true, what you just said, but there's something else."

He waited, knife in hand, and finally turned back to the table when there was no answer.

Lichine exhaled, as if there was something he could hold in no longer. "Marker came to see me," he said without preamble.

"Where?"

"In New York, about four weeks after . . . St. Thomas. Said he had to talk to me. I wasn't interested. I just wanted to keep working. He persisted. Said he was there for a few days checking out locations, and that he simply had to tell me some things. I would have preferred solitude or at least a good deal less heartiness on his part, but he insisted. He said that Horst Triga was responsible for the takeover bid for my company. And for Childs being found out by his wife. And for his getting the assignment for the picture. And," - he shut his eyes - "for Catherine's death."

"You okay?"

Lichine blinked and nodded. He stared at the wake, draining his face of expression.

"Marker didn't have any real proof, nothing that would hold up legally. But what he suspected, I confirmed. I don't have it all, but enough. My brother admitted dealings with the vice-president at Triga Associates. I talked to Mrs. Childs and to Triga's steward. There's a man to put faith in. Marker was paying him to spy, and he told me all about it for a few dollars more. The broker repossessed your uncle's boat and then turned around and sold it to Triga. The boat became both carrot and stick. Rumfeld admitted enough to make that clear, although he'd deny it. Tim Carey and Marker's agent in California opened up, too. For a price."

"You've been busy," Wink said, handing him a beer.

"It's all pretty tangled, and Marker isn't blameless, by any means. Given the resources, he was capable of doing it all himself. But it was Triga."

"Think a little about this, Ernie. I hate Triga's guts more'n anybody I ever met, but. . ."

The angler made an undecipherable gesture and went on as if he hadn't heard. "There's more. Someone closer. Someone you know. That woman Pia Cipolla."

"Bullshit," Wink bristled. "Pia hasn't the highest moral character, but I don't see too many saints in any of this."

"She kept popping up. She was there when Triga wanted to persuade your uncle to work for him. Sweetening the pot, I suppose, plus keeping Fowler in line and informing Triga of our moods and plans."

"Okay, maybe. But hardly a capital offense."

"That came later. Duncan, the steward, told me she visited *Highlander* on at least four occasions, once in each place we were fishing. Triga found himself trailing, and he got desperate. He started doing these other things.

"Mrs. Childs was in their Miami apartment on an impulse visit when a girl came in who acted like she'd been there before. According to Mrs. Childs' description, it had to be Pia. The mailgram that brought Mrs. Childs was sent from Miami. Supposedly, it was from Monty, but he was in Morgan Cay on that day. And why wouldn't he just have, called on the phone? Good-bye Monty. Marker was tougher. Even Triga doesn't have enough money to buy off Hollywood, but he lucked out. Marker got the film project on his own merits, although it didn't hurt that Triga offered to back a chunk of the production."

"So Theo's as good as he thinks he is."

"Apparently."

"But, Ernie, Triga hasn't had it all his way. His boat almost piling up in Cuba. Boots. Pat getting beat up looking for Pia." He stopped, remembering something.

"No, but as far as I can discover, those were accidents, random circumstances. Maybe Marker arranged for Pat's mugging, but I can't find any evidence to believe that."

Wink couldn't bring himself to ask the next, most obvious, question. He didn't have to. The man in the chair was purging himself.

"Triga had long before instructed Pia to ingratiate herself with Catherine. Just to keep an eye on her, I suppose. But Catherine maintained her lead, to his surprise. Catherine had... appetites of which everyone was aware. Except me. Triga took advantage of them. That day in St. Thomas, she made. . . an overture to Pia. I saw it. We argued."

Wink put his hand on Lichine's shoulder.

"No more, Ernie."

But Lichine went on compulsively, ignoring his mate.

"Catherine went a little crazy. I made it worse. The booze, the pills, that time with Cronski. We argued again. The second Monday, Pia was on *Zodiac Arrest*, and again Tuesday. Halfway through the day, Catherine went back to harbor. Her crew cleaned up. Catherine hadn't left her stateroom. Pia told Carey to return to the hotel. The last he saw, she was taking a bottle of brandy from the bar."

"So what now?" Wink asked when he was sure Lichine was done.

Lichine jerked his face around, as if newly aware of Wink's presence.

"Now?" he repeated dully. "Now? I said that none of this would hold up in court. That doesn't leave many options."

"What are you going to do, Ernie?"

"I think you know."

Sparky Thomas was assigned as umpire to *Adroit* for the final phase. That evening, Triga invited him to his stateroom for a predinner drink.

"I have the updated standings," said Thomas after he took a seat.

Triga handed the umpire his gin-and-tonic and took the sheet of paper. There was no introduction, just the names and point totals:

Triga 2,526
Lichine 2,214

Triga crumpled the paper and went to pour a glass of wine.

"Who would have imagined this last February, hmm? Mr.

Lichine seemed most unlikely to get so far," Thomas said, filling his pipe. "But it looks as if it will work out for you."

"Assuming that Ernest obliges by not catching anything big," Triga said sourly. He picked up the paper and smoothed it out.

"Well, now," Thomas said, tamping the tobacco, "that needn't necessarily apply. We're moving up to Ribbon 3 tomorrow. Perhaps your luck will improve. Neither of you have brought in a grander. Just one of those can put you out of reach."

"Assuming Ernest doesn't get two."

"Hm. Quite so. Indeed," said Thomas between puffs.

"Regrettably true. Yes."

"Sparky."

"Umm?"

"Stop nattering."

"Was I? Excuse it, old boy."

"I do not intend to be defeated."

"No, I assume not."

"And I require your assistance," Triga continued.

"Oh now, really, Horst. Steady on. You are well aware of my role here."

"I am. I expect you to continue performing it. You will simply not do so with quite the same precision."

"I protest your implication," Thomas said, rising, "and I have no intention of listening further. I will not be compromised."

"Sit down," said Triga, his tone unchanged.

He was holding out a small manila envelope.

Thomas permitted himself a moment of blustery indignation, then returned to his chair.

"I hope that is not what I fear it might be," Thomas said. "While I do not enjoy resources comparable to yours, you surely know that I am nevertheless quite comfortably situated. Money will have no effect on my. . ."

"Open it."

The contents were not as Thomas expected. There were photographs, affidavits. Thomas placed his pipe in the ashtray.

"How did you. . . how could you?"

"That is hardly germane, Sparky, now is it?"

"Nevertheless," Thomas said, attempting to recover his aplomb, "I doubt very much that such things as this will have the effect you desire. My marriage and professional position are much too stable to be as shaken by revelations of this. . . matter. . . as I expect you anticipate."

"Ordinarily," Triga said conversationally, "I'd be inclined to agree. But this extended relationship - from last November to the September seventeenth just passed, wasn't it? - does have that one intriguing variation. Does it not? Your good wife - and the several members of your board - might be able to find it in their hearts to dismiss this escapade as the last fling of late middle age, even considering its - ah - bizarre overtones. However. . ."

Thomas' shoulders drooped. He fumbled for the pipe. Triga knew.

"However," Triga continued, "the comely young man in question is, after all, the assistant to the president of your firm's major competitor."

"What is it you want?"

Triga went to the door and threw the lock.

By mid-afternoon of the seventh day, *Adroit* had hooked and released two small marlin. A third was on the line. It, too, was underweight and Triga was having little difficulty working it to the boat.

"Double line comin' up!" Grubbs yelled to Fowler on the bridge. "Slow it down, Cappy!"

Fowler cut the throttles, holding the boat on station.

"Swivel comin' up!" Grubbs shouted.

The fish, its mouth opened wide, rolled to the surface, belly up.

Triga wound in. The swivel connecting the line to the wire leader approached the rod tip. When it was two feet away and Grubbs was reaching a gloved hand far over the transom, the marlin heaved into the air and wrenched its head away. The leader snapped.

Grubbs tore off his gloves and whacked them against the covering board. Timmins threw the flying gaff to the deck. Fowler slapped the console, cursing.

Triga was strangely calm. Fowler saw his employer glance at Sparky Thomas. The umpire began to write on his clipboard. Fowler left the engines in neutral and went down. He walked over to Thomas, who looked up, startled.

"What're you writin'?" Fowler asked.

"Why, Captain, I. . . ah. . ."

Fowler snatched the clipboard away. His suspicion was confirmed. He turned to Triga, who was staring out over the water.

"What's goin' down, Triga?"

"I assume that Sparky was recording our catch."

"That wasn't no catch! The swivel has to hit the rod tip and the mate has to touch the wire."

"I do not require schooling in the conventionalities."

"Take it off," Fowler said to Thomas, shoving the clipboard at him.

"He will leave it as is," Triga said.

"It wasn't no catch."

"You're splitting hairs. The spirit of the regulations have been observed. A few inches more or less hardly matter."

"They do to me. Cheatin' is cheatin'. Take it off, Thomas."

"He will not."

"Then we're goin' in. Right now."

"Do that, and you'll be on the first plane home."

"Sooner that than let you keep on with what you're tryin' to do."

"There are other captains."

"Crews, too. I figure you'll have to replace Steve and Chuck, unless you come to a stop right now."

"That is no problem," Triga replied.

"It is with only three days left, and you know it."

"You will lose more than a pay check, Pat."

Fowler hesitated. Too long. "That's the way it goes," he said finally.

"It needn't," Triga said, swinging out of the chair. "Gentlemen, it is time we talked. Sparky, go up there and set the autopilot."

Triga went into the cabin and waited for them.

It took him only five minutes to make his proposal. He looked at his captain and at each mate. "Well, then. Do we have an understanding?"

Grubbs broke the silence. "I want to make sure I got you right, Mr. Triga."

"We're losing valuable time," Triga snapped.

"Won't take but a minute," Grubbs insisted. "You'll excuse me, but you do tend to circle around a point sometimes. What you're sayin' is, that if we - you - win this tournament, you intend to cut us in on the pot."

"That is correct. If I do prevail, I will share the prize with each of you. Two hundred thousand dollars. Each."

"Now that," Grubbs said, shaking his head in disbelief, "is a whole lot. I couldn't make that much in fifteen years."

"You'll have a certified check in that amount when we get back to Cairns," Triga said. "Assuming. . ."

". . . that we win," Grubbs said. "And all we have to do is look the other way now and then. Is that right? Like that last fish we didn't quite catch? And maybe we roll some extra-strong line on the reels? And like maybe when we need the points we count a fish that just took the bait and threw the hook?"

Triga was nodding with ill-concealed impatience. "Indeed." He put up a hand. "But no more than absolutely necessary, of course. There's always the possibility it won't be."

"Which we won't know until it's over," said Fowler.

"So it don't matter."

"I sure would like to be rich," Grubbs said. He sighed. "But I don't guess I can do what you want. I'm gonna hate myself, but I figure I'll just take what I'm owed and go."

Triga's face fell.

"As you wish," he said eventually. "And you, Chuck?"

"Whatever Pat decides," Timmins replied.

"I'll just go out there with Thomas," Grubbs said, standing. "Make it easier for you, Pat."

"Steve. . ."

"No big thing, Pat," Grubbs said. "I understand,"

He stepped outside and closed the door behind him.

"Pat?" Triga prompted.

Fowler carefully looked away from Timmins.

"I still get my boat back?" he asked.

"Of course."

"And my pay?"

"Yes."

"Both? No matter what?"

"Well. . ."

"Both?"

"Very well."

"I'll take that in writing."

"As you wish. When we get back."

"Now."

"All right."

"What about Thomas?"

"We have his cooperation," Triga blandly replied.

"I wonder what you used on him."

Triga didn't respond. He was writing. When he finished, he handed the paper to Fowler and said, "That should cover it."

Fowler read it quickly and put it in his pocket. Right then, the loathing began anew. For Triga. For himself.

Lichine was sitting on the icebox, back by the open cabin door. The sun was falling to the horizon. Nothing had happened since *Brain Soup* tagged and released two small blacks in late afternoon. Lichine was numbly monitoring the transmissions of the other boats over the salon receiver.

"*Mother*, this is *Adroit*." Lichine recognized Triga's voice.

The mother ship acknowledged.

"*Mother*," Triga continued, "we're coming in. ETA about seven-thirty. Plan on dinner for us about eight, if you will. Did the mail boat arrive?" Pause. "Good. Please ask the skipper to await our arrival. He'll have a passenger returning to the mainland with him. Understood? *Adroit* out."

"What was that about?" Wink said, glancing up from the table.

"Beats me," Lichine replied.

Wink sewed up the mackerel and tossed it in the ice chest. "Y' know, when me 'n' Pat first came down here in seventy-two, there weren't fifty black marlin caught in the whole world that whole year. And in seven days, just these two boats have done all that."

"So?"

"And so, our luck's bound to get better. I can taste it."

"Wish I could. And I wish I could share in your unflagging optimism."

"Always had it. Ask me how I got my name."

"Okay. How did you?"

"My Momma says that when I came popping out of her twenty-eight years ago, I didn't cry at all."

"You didn't?"

"Nope. Momma swears the first thing I did was wink at her."

When *Brain Soup* arrived back, *Adroit* and a small cruiser were standing to port of the mother ship.

As Doakes maneuvered forward of the mail boat to permit Lichine to debark, Steve Grubbs walked past, suitcase in hand. Wink went over and asked where he was going. Grubbs dropped the suitcase into the cockpit of the mail boat and swiveled around to see if anyone was within earshot. Then he said there was something Wink should know, but that he had to keep it to himself until the next day, when Grubbs would be on the plane home. Wink promised. With obvious misgivings, Grubbs told him.

24

Breakfast was at eight the morning of the eighth day. Despite the close quarters of the dining cabin and the presence of most of the participants, it was quiet. The Australian mate moved among the diners, his spoons clacking against the serving platters of eggs, bacon, broiled tomatoes, sausages, and browned potatoes.

Fowler and Timmims whispered to each other in one comer. The others ate mechanically, their faces bloated from sleep.

Horst Triga stared at the score sheet. His table partners, Thomas and Farrington, concentrated on their plates. He had done everything he could, Triga decided. He had ensured the collaboration of those participants who were both susceptible to persuasion and utilizable in his cause. If Lichine did not boat any fish in excess of one thousand pounds in the remaining three days, the contest was Triga's. The odds were in his favor.

Wink Andros entered the cabin and walked to where his uncle was sitting. He asked for a private conversation outside. Lichine saw them several minutes later, standing by the weighing gibbet at the stem. The soft wind caught some of their words and carried them back to Lichine, but the context was lost. Involved in his own thoughts, he went to his stateroom to prepare for the day.

"I don't get what you're talkin' about no better now than I did five minutes ago," Fowler was saying.

"I told you, Pat," Wink said, ignoring the denial. "I told you that sooner or later he'd pull this. If he couldn't win it straight, he'd try to do it crooked. He always has. And I know, Pat, what he's doing. For certain."

"Triga ain't doin' nothin'. Now drop it. I'm goin'."

Wink put his hand on Fowler's arm. "You can't let him do it."

"He ain't doin' nothin'," Fowler said, shrugging the hand away. ""Whoever said he was was talkin' out his ear. And I ain't listenin' no more."

"What else besides Pia?" Wink called after him.

Fowler stopped. "What about her?"

"You haven't seen her since St. Thomas. Why?"

"Don't push it."

"Because her work's over, is why."

"That ain't worth remarkin' on."

"She was around keeping you in line since day one. Even way back, who was in bed with you when Triga came to hire you? What else you think she did?"

"I"m takin' pity on you, Wink. Stop. Now."

"You've been thinking the same thing, else you would've tried to punch me out by now."

Fowler unclenched his fists. His head throbbed.

"How was it she knew you were in the hospital that time? You went all over trying to find her. How'd she know unless she was told by someone who knew what'd happened to you?" Wink had to shout, for Fowler was storming back to the dining cabin. "I guess it doesn't matter, Pat. Whether you tell Triga to stuff it or not, it's too late. He's had you by the short hairs and you been following and now I guess you don't know any other direction to walk." Fowler was at the door. "You're done, Pat! One way or another, you're going down with Triga. It's over. I'll make sure of that!"

Brain Soup left at nine. Doakes was running to Ribbon 10, a northern section of the Reef they were yet to explore. Halfway there, Lichine went to the bridge. Wink and Havens were preparing equipment and baits below.

"I have something I want to try."

"I'm listenin'," Doakes replied.

"We've been staying out only during daylight hours."

"More'n twice as much as Triga."

"But it hasn't helped much."

"Don't I know that? What you got in mind?"

"To increase our edge a little more. I want to stay out the rest of the time. All of it."

"Twenty-four hours? The next three days?"

"Starting now. Except for stopping back at *Mother* for fuel and provisions."

Doakes shook his head. "Ain't no point. Blacks don't feed at night."

"So everyone says. You were the one who told me that they could be had before noon when everyone said they couldn't. We went against that and we picked up a few."

"They don't feed at night," Doakes insisted.

"Maybe not. Probably not. But fish don't eat baits just because they're hungry, isn't that right? Sometimes they do it out of annoyance.

And they hardly ever caught swords off Florida until a couple of years ago. Then they tried nights, and it turned around. Same thing with the shrimp fisheries."

"Don't mean blacks'll be the same."

"Of course not But they could be, and we don't have anything to lose. I'll sleep in the chair and you guys can spell each other and. . ."

"Even if we did tie into one, we couldn't land it when it was dark. Not if it was of any size at all."

"So I'll just keep it at a standstill until daybreak. Then we'll boat it."

"You ain't got that kinda strength, Ernie. Not if it's a fish worth keepin'. Could be eight hours or more."

"You don't know that. Neither do I. The fact remains, we have nothing to lose."

"True enough." Doakes concentrated on his course for a moment.

"Would it help if I told you my intentions about your bonus, should we win?"

"Ernie, I purely wish you hadn't of said that. You oughta know better by now."

Lichine watched the mates rigging the baits. "You're right. Forget I said it. But I want to do it."

"They won't be on the surface."

"Okay. So how about we run south, right over the edge. Then we troll deep on the sea side and on the surface with the other and see what happens."

"You ain't carryin' a full deck if you think we're gonna hang a black in the middle of the night. Howsomever. Ain't nothin' left but fingerprint smears on the mirror. Consider us in agreeance."

The crew of *Adroit* spent the morning fishing for bait. By the time they circled back to pick up their angler and umpire at *Mother*,

Jeeter Doakes had called in two marlin releases. At dusk, long after the other boat had returned for dinner, Wink wired and released the fourth marlin of the day for *Brain Soup*. It was the best day for either angler since they arrived in Cairns, for it was not unusual for fishermen to come to the Reef and never see a marlin.

Yet it made little difference. The largest of Lichine's marlin was below the bonus weight. He had added only forty points to their score.

When they were fueling up the next morning, Doakes told Havens to sharpen all the hooks with the metal rasp. Wink used the time to disassemble the reels, one by one, meticulously cleaning each part and testing its action.

On *Adroit*, Horst Triga handed Timmins two boxes and instructed the mate to replace the monofilament on his reels with this new line. Timmins hesitated. The boxes were labeled "160 Super." Serious anglers rarely used line of that strength. It was regarded as unsporting, and if a record fish was caught with it, the IAA would not recognize it. Tournament rules expressly forbade it. None of these factors concerned Triga. The mate did as he was told and Fowler and Thomas pretended not to notice.

These preparations, extraordinary and otherwise, proved immaterial. The day was very hot and the water beyond the Reef was nearly as placid as that inshore. By nightfall, not a single catch had been registered. *Adroit* returned to the mother ship. *Brain Soup* again stayed out, and that made no difference either.

At dawn of the tenth and final day, *Brain Soup* returned to the mother ship for fuel and a quick breakfast. A darkening overcast screened off the sun, but the air was heavy with moisture. Lichine wiped the gloss of perspiration from his forehead and stepped back into his boat. Farrington was in the salon; the captain and both mates were on the bridge. He joined them.

"What's the verdict?" Wink asked.

"Triga won't agree to calling the day off," Lichine replied.

"But it's gonna be nasty out there, Ernie. Might even be a touch of that typhoon you were hoping for. We should be heading back for land, never mind just sitting here."

A fat raindrop splatted on his hat brim. Lichine turned his palms up.

"I know. But he has no reason to call it off. He has what he thinks is an insurmountable lead. He might not even go out, he's so sure he's got us licked."

"What about the umps? Could be they'd side with you."

"Farrington, maybe. But not Thomas. He backed Triga. So no tiebreaker."

"Okay," said Doakes with a sigh. "So what's the score?"

"We're at 2,764," Lichine replied. "They have 3,076."

Wink whistled softly. "All we need's a 1,313-pound black. Hope those are lucky numbers for you."

"We still have a chance," Lichine said.

"Always," Doakes agreed. "But you're still half a bubble out of plumb to go out in this, Ernie."

"Don't say too much for us, either," Wink said, moving to the ladder. "But what the hell, Grasshopper. You've run a couple tons of dope in worse'n this, and weather like this is supposed to bring the fish up. Head it for the peapatch, Jeet. Let's get this stubborn fucker a double thirteen."

Havens cast off and went to help Wink with the rod and baits. Doakes started up. Even inshore of the Reef there was a high, ragged chop, and the thunderheads piled on the horizon were coming in their direction. Lichine checked his watch.

"Nine hours," he said to Doakes. "To do what maybe twenty people have ever done."

"You been readin' up. But there's nothin' says you can't be added to the list. Hang Mo at one minute to final call and he still counts, even if it takes from now till Tuesday to get him in."

Doakes glanced down into the cockpit. Wink was trying on the gloves.

"You got 'em built up too thick," Doakes shouted. "No way you'll be able to feel the wire through those. Peel off a layer. And, Havens, grease up the seat of the chair."

"Why?" Lichine asked.

"Helps a little. Not much. The Aussie captains do it a lot. Makes it easier to slide back and forth when you're horsin' the fish in. That is, if you'll do what I been tellin' you for eight months and push with your legs."

"You fixin' on usin' the gin pole?" Havens asked. He was referring to the block-and-tackle contraption designed to lift fish over the transom.

"Shit no," Doakes answered. "Not after the other day. Thing's useless as tits on a boar hog. If we get the kinda fish we need, he'll snap it like a match. Less trouble to bring 'em through the tuna door."

Beyond the Reef, the crests of the waves were foam. Jeeter steered into a quartering course to slice diagonally through the seas. Before he completed the maneuver, he was caught in a long trough and water hammered the boat broadside, broaching the gunnel. *Brain Soup* yawed to port, then righted itself. Wink and Havens went sprawling.

"You incompetent cheechbug!" Wink howled. "Your feet stink, and you don't love Jesus!"

"Kiss my ass!" Doakes shouted. "I'm slidin' around so much the bottoms of my socks is wore through."

"When you're dumb, you gotta be tough."

The new course was comfortable enough, and the captain and mate stopped yelling at each other after a few minutes.

"This here's as good a place as any," Doakes decided.

"Get them lines out! We fishin' or not?"

"You want me to put out the teaser?" Havens asked.

"I guess so. In this sea, we need all the help we can get."

Havens hauled out two ropes with rubber squids affixed at one-foot intervals. He secured the ends to the first stretchers on the outriggers and threw the squids over the sides. They snapped out, churning along the edges of the wake.

Suddenly Doakes squinted and bowed over the wheel. "I'll be dipped," he said, and rammed the throttles forward. The boat sprang forward. "Ernie, you get on down there, now, and strap in."

"What did you see?"

"A dorsal stickin' outa the water as high as a palm tree. I ain't seen a black finnin' like that in years. Get on down there, son. You're 'bout to join that club!"

Horst Triga was pacing the deck of the mother ship, raging. His captain was in the bilge of *Adroit*, attempting repairs on the port engine. Time was slipping away. Triga went to the open hatch and thrust his head in, demanding to know how much longer Fowler would take.

"I don't know that, do I?" Fowler growled back, wiping the sweat away. "Leave me be, you prick, and let me get on with it."

"Our contract precludes insubordination," Triga shot back. "Keep a civil tongue."

"Goddammit, Triga! Get off my back! You're crazy to want to go out in this weather anyway!"

"I will not be intimidated. Tell me immediately how much longer it will be."

Fowler gritted his teeth and glared at the recalcitrant generator. "I'll have you out fishin' directly."

"Which means exactly how long?"

Fowler didn't answer. Triga gave up, and settled for reprimanding Timmins for urinating over the stern.

The thunderheads stacked on the horizon when they set out were nearly overhead now. The wind shifted, blowing across the current and whipping the waves into a cross-chop. The boat yawed sickeningly from side to side in a sea billowing into twelve-foot swells, and the stern alternately lifted skyward and fell back with jarring thuds. Several times, waves drenched Lichine and the two mates. They clung with fingers and toes, straining to keep balance while their eyes swept the water.

Doakes overran the place he had spotted the fin gliding through the bruise-colored water. He looked over his shoulder, and there it was, rising, fluorescing. The great dark shape accelerated.

"Get ready! He's trailin' the port bait!"

The fish slashed its bill at the darting mackerel. The line floated out. The bait was swallowed. The marlin pivoted and streaked off. The rod went down.

"NOW!"

Lichine threw the drag and flung himself back. Again. Again. The hook was set. Doakes had the boat in wide open reverse, engines roaring, cockpit deluged. The marlin was swimming away on an unwavering course, just below the surface. It did not sound or turn or jump. Lichine caught only glimpses of its tail and dorsal. The spool of his reel slowed. He eased back carefully, hoping to force the fish to interrupt its momentum. The line went slack for an instant and then came taut.

"Comin' up!"

Lichine had been told that black marlin were not as acrobatic as the blues off St. Thomas. That was confirmed by the ones he had caught here, so far. He was, as a result, unprepared.

The black exited the water on an angle and hung in the air for an impossibly long moment. It was fifteen feet long and twice as thick as his biggest blue, with pulsing purple bars sectioning its flanks. It lashed itself about as it fell. Head on, its shoulders were as broad as a bull's. It crashed into the water with the sound of a thunderclap.

"God! It is... everything!" Lichine breathed, certain his heart had stopped. He remembered to crank.

"Take it easy," Wink said, recovering his voice and feigning calm. "You're forcing."

"That was the most - frighteningly - magnificent - monster..."

"You've ever seen," Wink completed. "Me too. But save your breath. What you got on there is big as a Buick and damn near as heavy. But you work him the same as sail. Don't be afraid of him. Just respect him."

Apart from the one stunning leap, the black did not clear the water again. It greyhounded in shallow bounds, its rigid pectorals trailing through the crests before it dropped and lifted once again. It was zigzagging, stripping off line, but Doakes kept backing and Lichine retrieved a few feet each time. The reel was filling. Then the fish pulled away once again. There were many ways he could lose it. Accidents he could do nothing about. A sea turtle or porpoise or coral head could scrape the line and weaken or break it. Sharks might come. The engines could halt as Lichine was lifting back, placing unacceptable tension on the line.

But those things were not happening, and Lichine was doing everything properly. Right down to guiding the recovered line evenly onto the spool with his fingers. He was always forgetting that.

More, he was functioning on instinct, mind and body united. No conscious instructions to himself, no articulated reminders, yet he flowed into it, pumping and reeling without hesitation. Even the action of the pitching boat was made part of the rhythmic work, Lichine winding as the stern went down, lifting back as it rose. Now, after all these months, it made a kind of primal sense. It seemed the very first time he had done this.

"This one'll do it, Ernie. Never seen a bigger one." Wink yelled up to Doakes. "What do you think, Jeet?"

"That is one hellacious mother. Primo, Ernie, primo."

"The weight, Jeet."

"Fifteen, easy. Maybe a record."

The black was a hundred feet off, apparently tiring. Wink pulled on his gloves, smoothed them between the fingers. Havens readied the flying gaff. Doakes throttled down slightly.

"Why's he comin' in so easy?" Havens asked.

"Isn't in yet. And it's been nearly an hour."

"Yeah, but. . ."

"Ernie hooked him someplace it hurts. Most times you get them in the lips. All they feel then is the tugging of the line. There's a nerve at the base of the bill, in the roof of the mouth. Could be the hook's in there. Makes him numb almost."

The black saw the boat then, and with a mighty spasm, arched its back, flashed its belly, and sped away, flicking its scimitar tail. Line whizzed off the spool as angler and mates helplessly watched.

"Guess he isn't ready yet," Wink said mildly.

"Guess not." Lichine bent once more to his task. "Bastard."

"No sweat. He does this for a living. Wouldn't of got that big if he wasn't good at it."

The ominous clouds disgorged a heavy, nearly horizontal rain, but then passed. Doakes didn't leave the wheel, nor Wink the chair. Havens ferried drinks. Farrington watched from behind the cabin door. In the distance, lightning split the sky from time to time. No one suggested that they return to *Mother*.

Pat Fowler monitored the call from Doakes announcing the hookup. If Jeeter was correct on his weight estimate - and Fowler knew the other captain was conservative in that matter - and if they boated it in one piece, Triga was beaten. Only a grander-plus could save him. With barely a half day left, that was improbable, and there were rational limits to how many nonexistent fish Thomas could tally on his clipboard. With a relish moderated only by recognition of his own loss, Fowler shouted the news to his employer.

Triga blanched, his mouth moving convulsively. When he regained his voice, it was in shrill orders to Fowler and Timmins, spittle spraying. Little of it made sense. Finally he quieted, seething with impotence.

"It's done, Triga," Fowler said. "The kid's all but beat you. After all you done. . ."

Perhaps the bait made an intriguing hop. Perhaps it bounded into the middle of a school of rainbow runners that was at that moment under surveillance from the depths. Whatever, Triga found himself connected to what proved to be an exceptionally large marlin.

Triga pushed back against the harness and watched the line screech from the reel.

"Done, am I? Beaten?"

Doakes kept backing the boat, adjusting course to keep the black astern. The waves were higher, lathering where they broke over indigo water. The sky was dark as dusk, with an unearthly yellow cast. Raindrops stung their faces in quick squalls, ceased for a time, then pelted them again.

Lichine felt the familiar lancing pain across his back. His arms were leeched of feeling; his legs quivered; his flesh jumped with coursing chills. But he gave no thought to quitting, for the first part of his planned retribution was at hand. He horsed the black to the side twice more. Both times, the fish plunged away.

"It's so dark," he managed. "What time is it?"

Wink glanced at the cabin clock. "Two-fifteen. You've had him on over five hours."

Once more, the fish crested. It drifted now, belly showing. The double line cleared the water, then the swivel, the leader. Doakes chopped the engines and came down to handle the gaff. The mates pulled on their gloves once again. Farrington hovered.

"This time," said Wink, reaching for the leader.

Triga, too, brought his fish to the stern. Timmins stretched for the leader, but it was inches beyond his fingertips. The marlin pulled away, beating the water white. Triga was furious.

"You bungler!"

"It's green, Triga!" Fowler shouted. "You gotta wear it down more!"

"You will not tell me what to do! Back this boat down!"

Fowler yanked the clutches into reverse. The stern pounded toward the fish, and Triga recovered line as quickly as he could turn the handle. The leader came up. Again, Timmins missed it. The marlin rolled on its side, spent. Blood streamed from its gills.

Triga shrieked at Timmins, tore off the harness, lunged from the chair, shoved the mate aside, and grabbed at the leader.

"BACK DOWN! BACK DOWN! FASTER!"

The hook was imbedded in the nerve terminus at the base of the bill. It ripped free.

The fish sprang straight up. Its bill drove through Triga, right below the sternum. Fowler saw the point pierce through beneath the shoulder blades. The marlin fell back. Triga was dragged over the covering board, impaled.

Fowler watched the angler go over. Other images flashed behind his eyes. A man, his friend. A black-haired woman. The boat was still backing. His reflexes were quick. He had time to throw the throttles to idle and the clutches forward, halting the rearward momentum. Instead, he watched. The propellers passed over the fish and man.

Timmins reached for the flailing arm. He caught it and pulled, but there was no resistance. The water was a boiling scarlet and pink cloud and Timmins was holding the arm of Horst Triga. Nothing more. Fowler pushed the throttles forward.

The cockpit of *Brain Soup* was pandemonium, every one bellowing orders to everyone else. Lichine brought the black to the side, but as Wink touched the leader, it drifted away, out of reach. Oscar Farrington was shouting in Lichine's ear about what had just happened on *Adroit.*

Lichine grabbed the umpire's collar and yanked him close.

"Are you certain?" he demanded. Farrington nodded vigorously.

Wink caught the leader again and took a wrap. The fish thrashed against the hull and Havens raised the gaff, ready to send it home.

"Wait!" Lichine cried.

They froze. Faces turned to him, Wink barely maintaining his grip and Havens holding the gaff high.

"For God's sake, Ernie!"

A sliver of amber sky widened to the west and the sun dropped through the space.

"Ernie! We got to do it! Now!"

Lichine felt loss and relief and redemption.

"No," he said. "Let him free."

Printed in the United States
114450LV00004B/205-222/P

9 780972 856485